ONE NOTE MURDERS

CAT GABBIANO MYSTERY SERIES

BOOK 3

DONNA KEEL ARMER

RedPenguin
BOOKS

Red Penguin Books

Bellerose Village, New York

Library of Congress Control Number: 2025919313

ISBN

Print 978-1-63777-771-8 | 978-1-63777-772-5

Digital 978-1-63777-770-1

Music is the language of the spirit. It opens the secret of life bringing peace, abolishing strife.
— Kahlil Gibran

Also by Donna Keel Armer

Fiction

The Cat Gabbiano Mystery Series

The Red Starfish

Moringa ~ Tree of Life

Nonfiction

Solo in Salento: A Memoir

Un'americana in Salento (Italian Translation)

Anthologies

London: Smokes, Blokes and Jokes of Foggy Town
"Darkness Before Dawn"

Paris: Love, Loss, and Longing in the City of Lights
"If It Waddles and Quacks, Is It a Duck?"

Rome: Centuries of Stories of the Eternal City
"Rome: The Gritty City"

For All the Artists Who Create Beauty in a Broken World

&

Sempre Ray

Contents

Preface

In our first year of marriage, my husband and I created a tradition of attending midnight services and then returning home to open our Christmas gifts. It was Year Ten as the midnight hour struck on Christmas Eve. A glow from the fireplace spread warmth and cheer in the room as we sunk onto the sofa with glasses of Prosecco. With a huge grin on his face, Ray handed me a plain white envelope.

For a moment, Christmases past whirl through my mind. My daddy's sisters always added a white envelope to the gift box that held the granny style underpants they thought proper for young girls to wear. But inside that envelope would be a crisp five or ten-dollar bill which made the underwear tolerable and the writing of a thank-you note less painful.

The look on Ray's face told me this wasn't about granny underwear or dollar bills. I held the envelope for a few moments, running my fingers along the smooth edges as I considered all the possibilities. My imagination kicked in and danced through a list of prospects.

Delaying the delicious moment of discovery was part of the excitement for me, not so much for Ray. His nervous fidgeting broke through my lost-in-memories reverie. His patience was wearing thin as I dawdled, turning the envelope over and holding it to the light.

When I finally tore through the seal, I was speechless. It was the best and most meaningful gift Ray had ever given me: two tickets to a Luciano Pavarotti concert. It was a grand gift, not only because I'm a huge opera fan but also because Ray isn't. Willie Nelson would have been his first choice.

In the past, I have prevailed upon his good nature to take me to the ballet, the symphony, and particularly the opera. Of course, in return, I have attended football and baseball games, as well as country music concerts with him. But this gift had a more significant meaning as it was the beginning of Ray's operatic journey.

Opera, as long as I've known my husband, has been on his list of least favorites. That is, until 1997, when he first heard Andrea Bocelli on PBS. That chance click of the remote changed how Ray felt. It eventually resulted in a gift superior to the Pavarotti concert—a gift that took eighteen years to come to fruition.

Years later, on the occasion of a big-number birthday, I was handed a similar white envelope. This one contained two tickets to an Andrea Bocelli concert. But not just any concert—along with the concert tickets were two airline tickets to Italy to see the amazing Maestro in concert on his family farm in Lajatico (Tuscany), Italy.

Eighteen years after we first experienced Bocelli's magnificent voice, we sat in the orchestra section in the middle of the golden fields of Tuscany. We heard the roar of drums. We watched in awe as a full moon rose the moment Andrea Bocelli stepped onto center stage.

I wept with the first words of *Nessun Dorma*—

No one sleeps...no one sleeps...Even you oh Princess—

until the very last words faded—

Vanish, oh night! Set, stars! At daybreak, I will win! I will win!

Preface

And so, the third book in the Cat Gabbiano Mystery Series begins with the plans that Stella made (*The Red Starfish*, Book #1) for her and Cat to celebrate their joint 40th birthdays in Tuscany at a Bocelli concert. But it's two years later, and Cat is traveling alone to attend the concert.

Since Cat is a huge part of me, it's only fair that she has the same opportunity to immerse herself in the enchantment of Maestro Bocelli's magical voice.

Of course, her journey won't be as smooth as mine.

~ Donna Keel Armer 2025

Dark Lady
Whispers in the darkest night
Strange eyes watching
Cloaked in black
She murmurs in my ear
Whitest moon lights pallid face
Cold lips sighing
Gauzy cape twists in the wind
Her fingers float toward me
I flee down an empty alley
She waits for me under the lamp

~ Virginia Vogler Brown

Prologue

Darkness smothers me in black velvet. The empty cobbled passageways vibrate with the sounds of my feet. Running. A sudden chill engulfs me as the wind slaps cold air in my face and bids the last warmth of summer farewell. The moon tucks in and out of the gathering storm clouds. Silent shapes reach out to me. Shadows dance erratically to the wind's tune. They clutch at my hair with gnarly fingers.

The wind whips against my jacket. Shivers slither along my spine. My heart thumps loudly against my chest. Fear instead of blood pumps through my veins. I'm lost in a maze of tiny passages. I know this town so well, but tonight, the familiar abandons me. Do I keep straight? Do I turn? If I turn, which path do I take?

One moment, the moon shines brightly; the next moment, the blackness of night renders me blind. The weight of the 800 martyrs flees with me leaving behind a trail of fragmented skulls and twisted bones. Panic clenches my heart. It creeps into the edges of my mind. The shadowy creatures whisper, "Keep moving."

Once again, there's mayhem and murder in my life. The horror of what I've done renders my legs useless. I stumble. My body jerks in response. I cry out as the gash in my arm widens—the pain swallows me whole.

The metallic odor of blood follows me. The stickiness saturates my hands. A trail drips behind me. The cut on my forehead oozes into my eyes.

I merge with the night. The immortal soul of inhumanity rumbles through me, racing by my side through the narrow streets. I push forward into another dark passageway. The night thickens around me. It sucks me into its vortex of evil.

As I reach the piazza, the wind shifts. The clouds part to reveal dark figures moving in my direction. Fear cloaks me in her mantle. Shadowy arms reach out. They have come for me.

I am a murderer.

Part One

The Riddle of Turandot

Set in the eighteenth century, the opera *Turandot* is the story of Princess Turandot. She is a woman ahead of her time and is notorious throughout the Orient for her refusal to marry. Her father, the emperor, is fearful of losing his dynasty. He insists that she find a suitable husband. Thinking to outsmart him, she devises a series of riddles. She tells her father she will marry the first suitor who can correctly answer three riddles. If all three questions are not answered correctly, the suitor dies. Many have already suffered death's fate.

The exiled prince Calàf arrives and seeks to marry the Princess Turandot. She asks him the first question:

WHAT IS BORN EACH NIGHT AND DIES EACH DAWN?

Calàf correctly answers

HOPE

Act II ~ *Turandot* ~ Giacomo Puccini

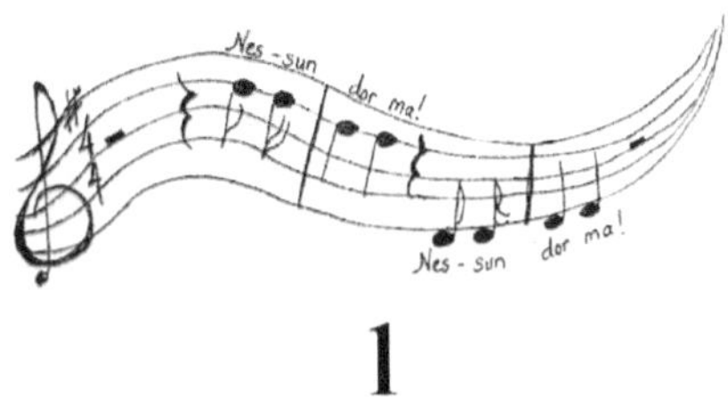

1

South Carolina Lowcountry

The swift current of the river beckons me outside, away from my thoughts of Italy. I open the French doors to the terrace and breathe in the fresh, salty air. A breeze tickles the sheer curtains, and the damp smell of earth steaming from an earlier rainstorm drifts inside. It mingles with the heavy humid air of the South Carolina Lowcountry.

I kick off my shoes and walk barefoot in the warm sandy soil. The stone pavers are cool under my feet. I pause to roll up my jeans. The stubby grass scratches against my bare soles as I tread my way to the edge of the river.

If only I could plunge in and swim away. Let the flow of the water wash away the pain and sorrow that calls my name. Instead, I gaze at the snowy white herons as they lift their long legs to wade through the marshy shallows. They patiently wait for the right moment to snare their next meal.

The mud squishes between my toes—black, thick and rich with the sulfurous smell of decades of rot in the saltwater river. The water calms me, anchors me, and takes me to a place of healing. The last few years of my life have spiraled out of control. Pain and sorrow have been my only companions. But in this place I begin again. In the midst of my grief, I find solace.

The shrill ring of my cell from inside the house disrupts the soothing lull of the river. I turn back but forget about the phone as the low, rambling structure comes into view. My Lowcountry home fills my heart with joy.

At one time, this place was a simple fishing shack, and then the add-ons came. Now it gracefully curves with the river, merging with the giant oaks and dangling Spanish moss. The weathered boards bask in a warm patina. The tin roof has softened to a rosy red that reflects each sunrise and sunset.

At the door, I wipe my muddy feet against the bristles of the mat. My footprints follow me to the bathroom. I sit on the edge of the tub and let the water pound against my feet. Weeks of tension ease up as the warmth curls around my toes and the mud slides down the drain.

A long-ago memory of driving the Natchez Trace with Sarah Tidwell Chandler comes to mind. We were roommates at UVA. One spring break, she invited me to her home in Natchez, Mississippi, with the promise of hiking on the Trace. Although late March, the sun held the summer's heat and relentlessly beat against our bare heads and shoulders. Our shorts and tank tops were soaked with sweat. Our feet were hot and burning with blisters. As the sun faded into the Mississippi River, Sarah grabbed my hand and led me to the water's edge. She shed her boots and clothes and flung herself into the river. I followed.

When she surfaced, she said in that honeyed voice so indicative of the deep south, "Now Cat, wherever you go, whatever you do, always remember this moment when we washed our poor aching feet in the river. Whenever you're tired, hot and bothered by life, jump in the water and soak your feet. If your feet feel good, you can tackle the world."

Perhaps it's true, I think as I dry my toes, retrieve my shoes and walk into the bedroom. My feet feel good, but do they feel good enough to return to Italy? To take this trip to honor my best friend, Stella Lombardi? Is it possible for me to attend the birthday celebration she planned for us before she was murdered.

Is it the right thing to do? It's one of those treadmill questions I can't shut off. *While my feet may feel good, what about the rest of me? Am I prepared to return to the place I left over a year ago? The place where pain and sorrow traveled with me? Am I ready to see Lorenzo after the silence that has grown between us?*

My almost-packed bag is open on the bed. Two passports lie next to it. The first one reveals the happy, unlined face of a younger Caterina Maria Lucia Gabbiano. The second one shows the same face with a few crinkles around the intense green, unsmiling eyes. One Italian passport and the other American. Passports, tickets, reservations—I'm ready to travel, even if my heart is undecided.

I slip the passports into my purse with the Italian one on top. The EU lines are always shorter and easier to maneuver. A half-laugh escapes as I recall my best friend Stella and I standing in line with our parents to receive dual citizenship. We were the only kids in our class with that status and the only kids who could brag about vacationing in Italy every summer.

Stella loved and fed off the attention. She turned the possession of dual citizenship into the beginning of her celebrity status. She seized on the fact that her name in Italian translated to *star*. It was an easy transition to promote herself as a rising star. True to her goals of fortune and fame, she ascended to great heights—first on the Italian modeling scene and then in the Italian film industry.

Those two little girls—so innocent, thinking life would always be fun and exciting as well as special because we were Italian-Americans. We were world travelers. In retrospect, it was easy to see Stella as the famous movie star she became—and me as the staid accountant.

Those years between idyllic childhood and responsible adulthood were full of confusion, painful and misguided decisions, and misunderstandings crammed into a few glorious moments. It was only a couple of years ago, during the trip to New York, that Stella and I rekindled our friendship and made plans to let go of past hurts and slights.

While in the city for Stella's award ceremony, she presented me with her plans for our fortieth birthday celebration in Italy. She excelled at providing the perfect surprise. She knew I was smitten with the great Andrea Bocelli. Attending his concert was her way of asking for forgiveness and seeking to restore our friendship. She had a habit of buying redemption.

During our time together we caught up on failed marriages, my divorce and the unexpected death of my parents. After my divorce, staid accountant no longer fit me. I threw caution to the wind and returned to school to become a chef. With all my possessions in my car, I arrived in the Lowcountry and created a new life as a caterer.

Stella considered my change of career as a small deviation that would soon be corrected. She always thought big and expected everyone else to do the same. Small time caterer in a backwater town didn't suit her. During our time in New York, she added further chaos to my life by pairing me with an up and coming chef in Castello del Mare so I could be something other than a small town caterer. Again she didn't ask—just waved her hand as I protested. It was easier for me to surrender and rearrange my schedule to include a sabbatical and hope my business wouldn't be in ruins when I returned.

As always, she took control of my life. The plans were made without any consent from me. Airline tickets purchased. Accommodations reserved. She squealed with delight when she showed me the fancy resort where we'd stay. She didn't ask for my input or if it was convenient with my schedule.

Most people would say I was lucky to have such a generous friend, but they didn't know Stella. Didn't know it was her way of ensuring she was in control. She promised it would be a clean slate for our friendship. Of course, I gave in and agreed to the trip. I mean, after all, it was Andrea Bocelli. But, like many things in our friendship, it turned out to be another misguided decision.

After New York, she returned to Italy and I to the Lowcountry. We continued our friendship with an occasional Zoom to discuss our pending trip. Each conversation brought more excitement as I relaxed and accepted my fate. After all, didn't I deserve a vacation?

Then the calls stopped. Weeks went by. My calls, texts and

emails went unanswered until one final message was left on my phone.

Cat, Help me!

I booked the next flight to Italy. When I buckled my seatbelt for takeoff, I didn't know it was already too late. I didn't know her story had ended and the terror of mine was just beginning.

Tomorrow, more than a year after the search for Stella ended, I'm returning to Italy alone. I promised Stella I'd go to the concert, but never once did I think I'd be celebrating our birthdays without her.

Stella is gone—lost to me at a time when our lives seemed to be gaining traction and smoothing out. I'd gotten over my schoolgirl crush on Lorenzo and Stella's betrayal when she slept with him. I'd married and divorced. Stella had dumped Lorenzo, who was now the Commissario of the Guardia di Finanza in Puglia. She married Antonio, the only doctor in the small village of Castello del Mare. She was persuaded by his connection to the royal family and his status in the community. She used him as another stepping stone to her stardom.

Affairs and drugs broke her marriage. The divorce left her free to be with Lorenzo, the man she and I both loved since we were kids. After her death, Lorenzo and I found each other, but even in death she still came between us. I shake my head to dislodge the continuous unhealthy soundtrack in my mind.

Events have changed me. I've successfully transitioned from accountant to chef. My catering business is thriving. I create fabulous food and events for all of life's special occasions. I'm far too busy to include heartbreak in my life.

Still, sadness surrounds me as I fold a cobalt blue sundress and tuck it into the bag.

Although Lorenzo and I reconnected after Stella's death, it hasn't worked out. The passion's there, but the commitment's not; neither of us are willing to leave our careers and make a permanent move to another country.

The summer sweater I'm folding drops to the floor. The memory of Lorenzo is painful and full of anger. Italy is my second home, too—

a country I love as well as my own. I have longed to return, but after what happened to Stella, and now Lorenzo, it isn't that easy. My emotions, my fears, and love are all intertwined with the small, walled village of Castello del Mare and the childhood Stella and I shared. And the man we both loved.

All that's left from those long-ago summers are faded images of us splashing in the Adriatic Sea. The images grow dimmer with each passing day. Since I returned to the Lowcountry, Stella's face comes to me from a watery tomb.

Those dark days when we searched for her are as vivid now as they were then. I stayed at Villa Fiori unaware it would become her gift to me. Nor could I have foretold the importance of Gino and Maria, the villa's caretakers, who have become my best friends and confidants. They embraced me and became the parent figures in my life because my own parents had perished in an automobile accident.

During our last Zoom meeting, they suggested that I not attend the concert. When I asked why, they gave me shoulder shrugs and pressed their fingers against their thumb to indicate fear. Gestures they won't or can't explain in words. When I told them I was returning because I promised Stella, they asked me to come to Castello instead of Tuscany.

I've given considerable thought to their request. Gino thinks Riccardo, although still in prison, will somehow hurt me if I attend. He believes the mafia, under Riccardo's direction, is watching for my return. The few times Lorenzo and I have Zoomed, he also mentioned that staying away from the concert venue might be a good idea.

Images and thoughts of Lorenzo roam freely in my mind—dark hair, hazel eyes, the stubble on his face no matter how often he shaves. As Commissario of the Guardia in Puglia, he's always in charge and always has the answers. He'll forever be the man I love.

Over the years, my toxic relationships with men are the sort that would not make for a Hallmark movie. Lorenzo falls into that same tangled, messy category. Last year, we were so close to being together.

But his job as a high-ranking officer and mine as a successful caterer created barriers that neither was willing to cross. One of us had to make major concessions. Risk-taking in all other aspects of our lives came easily—love and trust did not. For me, there's the angst of wondering if he'll ever recover from losing Stella. When we were together, she hovered in the background.

I pick the sweater off the floor, refold it and add it to the bag. I'm going to the concert. Stella went to great lengths to create this celebration for the two of us. I promised her I would attend. It's a promise I intend to keep—my last promise to Stella.

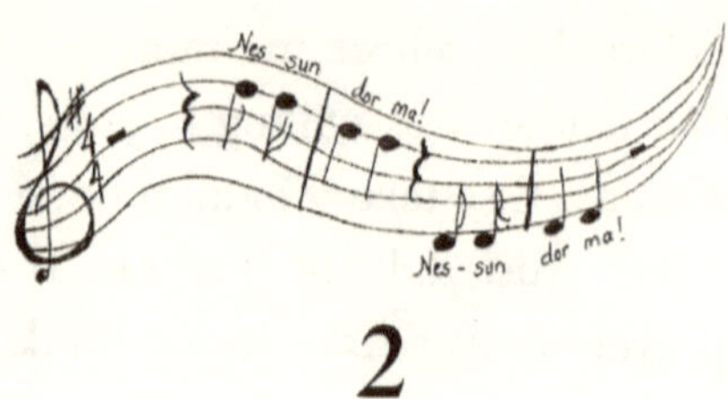

2

On the bed next to my luggage is a large box. It arrived from Italy a few days ago. Tears leak as I remove the flaming Dolce & Gabbana gown —Stella's dress.

Standing in front of the mirror, I clutch it against my body. The starfish necklace, centered by a rare red ruby and surrounded by clusters of diamonds, shimmers at my throat. The mirror's reflection magnifies its beauty. Custom designed for Stella, the necklace was Antonio's wedding gift to her—another thing she left me in her will. Once I wear the necklace, it will be retired—perhaps I will auction it and set up a college fund in Stella's name. It has brought nothing but bad luck to the wearer.

Of course, I'm taking it with me but not to wear. It would be tempting fate, as too many people want it. I smile inwardly at my devious plan, another aspect of this journey no one knows about. While my Italian friends may think my decision to return is foolhardy, I have taken precautions to protect myself and the necklace.

With tenderness, I caress the bodice of the dress with its elaborately twisted waist and godet hem. Stella wore this gown at the gala held in her honor at the Metropolitan Museum of Art in New York. She was the star that night. I was so proud of her and her accomplishments as an international actress. But all the accolades in the world couldn't save my beautiful friend. Closing my eyes, I monitor my breathing—in, out, in, out—just like Dr. Ginny taught me. After a few minutes, the internal trembling stops.

Is wearing the dress the right thing to do? Am I wearing it for the right reasons? The concert and the dress are all about celebrating Stella's life. But maybe I was wrong to ask Maria to send it to me. Or maybe I'm hoping she'll tell Gino, and he'll tell Lorenzo. I pretend to be brave, but am I?

Slipping the dress over my head, I stand in front of the full-length mirror. The silky material flares. The center-front slit swirls open. Tiny sequins twinkle in the gathering twilight. The starfish necklace sparkles as the last rays of sunlight dance across the clusters of diamonds.

The image of Stella standing by my side appears. She, strikingly gorgeous in the red dress with the magnificent starfish necklace at her throat, and me, standing by her side, looking like a proper starlet in my sleek black designer gown.

If only she'd confided in me that last night—told me about her affair with Lorenzo and how her drug addiction had ended the relationship. Maybe if she'd told me how, in desperation, she had turned to the mafia for drugs when her husband, Antonio, cut off her supply. Yet, his hand was only one of many which pushed Stella to the edge and walked away. At least he was punished. His license to practice as a doctor was suspended, and he served time for the illegal distribution of drugs. Maria says he's a changed man, but I'm not sure.

As I stare into the mirror, I wonder if I would have believed Stella if she had told me she was single-handedly going to bring down a mafia drug ring. *Would I have offered to help her, stuck by her side, downplayed her fears, or told her to contact the authorities?*

When her message, begging for help, appeared on my phone, I dropped everything to help her. But it was too late. By the time I arrived, she was gone.

All of us involved have suffered mightily—Stella with her life. If only she had confided in someone about her deadly plan to expose the drug smuggling ring. Maybe, just maybe, the outcome would have been different. But I'll never know.

My punishment is to be on the treadmill of rumination. Dr. Ginny is working hard to wean me off my poisonous, repetitive thoughts. Intellectually understanding the destructive patterns of rumination and trying to practice the steps to overcome the depression are two different things. Every time I think I'm making progress a major setback occurs—like this trip.

The fading light shines on the illusion of Stella by my side. I'm suddenly back in New York. Stella removes the starfish necklace from her neck and clasps it around mine. She leans toward me, our foreheads touching. She whispers, "One day, it will be yours."

She smiles, as only Stella can, and says, "The day will come when this necklace will belong to you. Wear it and remember me. If I can't make it to the concert, you must go without me. You must wear the necklace. Promise me."

She knew her days were numbered. I did not.

As quickly as Stella appears by my side in the mirror, she disappears. I chastise myself. *What am I doing?* I have a business to run. I have commitments. I don't have time to go running off to Italy to fulfill a promise to Stella. Yet here I am, wearing her dress and her necklace and remembering that promise. Shaking my head, I sink onto the edge of the bed. Tears for my friend leak from the corners of my eyes.

They no longer flow or bring on shudders or sobs so painful that they rack my body. My sorrows, like my memories, have softened into the haze of long-ago summers spent together, shared secrets, open wounds, and a friendship that bordered between love and hate. While Stella will never stray too far from my thoughts, the hard edges have been tempered by time. They have been replaced with a sweet bitterness that comes with ambiguous loss.

The red dress, with all its glitz and glitter, is carefully folded. I tuck it into the last space in my already packed-to-capacity luggage. Next to my suitcase is the packet of information for the concert—the occasion of our same-day birthdays is no longer a celebration, but a memorial service.

Next to the packet is the last letter Stella wrote to me. Even after two years, there's hardly a need for me to read the creased and tear-stained words. They are forever embedded in my mind.

...I was a fool. I'm so sorry for all the times I let you down. I never

meant to hurt you. I hope you'll stay and fight in my place. But if you believe your life is in danger, then Go Home Now! Whether you stay or go, live your life fully and beautifully for both of us.

I love you, my forever friend,

Stella

The packing is finished. I close and zip the suitcase. If I follow through with our plans to attend the concert, there's a certain degree of danger, but I assure myself it's not enough for me to feel threatened. The choice is mine to make. I have chosen to honor my promise to Stella.

♩

Castello del Mare, Italy

The dress was the clue. When Caterina asked for it, Maria and Gino knew she was making plans to attend the Bocelli concert. When they questioned her, she was vague and wouldn't comment. But in Maria's mind, asking for the dress was proof.

Maria clenches her fists and shakes her head. *Why hadn't Caterina trusted them enough to confide in them? She'd never been evasive before—why now?*

She pounds the dough for tonight's loaf of olive bread. Her chest rises and falls with deep sighs as she beats the already compliant slab into submission. She leans away from the counter, chuckles, and blows a strand of hair out of her eyes. Of course, she understands why Caterina didn't confide in them. They opposed her plan to attend the concert without listening to her reasons. Stella had been Caterina's best friend, and she was loyal even after Stella's death.

Instead of being supportive, they insisted she come to Castello instead of attending the concert. Perhaps it was because Gino had some knowledge of the mafia's activities. When he began to worry, Maria did too. Gino said that Riccardo's incarceration really didn't mean that much, because the family that Carlo Rossini had headed as *il padrone* before he was killed was still active. Gino knew that Riccardo had unofficially assumed that role, which made it easy for him to be informed when Caterina arrived in Italy.

Maria continues to pound the bread into the well-worn wooden table. She wonders what happened to change Caterina—to make her so fierce and adamant about this crazy promise she made to Stella.

She'd heard rumors that bad things had happened in the place that Caterina called the Lowcountry. They pressed Lorenzo for information, but he just shook his head and walked away. He knew what had happened, because he'd been on the first plane to South Carolina when he learned she was in trouble. The only thing he told them was Caterina was involved in breaking up a human trafficking ring. Maria wonders how someone who's supposed to be a chef manages to get entangled in such dangerous situations.

Maybe she is overreacting. She shakes her head with each slap of the dough against the wood. They've been through so much together. They came close to losing Caterina like they'd lost Stella. All they wanted was to keep her safe. She was like a daughter to them and a sister to their only daughter, Analisa.

She laughs out loud as she realizes she and Gino have become overprotective parents, shielding their baby girl. Caterina is all grown up. She's proven more than once she can handle herself in difficult situations.

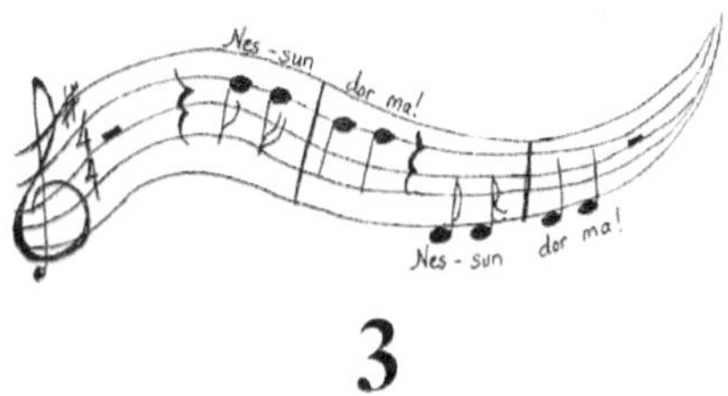

3

Rome, Italy

Every one of her days hums with the possibility
that she might be doing it wrong
~ Karen Thompson Walker, The Dreamers

For the tenth time since I checked into the Hilton Rome Airport Hotel, I open my purse. I'm jittery from lack of sleep and the six-hour time change. The packet is still there along with the tickets to the concert, the itinerary and the reservation at the posh Tuscan resort *Casali di Casole*.

As I've done many times since Stella handed me the large envelope, I examine the contents of this once-in-a-lifetime trip to Lajatico, Italy to attend an Andrea Bocelli concert. I still remember the dramatic flourish as she presented it to me. She was first and foremost an actress. While she hid her personal life, her behavior throughout our friendship was somewhat erratic and over-the-top. I wasn't totally surprised when she handed me the envelope stuffed with an amazing first-class trip to the concert. It was her style—her way of making up for the years of sporadic torturous friendship she'd bestowed on me.

We were born on the same day to mothers who were best friends. Our fates were sealed right from birth. From the beginning, Stella was in charge of her life and mine. She was everything I wanted to be —beautiful, popular, and without fear.

I was shy and reticent. I obeyed her every command.

When she handed me the packet in New York, I simply saw this expensive celebration of our 40th birthday as another way to be obligated to Stella.

But after her death, I discovered she had charted a new and better life for herself. Being named both the executor and benefactor of her will opened my eyes. A new Stella emerged—one who was working hard to change.

In addition to leaving everything to me, including her villa and priceless starfish necklace, she had left behind incriminating evidence against the drug smuggling ring. Once she decided to go after them, she began the arduous task of becoming drug-free. She believed if she could bring this part of the mafia down, she'd have a chance for a new life. If only she'd lived to see that her diligence and hard work decimated a large part of the local *Sacra Corona Unita*.

My fingers continue to sort through the packet until they stop at a colorful brochure of the resort. The photos are magnificent, with their sweeping views over the Tuscan hills, the private infinity pool, and the gorgeous villas.

Opening it to the center section, my eyes are drawn to the name of the villa Stella booked for us—Santa Lucia. My given name, Caterina Maria Lucia Gabbiano, has a long history in my family's DNA. I like to pretend that Stella remembered that small detail about my name—that she actually did care.

The edges of the folder are well-worn from my constant review of its contents. Stella's assistant, or used-to-be assistant, covered every detail with me numerous times. Still, I question myself. *Why do this? Why put myself through the agony—the reminder that Stella is gone?*

The answer is always the same. If the situation were reversed, Stella would do this for me.

Shoving the packet back into my purse, I scrounge deeper until my hand touches the three velvet jewelry bags. Once I'm satisfied they're safe, I resume browsing the menu as the crowd in both the lounge and restaurant grows larger and louder.

The Hilton Airport Hotel in Rome is always the same—chaotic and noisy. After the cross-Atlantic trip, I'm tired and wish I'd stayed in and ordered a meal delivered to the room instead of joining the boisterous mob.

The large, open room is packed with Americans—shorts, flip-flops, baseball caps, and captioned T-shirts—all smack Americana. Throw in the ear-splitting 'I'm from the USA' attitude, and you'd think you were in the middle of Times Square.

The Italian side of me often feels embarrassed for my American side. Of course, I know it's a cultural thing. Americans are expressive. They don't like long stretches of silence. They take up a lot of space, and they seem to think everyone wants to hear what they have to say. The behavior reflects the adolescence of the United States when compared to the longevity of European countries. Americans approach life naively and openly with a lot of optimism and in-your-face boldness. Somehow I inherited a larger portion of genes that cringe when I'm put in a room full of American extroverts.

I drop the menu on the table. The noise has dampened my appetite. I appraise the crowd from my seat in the raised cocktail lounge that overlooks the restaurant. At eight in the evening, every table is occupied. Several men with questioning eyes file past the vacant chair at my table. One is crass enough to place his hand on the chair and start to sit down. Each time I shake my head no. There is no room for a table mate, not because I'm a snob, but because I'm too tired to strike up a conversation with a person I'll never see again.

The chips, peanuts and pretzel mixture in a souvenir bowl featuring the Colosseum are quintessentially American. Yet I booked a room here knowing all this. It's an old habit—a hard one to break. Stella and I often met here to reconnect. Then we'd fly on to Brindisi, where her chauffeur would be waiting at the airport to whisk us to Castello del Mare.

Somehow, with Stella by my side, the place seemed okay. Of course, her stardom guaranteed we received the best service. She was recognized the minute she walked through the door. My problem is I lived in her shadow for so long that the habits have become engrained.

But where else would I stay? The Hilton Rome Airport Hotel is the most convenient and nicest place to stay when you're in-between flights. I try to shrug off my growing agitation, but without her I'm impatient with the boisterous voices and overly contrived outfits that scream a desire to look twenty to thirty years younger than the wearer actually is.

The face lifts, botox injections, and heavy eye makeup rob women of their natural beauty. The men are no better with their hair transplants or combovers, loafers without socks or sneakers without laces, and the ever present aviator sunglasses.

A bleached blonde sips a martini and clings to her decades younger escort. The laughter of a group of young women playing Balderdash pierces the air and catches the attention of passersby. Older men furtively glance around to determine if there's a possibility they won't sleep alone tonight.

A guy seated at the bar jiggles his right leg to some tune only he can hear. Flight crews, weary and ladened with luggage, make their way to the back room where a round-the-clock buffet nourishes their bodies if not their souls.

The Rosato I'm sipping, crisp with hints of strawberries and earth, doesn't soothe my disquieted spirit. Absently, I nibble on a pretzel while surveying the unruly crowd. Am I grumpy because I'm tired or because I'm lonely? If Stella were here, it would be different —maybe even worse with strangers stopping by our table to seek her autograph. Of course, when I was with her, she'd order lavish room service, and we'd catch up before having a nightcap in the bar so she could get her daily dose of admiration.

For a brief moment, my view of the dining area is blocked when the waitress leans across the table and asks if I'd like another glass of wine or something to eat. As she reaches for my empty glass, a slight movement behind her catches my attention. For a brief moment, my eyes connect with the eyes of a man seated at a table on the lower level. The too-long dark hair, the stubble on his face, the leather jacket, and the eyes—dark and brooding—latch onto mine.

There's instant recognition for both of us. I half rise from my chair as the waitress straightens up, once again obscuring my view. The eye contact is broken.

"Madame, do you wish anything else?"

"No," I murmur. I crane my neck.

She sighs, frowns, and moves to the next customer. But it's too late. The table where the man was seated is empty.

Grabbing my purse, I race out of the restaurant with the waitress trailing behind, calling, "Madame, madame, you haven't paid your bill."

The lobby is empty. I run from corridor to corridor. I push past people with startled expressions as they move out of my way. The waitress, flushed and panting, catches up with me and waves a ticket in my face. "Madame, please sign. I will lose my job."

Leaning against the wall to stop the spinning, I focus on her creased forehead and trembling lips.

"*Mi dispiace*—I'm so sorry."

I scribble my room number and signature before handing her a ten euro bill.

"Oh madame, it is too much."

"No," I respond. "It's not enough."

She nods rapidly and bolts away from me. The wall supports me as I allow the evil, sullen face of Riccardo to reenter my mind. He was at that table. I'm sure. It means only one thing. He's out of prison. He knows I'm here.

Yet I hesitate. My mind has let me down before. *While it's been a few months since the last flashback, could returning to Italy resurrect the old fears and brutal memories?*

Maybe it's jet lag or perhaps it's the familiarity of this place that conjured up the past. Or, maybe it wasn't Riccardo.

Like it or not, this once-in-a-lifetime trip begins now. I'm alone. Stella is dead.

4

The nightmare started when Stella was murdered. Two agonizing years since I was kidnapped and nearly killed. Two years, and I'm still confused about the gun battle that raged around me. It was only later I learned Riccardo killed Stella at Carlo's direction. There was no proof, but the incident set in motion the gun battle at the Zinzulusa Caves.

Nightmares surround that incident but the worst was learning that Riccardo was only sentenced to a maximum of ten years with parole or extradition a possibility within the first two years. Although he confessed to me, there was no proof he killed Stella. Her body was never found. *Where's the justice in that?*

The smooth, cream-colored walls of the hotel hallway close around me. My blouse is damp from being plastered to the wall. I watch with fear-filled eyes as the waitress rushes away from me.

The evil face I saw in the restaurant is still there. *Could it have possibly been Riccardo?* No, it can't be. He's in prison. When Riccardo was incarcerated, Lorenzo assured me he would stay locked up. Recently, through Gino, I was told that no court order had been filed to extradite him to Albania. *But what if something changed?* Maybe an early release or extradition was granted, and no one had the guts to tell me.

Only two people know I'm here—my best friend and business partner Cassandra (Cassie) Burton and my therapist Dr. Virginia (Ginny) Hollister. They wholeheartedly supported my decision to return and both swore not to reveal to anyone I planned to attend the concert. Yet here I am in the middle of a hallway in the Hilton Rome

Airport Hotel wondering if I've lost my mind or if I really saw Riccardo.

If Riccardo was released, how would he know I'm here? My mind scrambles to answer the question. Yes, of course, he knows. He's been waiting for me to return. The mafia will reach me no matter where I am. *Why was I naive enough to believe I'd be safe?* Gino understood that I wouldn't be and tried to warn me. *Did I listen? No, of course I didn't.* My determination to do what I think is right often gets in the way of rational thinking.

The neutral colors of the carpet and walls blend together. The chatter of guests fades into the background. The surrounding corridor empties. My body slides to a sitting position on the floor.

Being kind to myself has been the most challenging part of therapy. Dr. Ginny's voice admonishes me not to chastise myself. I quiet my thoughts and tune in to what she'd say to me in this situation.

"Cat, in your mind, you really saw Riccardo. Even if he wasn't there, he was real to you. You have to remember head trauma takes time to heal fully. Stress, anxiety and even lack of sleep will trigger these events. Your reality has been distorted. You've made tremendous strides, so let's work on ways to cope with these small setbacks."

The thing is, whether I did or didn't see him doesn't matter, as both options are scary. I begin the deep breathing exercises and clear my mind before considering my next steps. A calmness settles over me as I press against the wall and breathe, sorting through possibilities.

If I call Lorenzo and tell him I saw Riccardo, he'll know I'm in Italy. He'll be furious at me for not warning him. He'll insist on coming to my aid and providing security, whether or not I want it. He'll argue that I can't attend the concert unless he's with me. But if he's any good at his job, which I know he is, he already knows I'm here.

Then there's Maria and Gino—two incredibly kind friends who stood by me and supported me through every horror imaginable during my last visit. Maria risked being an accessory when she helped me escape the Guardia's notice so I could search for the information Stella had left behind. And it was Gino who came to my rescue when I was kidnapped. He and Lorenzo saved my life. They put their lives on the line for me.

And I decide not to tell them I'm coming? *Have I completely lost it?* Their opinions about the concert possibly being dangerous for me is not because they're dismissing me or Stella. It's because they care.

The thing is, this pilgrimage is difficult enough without all these dear people putting roadblocks in my way. I made the choice. Stella meant this concert to be a celebration of our lifelong friendship.

Returning to Italy is about my promise to Stella. I decided to come when Dr. Ginny indicated my nightmares and blackouts had grown increasingly rare. According to her, facing Stella's death is a huge part of my therapy. Honoring Stella will enable me to let go of some of the painful memories. I told her I was ready, and she agreed. But after seeing Riccardo, real or fake, my eagerness to honor Stella's wish is slipping away.

Pushing up from the floor, I trudge back to the lounge. The bartender's lips curl in a sneer. He turns away. It's clear the waitress reported my attempt to leave without paying the bill. He chats with every person sitting at the bar before arriving to take my order.

"I'd like an Aka rosato to take to my room, *per favore.*"

He shrugs and takes orders from several more patrons before opening the cooler and removing the bottle. While I wait, I glare at each person in the restaurant and lounge. My eyes linger on each face as I search for anyone who has the slightest resemblance to Riccardo. It's destructive for me to keep thinking that every shadow is a potential murderer and I'm a possible victim, but that's exactly what I think as I scan the crowd.

Did I really see Riccardo? My imagination, from time to time, conjures up ominous figures threatening to kill me. Shaking my head in an attempt to dismiss the negative thoughts, I turn to the table where I thought I saw him.

A couple now occupies the table. The man's arm is in a sling smudged with stains. The woman's scrunched-up face tells the world he's in a big heap of trouble. Red splotches appear on his neck as she ratchets up the decibel level of her voice. The conversation drifts across the restaurant and lounge.

"You idiot. You've spoiled our vacation. How could you be so clumsy? You said this would be a trip of a lifetime. Now look at you!"

The man hangs his head and doesn't respond. Yet I catch a smug look passing between them—a tiny thing that I'm probably imagining as well. The woman starts in again. A smile replaces my scowl. These two make me realize how thankful I am to be single.

I turn back as the bartender slides the bill across the bar. He holds onto the glass of wine until after I sign the tab. My hands shake as I grab the stem. Wine slushes over the rim. Seeing Riccardo or his lookalike had a greater impact on me than I thought. Holding the glass with both hands, I rush to the bank of elevators and the safety of my room.

5

Brindisi (Puglia)

Riccardo squirms in the cold metal chair. Although *Casa Circondariale* in Brindisi isn't a maximum security prison, any incarceration is hell. Thankfully, there are people on the inside and outside who take care of him. He's well supplied with life's necessities and protection.

His fingers drum on the metal table as if he's playing a grand piano. The small radio on the shelf next to his bunk is an example of one of life's necessities. Luciano Pavarotti's voice resonates against the concrete walls of his cell. Riccardo closes his eyes as the fevered climax of Nessun Dorma rises in the stale air.

Vincerò! Vincerò! I will win! I will win!

Carlo Rossini had been his *il padrone*—the boss of the mafia in Puglia. Riccardo had been his right hand man. He had treated Riccardo like a son, groomed him in all the ways of the mafia and all the niceties of good living. Drug smuggling, human trafficking, corruption, greed, and murder along with good food and wine, the arts, ballet and his favorite, opera.

Riccardo hums along with the famous aria from Turandot. He leans back in the chair and massages his neck before resuming his task. His nicotine-stained fingers stroke the little stack of white note-cards, waiting for him to write the messages.

He found the original card while foraging through the trash bin at Villa Fiori. Carlo sent him there to search for Stella's red starfish necklace. Instead he came across the note. The card shocked him and made him angry, maybe that's why he kept it. He never suspected Carlo was wining and dining Cat, much less sending her roses with love notes. He'd stuffed that note in his pocket—and then he filed it away with a premonition that one day it might be useful.

The note changed his relationship with Carlo. Riccardo felt slighted. When he flubbed Stella's death and couldn't find the necklace, harsh words were spoken between them. Although Stella was creating problems for the drug smugglers, Riccardo didn't want to kill her. Carlo had the power to wreck her career or smear her name—humiliate her in so many ways other than death.

Carlo's need to control and hurt Stella stemmed from a long ago insult when they were children. According to Carlo, she had deemed him unworthy to be included in her world.

Carlo often spoke of his childhood poverty and the many insults he endured as a result. But it was only Stella who had hurt him so deeply that he never forgave her. Stealing the necklace—the most valuable thing she owned—and killing her were his obsessions. Yet he'd assigned the task to Riccardo instead of doing it himself. Riccardo had botched the job by killing her without retrieving the precious jewels.

Carlo had raged when Cat, instead of Riccardo, discovered the necklace only a short distance from where Riccardo had shot Stella. He called Riccardo incompetent and lazy, a piece of Albanian trash. The bond that had been impenetrable was broken. Nothing he did after that appeased Carlo.

In the end, Carlo was killed, and he was hauled off to prison. Cat had managed to slip away. She returned to the US with the necklace. But he waited. He knew she would return.

He ran his fingers over the card's crisp edges. From his isolated prison cell, this small note would set a chain of events in motion—events that would ultimately lead to retrieving the necklace that Stella left for Cat. The one that would have made a difference in his and Carlo's relationship if only he had found it.

The best way to honor the memory of his *il padrone* was to follow through with the theft and the murder. He wiped tiny beads of sweat from his forehead. Carlo shooting him still caused him grief. He tells himself it wasn't vindictive, that it was necessary to the scene that was unfolding. Yet, he believes the whole business had been mishandled, and the memories still torment him.

He remembers how he waited, knowing he was the better shot. His bullet would have killed Carlo, but he gave Carlo time to shoot first. True, Carlo hadn't killed him, but he'd shot him without hesitation. A bond that had been so solid for years was wiped away because of Carlo's obsession with childhood pain. Riccardo shakes his head in disgust.

The SCU and Carlo had taught him that loyalty was the most important aspect of the brotherhood. Carlo had told him he was in line to take his place as *il padrone*. Instead, he had tapped an Italian protege with the explanation that as an Albanian, he didn't qualify. When Riccardo asked about his replacement Carlo refused to tell him.

That's when he discovered loyalty was nothing but foolishness. Yet he had stayed loyal to the end.

For a long moment, Riccardo thought about how he would have reacted if he'd known the truth. Would he have been so loyal? There was so much he didn't know about Carlo. Yet it was Carlo who saved him from death all those years ago when the overcrowded refugee boat from Albania capsized and was sinking off the coast of Castello del Mare. He'd been eight years old when Carlo took him into his home. He had treated him like a son, and in turn, he'd given Carlo total loyalty.

What hurt was how Carlo had played him, strung him along, letting him believe that someday he would become *il padrone*. Still he'd see this through to the end. That much was owed.

Once he killed Cat, he would slip away into the night. His life of crime and corruption would be over. Without Carlo, he didn't owe allegiance to anyone. The necklace and what he'd been saving on the side would give him enough to return home—to his own country and live a good life. His years in the SCU would vanish.

Riccardo picks up the note card and writes the same sentence that Carlo had written on the original card. The only change he makes is to add one tiny musical note next to Carlo's signature—his personal signature—a single note from Turandot. He wonders if Cat will notice. He loves playing games with his victim's mind.

He scoots his chair toward the cot and lifts the mattress. A cell phone nestles against the wooden slats. It was easy to buy off a prison guard. He'd been in this hellhole too long, but soon he'll be free.

He texts:

Need to see you tomorrow. I have a job for you.

6

Rome

Last night, I thrashed from one side of the bed to the other as nightmares invaded my sleep. Riccardo's black beady eyes infused my dreams. They hovered over the bed and watched my every movement. In my dreams, I ran without feet. I screamed without sound. I wept without tears.

At five, I struggle out from under the soft blue duvet and lean against the shower wall as the fiercely hot spray jolts my body awake. After a cappuccino and cornetto, I walk the short distance to the train station and position myself in a small knot of people. Turning my head slowly, I scan those waiting on the platform, although I have no idea what I'd do if those deadly eyes confronted me.

Everyone looks normal, but that's how we all carry our hidden-in-plain-sight secrets. No one is aware I'm frightened. The faces surrounding me appear serene, yet beneath the facade there could be fear, sadness, pain, or illness, or sometimes joy. But it's usually the negative sides of ourselves we hide from the outside world.

Standing close to one of the large columns about mid-way between the tracks and the exit, I check out the other passengers. My thoughts return to Riccardo. *Why,* I ask myself, *am I dwelling on the past when it only dredges up frightening memories?*

When I fail to answer the question, I resort to counting, a habit I thought I'd put aside. The numbers allow my mind the freedom to move away from the dark images of Riccardo. I count the number of columns, the light fixtures, and then move on to black luggage versus navy.

The sleek Leonardo Express glides into the station, doors open and in Italian style, without regard for lines or order, we all rush in simultaneously. I stow my luggage overhead and drop into 6D. Every person passing my seat gets a who-in-the-hell-are-you stare from me. I'm not only looking for Riccardo but also for his thugs.

The question is, how would I recognize a thug? What would I do if I did? I have no plan in place in the event a thug falls in my lap. These days, the mafia isn't the stereotypical Al Pacino or Marlon Brandon type. A well-heeled attorney, corporate executive or politician can easily be on the payroll.

The automatic doors shush together. The departure announcement begins. Throwing one last glance out the window, I continue to search for those eyes and that face. As we pick up speed, a man slouched against one of the concrete columns lights a cigarette. The hair is the same shade of dull black, long enough to tuck into the neck of a black leather jacket only a crazy person would wear in August or maybe a person who wants to be noticed. The sinister figure becomes a receding speck as I sink back into my seat.

Was it Riccardo or was it simply a lookalike with my imagination turning every black-haired, dark-eyed male in a black leather jacket into an assassin?

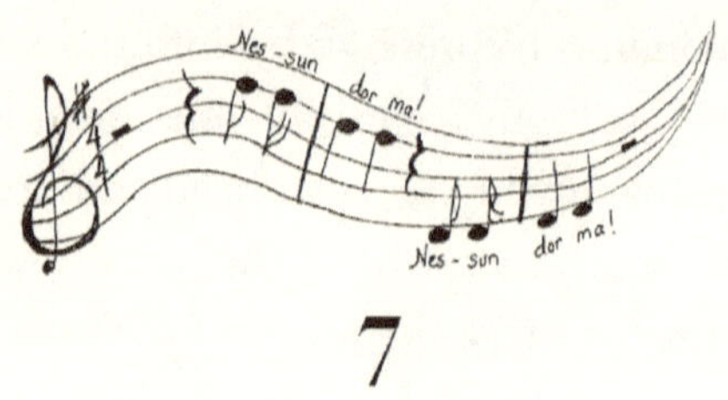

7

Florence (Tuscany)

As I step off the train in Florence, the usual lineup of chauffeurs with their signs gathers on the platform. Signora Gabbiano, in big bold green type, is easy to spot. I nod at the driver. He reaches for my luggage and points to a white limo parked across three spaces.

Fear has been building ever since last night's encounter. I'm not happy about getting in a car with someone I don't know. The driver is good-looking in that Italian way with a straight Roman nose, high cheekbones, a strong jawline covered in dark stubble, and bronzed skin. But it's not just the bulge in his jacket and his flexing muscles that ratchet up my anxiety level. He's a bit different from the usual driver. Although, after reading about how exclusive *Casali di Casole* is, I'm not surprised he's packing a firearm. Any resort frequented by celebrities is required to hire well-trained security personnel. But the concealed weapon is obvious to my untrained eyes.

On the passenger door of the limo is a discrete *Casali di Casole* sign in green script. The driver hesitates a second too long as he scans the crowd before opening the door. I slide across the cream-colored leather seat.

With my luggage still in hand he says, "I am Luigi. Would you prefer a glass of Prosecco? Or, perhaps wine, *signora*? Maybe sparkling water?"

"Water, no gas, please."

He nods, then realizes he's still hanging onto my luggage. *Mi scusi.*

He walks to the back and deposits my bag in the trunk. He returns and opens the door opposite me, reaches in, and unlatches a console. He fumbles around as it's the first time he's seen what's inside. Eventually, he locates and pours chilled water into a crystal goblet. He leans across the seat. His hand hits the headrest. Water splashes on my slacks. He grabs a small towel from the bar and looks at me uncertainly. I relieve him of the towel and blot the water from my slacks.

His voice is strained as he apologizes and announces as if memorized, "It takes approximately an hour to reach the villa. If you are hungry, thirsty, or need reading material, it's all available for you."

I glance around the vehicle to see if there's some script he's reading. His movements are clumsy as he unfastens another cabinet and points at the TV. In the space below, he points out magazines and newspapers. His face flushes as he opens several more doors and looks surprised at what's inside. One of the cabinets reveals a small refrigerator stocked with caviar, a truffled pâté, and several types of cheese. When I repeat I don't need anything, he says in the same scripted voice, "If you decide you'd like something, please use the intercom system."

My vivid imagination suspects he's either one of Riccardo's thugs or someone from the Italian security system. I'm not sure which would be worse, so I pretend he's a chauffeur just as he's supposed to be.

Even with the stopover in Rome and a few hours of sleep, my body tells me it's four o'clock in the morning on the east coast. Jet lag is in high gear. I place the goblet in the holder, unfurl the soft seafoam-green throw, tuck the pillow under my head, and push the button to recline the seat. I can only trust I'm safe in the chauffeur's somewhat shaky hands instead of in the hands of someone who might murder me while I nap.

♩

A gentle cough lures me out of my sleep world. My eyes open to paradise. A soft *WOW* escapes my lips. The dream continues as I gaze out across the paint-by-numbers landscape. The brochure in the folder Stella gave me doesn't do it justice. I had read the words numerous times:

Beautifully situated in the rolling hills of Tuscany on a 4,200-acre estate, Casali di Casole offers luxurious farmhouses, villas and penthouses with wood-beamed ceilings, stone walls, gourmet kitchens, dazzling mosaic tiles, travertine pools, and resplendent interiors.

The word resplendent stuck in my mind. I haven't had many occasions to use such a word. I repeat it under my breath as I try to imagine speaking to someone in one of those rather superior voices.

"Hello, Charlotte, did I tell you I'm flying off to Italy tomorrow to stay in a resplendent villa in Tuscany?"

The driver interrupts my fit of giggles with another discrete cough. He offers his hand to assist me from the limo. When I accept, he discreetly slips a business card into my palm. Perhaps he's a freelance chauffeur and has a private service on the side. I slide the card into my pocket and, still smiling, step out with the last sentence in the brochure lodged in my thoughts:

We will attend to your every desire during your time with us.

A man attired in true Italian fashion descends the stairs. He bows over my hand and says, "Signora Gabbiano, *benvenuti a Casali di Casole.* I am Marco Bianchi. During your stay, I will be at your disposal. No request is too small or too large. Whatever you wish will be made possible."

His good looks are fashion magazine quality. I wonder just what kind of "services" he might render in a resplendent residence—all of which has me hiccuping in order not to burst into out-of-control laughter. If Stella were here, she'd be dismayed at my outburst. She would be comfortable moving in this kind of environment. I am not. While my career as a caterer means I frequent the homes of the rich and famous, I am not one of the chosen privileged.

Marco Bianchi continues to hold my hand and my gaze while I

admire his smart resort outfit. White trousers paired with a royal blue and white striped shirt, sleeves perfectly cuffed to just below the elbow, along with Gucci loafers and belt. I'm betting his outfit cost more than my first-class plane ticket.

"Luigi will transport your luggage to Villa Santa Lucia, where Isabella will unpack and wait for your arrival. If you would come with me please, we'll finalize your registration."

I glance back at Luigi and catch his eye. His nod is reassuring or perhaps not. I have yet to decide.

We cross the terrace filled with enormous terra cotta planters brimming with sunflowers, carnations, and mandevilla interspersed with basil, rosemary, and various other herbs. The air hums with buzzing. Marco explains that they keep bees on the premises, gather the honey, and grow vegetables and herbs for the onsite restaurant.

I wonder if it would be in good taste to ask to see the resort's kitchen? Perhaps I could speak with the chef. I'd love to know which recipes he infuses with honey. Thoughts of food preparation seldom leave me. Even on vacation, my curiosity about food travels with me.

The ornate glass doors part effortlessly as we step into a magnificent reception area. Breathtaking vases of dahlias, calla lilies, and roses spice the air with soft scents. The stark white of the Calacatta marble floors flicked with gold pulsates with rays of summer sun shimmering down from the skylight. Magnificent works of art line the walls of the reception area.

This is the definition of resplendent. I've never had the luxury of staying in such a grand place. I don't imagine I will again. Although Stella made sure there were zero costs displayed in the packet she gave me, my curiosity sent me directly to Google. The villa she rented for us isn't something I could ever afford. Yes, this is a resplendent place.

Unfortunately, my descent into opulence is abruptly shut down when a shrill voice breaks into the magic kingdom.

"Neil Hickman, where are you going? Get back here now! You'll be sorry. You hear me? Neil!"

A flash of a blue shirt with an arm in a white sling whizzes past and disappears through the doors. Hot on the trail is a large woman with red splotches on her face that match the red floral print on her billowing caftan. I do a double take, as I'm pretty sure it's the same couple that were at the Hilton last night.

"Oh, shit!"

I gasp when I realize I've spoken out loud.

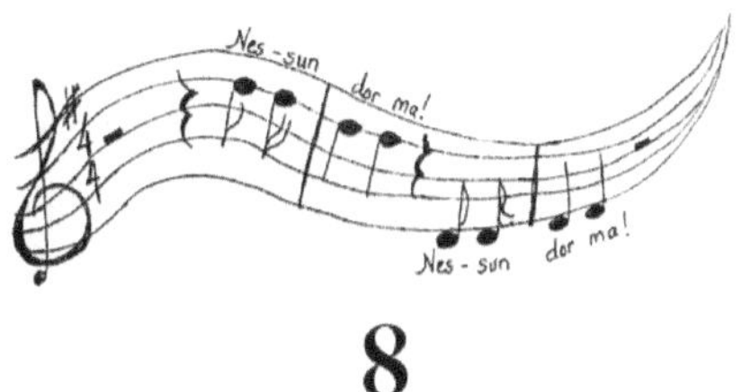

8

Casali di Casole

Marco rushes to Mrs. Hickman's side, "*Mi scusi, signora,* what's wrong? Do you need assistance?"

Anticipating more drama, I stay rooted in place. Marco escorts her to a seating area away from the entrance. He nods toward the reception desk. A woman glides across the floor with a glass of chilled sparkling water.

What are the chances that people staying at the same hotel in Rome where I stayed last night are now at the same resort? What if it's not a coincidence? Pivoting several steps closer, I take shelter behind a large marble column and eavesdrop on the conversation.

"Have a sip of water, Signora Hickman. There, that's better. Now tell me how I can assist you."

"There's nothing you can do unless you're willing to knock some sense into my idiot husband's head."

"Oh no, Signora. While I'm sure you're upset, there must be a better way to settle your situation without ruining your time at *Casali di Casole.* Would you like me to escort you to your villa? Perhaps a massage or a nap would be more relaxing for you? Or even better, why don't I send around a complimentary bottle of Prosecco? You can rest by the pool. You don't want to waste such a beautiful day."

Before Marco can finish his sentence, the woman is screeching at him.

"What? That's your solution? Imbibing in alcohol or letting some over-sexed man or even worse woman put their hands on my body. You think that's going to help? We're paying thousands to stay here.

Neil told me this is the place where the movers and shakers of the world congregate. Hmph! The only movers and shakers I've seen are the cleaning people. The only thing that will make me happy is a refund and a flight home. Now find my husband!"

"Signora, once your husband returns, you'll receive your refund. We do not wish for you to stay here a minute longer than necessary."

"My husband! You're telling me that a refund requires my husband. I'll have you know the only money he has is mine. Mine! Do you hear me? I want a refund now!"

"Signora, your husband made all the arrangements. The credit card is in his name alone. Your name does not appear on the registration."

"What? That's a lie! Why are you lying? Did Neil put you up to it? I'll just bet he did. He couldn't possibly have a credit card without my name on it. Well, what are you waiting for? Pull the file and show me every single bit of correspondence you've had with that miserable creature."

Marco's face, which initially held concern, turns a deep red, whether in embarrassment or anger, I'm not sure. He rises from the chair with a clenched jaw and nods at one of the drivers.

"Gaetano, please transport Signora Hickman to her villa while I pull the file."

"What? Oh no, don't think you can get rid of me that easily. I'm staying right here until you show me our account and that good-for-nothing man returns."

"Signora Hickman, I have other matters to attend to. I will pull your file and meet with you later. Gaetano can either take you back to your villa, or perhaps you would like to search for your husband. It's your decision."

"Well, I never! And what if I plant myself right here until you carry out my orders?"

Marco straightens his shoulders and stands, "*Signora*, you can either go with Gaetano, or I will call the local police and have you removed from the premises. It's your choice."

"You're a nasty bastard, just like Neil. As soon as I get home, you'll hear from my attorney. He will sue the pants off this establishment and you personally."

"That's your right, *signora*. Now you'll have to excuse me."

Marco backs away from the sputtering Mrs. Hickman. He spies me taking refuge behind the column and steers me to his office. The red hue on his face is replaced by a white one. I can almost feel the knots in the back of his neck.

"I apologize you had to witness that outburst, Signora Gabbiano. It's not the kind of behavior we usually see here."

"Please, call me Cat. There's no need to apologize."

I smile and continue, "I'm in the hospitality industry, too. I'm not sure how I would have handled the situation. You were calm and polite."

I pause, thinking of past clients, "I've often thought that rude people are unhappy people. The important thing is you didn't lose your temper. That was impressive given her stream of insults and threats."

"*Grazie, signora*—Cat. I appreciate your support. It's the first time since I was hired that I've had to deal with someone so uncivilized. The guests, like the staff, are supposed to be thoroughly screened. I'm not sure how these people made it on the reservation list. But I should confess that I've only been here a few weeks. I'm not aware of the previous management's protocol for accepting reservations. Sometimes, money speaks louder than the vetting process."

The frown on his face is replaced with a smile. He abruptly changes the subject.

"*Allora*, let's complete the registration so you can start your vacation. I only have a few questions."

He picks up and discards several files on the desk and then opens and closes several of the drawers. He shrugs and walks out the door. In a few minutes, he returns with a registration form.

"Sorry, I'm still finding my way around the place. This won't take long. Then you'll be on your way to a lovely vacation."

"It's okay. It's not much of a vacation. This was supposed to be one of those trips of a lifetime. A birthday celebration with my best friend, Stella. She—she's not coming."

"Yes, I see the reservation was made for two. Will anyone else be joining you?

"No."

"If you change your mind and want to invite someone, let me know. It would be okay. Everything has been paid for. Your friend's assistant explained the situation."

Marco's voice trails off. I can't speak. The silence stretches as memories of Stella's radiant face bring tears to my eyes.

"I'm so sorry. It must be a very sad time for you and certainly not the celebration you planned. Check-in will only take a few minutes. All I need is your passport."

I hand him my American passport—another advantage I have with two passports. No one at the resort is aware I speak Italian. I want to keep it that way—just in case.

Marco opens my passport to the photo page and looks around the office. It's almost as if we both discover the copying machine at the same time. After several seconds of examining the buttons, he manages to get the copier to work. He smiles sheepishly. I'm not sure whether to be amused or concerned. Weirdly, the manager of such a fancy place doesn't appear to know what he's doing.

The same is true of the chauffeur's unusual behavior. And the loud woman and her husband. *Who are these people? Or is this just me conjuring up things that aren't so?*

Marco slides my passport across the desk and says, "I apologize for the earlier disturbance. I'm also so sorry about your friend. It was truly a tragic event for the entire country, and I'm sure for you. Her death made the headlines in all the journals and on TV. Something about the mafia being involved?"

There's nothing I'm willing to add to the conversation. He glances up and slides the passport across the desk. I place it in my purse before asking, "Oh, do you have a vault?"

"Yes, of course. Would you like to settle into your accommodation first?"

"No, I'd like to secure my belongings in the vault before I go to the villa. I'm very tired, and need to handle this before I can rest."

"What size container will you need?"

"Something small."

We turn right out of his office and walk down the long corridor in silence until we arrive at a steel door. Marco unlocks it, turns the heavy handle, and follows behind me. The vault is a large walk-in with heavy-duty security along with a combination of safety features. Once inside, I select the size container I need. He uses his master key to unlock the box, hands me a key and says, "I'll wait outside. Let me know when you're finished."

I remove the three jewelry bags from my purse and place them in the container. After locking the box, Marco returns, double-locks the container, and places it back in its slot.

After the steel door thuds behind us, Marco says, "Are you ready for me to show you Villa Santa Lucia?"

"Yes, I'm so ready—not only to see the villa but to have a shower and a long nap before dinner. Is it very far?"

"Hmmm, not too far. Perhaps a mile or so. Is that a problem?"

"No, that's easily walkable, but I'd rather not walk for tonight's dinner."

He smiles, "Oh, you'll never have to walk. When you're ready, call the front desk. Someone will arrive within minutes to pick you up. Wherever you want to go, whether on or off premises, someone will take you and return for you. Walking is something our guests never have to worry about."

I nod. It's the first time I've stayed at a place where walking is something to worry about. I guess this is another aspect of resplendence.

"If you're ready, I'll drive you to your villa."

9

Casole d'Elsa

Neil Hickman shudders when the door opens. Although he's blindfolded, the brilliant sunlight penetrates the darkness. The gash across his cheek stings, and the pain intensifies whenever he lifts his head. He tries to track what they're saying, but there are multiple languages, some with soft, slurring sounds, while others are hard and clipped. He doesn't understand any of them, but he's fairly certain no one is speaking Italian or English.

Gaetano dropped him off on the outskirts of *Casole d'Elsa*. He waited until the driver was out of sight before following the instructions toward a series of dilapidated buildings enclosed by a high chainlink fence. A tattered sign above the gate *Fabbrica Tessile,* indicated the remains of an old textile factory. The gate was open, just a sliver. He pushed against the rusting structure. It creaked and groaned until it opened enough for him to slide through.

The directions said to look for a building with a green door. The narrow passageways between the buildings were dark and muddy, smelling of human and animal waste. He wasn't a brave man, but he was willing to do anything to get out of the mess he was in and to keep Gladys safe.

After stumbling around, he found himself outside a metal shed with a door that might have been green at one time but was now stripped of color by the sun. He turned the handle and walked inside. The door slammed behind him. He stared into blackness. A blow to his head dropped him to his knees. When he came to, he was bound and blindfolded.

The harsh voice with a heavy Eastern European accent interrupts his fog-filled thoughts. "Perhaps you're ready for a deal, Mr. Hickman?"

Neil's head flops down on his chest. His voice is small as he pleads, "I've given you all the money I have. Everything else belongs to my wife."

"Ah, so you don't care if we kill her. All of the money will be yours if we do, yes?"

It takes him a moment to realize the low moan filling the room is his.

"No, she has a trust fund. If anything happens to her, I don't receive anything. But if you let me go, I promise I'll get more money."

"The money is only the beginning Mr. Hickman. You seem to have forgotten you left Vegas without settling your debts. You disappeared. You thought we wouldn't find you. For that, the cost is more."

"What do you mean more? More money? Isn't what I gave you enough? It was the full amount I owed plus interest."

The fist came hard and fast. The hot, fresh blood flows from the cut on Neil's face.

"Please, I'll do whatever you want as long as you don't hurt my wife."

The heavy breathing fills Neil's ears. The smell of fried onions drifts in and out of his space as the speaker moves around the chair.

"There's a woman staying at the resort, a Signora Gabbiano. She has a priceless necklace with her—a red starfish—a rare natural ruby surrounded by diamonds. She'll be wearing it for the Bocelli concert. We know you have tickets and will be attending the concert and the event that follows. Make sure you're behind her at the entrance to the after-party event—a slight push on the steps is all that's needed. During the scuffle, we'll remove the necklace and vanish. Your wife will stay with us as insurance—in case you decide not to follow through."

"Gladys? Please, no."

"If you cooperate and agree to push the signora, Gladys will not suffer any harm."

"But there'll be thousands of people at the concert. Won't they notice?"

"That's not your concern. All you have to do is push; we'll do the rest."

"But what if the fall hurts the woman. I can't do that."

Another punch renders him silent.

"It's either her or your wife. Your choice."

♩

Gladys fumes as she pushes her plump body into *l'ape*.

"You stupid people call this contraption a part of your luxury deal?"

Gaetano stares straight ahead.

"Well, do you speak, or has your tongue been removed? I saw my husband get in this vehicle with you. Where did you take him?"

"Signora Hickman, I don't know what you're talking about."

Gladys glares at Gaetano and then stomps on his foot. The cart lurches off the path as he struggles to bring it under control. Beads of sweat form on his upper lip. He curses under his breath.

"Are you trying to kill us?"

"Fat chance of that. You tell me right now where you took that cheating lowlife husband of mine, or I will see to it that you lose your job along with that sorry Marco and anyone else who crosses me."

A wary, sullen look gathers on Gaetano's face, along with a scowl that would intimidate anyone but Mrs. Hickman.

"I took him to town."

"And just where is town?"

Casole d'Elsa.

"And?"

"I dropped him off."

"Good god, man, do I have to pry everything out of you? Where did you drop him off?"

"At the edge of town. He said he'd find a ride home, or he'd call the resort for someone to pick him up."

Gladys studies Gaetano's face. He's smart enough not to move a muscle or blink.

"Well, no point wandering around in one of your backward towns. Take me to the villa. Have that girl come and pack my bags. I'll be leaving in the morning. Tell that Marco fellow I expect him to change my flight and to arrange transportation to Rome. And remind him that he will hear from my attorney."

10

Casoli di Casole

Isabella's cell buzzes. The girl at the front desk texts that Marco and the guest are on the way to the villa. She removes the notes from her pocket and places one in each of the four vases of roses. The latex gloves are removed and placed in a plastic bag which she drops in her purse.

♩

Without further conversation, Marco and I walk to the golf cart. The silence continues all the way to the villa. He's deep in thought—perhaps murderous ones after the confrontation with Mrs. Hickman. Yet I have this sense something else is going on with him. As easy-going as he appears to be, there's an almost militaristic bearing about him, and there's definitely an edginess that seems out of place for a resort manager.

Since there's no conversation, I remember the card the chauffeur pressed into my hand. When I pull it out of my pocket, it flutters to the floor. The driver's name, along with the resort's name and phone number appears on the card. I flip it over, and in tiny print, I see *Lorenzo hired me. Don't trust anyone.*

"What's that?"

"Oh, nothing, just a business card from someone I met at the hotel last night."

I stuff the card in my pocket and force a big smile on my face.

What does the 'don't trust anyone' message from the chauffeur mean? Are there people at the resort spying on me? Or is this just Lorenzo's way of telling me he knows I'm here? Or is this just me with the world's largest imagination?

As Marco pulls into the parking space next to the front entrance, I dismiss my suspicious thoughts. Ever since Stella's disappearance and murder, I've been a bit paranoid. I'm here to relax, to celebrate. I force myself to look at the surrounding scenery.

The view is spectacular—rolling hills merge into mountain peaks. Lush vineyards, olive groves, and fields of sunflowers surround the villa. Centuries-old cypresses merge their blue-green needles with the sky. The air is flecked with gold dust, and flowers cascade over stone walls.

"You're staying in my favorite villa."

Not wanting to break the tranquility of the place, I don't respond. I let the beauty wash over me and soothe my broken spirit.

"Come on, I'll show you why it's my favorite."

He jumps out of *the cart* and reaches my side before I have time to launch myself out of the tiny vehicle. He offers his hand. I don't bat it away, which is my usual style. The door to the villa swings open, and a petite brunette, her bountiful hair cascading over her shoulders, calls from the terrace.

"Marco, where have you been? I've been waiting for the *signora*. When I called Gabriella, she said there was a problem. What happened?"

Marco hunches his shoulders and stuffs his hands in his pockets. "Not now Isabella. We'll talk later. Go back to the office. I'll show Cat—*Signora* Gabbiano the villa."

During the exchange, I watch Isabella's expression. It changes from delight to dismay as quickly as flipping a coin. The lovely young woman, dressed in a fashionably short black leather skirt and white silk blouse with plunging neckline, appears to be captivated by Marco. She waits until we reach the front door before glaring and storming off.

The air in the entrance hall is infused with the sweet scent of roses. A round mahogany table in the center contains a cut crystal vase with an arrangement.

"Oh, they're beautiful. Are they from the management?"

"Usually, but not these. Someone sent them to you. Perhaps an admirer? Would you like some privacy to read the card?"

I hadn't noticed the small white envelope tucked in the greenery. It's tempting to take a peek, but I don't. *Who would send me flowers? Who knows I'm here?*

"No, I'll check later. I want to see the villa. You said something about it being your favorite."

I follow him down the long hallway. Hardwood floors gleam against the cream-colored walls, which are adorned with tapestries and artwork. The aroma of roses drifts with us, as intense as a funeral parlor.

The hallway opens into a gourmet kitchen. I clap my hands with delight at the six-burner gas stove, the marble counters and a butler's pantry stocked for making feasts. After reading the brochures, I thought I'd be stuck eating all my meals at the restaurant. The thought of mingling with strangers isn't what I consider a vacation. Now I won't have to.

Marco beckons me to follow as he strides through the open French doors onto the back terrace. We stand at the edge of the infinity pool which overlooks the countryside. There's no need to say anything. It's magical.

Marco leaves me. The refrigerator door opens and closes. I hear the gentle pop of a cork. A crystal champagne flute is placed in my hand.

"*Benvenuta*, Cat. I hope your stay at Santa Lucia is perfect."

Our glasses whisper as they touch. The Prosecco is crisp, dry and lingers with the finish of honey-suckle nectar. Marco takes one sip and places his glass on the long wooden table under the pergola.

"I wish I could stay, but you can imagine what I'm facing back at the office."

"Yes, I understand."

I don't envy him as I remember without fondness one of my own unmanageable clients, Mrs. Randolph Augustus Harrington, who almost wrecked my business.

As Marco turns to leave, he says, "I meant it when I said whatever you need, call me—anytime. Will you do that?"

I nod. "What about security? The villa seems pretty isolated."

"This place is as secure as the Vatican Archives. It's patrolled by a security force you'll never see. There's motion lighting everywhere, and your intercom system has a big red button that will instantly connect you to our security office if you hear or see anything suspicious."

"Isn't that a bit much?"

"Oh, no, our guests require that kind of privacy."

Marco lifts his hand and nods before driving away. I close the door and face the vase of roses. If the management didn't send them, who did? No one knows I'm here but Cassie and Dr. Ginny. Neither are candidates to send me roses. My stomach tangles in knots as I approach the table and reach for the card. Hope rises that since Lorenzo knows I'm here, perhaps they're from him.

As I pull the note from the envelope, vile words jump out at me. I recoil as if attacked by a rattlesnake. The card flutters through my fingers and drops to the floor. The stark white rectangle against the golden hardwood stares back at me with words that are forever branded in my mind:

There are only eleven roses. To find the twelfth, look in the mirror. Bellissima Rossa!

Mi dispiace, Carlo

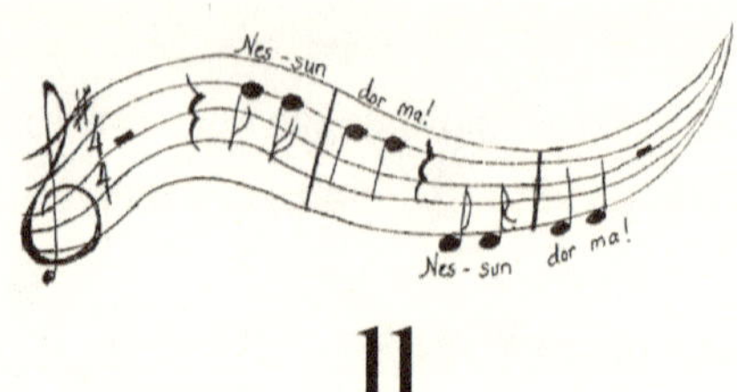

11

My entire world shifts, spinning out of control. Carlo is dead! Dead! My stomach heaves as the aroma of the blood-red roses permeates the air. My legs give out. I slump to the floor in a rubbery heap.

He can't be alive. He simply cannot be. But how do I know if he's dead? Perhaps that's what everyone wants me to believe?

Negative thoughts push through years of therapy and self-imposed barriers, the very ones I'm not supposed to dwell on unless Dr. Ginny is by my side guiding me through the maze. A low guttural moan rises from some dark place I've kept hidden away for years.

The memories dump out so fast my head reels. But nothing stops the boiling over of emotions long suppressed. Growing up with Stella's perfection had eroded my self-esteem. I stood in her shadow for years. There were so many small betrayals, but when she slept with Lorenzo, she crossed the line. She knew I was in love with him and laughed in my face. The summer ended with us barely speaking. I headed to college, and she to her modeling career. I met Richard at university and settled when he asked me to marry him. His abusive behavior tore our marriage to shreds. On my downward spiral, I grabbed at becoming someone else—someone clever, self-assured, independent, and bold. I attempted to model myself after Stella.

Excelling at everything I did from culinary school to my start-up business didn't help quell the emptiness that followed me wherever I landed. My parents were killed in an auto accident without time for us to make amends. I plunged into another sordid affair with John Ashley Williams, IV only to face another failure.

Then Stella and I attempted to reconnect, but it came too late.

My search for her was futile, and my tattered world continued to crumble. Then the day came when I woke up in a hospital bed and learned the man who killed Stella and tried to kill me was still alive. Riccardo. The name sucks me further into the abyss. Two years ago, I regained consciousness thinking both Riccardo and Carlo were dead until I discovered Riccardo had survived. Now, my trembling hand is holding a tear-stained card from Carlo. It can't be true.

More memories slide into view like a PowerPoint program. Rough hands jerk me from bed, my mouth is covered to quiet my screams and a shroud is pulled over my head. I wake up in a cave with my arms and legs bound and water rising—the nightmares are as vivid as the day it happened.

The image of Carlo's knife dripping with my blood as he split my forehead open is more real than the sunflowers nodding right outside this door. The heat of my blood oozing returns. If I were to wipe my hand across my face, I'm sure it would come away with sticky wetness.

The pain of reliving so many tragedies rolls through my mind like one of Evel Knievel's death-defying acts. Carlo's cruel smirk lunges at me from the corners of the room. He's here in front of me with a knife blade pointed at my face as he brags—*Sono il padrone*. I am the boss.

In that brutal moment, he tells me he was the one who ordered Riccardo to kill Stella—this man who held my hand and kissed my lips so tenderly. The agony is as sharp today as it was then.

On that never-to-be forgotten day when I learned Stella was dead, a fatal gun battle followed. Carlo, Riccardo, Gino, Lorenzo and even I—all of us were dead—that had been my last thought. The bodies fell one by one as bullets ricocheted off rocks before my head slammed into a boulder.

When I woke up in the hospital, I was told that Lorenzo, Gino and Riccardo survived. Only Carlo hadn't lived.

But what if Carlo wasn't dead? What if he had been spirited away to live another day?

Damn it! Two years, two whole years have passed since Carlo

sent me the roses with the identical message as the one lying on the floor in front of me. For two years, I believed he was dead. I thought I was safe, and he could no longer hurt me.

Is this a sick joke? Lorenzo wouldn't lie to me about Carlo's death. Or would he?

My thoughts flit like a swarm of gnats.

If Carlo is dead, who would send me such an evil message? Who would want to frighten me? Who knows that I'm back in Italy? Who would know about the note?

Lorenzo and Gino assured me that Riccardo's in prison, but maybe it's true that the long arm of the mafia is not a cliché. Riccardo's orders could easily be followed—even from jail.

But still, how would he know about the roses and the message on the card?

It doesn't make sense. My sobs become random hiccups. I can't live in fear or stay on the floor forever. I scramble up and place the note on the table. It falls open. There's a single musical note in the corner. That tiny note wasn't on the original card. I'm sure of it. I drop the card back on the table and race to the kitchen.

After locking the door to the terrace, I drain my unfinished glass of Prosecco and tell myself to be calm. I'm not frightened as it's daylight, and this place, according to Marco, has security like Fort Knox. Security cameras and motion-active lighting are everywhere. But I'm alone in the middle of nowhere.

The question is who at this resplendent place is my friend, and who is my enemy?

The throbbing from the long-ago head injury returns. Sucking in a deep breath, I push the fear back. I can't live in the past. It's lack of sleep, jet lag and exhaustion that have my imagination running wild. My mind will be clearer after a shower and a nap.

Pushing open the door to the suite closest to the kitchen reveals shades of contrasting greens— celadon against emerald —colors that calm and invite the outside world to enter through the bank of windows. There's no sign of my luggage in this room, so I pass through the butler's pantry and open the door to the second suite.

Another spellbinding view. The sun sparkles against the room's pale palette of yellow and cream. There's a writing desk and a chaise lounge. My toiletries are neatly lined up on the boudoir table. Before taking a shower and a much-needed nap, I return to the living room to make sure the deadbolt on the front door is secure.

As I enter from the hallway, the room opens into a large living space full of air and light—all cream, taupe and dark chocolate. The stunning view of the countryside is a mirror image of the other rooms. The tension in my neck and shoulders lessens as I gaze at the tranquil scene outside the large expanse of windows. I practice breathing until my balance is restored. I soak in the view until my tumble of emotions settles into a steady hum. The funeral home aromatic of roses has me gasping for breath. Turning away from the bank of windows, my heart leaps in panic. Fear rears its ugly head.

Strategically placed around the spacious seating area are three more vases of red roses—the piano, the mantle, the coffee table—all with little white cards tucked into the greenery. It seems like forever, but it must be only seconds before the adrenaline kicks in. I race across the space to the front door and secure the deadbolt. I pluck the cards from the roses. Each has the same message in the same script, identical to the one Carlo had written so long ago. A spine-chilling scream leaps from my mouth.

Someone wants to push me over the edge. Someone who knows my history. Someone who wants me dead. Riccardo—it has to be. With trembling hands, I stack the cards. Each one contains the same words and the same tiny musical note. Focusing on the note brings me back to what I'm good at—unraveling puzzles.

Why a musical note? Why only one? What game is being played? Who might have answers?

I text Marco.

The roses? Who delivered them?

After the lock clicks into place on the bedroom door, I sink onto the bed. Isabella has unpacked my luggage and has even chosen something for me to wear for tonight's dinner. My cobalt blue sundress hangs on the wardrobe door—something elegant and understated but not resplendent. That will wait until I dress for the concert. The concert—what a joke!

Is it worth risking my life for a promise I made Stella? Are the roses a threat to keep me from going or a challenge to go?

I check my phone, but there's no response from Marco. *Should I call Gino?* He knows my story. *Or is Lorenzo the better choice?* The problem is Lorenzo would drop what he's doing and book a flight. He'd insist that I pack up and leave, or even worse he'd stay. Facing him is not on my list of things I want to do.

Our situation is awkward. All the plans we made last year to see each other didn't happen. Either his work or mine had us rescheduling until the spaces in between our rendezvous became longer and more problematic. Reassurances that Carlo is dead and Riccardo is still locked up are all I want. If I have that, then I'll find a way to interpret the roses and the message.

I click on Gino's name. The call goes to voice mail.

12

When Neil stumbles through the doorway, Gladys doesn't look up from where she sits on the bed, surrounded by a sea of shimmering jewels.

He hesitates a moment and wonders if their playacting has gone too far. She's so absorbed in admiring her gems that she doesn't notice his return, or that his face is a bloody mess. He watches as she sorts through another bag, pulls out a gigantic emerald ring and aligns it with a matching bracelet and necklace.

He sighs loud enough for her to look up. A tiny cry escapes from her mouth as she takes in his bleeding cheek and black eye.

"Neil?"

Nodding makes his head throb. He eases down on the bed. She places her arms around him.

"What happened? You said you were meeting some people to clear up any misunderstanding about your gambling debt. This is far more serious than what you've told me, isn't it?"

He nods. Gladys pushes her jewelry aside and reaches for his arm. He winces and pulls away. She pushes up the sleeve of his shirt to reveal the rope burns.

"Oh, Neil. Don't move."

He closes his eyes and listens to the sound of cabinets opening and closing and the clicking of her sandals as she moves back and forth. She returns with a first aid kit.

"You need a doctor. The resort probably has one on retainer. Let me call the front desk."

He shakes his head, which sends a throb of pain ricocheting down the side of his face.

"Maybe later. Stop the bleeding if you can, and give me a couple of those pain pills. I need to rest and figure out what to do."

Gladys pushes a stray strand of hair out of her eyes and surveys the field of gemstones.

"If you think it's necessary, I can sell some of my jewelry."

"No, Gladys, your daddy gave you the jewelry. In spite of everything, you still hope he's not behind this scheme to ruin me. Anyway, it's not your jewels or money they want."

She interrupts him with a vicious shake of her head, "I've got to grow up. I'm not Daddy's little girl anymore. You're right! He's behind this scheme to discredit you. I should never speak to him again, but you have to understand he thinks he's protecting me."

"Do you really believe that? If you do, maybe it's best you go back to your daddy."

Gladys wants to scream, but she's too weary.

"You don't mean that. We're in this together. Lie down. I'll look through the jewelry and find some pieces that don't have any sentimental value."

Neil pulls a pillow behind his back and leans against the headboard.

"Gladys, you're not listening. I paid them back, but they want more."

She moves her hands through the dazzling stones before it registers.

"What do you mean? More what?"

She turns to look at him and notices the cut on his cheek is still bleeding. She dabs at it with a damp cloth.

He pushes her hand away, sucks in his breath and says, "It's the pretty redhead we saw at the Hilton. She's here at the resort. How in the hell can I possibly tackle her in a public place? What if my attempt to steal her necklace injures her? It's insane what they've asked me to do!"

Gladys' head is bent over her display of jewels. Without looking up, she says, "Neil, you're not making sense. What woman? What necklace? What have they asked you to do?"

Neil sits up and reaches for her arm. "Gladys, I'm a lot of things, but I'm not a thief. I've never assaulted anyone in my life. I was a gambler, a liar, and a cheat, but I promise you I'm none of those things now. I can't attack this woman."

Gladys' face scrunches up in bewilderment.

"What are you talking about? Who are the people asking you to do this?"

"The lady we saw at the hotel in Rome. She's here. She's also going to the concert. She apparently has a priceless necklace, and these people want it. I'm supposed to push her and steal the necklace."

Gladys' bewilderment is replaced with anger. "That's just stupid. Why in the world do they want you to steal her necklace? Why don't they steal it themselves?"

"I'm talking about the mafia. We're staying at a high-end resort, which means they can't barge in here and attack a guest. The concert gives them their only opportunity. They are using me to attack her."

"Well, if you're careful, maybe she won't be hurt. If that necklace will save our lives, don't you think you have to take that chance?"

Neil reaches for her hands.

"I can't put someone else's life on the line. Having yours there is already too much."

She looks at him and sighs.

"What if we go home? Talk to Daddy? You described these people as foreign thugs, part of the mafia. Daddy isn't involved with the mafia."

"Gladys, look at me. Look at my arm and my face. These are people your daddy hired to ruin me."

He pushes away from her. His head drops into his hands. He moans.

"You have to understand. I didn't trip and fall in Rome. I was pushed. I didn't fall on the way into the village. With the mafia, it makes no difference whether it's in Italy or in the States. They're connected. They're here."

Gladys shakes her head in disbelief, "What are we going to do?"

"We're going to stick to the plan. Finish dressing so we can join the group for dinner. By now, you've got the loud, dissatisfied wife role down pat. You've become so good at it that sometimes I forget you're playacting."

She squeezes his hand, "This is such a dreadful way to present ourselves to other people. They think I hate you. It's exhausting. How long do we have to continue this charade?"

"We have one last performance tonight, so no one will be surprised when you leave. Once you're on the train and safely in Rome, you'll go directly to the American consulate. You have an appointment for tomorrow afternoon. It will all work out. I promise."

She shakes her head. A big tear plops on her hand.

"What if it doesn't? What if they hurt you? What if the woman doesn't show up for the concert? What if—?"

"Stop! We can't go there. We have to focus on it all working out."

Gladys scoops up the jewelry and pushes it in his direction.

"Take it. All of it. My entire life I believed my daddy loved me.

Her voice drops to a whisper.

"But he doesn't. The jewelry is about his control over me. Every conversation is about how much he's lavished on me and how disappointed he is that I married you. I should have told him off a long time ago. It's just that the jewelry is my—our safety net. Once it's gone, there's nothing left."

Neil wonders if she really understands what's at stake. Probably not, and there isn't time to make her understand. He gently squeezes her hands.

"All I have to do is give the woman a little push and create a bit of confusion. No one will get hurt. Then I'll join you in Rome. You have the reservation for the hotel. Wait for me there. Day after tomorrow, we'll start our new lives."

He smiles, touches her chin, and brushes his lips against her cheek.

"No one will find us once we leave Italy. I've hired a driver in Rome to pick us up. In seven hours, we'll cross the border to Slovenia. We can stop there, or we can keep going."

Gladys shrugs.

"Why don't I wait? We can leave together after the concert. I know this sounds selfish, but we paid an exorbitant amount for the tickets."

"No, sorry sweetheart, it's better if you leave before the concert. I can't be distracted. If you were there, you might be hurt. Please, Gladys."

"I'm frightened. I don't want to leave without you."

"It will be okay. In a few days, we'll be sipping wine in another country and our new life will begin. You stayed with me after I betrayed you and our marriage. We're starting over. Your daddy and the mafia can go to hell."

Gladys pulls him into her arms and whispers, "Okay, let's do it."

13

Much to my disappointment, I'm picked up by Isabella instead of Marco. The drive to the restaurant seems far longer than a mile. Isabella's furtive glances when she thinks I'm not looking are enough for me to feel like I'm being stalked.

After thanking her for unpacking my luggage and selecting my outfit for tonight's dinner, I try a variety of topics. She ignores all my attempts. The silent treatment continues when she stops in front of the main reception and points to the well-lighted terrace sheltered by a flowering pergola. The sneer on her face is obvious. The only reason that comes to mind is Marco.

In a tone devoid of emotion, she says, "Enjoy your evening."

I have a reasonable amount of nosiness and ask, "Won't you be joining us?"

The scowl that's been on her face the entire drive deepens. Her scorn is evident when she says, "It's part of my job."

♩

Events that include meeting new people are miserable for me. I don't have a knack for chitchat or socializing. The only reason I'm here this evening is pure obligation. Stella would insist I show up at the first meet and greet. Marco would have someone banging on my door if I stayed away.

A small part of me feels bad as this resort is all-inclusive. Stella would have dragged me to every meal and social gathering. She would have charmed everyone around her. I would have hung out in the darkest corner, hoping not to be noticed.

With such a well-stocked pantry at the villa, my first choice would be to stay in and prepare a resplendent meal all by myself. I plaster a smile on my face and join the small group of guests clustered around the bar.

The cocktail hour passes without incident as neither Neil nor Gladys put in an appearance. Prosecco is poured and appetizers—each one delectable—are passed. I poke, prod, sniff and taste each morsel. There are crostini Toscani which is the traditional chicken liver pâté. The spread is smooth, velvety with hints of anchovy, sage, garlic and lemon. I take a second one to make sure I correctly identified the ingredients.

Next are tiny wedges of melon wrapped in prosciutto. Simple and one I use often at my own events. *Bruschetta al pomodori* bursts with the taste of perfectly ripe and just-picked tomatoes loaded with minced garlic, black pepper, and a hint of mint.

The last bite I take is a sliver of soft, fresh pecorino cheese drizzled with honey—a melt-in-your mouth tidbit. One I will add to my list.

Marco and Isabella circulate and introduce guests. Awkward exchanges morph into conversations once common ground is discovered. Since I prefer to observe rather than socialize, I wander to the large expanse of windows overlooking the valley and the setting sun.

My thoughts are disrupted when a hand touches my shoulder.

Marco produces a bottle of Prosecco and refills my glass. "I'm sorry I didn't get back to you about the flowers."

Before I can speak, he shrugs his shoulders and says, "I was busy all afternoon with the Hickmans. They've decided to stay for the concert and then leave. *Mio dio*, what an exhausting pair they are."

I nod in agreement. He leans in closer. "Can you stay after dinner? I'll fill you in about the flowers."

"Yes, of course."

He smiles and moves on to the next group. As the evening

progresses, he flits from guest to guest like a honeybee to flower. Are they pleased with their accommodations? What else can he do to make their stay perfect? I don't envy him as it seems the more money people shell out, the more demands they make, as if it's their right to be pushy and rude.

Out of curiosity, I observe him. He often defers to other staff members to answer questions. It surprises me that a place like this would hire someone who doesn't seem to know much about the resort's operation. While he said he's only been here a few weeks, I'm sure he wouldn't have been hired without having an extensive background in hospitality management. He dresses and acts the part, but he doesn't fit the profile for this upscale resort. Sure he's handsome, elegant, charming, and his manners are top-notch, yet he's hesitant and often appears confused and uncomfortable.

Then there's Isabella—I give her two adjectives—sophisticated and arrogant. She plays the role of a posh resort employee better than Marco. Her function appears to be one of expediency and efficiency, as well as sniffing out Marco. These traits do not convey a warm or welcoming vibe.

Oh dear, here I go again—trying to create intrigue where there isn't any.

I tell myself to stop this nonsense. As a caterer in the South Carolina Lowcountry, I understand the amount of effort it takes to keep people happy when they're shelling out a lot of money. Most of my events run smoothly, but I've had my share of people like Gladys Hickman.

At the end of a long day with surly clients, murder is often on my mind or at least a slap to the head. So Marco and Isabella's predicament is understandable. I dismiss my unease.

♩

Tiny twinkling lights weave through the pergola. They compete with the stars. Candles glimmer across a long table set with elegant linens and china—not exactly the Italian family-style meal I prefer.

Marco seats me on his right, and a lovely blonde, attired in a violet sundress and dripping with jewels, sits on his left. The other elegantly dressed guests find their places around the table. Isabella is visibly absent. Two spaces remain empty—probably for the Hickmans.

As the wine is being poured, a movement in the far corner of the terrace catches my eye. It's a dark corner, but the shimmer of Isabella's yellow floral maxi shift attracts my attention. If Stella were with me, she'd say, *That bitch has style and more money than class to wear that Carolina Herrera dress to a party when she's an employee and not a guest.*

I wouldn't have responded because it would have only agitated Stella, and she would continue. She never wanted to be in a room if another woman had the potential to outshine her. Tonight, Isabella could have been that woman.

The first course arrives—a scrumptious plate of burrata and prosciutto, and the last of the summer tomatoes. The dish is drizzled with olive oil and topped with a chiffonade of basil. Next, the pasta course arrives topped with shaved truffles. Murmurs of approval are interrupted when a ruckus causes everyone to stop eating and look in the direction of the commotion.

Mrs. Hickman half drags and half pushes Mr. Hickman across the terrace as she yells, "You stupid fool. How could you fall again! Look at you—a broken arm and now a stitched-up face. What are you planning to do for your third act? Break a leg?"

Every head in the group turns to Neil. With his arm in a cast and a bandage covering half his face, he looks like a victim of torture. Marco rises halfway out of his chair. His face darkens. His hands curl into fists.

Gladys strides across the terrace, never letting go of Neil. He stumbles as she yanks him along. She pulls out a chair at the end of the table and pushes him into it. Before sitting, she surveys us with eyes squinting out of puffy, quivering cheeks.

"You people started without us? You know how much money we've paid to be in this rat trap, and you don't have the decency to wait? Well!"

She doesn't pause for a reply but makes a sort of snorting noise before she continues, "You!"

She points at Marco who has straightened into a full-standing position. His clenched fists graze the top of the table.

"Yes, you! Where's our food? Don't just stand there! I want to see the million-dollar service I've paid for. Where's the wine? I want a bottle of red right now!"

Marco is paralyzed. I glance around in search of Isabella. Surely, she'll come to his rescue. But it's the chef and the wait staff who appear with two plates piled high with antipasti. Shortly after, Isabella follows with a bottle of red wine and two glasses. Her eyes connect with Marco. She gives a tiny nod before opening the wine to total silence.

All eyes are locked on the Hickmans to see what will happen next. I feel sad for them. I wonder what traumatic event occurred in her lifetime to create such an abrasive and on-edge personality. There's some serious stuff going on in their relationship.

From my own experiences, I've learned that our lives contain secrets we keep hidden from the world. Gladys' strident voice and erratic behavior seem to me a shield against her deep-seated insecurities. I relax. Reaching out, I touch Marco's arm. His fists uncurl, he smiles and sits down.

Conversation resumes for a few minutes before Gladys, after downing a large glass of wine, begins another tirade. First about the food, then the wine, their accommodations, the expense and her lowlife husband. I try to tune out and start a conversation with the man sitting on my left. But he's locked into what's happening at the other end of the table and doesn't bother to answer my half-hearted question.

It's impossible not to listen to her loud Texas twang. The harsh sounds bounce off the old stone walls and vibrate around the terrace. The words are unrelenting with their criticism of the entire world this woman lives in.

I whisper to Marco, "This little scene is only going to get worse. Forgive me, but I'm going to skip dessert. Is there someone who can drive me to the villa?"

He leans close and says, "Please don't leave. I need support to cope with her. If she decides to sue, I'll need witnesses."

I take a swallow of wine. What are the odds that Stella would have chosen a posh resort that's overflowing with trouble?

Marco doesn't notice I'm lost in my own thoughts. He continues, "I also want to give you the information about the roses. There's a side terrace through the dining room on the right. Please wait there for me. As soon as the group finishes dessert, I'll take you to the villa. We can talk about the flowers on the way."

I nod and push back from the table. Before I can stand, Neil jumps up, and knocks over his chair and stumbles against the table. His hand grabs at the glass of wine, but it's too late. It tilts in slow motion before tumbling into Gladys' lap.

She shrieks, "You stupid fool! Look what you've done! My daddy warned me about you. Neil Hickman, this is the end. You paid for this place with my money—my money! You're a leech, but you're not going to bleed me dry."

"Damm it, Gladys! If you're so unhappy, then leave. I'm sick of listening to you complain. Everyone here is sick of listening to you."

There's a collective sucking in of breath around the table. It's a miracle we don't all stand and applaud. Instead all heads turn and focus on the standoff. Gladys' eyes, almost buried in her pudgy face, open wide. They glance around the table before settling back on Neil. She stands and pushes the table as hard as she can. Wine glasses tumble as the table slams into Neil.

"How dare you humiliate me! You are going to regret every word."

She gathers her flaming red shawl off the back of the chair, flings it around her shoulders and stomps past all the downcast eyes. She pauses by Marco.

"Don't think for a minute that you're off the hook. You'll be hearing from my lawyer. This place is nothing but a scam. Luxury, my foot! You people don't have a clue!"

After a period of stunned silence, when even the cicadas are quiet, Mr. Hickman stutters an apology and disappears off the edge of the terrace into the darkness. The staff whisk away overturned glasses, remove plates and utensils, and strip the table as Marco gathers us in the bar. Everyone passes on dessert, but no one turns down a glass of limoncello or Vin Santo. The conversation is muted. The atmosphere is full of tension. Within minutes most of the guests, with Isabella's help, quietly drift away.

With a glass of Vin Santo, I head for the side terrace. As I approach the door, a hand reaches around me and opens it. I look back, expecting Marco. Instead, it's the man who was sitting next to me at dinner—the one who ignored me. I nod and say thank you. After slipping through the opening, I walk to the low stone wall and gaze across the valley. The town of Casole d'Elsa lights up the hillside.

I keep my back to the restaurant and hope the guy who came through the door with me will go away. But it's not my lucky night.

"Beautiful evening."

Not wishing to encourage conversation, I don't respond.

"Sorry, am I disturbing you?"

"Actually, you are. I was hoping to have some time alone before I return to my villa."

"Well, that's honest. I'll leave you, but for granting your wish, you need to grant mine."

"What?"

"Don't look so surprised. You tried to engage me in conversation during dinner. I apologize for ignoring you, but entertainment like the Hickmans couldn't be missed. My name's Frank, Frank Woodlee. My wish is that you let me escort you back to your villa."

"Mr. Woodlee, you're most kind, but I already have a ride. If you don't mind, I'd like to enjoy the view alone."

"Oh, but I do mind. You're too lovely to be alone."

He moves into my space. The nastiness of cigar smoke embedded in his jacket makes my nostrils flare.

"But I choose to be alone."

He caresses my shoulder.

"Don't touch me again."

He reaches for my arm just as Marco barges through the door.

"Signora Gabbiano, if you're ready, I'll drive you back to your villa. Signor Woodlee, please excuse us. The bar is still open if you'd like another drink. Isabella can assist you. Enjoy the rest of the evening."

Marco offers his arm, but I ignore him. I hold my head high and walk with what I hope is my best strut.

When the door closes behind me, Marco asks, "What was that about?"

"Thank you for your timing. It was perfect. Otherwise, that man was just about to see Krav Maga in action."

Marco throws back his head and laughs. "You are full of surprises. I would have never suspected that you practice Krav Maga. Good for you! If that *buffone* gives you any trouble, let me know. But I'm guessing you can handle him. Tell me why you know Krav Maga."

"A course in self-defense seemed like a smart thing to do when I discovered human trafficking was taking place on a property I was checking out for an event. There's a studio close to where I live that offers a variety of martial arts. The owner suggested Krav Maga."

Marco stops and turns to face me.

"Are you serious? You're a caterer, right? That doesn't sound like a dangerous job. So how does a caterer get involved in human trafficking?"

"That's a very long story, and I'm too tired tonight."

"Can you at least tell me if you've used Krav Maga?"

"I have. One time, it worked and another time it didn't, but I was at a disadvantage. What about you?"

For a moment, Marco's discomfort is obvious. He hesitates too long and looks over his shoulder before answering.

"Yeah, but it's been a while since I've practiced. I'm a little out of shape."

He doesn't look out of shape to me. My cell vibrates as we reach the cart. After I'm settled in my seat, I check. Gino's message says to call him no matter how late.

14

Frank Woodlee stands in the shadows and watches as Cat and Marco drive off into the night. He slips a gold, embossed cigar case from his jacket and clicks on the small notch. After examining the contents, he selects a slender Cohiba Behike Cuban from the group. He places it under his nose and inhales before trimming the head. The flame of his lighter caresses the foot before lighting. He gently draws in the smoke and lets it rest in his mouth. He savors the rich, complex flavors.

He pulls out his mobile and places the call. "She's here. She's feisty, maybe more than you bargained for."

♩

Marco is quiet on the drive to the villa. The moon is a sliver shy of being a brilliant orange harvest orb. Based on its trajectory, it will be gloriously full on the night of Bocelli's concert.

Should I go?

It's the question I ask myself over and over. Perhaps after speaking with Gino, I can make a decision. I squirm, trying to locate a more comfortable position on the rock-hard seat. The cart bounces against the gravel pathway as I think about tonight's fiasco with the Hickmans and that Woodlee man. I'm ready for PJs, soft music, and a cup of tea.

As we approach the villa, automated lights inside and out accentuate the entire house. It's easy to see no one is home. A chill settles across my back. I shiver.

Marco glances over, "What's wrong, Cat?"

"I'm spooked by the roses. What did you find out?"

"Not much. They were sent through Interflora from a shop in Milan. It seems a young woman placed the order and paid cash."

"A woman bought the roses and sent them to me? That's unusual."

"She was sending them for someone else."

I wait until Marco pulls into the parking space.

"I don't understand."

He leans back against the seat and turns toward me.

"When she was asked to provide the sender's information, she said she couldn't. She told the shopkeeper a man stopped her on the street and offered her fifty euros to order the roses. She's a student, so that amount of money was significant to her."

"How strange. It sounds so mysterious."

He nods as he runs his fingers through his perfectly coiffed hair. He's nervous about more than my flowers. But what, I wonder?

"Once she agreed, he handed over the cash for four dozen roses plus the 50 euros for her. When questioned further, she said he asked her to remove one rose from each vase and keep those for herself."

"Gracious, that sounds like a made-for-TV movie. But what about the note cards? Did the local florist who received the order write those? Who gave the instructions for the notes?"

"We checked with the local florist. They said there were no notes with the order. All they received was a request for the four dozen roses with only eleven roses in each of the four vases. The resort was called. It was Gaetano who picked them up and delivered them to your villa. He said no notes were in the vases."

I think back to my arrival. Isabella was the only one in the villa. *Is she involved? Or Gaetano? Or even Marco?*

The night air feels oppressive as he continues, "Our security talked to the shopkeeper in Milan. She said the young woman refused to give out her personal contact information. They pulled the footage from the security camera."

"What did they find?"

"Nothing they could use. The photo showed a male in jeans and a hoodie talking to the girl. They were turned away from the camera, so their faces were blurry. We're checking the area for other cameras, but it's doubtful we'll come up with anything."

"And the local florist?"

"They just received the order from Milan minus notecards. Do you want me to pursue this? I can involve the police."

Now what? My mind skips from one what-if to another. *Could it have been Riccardo? I can't keep thinking Carlo has returned from the dead, can I?*

I turn to Marco. "Maybe it's best if I sleep on it and make the decision in the morning. Do you have any thoughts?"

"Well, Cat, you're a beautiful woman. Any man who knows you might want to send you dozens of roses. I'm guessing you have an admirer. Perhaps someone you left back in South Carolina or someone here?"

The question hangs between us as he slides from behind the wheel and walks around to my side. He leans in and smiles before offering his hand. I can't think of a clever response, much less a face-saving one, so I don't respond.

"Cat?"

"Yes?"

"I sent Isabella around during dinner. She removed all the roses. Is that okay?"

A big sigh of relief wells up in my throat but only for a moment. While I'm thankful the flowers won't be there, it means Isabella has a key, along with Marco and possibly others.

When we arrive at the front door he takes the keys from my hand and unlocks it. "Why don't I check out the premises? I can stay for a while if you like."

"You're incredibly kind, but I'm okay. You're probably right about it being someone I know. I'm really tired and still have the jet lag thing going on. I need sleep. I can't show up to see Maestro Bocelli looking bedraggled."

Taking the keys from his hand, I say, "*Buonanotte. A domani.*"

I watch as he backs onto the path and turns around. I wait until the taillights disappear before locking the deadbolt in place. I kick off my shoes and click on Gino's cell number.

15

Gino picks up on the first ring. He puts me on speaker. Maria's voice gathers me in her warm embrace.

Mia cara ragazza, dove sei? Sei qui—in Italia, vero? Perché non ce lo hai detto?

The disappointment in her question reaches through the phone as she asks why I returned to Italy without letting them know.

How do I tell her I didn't want anyone to know? One of the last things they said to me before I returned to the States was that they didn't want me to go to the concert because they had a bad feeling about it. Italians are adamant about bad feelings. Now Maria is upset.

"Maria, I'm so sorry, but I didn't decide until the last minute."

"No, Caterina, you decided the day you asked me to mail you Stella's dress. I knew in my heart you would attend the concert. Why didn't you trust us enough to tell us?"

Before I can explain, the speaker is turned off, and Gino speaks.

"She's upset, Caterina. She'll be okay."

"I'm so sorry, but I simply couldn't argue with you and Maria about my decision. I'm not doing this for anyone but Stella. Maybe one day you'll understand."

"Caterina, we do understand. We know how close you and Stella were. But after what happened to Stella, Maria worries that something will happen to you. When Maria gets these bad feelings, she won't let go. She comes from a superstitious family. But it will all work out."

I kick off my shoes and fidget with the zipper on my sundress.

"I hope so, but that's not why I called. I need your help, Gino."

"What's wrong?"

"Nothing's wrong. Well, except I think I saw Riccardo—more than once. In a hotel in Rome and at the train station. Can you confirm that he's still in prison? He is, isn't he?"

"*Certo*, he will be in prison for a long time. If it makes you feel safer, I'll check in with Lorenzo. But he would have contacted me if there had been a change in Riccardo's status."

"I was hoping you could snoop around without letting Lorenzo know. You have a lot of contacts. Maybe there's someone else you can ask?"

"Sì, sì, Caterina. You and Lorenzo, what's wrong?"

I squirm out of the sundress and watch as it falls to the floor in waves of blue.

"We tried, but we're both stubborn. Neither of us is willing to give up our careers and make a permanent move. It isn't going to work out."

Silence gathers before he says, "I'm sorry. Okay, I won't contact him but don't be concerned. I would have heard if Riccardo had been released. I'll check around and call you back. Are you okay? Do you feel safe where you are?"

I hesitate for a second too long.

"Okay, tell me what is going on?"

"I'm not sure. No one in Italy is supposed to know I'm here. But when I arrived at the resort, four vases of roses were waiting for me. They each had a note signed by Carlo."

Gino's intake of breath funnels through the speaker.

"Carlo's dead—right? You killed him! Didn't you?"

There's a long pause before Gino answers, "The notes can't be signed by Carlo. Of course, he's dead. Lorenzo identified him at the morgue. He is truly dead. There is no mistake about this. Someone is playing tricks on you."

"Are you sure? We were both severely injured and carted off in ambulances. Did you see Carlo's body or witness the burial? I can't fathom who would want to scare me?"

"What about the people at the place you're staying? The arm of the mafia is far-reaching, and you can be sure Riccardo is fully functional even from his jail cell. Perhaps someone at the resort is watching you."

I place the phone on the bed and hang my dress in the wardrobe.

"Caterina, are you listening? This is why we didn't want you to attend the concert. Riccardo swore he'd kill you to revenge Carlo's death. You don't have any protection at that resort."

The bed has been turned down—my night clothes laid out.

"Caterina. What's wrong?"

"Gino, something is going on, but I don't know what. There's a chauffeur at the resort who says Lorenzo sent him to guard me. He drove me to the resort, but I haven't seen him since. I'm not sure if this man is who he claims to be. If he is, then Lorenzo knows I'm here. Then there's the resort manager and one of the employees. They seem like misfits."

"Hmmm, Lorenzo probably does know you're here, and it would be like him to send protection. I don't know about the others, but I think you'd be safer in Castello."

"Gino, I need to do this one small thing for Stella. I promised her I would attend."

"But you made that promise before Stella was murdered. It's not a safe place for you after what happened. The odds of something happening to you at the concert are strong."

"Well, I'm here, and the resort appears to be secure. There are cameras everywhere, as the guests who stay here want their privacy guaranteed. I promise that once the concert is over, I'll be on the morning train to Castello."

Gino is silent. Finally, he says, "I'll check on Riccardo tomorrow and call you before the concert. Cat, take every precaution. We'll be waiting for you."

"*Grazie*—Gino, whatever you do, don't bother Lorenzo. If he sent Luigi to protect me, then he knows I'm here. All I need to know is if Carlo is dead and if Riccardo is in prison. Okay?"

16

Their heads are a whisper away from touching. Heat radiates between them as Isabella runs her fingernail down his spine.

He jumps and sputters, "Stop! Someone will see us."

She giggles, "Last night, you begged me not to stop. Have you forgotten?"

He shrugs and moves away from her.

"Look, Isabella, we agreed that our personal lives wouldn't interfere with our day-to-day working relationship. Don't mess around with me during business hours. Do you understand?"

Her lips pout prettily for a moment. She squints her eyes.

"Well, what has happened to the charming Marco? Maybe it's the new guest. I watched your eyes on her last night. I guess when you drove her back to the villa, she didn't invite you in? Was I second choice?"

"Don't be foolish, Isabella. We're adults. We agreed there would be no strings."

"Ah, I see. Don't push me, Marco. I'm in a better position than you to walk away from this. Many people would be interested in knowing who you really are. It's much easier for both of us if you play nice."

She flounces off, hips swaying to some tune heard only in her head. She pauses, then turns around just before opening the door to the hallway. Her lips curl in a cruel smile. She blows him a kiss and whirls through the door. The tap of her stilettos and the sway of her hips are in perfect alignment.

Marco snarls under his breath, "Ah shit! I'm an idiot! I let something other than my brain dictate my actions."

While managing the resort and Isabella presents a difficult situation, his bigger problem is his boss. If the commissario finds out he's been intimate with someone on staff who isn't who she says she is, he would be in a shitload of trouble.

17

Florence Train Station

Gladys boards the train to Rome. After storing her tote, she lifts the shade. Neil is standing on the platform. *Why is he still there? And why is he looking like he'd just seen a ghost?* She gestures for him to move away, but he doesn't. His body is poised as if to leave, yet he seems frozen in place.

The seat next to her heaves as a body drops into it. Out of the corner of her eye, she sees a muscular man dressed in black slacks and a black turtleneck. His eyes furtively observe her from under bushy eyebrows. She shifts her gaze out the window. Neil is no longer on the platform. Relief replaces her fretting. She's thankful he finally moved on. She removes a copy of *Donna Moderna* from the side pocket and pretends to be interested in the slick magazine.

A tear slides from the corner of her eye, but she pushes it back. The seat across from her shifts and huffs as it's forced to adapt to the body sliding into the imprint left by the previous passenger. She looks up and encounters a gangly young man. Fresh out of university, she thinks, and bound for a job interview. He fidgets, picks at his cuticles, and licks his lips—clearly, he's nervous.

She tries to re-focus on the magazine as if she can actually read Italian. She slouches a little lower in her seat and wishes she could disappear.

The aisle seat is now occupied. A businessman? Must be since he's well-dressed in a pinstripe suit, a nice tie and a good haircut. He and the university student make her feel safer.

Maybe all of Neil's warnings are for nothing. Still she considers getting off the train. She wants to be with him at the Bocelli concert. But Neil, who has always been her strength and courage, is frightened. Would those mafia types really let him go once he steals the necklace? Although she isn't sure it's the right thing to do, she stays on the train.

Her stomach clenches. She's afraid for both of them.

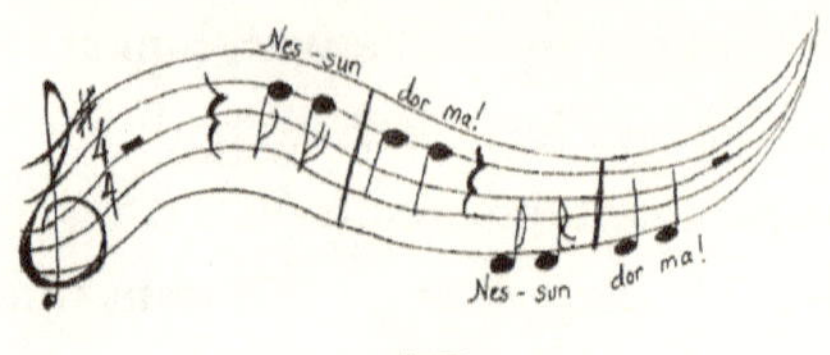

18

Casali di Casole

After a decent night's sleep, I plunge into the pool and swim laps until I'm exhausted. My body responds to the release of endorphins. Anxiety that has haunted me since I boarded the plane eases as I gaze at the peaceful and nature-filled landscape. A heavy sigh settles into calmness.

The luxurious bath towel—the kind I'd like to stow away in my suitcase—swaddles me as I sit on the edge of the pool. The sun peeks over the crest of the hills. Fiery red tentacles dance across the tree-tops. Threads of gold stitch the morning sky. The sun toils towards its highest peak. The valley blazes with an ethereal glow.

This simple moment of perfect peace protects me before another tempestuous volcano erupts. I let the sun's heat warm my body along with a cup of cappuccino before taking a long shower.

As I dress, my stomach rumbles. Foraging in the pantry and fridge, I find everything I need to make shakshuka, one of my favorite Middle Eastern dishes.

With olive oil warming in the skillet, I chop onions and garlic and scatter them in the pan. Diced tomatoes, smoked paprika, oregano, cumin, chili powder, and salt and pepper are added. During the slow simmer, I slice avocados and crumble a chunk of feta. After twenty minutes, I use a large serving spoon to create indentations in the sauce and slide in a couple of eggs. After another eight minutes, I turn off the heat and add the feta and avocado.

With thick slabs of crusty bread, I move myself and the skillet to the table and dig in. The only sound is my munching and an occa-sional sigh of contentment.

With my stomach happily full, I lace up my walking shoes and head to the resort center. After so much turmoil in my life, walking has become a natural healing experience for me. This morning I attempt to untangle my conversation with Gino, but a solution doesn't magically appear before I arrive at the reception. The ques-tion of whether or not I saw Riccardo continues to haunt me. If I did see him, then I'm in trouble. If I didn't see Riccardo, then it must be my mind playing tricks. Either answer is scary.

The automatic doors swish open. Marco looks up and moves away from Isabella. She scowls when I join them. The frown on Marco's face is quickly replaced with a smile—one that isn't as welcoming as his normal what-can-I-do-for-you smile that he's perfected.

"Cat, why didn't you call for pickup? How did you get here? You didn't walk, did you?"

I wonder what it might be about my walking shorts and shoes that he doesn't understand.

"Buongiorno, Marco. Yes, of course, I walked. Is that a problem?"

He flushes and mumbles, "No, I'm sorry. I thought you'd call me. Rarely do our guests walk."

I raise an eyebrow as it continues to sink in: I'm out of my element. *Guests who don't walk!*

Marco glances in Isabella's direction. She turns away and begins to sort through brochures. As she realigns pamphlets, her eyes stay glued on Marco's back. She isn't aware her feelings for him radiate like lightning strikes. As I watch the interaction, I notice that there's something else besides jealousy seeping through. It's an instinctive feeling on my part. I need to tread cautiously.

Marco loops his arm through mine and escorts me to the break-fast room. He closes the door between the reception area and the hallway.

"The Hickmans checked out. Well, at least Gladys did."

"What? When?"

"Sometime during the night. Gaetano was on duty last night. The problem is he didn't call me until early this morning."

"What happened?"

Marco runs his fingers across the dark stubble on his face. It's clear he hasn't had much sleep.

"Cat, in my capacity as manager, what I'm telling you is confidential. I guess I'm telling you as a way to protect myself. Does that make sense?"

"What? Well, I guess it does. Perhaps your boss would be a better sounding board?"

"No, that's just it. They don't want to be bothered. I'm paid a lot to keep things running without asking for assistance. I need someone objective like you in case I need a witness later on. I do believe that woman will try to sue us. I'm limited in what I can tell you, but it would help if you could listen."

"Okay," I say with some hesitation. I remind myself that I'm on vacation and listening might not be the best choice.

"But perhaps there is someone else who might be better qualified if this is confidential."

Marco shakes his head.

"There is no one else, and you understand the hospitality business."

"I do understand what it's like not having someone to confide in. It's often the same for me. Whatever you tell me won't be repeated."

Marco adjusts his shirt sleeves against some imaginary line on his arm.

"Thanks, Cat. I feel foolish as the situation with the Hickmans seems to escalate of its own accord. Gaetano told me that he received a call from Neil around two this morning. Neil asked him to open the front gates. Gaetano asked if he could help or if Neil needed transportation. Neil said no and hung up."

"So Gaetano opened the gates?"

"Yes, he did, but he knew I'd want some answers to this mysterious departure in the middle of the night. He walked to the entrance and found a taxi idling outside the gate. The driver said he was waiting for the Hickmans. Gaetano's no dummy so he asked the driver where they were going. It turns out that he was driving them to the train station in Florence. Gaetano asked the driver to find out what train they were taking and any other details that might be helpful."

"And the cab driver agreed?"

"Of course. It was to his benefit."

"Oh, you mean Gaetano made it worth his while?"

Marco shrugs.

"The driver sent Gaetano a text saying Signora Hickman left on the train, but he returned Signor Hickman to the entrance."

"Gracious, why would they sneak out in the middle of the night, and why would Neil come back? Did the driver say which train Mrs. Hickman took?"

"The train to Rome."

"So where is Mr. Hickman?"

"That's the problem. We can't find him. We guess Gladys is on the train, so that's one less person to worry about. There's no sign of Signor Hickman. Gaetano sent a text back to verify that Neil was dropped off, but there was no response. It turns out the driver used a burner phone."

Some part of me believes the Hickmans are having more than marital problems. And I'm not sure why Marco's asked me to be his confidant since I'm a paying guest.

I sigh loudly. Marco stops talking.

"I apologize for involving you. By talking out loud, I thought perhaps I could come up with a plan. If you'd rather I stop."

"No, go ahead."

But I think it's not okay. *Who is Marco?* While he possesses the looks and style of a posh resort manager, he lacks the necessary expertise. It's weird that he's drawn me into this strange situation with the Hickmans.

"Is Gaetano sure Gladys was the only one on the train going to Rome?"

"That's what the text said, and he verified that with the station manager. Of course, the taxi driver isn't to be found. The tag number that Gaetano captured on his phone was a stolen plate."

I stretch my shoulders and neck and move to a sunny spot by the window.

"So maybe Neil is in trouble, or maybe he rented a car? Sneaking out in the early hours before dawn seems weird. You could call the police, but so far, a crime hasn't been committed. Has anyone checked their villa?"

"Gaetano stopped by early this morning. No one answered the door. He said it was all very quiet—too quiet. I'm going to drive over there now. I'm also debating whether or not to call the police."

Marco hunches his shoulders. Worry creates small lines around his mouth and across his forehead as he continues to speak.

"The Hickmans are adults. There doesn't seem to be a good reason to intervene except I think something's wrong. Do you know anything about the Hickmans?"

My misplaced frustration at my own life creeps into the conversation.

"Are you asking me because I'm American, and they're American? I don't know anything about the Hickmans."

I blush all the way up and down before saying, "Oh, sorry. Maybe I do."

Marco frowns.

"Maybe you do? What does that mean?"

"It means I saw the Hickmans in Rome. They were staying at the same hotel. They were having dinner in the restaurant."

"Did you say anything to them?"

"No! Why would I? I don't know them. Besides, they were arguing. She said something about him ruining their vacation when he broke his arm."

Relief settles on Marco's face. He grins and says, "You had me worried. I thought you really did know them."

"Oh gosh, no! I'm sorry, but I didn't think to tell you when I checked in. It didn't seem important."

Marco places his hand on my arm. "Don't worry about the Hickmans. Like I said, they're adults. Based on their behavior, I think they are on the verge of divorce. That's not our problem. How about some coffee?"

I shake my head, and we walk over to the sleek bar.

"The only thing about the Hickmans that seems strange to me, other than the public fighting, is leaving in the middle of the night. That implies they have something to hide, or they're skipping out on the bill."

"Fortunately, I don't have to worry about the bill as everyone is required to pay upfront."

19

The gambling and golfing weekends in Las Vegas had been his downfall.

Neil shivers. The damp ground seeps through his lightweight trousers. He buries his face in his hands. Tears leak through his fingers and fall with loud plops onto the crudely written note.

WE HAVE HER

Years melt away to their wedding day. She married him against her father's wishes. He was poor, working-class—she was upper crust. They met by chance at Carnegie Hall—a free concert by the Prague Philharmonic Choir. She attended as the committee chair for the fundraising event. He was there because it was free. He remembers how she stood at the door in a pale blue grown with her hair swept up to reveal a lovely neck and soft, smooth shoulders. She asked for donations. He gave her all his money, including change. She recognized his needs were greater than the charity's and pressed some bills back into his hand. When he questioned her, she said casually, "For later when you buy me a drink."

Her father was less enamored. He did everything to prevent the marriage and had sworn to break them up, but Gladys prevailed. When Neil signed the prenuptial papers without any regrets, her father appeared to relent and offered him a job in one of his satellite companies. As time went on, he realized Gladys' father would never accept him. In fact, he made it his mission to derail their marriage.

The group of managers he worked with made overtures of acceptance. He was invited to join the country club and become part of the management golfing group. He was uneasy about accepting, but Gladys pushed him. She didn't seem to mind that his weekends would be spent with work colleagues and not with her. She believed it was the first indication of her father's acceptance of her much-beloved husband. She was welcomed back into her circle of society friends. Neil was included.

The weekend golfing trips turned into chartered flights to Las Vegas. He was not a gambler, a drinker or a womanizer, yet he found himself in the company of all three. His resolve to stay away from these vices broke early with the slot machines. He liked the high energy levels and the excitement that came with the bells and whistles indicating he'd won. He won often.

With encouragement from his colleagues, his gambling ratcheted up to roulette tables and all-night poker games. His descent into hell was swift and painful. For the first time in their marriage, he didn't confide in her. How could he tell her that he'd gone through their savings and taken a second mortgage on their home?

Neil's shivering brings him back to the present. He tries to stand but his legs collapse. He's not sure where he is. His eyes scan the surroundings as he wonders how long he's been unconscious or how far the resort is.

When he devised the plan to send Gladys on the train to Rome, he believed it would guarantee her safety. Now, he knows even if he follows instructions, they'll never be safe. He looks at the note with understanding. The mafia has his wife. The whole thing was a setup. The taxi, the beating, and the note all tell him Gladys is no longer on that train to Rome.

He tries to move, but pain invades his body. He presses on his ribs. They're bruised and tender. He inches out from under the brush and brambles and crawls to the edge of the road. Shivers continue to rack his body. When he touches his face, his hand comes away with blood. He needs to move to find his way back to the resort. He needs help to save Gladys.

20

The door to the hallway swings open. Isabella screams, "Mr. Hickman's hurt."

We run behind her as she leads the way to the crumpled figure lying on the white sofa, now splotched with blood.

"I've called *il dottore*. He's on the way."

I kneel next to the body.

"Mr. Hickman? Neil? Can you hear me?

A grunt and mumble indicate he's alive. There's a large, ugly gash on his forehead that shows signs of bruising and swelling.

"Get ice, a towel, some warm water, and some water to drink. He's probably dehydrated."

Isabella disappears and returns just as the doctor arrives. We back away to give him space. He pulls up each eyelid and squints into Neil's eyes with a tiny flashlight. Neil grunts and swats at the light with his good hand.

The doctor nods at Marco. "Help me sit him up. What happened? Why is his arm in a cast? Some of these cuts aren't new. What's going on?"

Marco updates the doctor as they hoist Neil into an upright position. After adjusting Neil's broken arm, the doctor turns his attention to the large gash on his forehead. Then, he cleans the old wound on his cheek and dabs at the various other cuts and scratches before administering an antibiotic shot and one for pain.

"He needs to rest. He doesn't appear to have a concussion, but someone needs to stay with him for a couple hours to keep him awake. His ribs are bruised, and these cuts need to be kept clean.

Have you called the police, or did he take a bad tumble and you're handling it yourself?"

Marco shrugs. "I'll have to call my boss before I make a decision. We don't want any bad publicity. It seems Mr. Hickman manages to fall wherever he goes. He arrived with that broken arm, and at the end of the first day, he had that nasty gash across his cheek. Supposedly, that happened from a fall in town."

"Well, call me if he doesn't improve. Based on my assessment, he'll be up and getting into more trouble by noon. He'll be sore and a bit incoherent from spending the night outside, but with fluids and rest he'll be fine."

As soon as the doctor leaves, Marco calls Gaetano.

"Come to the reception area. Mr. Hickman is banged up a bit. We need help getting him to his villa."

After hanging up, Marco turns to Isabella and me.

"Okay, someone needs to stay with him for a couple of hours. Isabella? What about you or someone on staff?"

Isabella frowns, "I'm supposed to take guests into town, but let me call around. Maybe I can find a nurse. That could take a while. I'll check with the staff first."

Marco sighs and mumbles, "*Merde*, I don't have time to babysit. Who knows how long it will take to find someone."

I don't say a word and back away from the little scene that threatens to claim my afternoon.

"Cat, can you stay with Neil for a few minutes? Isabella, come with me."

I nod. He walks away but then turns back. "Cat, you wouldn't, couldn't, maybe stay with him until we can find someone. No, I'm sorry. Forget I asked. It's totally inappropriate. You are a guest here."

I almost let him go as I don't need or want to be involved in whatever mess the Hickmans are dealing with, but the nicer part of me that often forgets to set boundaries nods.

"If you can find someone quickly, I'll stay with him."

"Oh, Cat. *Grazie mille.* I owe you. We'll find someone right away.

I promise. Isabella's suggestion to find a nurse is the best solution. We'll get right on it."

Marco looks like he's going to embrace me, so I move away and say, "Gaetano's here."

Between the two of us, we shuffle and drag him outside. Marco and Gaetano, with much huffing and puffing, maneuver Neil into the limo. Marco thanks me again and rushes through the doors toward his office with Isabella trailing behind. I scoot in next to Neil. We eyeball each other with trepidation.

21

Marco's promise to find someone to relieve me echoes around the room when no one shows up. Most promises are like that. Yet we continue to make them as we're running out the door—without a thought to the possibility of life intervening. It's no wonder promises are broken more often than they're kept.

Today, I have plans. I arranged a ride into town for a leisurely lunch before spending the remainder of the day at the spa. Tomorrow night is the concert. I'm in desperate need of a spa day.

Instead, I'm babysitting Neil. He's slumped on the sofa, his face and body crumbled. What am I supposed to do? Time is passing without a text or call from Marco.

"Mr. Hickman? Neil? Can you manage for a few minutes? I'm going to make us a cup of tea. Is that okay?"

He mumbles something unintelligible and nods.

The layout of the villa is similar to mine. In the pantry there is an assortment of teabags. While the kettle comes to a boil, I load a tray with cups, spoons, sugar, honey, lemon, and cream. The man probably hasn't eaten in twenty-four hours or more. I add pastries along with some salumi, cheese and fruit.

The sun casts warm streaks of light across the kitchen floor. As I move back and forth, it follows me. I poke around in the pantry and discover other culinary delights to tempt Neil. The electric kettle hums. My thoughts keep time. I'm annoyed with myself and the situation. Tension settles across my shoulders. I shrug and push it aside. The Hickmans are in a precarious situation, and so am I.

A cloud smothers the sun. A glint of light catches my eye as it blinks on and off against the side of the kettle. Hairs stand on the back of my neck. With purpose, I walk into the pantry. I shift my head in all directions. A barely discernible thin black wire snakes across the ceiling. It leads to a small black object next to the smoke detector. I'm not an expert, but the thought of this villa being wired jolts me. *Is this the norm for all the villas, or is this an invasion of privacy or something worse?*

My head is full of possibilities as I fill the porcelain tea pot with boiling water and take the tray to the living area. Neil hunches in front of the window, oblivious to my presence. A horrible sob escapes from deep inside of him. I place the tray on the table and join him at the window.

"Neil?"

He doesn't look at me or say anything, but the dry, hacking sobs continue. Finally, he catches his breath and says, "She's dead. I know she's dead."

"Who's dead? Gladys?"

When he doesn't answer, I put my hand on his arm and say, "Come away from the window. The tea is made. You must be hungry. It's a lovely day; let's sit outside."

He hesitates, then follows me. I set the tray on the table. He sinks into the closest chair and drops his head into his hands.

"Is there anything stronger than tea?"

"Of course. What would you like?"

"Bourbon. Neat."

Inside, I rummage through the impressively stocked bar and find a bottle of Woodford Reserve Double Oaked Bourbon. I struggle a bit with my conscience about giving him alcohol. He's dehydrated, and he's had pain medication. But after all this poor man has been through if this is what he wants, then he gets it. I take the bottle and glass outside and pour him a big slug.

"Mr. Hickman? Neil? May I call you Neil?"

He jumps at the sound of my voice.

"What?"

"Here's the bourbon. We haven't been formally introduced. My name is Caterina Gabbiano. I'm also staying at the resort. I saw you and your wife in Rome at the Hilton. I spent the night there like you two did before coming to the resort."

He mutters something and returns to studying the table, or maybe it's images in his mind that I can't see.

"Where is Mrs. Hickman?"

"Gladys?" Another big sob escapes. "I doubt I'll ever see her again."

He pulls a wadded-up piece of paper from his pocket and drops it on the table.

I pick it up, smooth it out and read the big, bold type:

WE HAVE HER

For a moment hopelessness renders me speechless. The crumpled piece of paper reminds me that I received notes with the roses. *Is there a connection?*

"When and where did you get this?"

He shrugs his shoulders and pushes away from the table.

I grab his arm, "Neil, you have to talk to someone. If not me, maybe Marco? He can call the police."

He collapses back in the chair and says, "No, no, don't do that. They'll kill her for sure."

I lean back in the chair.

"Tell me what happened."

"Last night, I took Gladys to the train station."

"Did she get on the train? Did she arrive at her destination?"

He presses his fingertips into his head. "I put her on the train, but this note makes it clear she was kidnapped."

"Who would do this and why?"

"Because they want me to do something. She's the guarantee. Someone must have been waiting for her on the train. I've tried to reach her, but there's no response."

Time lags as Neil struggles with his emotions. I make another attempt.

"Neil, if you think Gladys was kidnapped, the police need to be involved."

"No," his voice booms out unexpectedly. "No, I can't do that. They have her. That's what the note means. They're going to kill her unless I give them what they want."

"Tell me what happened to you and what these people want."

He shakes his head, "On my way back to the resort, the taxi was flagged down by a motorist with car problems. When he stopped, men with guns ran out of the woods. They dragged me from the car. Kicked me. Then forced this piece of paper into my hand and disappeared along with the driver."

So, the driver lied to Gaetano when he said he dropped Neil off at the front gate. *Where is Marco?* This is going to end badly, and I no longer wish to be involved. Yet I keep asking questions.

"Can you describe the driver or the others?"

He thought for a moment. "The driver was short, thin. He had on dark glasses and a cap pulled low. I didn't see his face. The others had on masks.

"How did you get back to the resort?"

He shrugged and continued his story as if I'd never spoken.

"I was unconscious for a while. When I came to, I had no idea where I was. I figured if I walked on the road, it might lead to the resort. At some point, I must have fallen. I can't remember much about how I got back."

"Neil, let me call the police."

"No," he whispered. "I can't. Perhaps there's a slim chance she's not dead. They said if I did what they asked, they wouldn't kill her. I have to give them what they want. I'm so sorry."

"Neil, you're not making sense. Why are you sorry?"

He doesn't respond, which makes me think I'm asking too many questions. I try a different approach.

"Neil, look at me."

He turns his head in my direction, but his eyes are vacant. The glass of bourbon sits untouched. I place it in his hands and say, "Take a sip."

He lifts the glass and gulps. He sputters and coughs, but his eyes focus.

"Okay, now tell me why you keep apologizing to me?"

He takes another swig of bourbon and begins.

"We're running away."

Oh, gracious, I think. Two slugs of bourbon with a pain injection must have made him incoherent.

"What do you mean?"

"Gladys and I. She's doing this for me. I'm in trouble. She's in trouble. Now you are in trouble."

The air in the room feels heavy. Oppressive. I don't want to hear what Neil has to say, yet I'm not surprised to learn that somehow I'm involved. The past few years have catapulted me from one traumatic event to another. I've come to expect that I will be in the middle of whatever catastrophe is occurring. This time, I have enough sense or maybe experience to be frightened.

"Neil, Marco is looking for someone to replace me. That could happen any minute. You have to give me something to go on."

He nods.

"I was running away from my gambling debt. Gladys agreed to come with me. Her father is behind everything bad that's ever happened to us. But so am I."

He slumps in the chair with his head in his hands. Another slug of bourbon, and he continues, "I lied about the gambling. I mortgaged our house. Our marriage was falling apart. That's what her father wanted. He set the trap, and I walked right into it."

"But her father wouldn't have her kidnapped. Would he? Neil, if you want me to help you, I have to know what's going on."

"It's useless to continue. You won't believe me."

A wayward chuckle or hiccup escapes from my lips.

"After what I've been through, I'm the one person who will believe you. Tell me the rest."

He takes another slug of bourbon and begins.

I listen as he tells me the story of their courtship, the issues with his father-in-law and the gambling.

He stops, wipes his hand across his face and shrinks into the cushion. He moves the glass of bourbon back and forth between his hands. I want to push him to continue as time is running out, but I'm afraid he'll clam up if I do.

"I tried to stay clear of the booze, the gambling, and the women, but the guys put so much pressure on me. My father-in-law was right about me—I am a loser and Gladys deserves better."

"How was he right?"

"He said I was weak and not good enough for Gladys."

He pushes his glass in my direction. I pick up the bottle of bourbon and pour.

Although I know the answer, I ask, "And Gladys—did she know what you were doing?"

"Not at first."

"So your father-in-law must have given you one free 'get out of jail' card. Is that right?"

"You guessed it. The thing is, Gladys might have understood and forgiven me for the gambling. But we'd drifted apart."

"A call girl?"

"Yes, that was arranged too, but I couldn't prove it."

I want to say *why were you so stupid*, but I've done more than my fair share of stupid. I nod. Neil continues with the pathetic story of his descent into hell.

"I was desperate. When I woke up, this woman was in bed with me. I'm sure I didn't have sex with her, but the photos looked otherwise."

"Your father-in-law left you without any options."

"You bet. His goal was to make me disappear. I decided since I had already lost everything, I would confess to Gladys. I thought if

I was honest with her, there might be a slim chance she'd forgive me."

"Since you're here, she must have forgiven you."

"Yes, she decided in my favor. Coming to this fancy resort was a way of misleading my father-in-law. He thought we'd be in hiding in some sleazy hotel. My mistake was using a credit card in my name. Since all the credit was in Gladys' name, I thought he wouldn't think to search for us at a high-end resort."

I glance at my phone. Still no text from Marco.

"The truth is, I thought I could outsmart my father-in-law. That tells you how stupid I am. Of course, when he discovered we'd left the country, he sent his henchmen after us. They found us at the airport in Rome before we had time to pick up the rental car. I was pushed down a flight of steps, but the commuters intervened. Everyone thought I'd stumbled."

Tears well in his eyes. He reaches for the bottle.

"Right after we arrived at the resort, I received a threatening text to come to the village if I wanted to keep Gladys alive. They worked me over. I thought they would kill me."

I pour more tea into my cup and push the plate of food closer to Neil. Still not sure where all of this is leading, I say, "But they didn't. Why? What do they want?"

Neil looks up, and for the first time, I see the pure agony in his eyes. In a whisper he says, "I've given them plenty of money. Now they want something else."

I wait. Fatigue etches tiny lines around his mouth. Dark, puffy bags hang under his eyes.

"What I've learned is my father-in-law isn't just mean, he's ruthless and corrupt. He has strong ties to the mafia. Ruining me has been a primary goal ever since Gladys and I married."

A story begins to form in my mind, as if I already know where this is leading. The long arm of the mafia has reached from one country to another. That's the reason he says I'm in trouble. Riccardo's face flashes before me. Yes, we are all in trouble.

I pick up on the conversation as Neil says, "Problem is, he's not as smart as the mafia. They must have assured him that Gladys wouldn't be hurt. They probably told him that kidnapping her was necessary to get to me, or maybe she's part of the scheme. Gladys is the only weapon they have to ensure I'll get them what they want."

Although I know the answer, I still ask, "And what do they want?"

He bows his head and another big sob escapes.

"Your necklace."

22

The vibration of my phone startles us. Marco's text is a welcomed relief.

nurse on way

"Okay, Neil, the nurse will be here shortly. We've covered as much as we can. But without knowing exactly what's in store for us, we'll have to work it out as we go. Our main goal is to prevent Gladys from being killed. Well, us too."

Panic fills Neil's eyes. "We need more time."

"We don't have it. Give me your glass. You don't want the nurse to know you were alert enough for a conversation, much less a glass of bourbon. While our plan isn't ideal, it's workable. For now, we must avoid each other. Do you understand?"

Neil struggles to stand. "But there are still loose ends. So much could go wrong. We must talk again before the concert."

"Neil, we're being watched. All our activities are being reported to the kidnappers."

"How do you know that?"

"Your place is wired. Mine might be, too. If that's the case, we simply can't afford to speak again or be seen together. You gave me the instructions the kidnappers gave you. I'll follow through on my end."

"What do you mean wired—like security cameras?"

"I mean top-of-the-line spyware. I spotted one in the kitchen. The devices are likely to be throughout the house. That's why I suggested we move outside. As soon as the nurse arrives, I'm headed back to my villa to check it out."

"Cat, this won't work. I can't ask you to put yourself in danger. You don't know us, and what little you've seen hasn't been pretty. I'm not thinking straight. I'll be in better shape tomorrow. Let's meet again. We can't go into this blindly or without a backup plan."

Without responding, I stand and rearrange the tray, taking deep breaths to keep my composure. Panic is stuck in my throat, but I can't second guess what will or won't happen.

"Neil, I'm sure there are people on staff that aren't employees of the resort. If we're seen together after today, they will become more suspicious than they already are. Let's stick to what we discussed. Gladys' life is at stake. We have to be very careful from now on."

He moans. "What about your necklace? I can't let you get involved. I'm guessing it's extremely valuable; otherwise, they wouldn't want it."

"Oh yes, it has a large price tag. But it's the sentimental value that's significant. The necklace belonged to my best friend. She was murdered because of that necklace. Neil, this is not just about you and Gladys. It's also about my friend Stella. It's about revenge. All that matters now are our lives. I'll give them the necklace."

I grab his glass and the bottle of bourbon. He picks up the tray and follows me. Before we enter the house, I say, "Eat a pastry or some cheese, so you don't reek of bourbon."

He nods and stuffs a couple of slices of cheese in his mouth.

"Okay, now slump down on the sofa and don't speak to anyone. When they arrive, ignore them. Don't answer questions. The doctor will stop by later. When he checks you out, be alert enough so he'll release you. Okay?"

He nods, heads to the living area, and collapses on the sofa. I scurry to the kitchen, wash and dry the glass, and put the bourbon away.

As I return to the living area, the front door opens. Isabella, all smiles and goodwill, rushes in followed by the nurse.

"Well, Mr. Hickman, you look so much better. There's a little color in your cheeks. Signora Gabbiano took good care of you. Why, she even prepared you tea. How kind of her."

Of course, her reptilian eyes reveal just the opposite. She turns her back to me and continues to speak to Neil as if he's a three-year-old.

"This is Marta. Say hello to Marta, Mr. Hickman."

Neil doesn't move, doesn't turn his head, and doesn't acknowledge either of them.

"Come on, Mr. Hickman. Why don't I help you sit up?"

When he continues to ignore her, she nods her head toward the kitchen and whispers, "*Marta.*"

I wait until they're out of sight before slipping into the butler's pantry. Since Luigi met me at the train station, I've spoken only English, other than an occasional touristy word in Italian. No one at the resort knows I speak Italian. I plan to keep it that way. From my vantage point in the pantry, I can't see them, but I can hear them.

Scopri cosa puoi. Va bene?

Fear kicks in as I struggle not to read too much into her command to Marta to *find out what you can.*

As the conversation wraps up, I tiptoe into the hallway bathroom, flush the toilet, and turn on the spigot. I plaster a big smile on my face and return to the living room just as Marta and Isabella return from the kitchen.

"Can you drive me back to the villa, or do you plan to stay with Mr. Hickman?" I ask.

Isabella turns her glassy eyes on me. They brim with malice. It seems from day one she hasn't liked me. Her voice is syrupy sweet, but her eyes remain flat and lifeless.

"Of course. Give me a minute to show Marta where everything is located."

She places her hand on Marta's arm and gives her a tour of the villa. While they're out of earshot, I use the time to reinforce Neil.

Pulling a throw off the sofa, I wrap it around his shoulders. I lean down and whisper in his ear, "Don't say anything, Neil. Do you understand? No matter what they ask you. Okay?"

He nods, grabs my hand, and murmurs, "Thank you."

I back away as the voices drift into the room. Isabella continues in her condescending tone, "Marta will take care of you, Mr. Hickman. She'll make you comfortable. If the doctor releases you, she'll leave. But if he thinks you're not fully cognitive, Marta will stay. Is that okay?"

Neil grunts, nods, and turns his head away.

As we walk out the door, Isabella turns to me, "Well, I'm not sure he's improved. What do you think?"

"I have no idea. I'm not in the medical profession."

"Did he speak to you at all? Tell you anything about what happened? Does he know where Gladys is?"

A seasoned interrogator comes to mind as I respond, "No, he said nothing. I made him tea, which he didn't drink. He did eat a slice or two of cheese but nothing else."

All the way back to the villa, she grills me over and over like the drip, drip of water torture. She's unrelenting and asks multiple times in multiple ways if he said anything. My answer remains the same.

A golf cart is parked in front of the villa. Isabella's scowl tells me it's Marco. She's not happy to see him at my place. As we pull up, he hops from his vehicle with a big grin.

"So how's Mr. Hickman?"

I wait for Isabella to speak, but she says nothing.

"Well, he's alive but still groggy. Has something happened? Is that why you're here? Do you have news of Gladys?"

He loses the grin, "No, there's nothing new. It's been such a hectic morning. I thought you might like lunch, and I owe you for sitting with Mr. Hickman. I made a picnic."

He reaches into the back of the cart and pulls out a large wicker basket and a small cooler.

Before I can respond, Isabella snorts, "I doubt she's hungry. She made tea and a large tray of food for Mr. Hickman."

I step out of the vehicle and return Marco's smile, "Oh, this is splendid. I'm starving. You are so kind."

Why don't I keep my mouth shut? Why do I antagonize Isabella? Of course, I'm not hungry. It's only been a few hours since I ate a huge breakfast. Isabella's rage is close to the surface. She stomps away. A plume of dust is all that remains as she and the cart bounce with gusto onto the gravel road.

"What's wrong with her?"

"Hmmm," I say with a big smile, "I don't have a clue. But if I were to guess, I'd say she's a bit jealous you prepared lunch for me."

Marco shrugs as he hands me the small cooler.

"Come on. It's a beautiful day. Let's enjoy it."

The sun sparkles on the pool, belying the intense heat building up. Marco sends me to the kitchen for wine glasses while he sets up the picnic under the pergola. The setting is magical. The table is shaded by a tangle of green vines that weave into an overhead canopy. The fans whirl, sending a cool breeze from the gurgling fountain.

Marco refuses to let me help. I watch with admiration as he pours a Trebbiano white into the hand-painted Murano wine glasses. A carafe of chilled water is cradled in a clay pot. He arranges platters with grapes and small wedges of different cheeses. There's grilled bread surrounded with little bowls of fresh tomatoes, basil and garlic, and pureed fava beans studded with black olives. Sliced sausages peppered with fennel seeds line up along thick slabs of frittata. For dessert, there's a cherry tart and hazelnut gelato.

He fills my plate with bites from each platter. We settle against the cushioned bench, and for a few minutes I forget about Neil and Gladys and what awaits me tomorrow night. That is until Marco starts with the twenty questions. He's much smoother in his approach than Isabella, but it's still an interrogation.

How is Neil feeling? What did he say about Gladys' disappearance? Do you think he made up the story about being attacked? Is his cognitive ability really a problem, or do you think he's pretending? It doesn't make sense to attack a man with a broken arm, does it? Did he describe the attackers or say what they wanted?

I put the same *I-am-stupid* look on my face and respond as if it's a subject I know nothing about. Fear piles up. *Are Isabella and Marco some kind of tag team? Is Marco grilling me for the sake of the resort and the fear of a lawsuit or something far more sinister?*

His questions wind and rewind in my mind until I blurt out, "What's wrong with you? Why are you interrogating me?"

A crimson flush infuses his face. "What? Oh, sorry. I didn't mean to make you feel uncomfortable. My boss is making my life difficult. I was hoping maybe you had some answers."

No answers come to mind as to whose side he's on, but I'm reasonably sure Isabella isn't on my side. Whatever is going on isn't in my best interest.

And then I remember Luigi's warning—*trust no one.*

23

Castello di Mare

Maria is puzzling over what to have for dinner when the door bursts open and little Gino rushes in, followed more slowly by his mother.

"Nonno, look what Papa bought me. We built it last night. I stuck the stickers on the wings. Come on Nonno. Let's make it fly."

He races out the back door and through the vineyard with his airplane. Analisa pats Gino on the shoulder and laughs.

"Papa, put your shoes on and go after that boy."

Gino shakes his head, "What kind of medication did Dr. Tony give him? I'd like some of his energy."

Analisa nods her head, "I don't know, but isn't it wonderful? I can't believe he's well enough to attend school. No more homeschooling. And guess what? I've been hired part-time as an assistant librarian at the high school. I'm so excited to be working again."

Maria's first reaction is to frown. Their daughter does not need to work. Analisa's husband Enrico is a good provider. She believes her daughter needs to stay home and care for her husband and her son, but she knows when to keep her mouth shut.

Analisa notices Maria's frown. "Oh, Mamma, it's a great opportunity for me. I start right away. I have flexible hours. I can drive little Gino to school and pick him up from the after-school program. And listen to this—his school is going to hire more teaching assistants."

Maria smooths her hands over her apron and examines a minuscule speck of food.

"And guess what? The principal asked me to be part of the inter-

105

view panel. I'm meeting with the director and some other staff members this afternoon to compile a list of questions. After that last mixup with his meds, they want to make sure I endorse anyone they consider hiring."

Maria smiles, "Well, that's a good thing, isn't it?"

"Hmm, I don't know. Maybe. How can you tell if someone who looks good on paper is really reliable?"

"Analisa, you're smart enough to figure that out. Is that what's bothering you, or is there something else? Come on in the kitchen. We can talk while you help me finish putting lunch on the table."

As the two women move toward the kitchen, little Gino runs back into the house and announces, "Don't call me little Gino anymore. I'm big now. I'm going to school. The kids will tease me with a name like *Little Gino*. My name is Giorgino. Come on, Nonno, help me fly this plane."

Gino grunts and pushes up from the chair. "Thank goodness you only have the one child, Analisa. I'm too old to be running after that boy of yours."

Analisa and Maria chuckle as they link arms and walk into the kitchen. While the two women prepare lunch, they discuss the day Dr. Antonio Morelli was released from prison.

Maria shakes her head and says, "I couldn't believe it when he apologized, and not just to us but to the whole town. He said he spent his time in prison reading, studying and researching sickle cell anemia. And to think that he discovered alternative treatments, and they're working on our little boy. I'm glad everyone is willing to give him another chance."

"Oh, Mamma, Giorgino wouldn't be racing around like he is without Dr. Tony. I'm thankful everyone was willing to put the past behind them and welcome him back. I know you loved Stella, but the time for your loyalty to her is over. Thank goodness that nasty nurse of his left the area after he was indicted. She was the real culprit, the one who destroyed Stella and Dr. Tony's marriage and his practice.

Maria looks up from rolling out the pasta. Her flour-caked hands move with ease from years of practice. She didn't see the need to fill in Analisa about the real story of why the marriage failed.

"I guess good things can come out of total chaos."

"What do you mean, Mamma?"

Well, don't you think it's a miracle Chiara arrived in town at almost the same time Antonio was released from prison. They are good for each other, although I do wonder why such a lovely woman from Milan would move to our small town and open a mosaic shop. I haven't asked her yet, but I will."

"Oh, Mamma, you are so nosey. Leave them alone. You've already interfered by introducing them."

"Analisa, I did no such thing. It was just a small dinner to welcome Antonio home and to befriend Chiara."

Analisa shrugs, "Well, you know she's world-famous, don't you?"

Maria rolls the pasta and begins to lob off pieces the size of her pinkie.

"Seems like you have more time to spend with that computer than you do with your family."

Analisa pretends she doesn't hear and continues, "She's a master mosaic artist and restores mosaics at grand cathedrals all over the world. Do you think she has something to hide, or maybe she's running away from her past?"

"Analisa, your imagination is out of control. Put it away. Chiara is the best thing that's happened to Antonio. It doesn't matter why she moved here. She's here. That's all you and I need to know."

Analisa nods her head in a circular motion, not agreeing or disagreeing.

Maria continues, "Antonio has grown wiser and kinder during his time in prison. Word got back to Gino that during his incarceration, he volunteered to treat the inmates as well as finding time to study and research."

Analisa twists her hair into a coil and secures it with a clip.

"Well, you know how I feel about him. He's wonderful to our little Gino."

Maria straightens her back and places the orecchiette on a cookie sheet to dry.

"The sad thing is his family turned their backs on him, but perhaps that's for the best. The good news is that with Chiara around, maybe he can forget Stella. He needs goodness in his life."

24

Casali di Casole

Marco's golf cart bumps down the road. Dust swirls in the still air. I watch the brownish cloud billow, then settle to earth. There's no sound except the drone of bees as they meander from blossom to blossom.

Once the cart disappears, I stroll through each room. There are no wires or cameras. Relieved, I return to the pool deck, retrieve my phone from the table and click on Gino's number. I move further away from the house in case I missed a listening device.

"*Buongiorno* Gino. Marco just left. None of this may work, but this is the plan Mr. Hickman and I put together. A lot could go wrong, but I think it's possible to pull this off without anyone getting hurt."

Gino listens as I briefly describe the attack that's supposed to take place after the concert.

"Caterina, this is crazy. You'll get yourself killed. If you don't contact the Guardia in Tuscany, then you must tell Lorenzo. Give him a call."

I chew that over for a few seconds.

"Gino, I can't. He'll be furious. I'd far rather talk to him after it's all over. In America, there's an expression. *Don't ask for permission, ask for forgiveness.*"

"I don't know what you mean, but the Guardia would not agree with you. If you don't contact Lorenzo, he'll be way beyond angry with you. I want to help you, but I don't have the authority to attend the concert with a group of my friends. We'll be turned away without law enforcement credentials. You've got to call him."

Glancing at the valley below and the mountains in the distance, I wonder how I can be having this kind of conversation on a day as beautiful and serene as this one.

"Gino, I haven't spoken to Lorenzo in weeks. It would be awkward for me to call him out of the blue and ask for help. Can't you call him? Hearing my crazy plan from you might soften his response. Please?"

The low, guttural sound of Gino's laughter fills the air.

"You know that isn't true. It will make him madder if I call instead of you. He knows you're here. He's known since you stepped off the plane. Your only other choice is to contact the Guardia where you are."

"But if I call the Guardia in Tuscany, it would take forever to fill them in on all the connections and why I'm involved. Even if they believe me, they might close down the entire concert. That wouldn't solve anything for the Hickmans. Either Neil delivers what they want, or they'll kill Gladys. There's a slim chance our plan might work."

"Caterina, do you know how many things can go wrong?"

"I do, Gino, but it's the only thing we could think of on short notice. Do you have a better idea?"

The silence on Gino's end goes on for a while.

"I guess not. Before I forget, here's the layout of the vault. Don't ask me how I know. There are a couple of blind spots that make it difficult for the camera to pick up what you're doing. If you keep your back to it at all times, it won't look suspicious. Do you really think someone is watching you?"

I jot down the key points as Gino provides the details.

"Thanks, Gino. Maybe I'm wrong, but the behavior of some of the employees at this plush resort seems suspicious. I don't think either Marco or Isabella is a regular staff member. And there's the chauffeur, Luigi. He drove me to the resort and then disappeared. It might be my imagination, but something else is going on."

I wait, but Gino doesn't say anything.

"You and I are the only two people who know what I'm going to do and why. It's important for you to know just in case anything happens to me."

There's another long silence before Gino says, "I'll call Lorenzo, and then I'm coming. You won't see me. But if you do, don't acknowledge me. I'll think of other ways to protect you. I'll be close by. Once I talk to Lorenzo, I imagine he'll call you. Be prepared."

Having a conversation with Lorenzo is not what I want. Right now, my idea of happiness is to curl up in bed and wake up after the concert is over.

How did a trip I longed for turn into this nightmare? How will I honor the memory of Stella when I'm going to be strung out like a kite?

25

Castello del Mare

Lorenzo's eyes lock on the extradition notice on top of the pile of paperwork his assistant left on his desk this morning. *Merde!*

He shakes his head. Cat will be furious. She'll believe he knew about the extradition the entire time. She will accuse him of being an active participant in Riccardo's release. *Mio dio*, she's so damn stubborn. Even when he tries to explain he was under orders to sign the paperwork, she'll say he had a hand in making it happen.

He picks up the notice and rereads it. He spent months fighting the extradition, but his superiors in Rome wanted to create a better relationship with the Albanian authorities. The politicians on both sides thought the two countries would work more cohesively on the drug smuggling operations if Italy was willing to cooperate with prison exchange. The Italian government thought it was worth giving up Riccardo to establish closer ties.

Lorenzo tried to find a loophole. He delayed signing the paperwork, but he'd been met with roadblocks every step of the way. Now, it was signed. Riccardo would be released to the authorities in Albania.

He sighs and brushes his flop of hair out of his eyes, realizing he's overdue for a haircut. Cat is going to be madder than a nest of tangled asps. His thoughts flood with the curve of her cheek, the splash of freckles on her nose, and the way she bites her lip when she's concentrating. He swears and abruptly pushes back from his desk and walks to the broad stretch of windows. His gaze lingers on the fields of golden sunflowers. They flow like honey across the land until they end abruptly in the karstic rock that plunges into the crystal blue Adriatic Sea.

He'd waited for Cat to meet him halfway. The Zooms were frequent a year ago, but they soon faded into random texts. Their conversations no longer include the possibility of a life together. Instead, he talks about his need to be at his post with the Guardia di Finanza. She speaks about her thriving business. There are fewer times "we" is mentioned.

It's already mid-August and last year's agreement to vacation together in September is a forgotten dream. Perhaps the real or imagined memory of Stella will always come between them. For Lorenzo, Stella's voice is as strong from the grave as it was during her lifetime. Lorenzo rakes his hand through his hair. He's a bit late in finding happiness and creating a family. He'd hoped it would be with Cat, but that's not going to happen. He needs to get Cat out of his mind and out of his life. And just when he thinks it's possible, she returns.

A gentle knock on the door reminds him he's having lunch with Sofia. He wipes the scowl off his face and replaces it with a smile, one that involves his lips but not his eyes.

Entrare prego. "Come in, please."

The door cracks a sliver and Sofia's face, surrounded by masses of blonde hair pulled back in a loose knot, peeks in. For a moment, all he sees is Cat's red curls and her spirited eyes full of sparks and passion.

His phone vibrates. *Why is Gino calling me?* He hesitates for a second. Gino rarely calls, and when he does, it usually means the news isn't good. Maybe he's heard about Riccardo's extradition and wants to know the details.

When Lorenzo looks up, Sofia is already seated, elegantly outfitted in a pale blue silk dress and navy blue stiletto heels. The dress has a front slit that opens to reveal long, slender legs. A navy leather belt cinches her tiny waist and silver jewelry gives her the look of a fashion model or celebrity. She was recently in Milan, where this outfit would be the norm, but not here in Castello. The restaurant he's chosen for lunch is a nice enough restaurant, but surely she knows something less ostentatious is more suitable.

Cat would show up in casual clothes that gave the look of being swept together by the wind. A tumble of red hair against a cobalt blue shirt paired with tight jeans and flats or walking shoes were always perfect for lunch on a wind-swept terrace like L'Aragosta. He's seen Cat dressed as glamorous as any film star, but he prefers her casual style over the opulence of Sofia's wardrobe. If he stops to think about it, Sofia reminds him too much of Stella.

He mumbles to Gino to hold on as he wants to take the call in private. He nods to Sofia, indicating his need to be alone. He holds up a finger to suggest he'll only be a minute. He turns away and walks back to the window before speaking in generalities while he waits for the door to close.

Sofia reaches for her purse. In her hand is a small black recording device that has already been activated. She slips it under the desk and presses the device against the wood until it adheres. She closes the door firmly behind her and sighs with relief.

She hates situations that require her to be personally involved, but she doesn't yet trust those working for her. None of them would have been given the easy access to his office like she has. Lorenzo is a nice guy, but she has no time for nice guys. He's in her way, but he won't be for long.

Once the door closes Lorenzo says, "Okay, Gino. I'm alone. I'm sure whatever you have to tell me has to do with Cat. I'm listening."

Heat rises in his face as Gino explains Cat's attempt to help the Hickmans. He's never met anyone in his long career with the Guardia who was capable of finding so much trouble as Cat. He's too angry to deal with her now. It has to wait.

Ten minutes later, he's still sitting at his desk. On the other side of the door Sofia is waiting for him. He met her in Rome a few weeks ago at one of the Guardia functions that required mandatory attendance. The commissario of the Rome Guardia had introduced them. At that event, she had smiled and tucked her arm through his, suggesting they order a drink. She was elegant, sophisticated, and beautiful with a great family pedigree. For some reason, she had chosen to shine her golden light on him that evening. After the drink, she moved placards so they could be seated together at dinner. When the music began, she reached for his hand and led him to the dance floor. The night ended in her apartment. Since then, she'd rented a place in Castello and showed up every few weeks. He had no idea what she did with the rest of her time.

When he quizzed her about how she occupied herself, she'd laughed and said, "Oh, I'm in the hospitality business—food, wine, the usual. It requires me to travel a lot. And when I'm not working for pay, I'm volunteering. I suppose you could ask me what committee I'm not on. In my family, we were raised that it's our duty to be philanthropic."

He didn't feel the need to ask any further questions—not yet. Although his heart isn't in it, he needs to consider her as a possible life partner. But he has to complete a background check. It's required before anyone gets too close.

He stands and walks slowly across the office, pulling the door open. Sofia laughs and sputters as she tumbles into his arms, and gives him a lingering kiss. He briefly wonders why she was leaning against the door, but her body pressing against his removes the thought as quickly as it appears.

She pulls away and brushes back his hair with her hand—a gesture that annoys him. He scowls as he takes in her perfect makeup, salon-styled hair and dark blue sardonic eyes that he's sure hold undisclosed secrets—so unlike Cat's wide open smile and her eyes full of warmth and sincerity.

He shakes his head to clear his mind of Cat so he can focus on Sophia. He thinks she possesses the qualities that might be suitable for a relationship. She would be an asset. She's independently wealthy, has important connections, from a good family and she's beautiful. But, before the relationship goes deeper, the background check is his priority.

26

Brindisi

When the cell door opens, Riccardo clamps his mouth in a straight line to stifle the smile snaking its way across his face. Freedom is only a few steps away. After he's cuffed, he's led out of the cell. He shuffles behind the guard as they walk through the endless gray prison corridors. Inmates peer out of their cells and nod as he passes.

The lock clicks open on the last door. Riccardo's first glimpse of the outside world is filled with darkness. The guard takes his sweet time unlocking the shackles around his ankles. Riccardo steps through the narrow opening. He stops. The early morning breeze caresses his face. Two years in that hell hole is a small price to pay once the necklace is his and Cat is dead. He will avenge Carlo. Then he will disappear. His plan is already in motion.

He chuckles, knowing Lorenzo fought signing the extradition papers, but in the end, he was forced to do so. The two burly guards behind him allow only a few seconds before pushing him toward the white van. He clutches at his wrists when the manacles are removed. One of the guards grabs the back of his shirt and half pushing, half lifting, hoists him into the back of the van.

The guard inside seizes his arm and clasps one cuff around his wrist and the other around the bar above the bench. The sound of the engine turning over is sweet music to Riccardo's ears.

In less than fifteen minutes, the van rolls to a stop. The paneled doors swing open to the night. He figures it's somewhere between midnight and two in the morning, maybe later. Moving prisoners always takes place under the cover of night. The cuff is removed. He's jerked to the ground and re-cuffed. When he looks up, Lorenzo is standing before him.

Se torni, sei morto! "If you return, you're dead."

Riccardo's mouth twists into a smiling snarl. *Nessun problema, Lorenzo. Non sei tu che voglio. Ma dì a Cat che la vedrò presto.* "No problem, Lorenzo. It's not you I want. But tell Cat I'll see her soon."

His spittle flies across the space and lands at Lorenzo's feet. Lorenzo takes a step forward, but his friend, Commissario Davide Faena from the Toscana Guardia, places a hand on his arm and shakes his head. The guards yank Riccardo toward the marina. He stumbles between them until they reach the end of the dock.

He searches the water until his eyes catch sight of the red Albanian flag with the two-headed eagle flying high. A dingy waits at the small dock. Papers are exchanged, and his manacles are removed by the Italian guards. The Albanian police secure his hands in front of him, a much less painful position. With their assistance, he boards the bobbing rubber boat.

He sits with his back to the dock as the boat putters toward the Albanian patrol boat and his freedom. Once alongside the larger vessel, he eagerly accepts the hands reaching to help him up the ladder. The dinghy is pulled on deck and secured. The idling engine roars into life. With its red flag fluttering, the boat heads out to sea.

Lorenzo trains his binoculars on the vessel until the boat fades in the distance. Riccardo doesn't move until they round the bend and pass by *Torre del Serpente* and the all-clear signal is given.

Police uniforms are discarded and dropped into the sea. Riccardo's hands are unshackled. He checks out the backpack that's waiting for him. It's full of food, water, a gun, and the various other supplies he requested.

The patrol boat's engines slow to a murmur. The dingy is lowered. Riccardo descends the ladder. A crew member leans over the railing and shouts—*paç fat*—good luck, as he throws the rope into Riccardo's waiting hands.

He moves the throttle from neutral to reverse and backs away from the boat. The engine idles as he waits. The two-headed eagle flaps as the boat turns and heads across the Strait of Otranto to Albania. Soon, he will follow, but for now, he has work to do. Once he avenges Carlo, he will leave Italy and never return. Stella's priceless necklace, along with his investments, will ensure a good lifestyle. The only thing he'll leave behind is a dead Cat.

Navigating the boat out into the Adriatic, he heads up the coast to where his men are waiting with a larger boat for the journey to San Marino. Once there, he will travel across land to Lajatico. That will be the tricky part, the time when being sighted is a greater risk.

Cat is already in Lajatico for the concert. His people informed him of her travel plans, which made it easy to position Isabella at the resort. Everyone was in place, including the team that would attend the concert. His encounter with Cat will be quick, and only meant to scare her, to create an anticipation of panic so that after the concert she will be looking over her shoulder. Fear will be her companion everyday until he kills her.

That's the part he thought about every day in his prison cell. He envisioned her begging for his mercy. He would show none.

After he retrieves the necklace, a vehicle would take him to a boat located in a small cove on the Ligurian Sea. His destination will be south, back to Castello del Mare—the place Cat will head after the concert. She'll be frightened and want to be with her friends. She isn't smart enough to know his people are already waiting for her to arrive. She'll learn soon enough that he's watching her every move. One by one, he'll kill the people she loves. Everyday, she'll know it's her fault. And when the time is right, he'll slowly and painfully kill her.

27

Casali di Casole

The call I've been dreading comes. The steely undertones of Lorenzo's voice make it clear this isn't a social call. No hello. No how are you?

"What the hell do you think you're doing? Why haven't you called me?"

The second question confuses me. Is Lorenzo asking why Gino called him instead of me, or is he asking why I haven't called for weeks? Before I can reply, he says, "No, don't bother to explain. While I may have thought you were misguided in some of your past decision-making skills, I never believed you would intentionally plan something so stupid!"

I let him rant. When he's quiet, I say, "If you're finished, Commissario, I have a few things to say to you. You promised to tell me when Riccardo was up for extradition to Albania. I believed you. Yet, I find out from Gino that the extradition has already taken place. Exactly when were you going to tell me?"

"Damm it, Cat, it just happened last night. Let me explain."

"Explain what? That I wasn't important enough to keep informed?"

"You know that's not true."

The muscles in my neck tightened. The words sputter out like an out-of-control geyser without any assistance from me.

"Maybe, maybe not, but I don't really care, Lorenzo. You knew it was going to happen, didn't you? If you had called and told me there was a strong possibility Riccardo would be released, I wouldn't be here. And you say I'm the one making misguided decisions."

I bite my lip to stop the flow of angry words. There's silence except for our intense breathing.

"You're right Cat. I thought I could stop the extradition. I tried right up to the final second, but it happened anyway. You were already here. I didn't want to frighten you. Commissario Davide Faena is a friend of mine with the Tuscan Guardia. He's putting together a plan to protect you, but now you've come up with this foolish scheme to rescue people you don't even know."

"And your point is?"

"Why didn't you call me directly instead of Gino? I thought you trusted me."

"You promised to let me know if Riccardo was released from prison. A broken promise of this magnitude doesn't deserve trust. Do you understand? Tell your friend I don't need or want his help or yours."

Tears are dripping, and I desperately need a tissue, but I have to keep on. If I stop, I'll lose my nerve.

"In a moment of panic, I called Gino. That was my mistake. I thought if anything went wrong, it would be smart to let someone know. You don't need to remind me that my current plan is stupid. Your lectures won't help me or these people survive. They are my only objective. If there's one chance in a million Mrs. Hickman will be released, I'm willing to take that chance."

He snorts. I don't blame him. My words are lame. Our plan is foolish. Everything can and probably will go wrong. I realize the odds are small that Mrs. Hickman will be released unharmed. But if there's a small chance to save another person's life, even a person I don't know, the risk is worth taking. Yes, it's probably a setup. Yes, I could be killed. My own life has been on the edge more than once. That's why I'm willing to try. I fully understand what it means to be rescued from the clutches of death..

While Lorenzo is my last hope, I'm not surprised he let me down.

His anger, like his passion, stays submerged. We didn't fight; we simply drifted away. Our time has passed. Now we are more adversaries than lovers or even friends. The pause drags on with only an occasional deep breath from one or the other of us.

"Cat, don't do this. Let me help. Don't push me away. We can make this work."

"Do you mean us or rescuing Mrs. Hickman? You and I can't be rescued, but there's a possibility she can be saved."

Again, silence. Finally, Lorenzo says, "*Mi scusi.* You're right. It's not my concern. It's out of my jurisdiction. Don't worry. I won't come to your rescue. You seem to manage quite well without any help from me."

There's a click and then nothing. The connection, in more ways than one, is truly dead. My tears flow.

Part Two
Night Music

The second question asked:

What flares warm like a flame, yet it is no flame?

Calàf hesitates, then answers

BLOOD

Act II ~ *Turandot* ~ Giacomo Puccini

28

South Carolina Lowcountry

Sheriff Blackwell's office, positioned in the front room of what used to be the old federal courthouse, gives him a 180° view of the surrounding area. He requested this room for his office along with specific renovations to open up the space with a series of windows—some facing the intersection of Bladen and North while others looked out over Bay Street and the river. He glances across to Herban Market. It's one of his small pleasures to pause every once in a while during his long work hours and watch the outside patio fill up during breakfast and lunch.

Today, Cassie and Chuck are seated at a table with their heads almost touching and their hands clasped as if they each feared the other might bolt at any moment. He shakes his head and smiles. He loves watching them and knowing that Cassie is happy. After her disastrous affair with that buffoon senator, he didn't want Cassie to be hurt again. He checked Chuck out. Went so far as to drop in on his martial arts studio on Sams Point Road to take a look around. During his chat with Chuck, he let him know he couldn't mess around with Cassie's feelings. He's satisfied Chuck is one of the good guys.

He smiles even wider when he thinks about Cassie's friend Cat, the red-headed wonder. He can't keep up with that gal. Heard she'd gone off to Italy again. It was easier keeping up with Cat's protégé, Diana. That girl is a sweetheart. Problem is she brings him something delicious to eat every time she drops in to see him. She says it's her way to thank him for saving her life. Makes him feel good, but his wife is now making comments about his expanding waistline. Lordy, that girl can cook. He's pretty pleased she got on with her life after the horror of the human trafficking situation. She's finishing up her last year at Johnson and Wales and is already working in Cat's catering business.

He turns back to the stack on his desk and pulls out the sheet with his half-finished letter of resignation. He loves this town, but he's plum worn out. The young ones are encroaching. They know all the technology mumbo jumbo that takes him days, weeks and sometimes months to figure out.

Looking at what he's written so far, he decides to wait until after the first of the year. Spring might be the right season to resign. Just in time for fishing weather. He knows just the friend who is eager to go with him. He figures it's about time to introduce his friend to his favorite fishing spot. Together, they can check out some of the places he hasn't visited since his childhood. Funny thing about Count Alfonso—a real Spanish count who's now a fishing buddy. He's a heck of a nice guy—doesn't seem like royalty at all. However, he's not exactly sure what it means to be royalty. But fishing he knows all about. Yes sir. Spring will be the best time to retire.

He sticks the incomplete letter in his desk drawer and turns back to the window.

29

"Chuck, I'm worried."

"Oh, Cass, you're always worrying about something. What now? Did you and your daughter have a spat?"

"Oh gosh, no, Sam's fine. It's Cat."

"Huh?"

"The trip to Italy. She insisted on going alone."

"Cass, we've beat this subject to death. Cat wanted to go alone. You told me yourself that it was something she planned to honor her friend."

"Yeah, I know. Guess I shouldn't worry, but."

Chuck takes a large bite of the sticky bun and mumbles, "Plus, with your new partnership, she's counting on you while she's away, right?"

"Hmm."

"Sounds like you're not satisfied with carrying the load. Is that why you have a scowl on your beautiful face?"

Cassie reaches over and wipes a crumb from his mouth. It's a tradition for them to stop by Herban Market and have a cappuccino and sticky buns every Wednesday morning.

"No, I don't mind being in charge for a short time, although it's not something I want to do permanently. What's bugging me is when I asked if I could go with her, she laughed. It wasn't a happy laugh. Then she drifted off somewhere. I thought maybe she was upset with me for asking. Finally, she looked at me and said she had to go alone."

Cassie looks at the river, but her eyes don't see the idyllic setting —blue skies, warm sun, light breeze, massive oaks dripping with

Spanish moss. Instead, she sees her best friend stumbling into trouble. Without fail, Cat seems to attract trouble wherever she lands.

She pushes aside the plate with the half-eaten pastry and looks at Chuck.

"She said she didn't want to hurt my feelings, and mumbled something about not needing a chaperone. She and Stella were supposed to attend this concert together. It was supposed to be a celebration instead of a funeral dirge."

Chuck doesn't interrupt. Cassie's wellbeing is all he's concerned about. He truly believes Cat can take care of herself, but he isn't about to say so.

"I can't help wondering if it's safe for her to return. Cat is so upbeat, but this trip was weighing heavy on her. Now I have this big knot in the pit of my stomach."

Chuck places his hand over Cassie's. Her restless hands stop spinning her coffee cup. She gives him a tortured smile.

"I never understood Cat's friendship with Stella. It wasn't healthy, as far as I could tell. Stella always had the upper hand. Cat was so loyal and remained loyal even after Stella's death. Oh, Chuck, I wish I had hopped on that plane with her."

Chuck tightens his grip on Cassie's hand, "It's not too late."

"Yeah, it really is. As you pointed out, I'm running the business while she's away. We're partners now. I don't want to do anything to jeopardize that. She'd be madder than a wet cat if I closed shop and showed up in Italy. In her mind, it would be unforgivable to put our business in jeopardy."

"Cass, maybe it's time for Sam and Diana to have a chance. Would you consider leaving them in charge?"

Cassie stutters, "Well, no, no, I mean, they're so young. What if something major happened? Who would they turn to? It doesn't seem like a good idea to throw them out there without any guidance. Cat would never forgive me if the business went belly up while she's away. I can't do that to her—or myself. It's my business too."

"Quit thinking of Sam as your little girl. She's all grown up. She's a hard worker and reliable. I bet she and Diana would jump at the chance. Sam's been working with y'all since she was sixteen. She graduated from culinary school last year and has been working with you and Cat full-time. Diana is finishing up her last year, and she's already working part-time. Both these kids take the responsibility seriously."

Cassie nods and considers the possibility. She tries to think how Cat would view her leaving the business in the girls' hands. Chuck interrupts her thoughts.

"What about Count Alfonso? Could he supervise them? He loves those girls. And what about me?"

Cassie's laughter has heads turning.

"You? Gracious, Chuck, you don't know a thing about catering. You can't even turn on a stove without burning yourself."

"Okay, so I'm not a cook, and I don't know a duck breast from shoe leather, but I can be the guy who keeps everyone calm and on task. At least think about it."

Cassie squeezes his hand so hard he's sure the blood flow has stopped. She continues to nod her head three or four times before she says, "I haven't seen Al around lately. His father is ill. His family needs him in Spain. This might not be a good time. But it can't hurt to talk to him."

Chuck pushes back his chair.

"Why don't we drive over today? And before we leave here, let's walk over and talk to Sheriff Blackwell. He'd be happy to check on the girls while you're gone."

Cassie grabs his hand and says, "I could rearrange some of our events that aren't date-driven. The last two weeks in August aren't too busy, but we crank back up by mid-September. But what would Cat think? I'm not sure it's the right thing to do."

Chuck frowns before he says, "Is there something going on with Cat that you haven't told me? Have you heard from her since she arrived?"

"No, that's just it. Two years ago, when she was in Italy, she kept in touch with me and Dr. Ginny. I've not heard a word from her. Well, she did text when she arrived at that fancy resort. But there's been nothing since. She doesn't answer my texts."

"Is that a bad thing? I mean, she's been working nonstop—right up until she left. She probably needs a break from the business and from us. She loves Italy. Don't you think she's having a grand time?"

Cassie shrugs. "I can't explain it. Maybe it's just that we've grown so close. We pick up on each other's vibes. She was nearly killed on her last visit, so I'd say she's frightened. And there's Lorenzo—he's a big part of what's going on."

Chuck looks surprised. "I'm not sure I'm following. I thought they were good."

Cassie picks at the sleeve of her shirt. "You men have no powers of observation. You haven't noticed Lorenzo's absence? He hasn't been here since the human trafficking gang was shut down. Their plans to meet haven't happened."

"Ah, well..."

"Ah, well, is right. You probably didn't notice Cat's personality change either. She's been quiet and sad. On the drive to the airport, she was silent. She's a nervous flyer and usually chats nonstop. Not this time."

Chuck stuffs the rest of the sticky bun in his mouth and waits for Cassie to brush the crumbs away. She doesn't.

"Cassie?"

"What? I'm sorry, Chuck. I'm worried. Maybe it wasn't the right thing to do, but I called Dr. Ginny. She hasn't heard from her either. Their first Zoom is scheduled for next week. If she shows up for the Zoom and Dr. G tells me there's no reason to be concerned, then I'll be fine."

Chuck nods. "That's a good idea. If Cat doesn't show, you could text her. Since she hasn't answered your other texts, make it a little stronger. Maybe all she needs is a little motivation to answer."

"Oh, Chuck, that's a great idea. Wait a sec while I come up with a draft."

Cassie types furiously for a few seconds.

"Here, what do you think?"

If I don't hear from you today, I'll be on a flight tomorrow.

"That's good. If Cat doesn't show up for the Zoom, then send the text. That will get a response. If it doesn't, then pack your bags."

30

In the early morning light, Count Alfonso stares at the young Moringa trees. Thousands of them ripple in the light breeze. The miniature trees are almost ready for harvest and shipment to Arizona where they'll be replanted in ideal conditions. They'd flourish and develop into full-grown trees. Soon it would be time to plant the next crop.

What a wondrous sight. The field of small saplings—their bright green leaves lifting toward the sunlight. The slightly spicy aroma mingles with the sulfurous odors of the marshes. He longs for Cat to be standing next to him. She was his biggest supporter in this undertaking, the only person who believed he could get these trees to grow in a different climate.

He shades his eyes with his hands and wonders why she'd left town without letting him know she was going or how long she'd be away. After all this time, he was sure their relationship had strengthened. Clearly, she did not.

He glances down at the carefully scripted note that Diana delivered last night.

Dearest Al,

Although he's hurt that Caterina sent him a note instead of having a conversation with him about her plans, he's able to smile as he opens the card. From their first meeting, when he had introduced himself to her as Count Alfonso Fernando Felipe Francisco Perez, she had joked about his name. On that night, in Mrs. Fitzhugh's kitchen, she had designated him as *Al* from the "You Can Call Me Al" song off of Paul Simon's *Graceland Album*.

That's what he loved about her—one moment sad and serious and the next moment she was laughing and playful.

The letter in his hand flutters in the breeze.

> *Dearest Al,*
>
> *This trip will seem sudden to you, but not to me. Stella and I planned this birthday celebration before her death. I promised her I'd show up for the celebration even without her. I'm not asking you to understand—only that you let me explain when I return.*
>
> *Cassie will handle the business, but I'd appreciate it if you'd stop by from time to time to see if she needs anything. She, of course, can help you whenever you need it. Diana and Sam can use your guidance as well.*
>
> *You have been my rock this past year. Thank you for that.*
>
> *Fondly,*
> *Cat*

Al is sure that whatever the celebration is about, it's in Italy. Although she hasn't mentioned Lorenzo in a while, it could mean he's in the picture again. He'd been hopeful that maybe, just maybe, she was over her Italian lover, Lorenzo.

After all, being present in another person's life is supposed to count for 75% of a relationship, isn't it? After the horrendous encounter he and Cat had with the human trafficking gang, Lorenzo hadn't hung around.

Rumors say they're together, but Lorenzo hasn't returned to the Lowcountry, and Cat, until now, has stayed away from Italy. He had taken advantage of every opportunity to be with her, but this note put a damper on his hope.

His smile widens, thinking how she cast her spell on him the first evening he met her in the Fitzhugh's kitchen. Her hands were submerged in sudsy water when he popped in to meet and thank the chef who created such a splendid Spanish meal. When she turned to see who had barged into her domain, her rebellious red curls swirled around her face. Her soft green eyes had been full of laughter and joy. His heart told him she was the one.

Oh, she'd kept him at arm's length, but recently he'd noticed she was happy when they were together. Still, he doesn't think she is ready for what he wants from the relationship. He wonders how long he has to wait.

His mind conjures up her image. Sassy is the word that best describes her. She's kind but dogmatic, all lightness with dark edges. She bubbles with laughter with just a hint of rain and stormy days. Her strength, independence, and courage, infused with the joy of living, is exactly what he wants.

He sighs deeply because circumstances are pulling them apart. Cat's in Italy, and his father is ill. His mother has asked him to return to Spain, and he needs someone to take over his business while he's away. He wants that person to be Cat. If she doesn't come back soon, he'll have to hire someone.

He shakes his head and turns away from the field of saplings. He wants her to be his full-time partner—a 50-50 deal, but the opportunity to tell her didn't work out before she left. And now he may have lost her to Lorenzo and to Italy.

He picks up his mobile and searches for Cassie's name. Although he's sure Cat has returned to Italy, he needs confirmation. Knowing Cat, she's sworn Cassie to secrecy, but he still wants to quiz her. While Cassie will protect Cat's privacy with her life, her voice will give her away.

Just before clicking on Cassie's name, he checks the time. Six thirty-seven in the morning is probably not the best time to place a call.

He rereads the note, looking for some sign that Cat has feelings for him. *Fondly* isn't it.

31

Casali di Casole

After a sleepless night, I plunge into the pool. Perhaps vigorous exercise will ratchet up enough adrenaline for me to face the day. The water is soft, salty and cool. It slides over me like a loving caress. I plow back and forth until all my body parts are rubbery with fatigue.

My phone pings several times as I climb from the cocoon of the swimming pool. Marco texts:

> excited about the big night?

I text back a yes and add that I'll be stopping by to retrieve some personal things from the vault. With a smiley face, I tell him I'll be walking, but I'd appreciate a ride back to the villa. There's no point in asking for trouble by toting around a bag of jewelry.

Right after I hit send, another message pings.

> You missed your Zoom with Dr. Ginny. If I don't hear from you today, I'll be on a flight tomorrow.

Oh crap, I think, *that's the last thing I need—an innocent like Cassie coming to my rescue.* I text her back.

Sorry to be out of touch. Needed time alone to detach from everything. Swimming every day, eating the best food and sipping the best wine. I'll text Dr. Ginny with my apology, as I totally forgot. The resort is gorgeous. No worries, a friend is going with me to the concert tonight. Taking the train to Castello di Mare tomorrow. Let's Zoom once I'm settled. Home soon. xoxo

I hate lying to Cassie, but I can't put her or anyone else at risk.

After showering, I dress, tie the laces of my walking shoes, and head out. The path glistens with morning dew. A haze wraps around the valley as I crest the small incline leading to the resort center.

The morning shimmers in innocence. For a moment, I pause and breathe deeply. The tranquility surrounds me and seeps into my bones. I let go of what's to come. The world becomes a small, safe place. The sounds of morning music reinforce me—the coo of doves, the drone of bees, the splash of water flowing over rocks—nature at her best.

A car door slams, a motor revs and the magic fades into fields of golden wheat. As I approach the bend in the path, a sleek limo glides through the open gates. They close with a clang. I walk on.

Marco waits under the portico. Our conversation lulls as we walk down the corridor and stop in front of the vault. Once inside, he removes the metal box and inserts his key. He places the metal box on the table and says, "Let me know when you're finished."

I nod and then check out the position of the cameras. They're exactly where Gino said they would be. Once Marco's back passes through the door, I let the tension in my shoulders relax. I'm alone except for the cameras. Nonchalantly, I move the container closer to my body so it's hidden from the camera. After unlocking the box, I reach in and scoop out the three pouches. One bag contains the starfish bracelet, and the other two bags hold identical necklaces—one real, one fake.

I slide the bracelet out and clasp it around my wrist. There's always this moment when it first touches my skin that I experience a warm vibration—a sort of tingling runs up my arm. My fingers wrap around the starfish set in small clusters of diamonds.

My arm flexes for the camera as I admire its beauty. While I'm modeling the bracelet for the camera, I nudge the other two bags close to my body until they're out of the camera's range. Once I'm sure the bracelet has been recorded, I slide it back into the pouch. I won't wear it tonight as I can't take the chance it might be lost or stolen in the scuffle.

With my body leaning over the bags, I tuck one against my stomach. The other velvet pouch I open and position the necklace in a spot visible to the camera.

I place the bag containing the bracelet on top of the bag next to my stomach and drop them both back in the container. The necklace in view of the camera is returned to its bag and stays on the table. I lock the box and text Marco I'm ready to leave. I make sure the camera catches me sliding the pouch I left on the table into my pocket.

I focus on keeping my movements smooth without suspicion. I have a strong feeling that the video will be reviewed. While it's just a feeling, it's a mighty strong one.

When I decided to attend the concert, it made sense to bring both necklaces. If I'm lucky, I can pass the fake necklace off to the kidnappers to save Gladys. The real necklace I'll hold onto as it might be the only bargaining chip left to save my own life.

Marco and I step into the corridor. A slight movement where the two hallways intersect catches my attention. The back of a three-inch black heel pivots out of sight. The staccato tap, tap, tap is loud as the person disappears around the corner. I rush after the sound but only catch a glimpse of what might be the back of Isabella as she slips through the door connecting to the reception area. *Why would she be in the corridor to the vault at this particular time?* As I ask myself that question, I think I already know the answer.

"Was that Isabella?"

Marco catches up with me and says, "I don't know. I didn't see anyone."

32

East Coast of Italy

Riccardo maneuvers the dingy into a secluded cove just north of Pesaro. The night air is heavy with humidity as he hauls the boat into the tree line. He retrieves the backpack and spends a few precious minutes camouflaging the boat with a tarp, rotten tree limbs and brush.

He breaks into a trot but keeps off the road. The nondescript car is parked in a vacant lot outside a small village. He squats beside the almost-new tires. He reaches under the left rim until his hand grabs the magnetic box. With keys in hand, he opens the door and slings his backpack on the seat. It's the first time since he was released from prison that he takes a deep breath.

When he turns the key, the car roars to life. He attaches the GPS to the dash, punches in Lajatico, and coordinates the time. If he keeps to the backroads, it will take him about four hours to reach his destination. Dawn will be breaking as he arrives. He fires off a text to his cousin, Roan Driton.

On the way

He shifts into first and pulls onto the road. His smile widens when Roan texts back and describes how he stalked Cat at the hotel and train station.

One Note Murders

It was fun. I let her catch glimpses of me.
Wish I could have taken photos of her face.
She was petrified. It won't take much to
push her over the edge. Everything's ready
for your arrival.

Donna Keel Armer

The hot breath of summer blows across the Tuscan hillside.
The heavy air huffs around the empty benches
and shuttered shops.
A handful of pamphlets scuttle in the piazza.

They lift on the wind--flying, swirling, dancing, hovering.
The dense air keeps them afloat.
One pamphlet strays from the group.
It flutters and drops at my feet.
The wind holds its breath.
The great Maestro Bocelli's face, surrounded by musical notes,
flattens against the steaming pavers.
It lingers, still as death.

It's only a second--a slight pause
before the searing, summer wind
heaves it back into motion.

Life or death sails on these words—

NESSUN DORMA ~ NONE SHALL SLEEP!

~ Donna Keel Armer

33

Casali di Casole and Lajatico, Italy

It's time. The full-length mirror reflects a woman I don't recognize. The red dress, the upswept hair, the touch of makeup and the starfish necklace. *Who is this stranger staring back at me?*

I'm a fool. There's nothing else to say. If I had any sense, I'd have on jeans and sneakers. Or if I were really smart, I'd be on a train to Castello del Mare or a plane headed to the South Carolina Lowcountry.

Stella's image, which fades in and out of my life, looks on as I adjust the necklace. Her gaze is unwavering. She was the one with a brave heart. Me, not so much. She'd be pleased with my plan to keep Gladys from harm as well as safeguard the necklace—her legacy to me.

My pathetic mind has determined that while it's possible to be murdered in any old place, I'm reasonably sure it won't happen at a Bocelli concert. Still, this event is probably the prelude to the end of my life. It's Riccardo's way of thumbing his nose at me and the Guardia. His desire to instill fear until the exact moment and place are arranged for my demise is much like an opera. He will torture and kill me at his leisure.

A loud knock on the front door startles me out of my reverie. Glancing out the window, I'm startled to see Marco in what, to my eye, is a custom made tux. *Is he going to the concert?* Funny he didn't mention it.

"Marco, you didn't tell me you'd be at the concert, too. How nice."

He tugs at his jacket sleeve and laughs. "No, I'm just your fill-in chauffeur."

"You're joking. You must have better things to do with your time than drive me back and forth to Lajatico. Why are you here? Where is Luigi? Or Gaetano?"

The pasted-on smile doesn't change. His eyes don't reveal anything when he says, "Managing the resort requires me to fill in from time to time when employees don't show up at the last minute. I hope you don't mind."

My mind scrambles to make sense of what Marco is saying. Since Lorenzo hired Luigi to safeguard me, I was sure he'd be my driver. *So what is Marco's role? Mafia? Guardia?*

Marco waits for my response.

"Well, I'm surprised but delighted, Marco. I'm sure you've been to one of these concerts before. You can fill me in on the drive over."

Why would this happen tonight? Driving someone to a concert and waiting to drive them home is an easy duty. I don't know about Gaetano, but Luigi wouldn't have bailed on this assignment unless he was forced to or he wasn't asked. *And why is Marco the replacement?* He's the manager of this resort. Or maybe he isn't. I either need to be worried or feel safe. I'm not sure which.

He holds the door open and says, "WOW! You are radiant. And that necklace! Stunning! Such a unique design; there must be a story behind it."

There is, but I have no intention of sharing it with him. Instead, I smile and move ahead to the waiting limo and say, "I hope you don't mind if I sit up front with you. It's ridiculous for me to ride in the back seat, don't you think?"

He shrugs with indifference, but his eyes blink rapidly. He closes the back door and opens the front passenger side.

Although the drive is an hour, we don't talk very much. A couple of times, we start sentences that trail off. I ask a few questions about the layout of the activities. He mentions that everything takes place in a big field with bales of hay and jokes about watching out for sheep and cattle mingling with the guests. He suggests I wear something other than my heels. I had thought of that, and my foldable flats are tucked into my small purse.

My mind just keeps asking questions: *Why is he here? Is he part of the scheme to steal the necklace, or is he part of some protection program that Lorenzo put in place without letting me know?* There are too many moving parts. I can't tell the good guys from the bad ones. I'm operating with very little information.

Marco parks the limo in a field close to the entrance for the executive cocktail party and insists on walking me to the gate. He even asks for my ticket and presents it to the gatekeeper.

"Okay, I'll leave you here. I'll be waiting for you in this spot when the party after the concert ends."

"*Grazie*, Marco. I only plan to stay long enough to see the Maestro so you won't have to wait too long."

He nods and disappears into the crowd.

My stiletto heels wobble on the closely mown field. There's no time to switch to flats as the crowds jostle me forward.

Marco is right about the giant bales of hay, but so far, no cows or sheep are waiting to ambush me. The hay creates barriers to prevent party crashers and also serve as tables. I'm so busy trying not to fall, I don't immediately notice the impressive array of food and beverages.

Turning another corner in the hay maze, a sign announces Italian caviar. What a surprise. I've been coming to Italy for years and never knew caviar was produced here. The vendor is all smiles as I approach the table housing a large exhibition of the history of caviar production in Italy.

"Buongiorno, signora. Please, you would like a sample? It's the finest caviar in the world. Italy produces 50% more caviar than Russia."

I nod in appreciation and chuckle. The sound of my laughter provides a bit of comic relief. After all, I'm standing in a field discussing caviar when the possibility of being murdered could be around the next haystack. Or, at the very least I could be trampled by sheep and cows. Laughter is good although perhaps a little misplaced.

The vendor continues, "Our caviar is exceptional, because our government has restricted fishing of the sturgeon. Most countries have no limit on the fishing season. They overfish and destroy much of the sturgeon population. Our restrictions give our fish the chance to thrive and produce not only large quantities of the eggs but also a better quality."

He finishes his speech with a flourish, then opens a jar and waves it under my nose. l wait with anticipation and perhaps a drool as he dabs a generous portion on a crispy toast and hands it to me. I close my eyes and experience the slight pop and salty burst as the caviar explodes in my mouth.

When I leave, I have a handful of brochures, business cards and a lovely gift of a half- ounce container of Beluga hybrid inside a dry ice pouch. I also have a name and a direct contact number to purchase the caviar. Recipes are already forming in my head for my next event. Ahhh, another reason to stay alive.

Numerous sponsors featuring their products are lined up in between the hay bales. The next exhibit that catches my eye is a huge wheel of parmesan. A handsome man is carving the cheese into chunks and passing it around. A large chunk lands on my plate. Next, I stop at a table with a variety of tramezzini. Platters are stacked high with these delectable little sandwiches. I select one with tuna and prosciutto, and another with artichokes and sun-dried tomatoes. Then a ricotta cheese and honey one is a must. My last addition is roasted red peppers and olive tapenade. With a glass of Prosecco in one hand and a full plate in the other, I locate a vacant bale of hay.

I sample each sandwich and file the ingredients away for when I return home. These will be great for wedding receptions. The Prosecco adds a layer of calmness until Neil appears out of nowhere. He stands too close and speaks in a not-quite-whispering voice.

"Cat, we need to talk."

I hiss, "Go away, Neil. We agreed not to speak or to be seen together."

Sweat collects on his forehead. He pulls out a handkerchief and mops at the drops trickling down the side of his face.

"Please, Cat. They called again and threatened to kill Gladys. I can't stand it. I've changed my mind. I'm going to the police."

"Neil, if you want to call the police, do it now, so I don't have to go through with this charade. What we're doing is dangerous, so if you've changed your mind, tell me now. But what about Gladys?"

I try not to look at him and move my plate to the other end of the hay bale, but he follows.

"Neil, these people are already here, probably watching us right now. Go away. If you don't want to do this, tell me what you want me to do."

Neil's pasty complexion morphs into red blotches intermingled with sweat. "I don't know. I can't make up my mind."

Shaking my head, I glance around the hay-filled space and wonder if one of these beautiful people is actually a murderer. For a second, beady black eyes meet mine. They morph from Riccardo's face to Marco's. I'm seeing people who aren't here. Helping others is supposed to be a positive experience, not a life-threatening one.

"You have about five minutes to let me know. I'm refilling my glass, and then I'm finding my seat. It's your call, but it's Gladys' life."

I disappear into the maze of hay stacks until I'm sure he isn't following me. I swallow all the Prosecco and dump my plate in a trash bin. I pull out my ticket and follow the signs to the orchestra seats.

Minutes later, Neil shuffles into the row behind me. His seat is slightly to the left. With my head on a tilt, I can see him. I let my program flutter to the ground. Before I can reach for it, he grabs it and taps me on the shoulder.

Without turning around, I say, "Well?"

He leans forward and whispers, "Okay, let's do it. You're right. This is about saving Gladys."

I nod and turn my attention to the stage. The empty seat where Stella should be sitting is a reminder she's lost to me as well as an acknowledgement to myself that this pilgrimage is not the smartest thing I've ever done. In fact, it borders on insanity. But I'm here. Sweet memories of Stella fill the empty space in my heart. And there's Gladys. For all her hot air, she doesn't deserve to die. Neither do I.

The concert blurs into the soft summer night. A full moon rises, stars sprinkle fairy dust, angels join the musical choruses and musicians play as if only the gods can hear. I bask in the magic of each moment.

The finale comes too soon. The Maestro moves to center stage. The beginning notes of "Nessun Dorma" swell. The sweet richness of his voice and the words fill my heart with joy and my eyes with tears.

Dilegua, o notte!	Vanish, oh night!
Tramontate, stelle! Tramontate, stelle!	Set, stars! Set, stars!
All'alba vincerò!	At dawn, I will win!
Vincerò! Vincerò!	I will win! I will win!

34

With my eyes closed, I let the music wash over me. The notes linger as I relish this last bit of happiness before throwing myself into danger. The applause is thunderous and continuous for at least ten minutes.

The last sweet notes disappear. Neil twists and turns in his seat and develops a hacking cough. Even with one arm in a cast, his hands shred the program until it's reduced to a small pile of white flakes at his feet.

He leans forward and whispers, "It's time."

I don't move. Once I leave this seat, there's no turning back, no rethinking, no let's call the police. Before standing, I watch the crowd filtering into the fields like swarms of bees. Those from the orchestra seats who are not staying to meet the Maestro drift to waiting limos. Engines come to life, and headlights create golden globes across the fields. Still, I wait.

My heart rate accelerates. Small pieces of trivia creep into my mind. I center on the packet Stella gave me. She had scribbled a note telling me that the after-party event with Bocelli is priceless. Only a small number of guests are admitted backstage after a concert because the maestro is tired. He will meet with the group briefly before disappearing. Members of the orchestra, other singers and staff will stay to mingle with guests who have paid for the privilege.

While this review of Stella's note doesn't change the perilous situation Neil and I are facing, it distracts me—calms me much like my counting.

The musicians pack up. My purse and the bag with the caviar are on the seat next to me. The caviar seems like a bad joke. I'd rather not be found with caviar when Neil pushes me.

The couple directly in front of me are still seated. I've been fascinated by the intricate hairstyle of the woman. Her long blonde tresses have been braided and twisted around jeweled ribbons. I tap her on the shoulder. When she turns, I'm transfixed by the most intense navy blue eyes. Her gown is the same shade. She's stunning.

She doesn't smile. She looks annoyed, as if I've interrupted a very important conversation.

"Yes?"

"I'm sorry to interrupt, but I was given this lovely caviar from one of the vendors. Since I'll be traveling once I leave the concert, I was wondering if you'd like it?"

Her look changes from disinterest to contempt. For a second I think she might roll her eyes.

"Oh dear, no, of course I don't want it. I'm sure it's inferior."

She turns away and whispers to her companion. He glances at me like I'm a pesky mosquito. He stands and offers the woman his arm. "Come, Sofia. It appears even the best seats are open to *la classe inferiore*."

Lower class—that despicable man just referred to me as lower class. My laugh borders on hysteria. The insaneness of what we're doing rolls over me like a giant wave.

With much regret, I leave the caviar on the chair. I nod at Neil. I'm ready.

We move as one person toward the small sign that says *Dopo la Festa del Concerto*—After Concert Party. My stiletto heels have been replaced with ballet slippers. My dress brushes against the ground. Neil's breathing is harsh and labored.

We mingle with the group, moving to the left of the stage. Crowds are difficult for me, and Neil is making me nervous. He's so obvious. His eyes dart in every direction. His raspy breathing is loud enough for a glance or two from those walking next to us. His cast nudges against my back. My steps become slower, smaller as I reconsider—maybe it's not too late to change my mind. When my heart gallops to an untenable speed. I stop. Neil plows into my back.

"Why did you stop?"

"You're walking too close to me," I whisper.

During our exchange, four muscular men dressed in dark suits join us. Neil's eyes bulge and his hands flail wildly. In panic, he jerks away.

Wrong move. A wicked-looking knife flashes before disappearing into Neil's side. A low moan rolls out of his mouth as pain flits across his face. Two of our burly companions lean in to keep him from falling. After a brief conversation, they nod at the two men who are glued to my side.

We are separated. Neil stumbles as they move swiftly away from us. His face, under the glow of a rigged light over the side stage, is pasty and drenched in sweat. He vanishes in the blackness.

My mind scrambles in numerous directions. Nothing about this makes sense. *Why don't they take the necklace now? Or walk me away from the crowd and take it?*

Instead, forceful hands push me toward the steps. I stumble as my foot catches in the hem of my dress. Seconds before my head cracks against the ground, a beefy hand grabs me. I jerk away, but I can't break the steel-fisted grip.

I'm forced toward the steps.There's a strange craziness in every part of this drama, as if it's been rehearsed by everyone but me. As we approach the narrow, wooden steps, I consider racing up them and merging with the partygoers.

As if reading my mind, one of my escorts slides in front of me while the other keeps his massive hand pressed into my back. The nose of a small gun presses on my spine and blocks whatever stupid plan I was creating. The chatter of the crowd is loud, full of excitement and energy. A plea for help would fall on deaf ears and would probably get me killed.

The familiar first notes of "Nessun Dorma" float on the air like a death march. Two steps from the top, I freeze as a hand reaches out for me. My eyes lock onto Riccardo. The black leather jacket and the dark, slicked-back hair are just as I remember. His ebony eyes and evil grin are the same, except for an addition of a narrow slit of a white scar which twists his mouth slightly off center. He's familiar but not familiar, but there's no mistaking who he is and what he wants.

His eyes, full of loathing and triumph, suck me back to the Zinzulusa Caves. My knees turn to mush. Hands on my back push. I stumble again. More hands slow my fall before I hit the stage. A sharp sting penetrates my neck. I collapse in slow motion against the wooden boards. My hand flutters up, but the necklace has already disappeared.

Blackness descends, but not before Riccardo's face swims into my blurry vision.

"*La collana è mia. A presto.*" he laughs. "The necklace is mine. I'll see you soon."

The kick in my ribs should hurt, but I feel nothing. I float in the deepest depths of the ocean. I no longer care.

♩

Neil struggles to stay with Cat. He promised her. The warm bleed seeps down the leg of his trousers. He tries digging his heels into the soft soil to slow down and glances back. The knife pings against his skin for a second time. The warm rush of blood quickens his pace.

The dark van is parked at the edge of the woods, far away from any other vehicles. The knife moves to his back as he's forced inside the vehicle. A hulking figure slides in on either side. Their bulky bodies smash against him. The knife hovers, never far away.

The driver backs onto the gravel road and turns the car around. The route takes them on narrow roads that curve and dip. The scrubby landscape of the coastal area changes into massive stands of umbrella trees as they move inland. No words are spoken; only the sound of his heartbeat and heavy breathing fill his ears.

Too soon, they swerve off the paved highway onto a dirt road. With every bump, the warm wetness of his blood oozes. The pain brings on seconds of darkness where Gladys' face flashes in his mind. The car rolls to a stop in front of a giant pile of rocks. The headlights flash against a broken tumble of ancient stone walls—an abandoned fortress like so many scattered across the Italian landscape.

"Esci adesso!" "Get Out Now!"

Neil's feet slip out from under him as he's half dragged, half pushed inside the crumbling walls. With every ragged breath or jolt to his body, the seeping wound in his side grows larger, and the sharp sting of pain intensifies. Once inside the half-standing walls, duct tape is pulled taut across his mouth. He gags. His feet catch in the cracks as he's yanked across the broken stones. The recesses of the old ruin reek of wild things.

A torch clicks on obscuring his vision. His eyes close to the harsh light as he tries to forget the crumbled body of a woman.

His tongue twists in a hopeless attempt to call her name. His mind screams, "Gladys!"

She lies across the broken stones splayed on her back. A pool of black blood congeals under her left shoulder. Over her heart, a piece of blood-soaked paper flaps in the light breeze— held in place by a dagger. One large musical note covers the paper.

Neil's thoughts wobble close to the edge of insanity as he wonders if the note is significant. Tears slide from his eyes and trickle over his taped mouth. The world spins into darkness as he slumps against the cold stones. He notices the weeds growing in between the cracks and a tiny white flower. They are the last thing he sees before the knife is plunged into his own heart. He doesn't see or feel the duplicate musical note pinned to his chest.

35

Lajatico

Shadows cover my eyes—thick like morning fog. Macabre shapes surround me, shifting and rearranging. A hand on my arm rocks back and forth. I jerk away. If I open my eyes, Riccardo's evil face will be the last thing I see. I keep them closed.

The hand continues to shake me, gentle but solid. The jiggling becomes insistent. A low, urgent voice whispers in my ear.

"Wake up."

"What?"

The word slides out of my mouth, although I'm sure I didn't speak.

"Please, wake up. I need to get you out of here, fast. You have to help me."

My head is heavy and rolls loosely on my neck. I swat at the hand, willing it to go away. I sink deeper into the dark womb of safety. The shaking continues, insistent and forceful. The voice comes closer. It's deep, husky and intense as lips move against my ear.

"Caterina, wake up! I am Commissario Davide Faena. Lorenzo sent me. I have to get you out of here. We can't stay. It isn't safe."

"Go away!" I slur and bat at the hands trying to lift me. An ID of some sort is waved in front of my face. The voice is persistent. I peel one eye open to squint at the document.

"Put your arms around my neck. I'm going to shift you into an upright position. Someone in the crowd called for a doctor and the police. We must leave before they arrive."

Some of the fog lifts from my brain. I protest. "Aren't you the police?"

"No, not the municipal police. I'm part of the Guardia di Finanza di Toscana—like Lorenzo in Puglia. If we wait for the doctor, you'll be hospitalized. That would be a dangerous place for you. Riccardo's men are somewhere in the crowd watching. They'll come after you. We need to leave now. If you struggle, the crowd will misunderstand and try to block us. Are you ready?"

My head, without any help from me, must nod as arms slide under my body.

"Now I'm going to lift you. Okay?"

He swoops me up. The sudden movement jolts me awake. As my eyes focus, they latch on faces in the crowd. Thankfully, I don't see Riccardo's, but one face jumps out—the man at the resort who accosted me. My foggy mind won't conjure up his name, but I know he's not a friend. He disappears as a path through the onlookers opens. There's murmuring, but no one stops us. A limo idles in the field. The door is open. Marco stands next to it. Is he part of this? Am I being kidnapped? I throw a punch at the man who's carrying me.

"*Merde!*" he growls.

He drops me on the seat. Other hands place a pillow under my head. A soft blanket covers me. A car door slams. The motor vibrates. We're moving before I can protest. My body rolls. A hand prevents me from falling to the floor. I wince from the contact but refuse to open my eyes. I fear who I'll see. *Who are these people? Where are they taking me?*

A vague image of Gino's face lingers as I sort through the faces leaping around in my brain. *Did I see him or imagine him? Did I see Marco?*

I fight my way out of the dark hole. My head throbs. My fingers press against my temple and come away, sticky with blood. I reach for the necklace. It isn't there. It doesn't seem to matter as the world sinks into blackness.

♩

Casali di Casole

Quiet whispers sail over my head. Voices discuss someone's medical condition. A hand rests on my shoulder, and a cool cloth is draped across my forehead.

"How much longer will she be unconscious?"

"Not much longer. She was injected with methohexital. It's fast-acting and usually dissipates quickly, but she was administered a large dose, much more than needed for her size. That's why she's still out."

Another voice interrupts.

"What's the prognosis?"

"She'll be fine with a little rest and lots of fluids. It's a great drug if used properly—fast-acting with no side effects. She has a bit of a bloody bump on her head but no concussion. She might have a headache for a few days. There's also a small wound at the site where the needle was jerked out. I patched up both of those. If you want, I can stay."

"No *dottore*, we'll take care of her."

"Well, if she isn't fully conscious in an hour or so, call me."

"*Grazie, dottore.*"

Conversations drone around my head. My thoughts gallop in all directions without the ability to settle on one thing until the necklace is mentioned.

"They must have stolen the necklace and the bracelet."

"Maybe she didn't wear the bracelet. None of us thought to check. Remember to ask when she comes to. By now, the necklace has been disassembled and the jewels are already being sold on the black market. It won't ever be recovered. I suppose she has insurance."

"Well, at least they didn't kill her."

"No, not this time."

Are they talking about me? The necklace is gone, but that's okay, as it was part of the plan. I move my hands under the blanket. My fingers move up and down my empty arm. *The bracelet is gone?* But no, that's not right. I didn't wear the bracelet. It's still in the vault because I didn't want to risk it being lost or stolen. It's part of Stella, like the necklace. I stifle a smile and keep my eyes closed. Only Gino and I know the real necklace wasn't stolen.

36

The phone call comes early. Riccardo is angry. Isabella knows something went wrong at the concert, but she doesn't know what. Marco is back with the Guardia and hasn't responded to her texts or calls.

She knows better than to question Riccardo's instructions. She's to leave immediately for Castello del Mare. She opens the wardrobe and pulls out the backpack he said would be there. The paperwork includes her new identity—Lucrezia Cristina Barone.

She glances over the resumé. The employment history is excellent, but the new photograph is going to require a lot of effort on her part. The woman staring back at her is plain, matronly with hair pulled back in a severe bun. Her eyes are covered with oversized glasses, and she's dressed in drab and out-of-style clothes.

After rummaging through the backpack, she finds oversized eye glasses, some frumpy clothes and an itinerary. She sighs letting frustration take over for a second. She's vain about her looks, and this makeover isn't something she likes. She sinks onto the bed. Now is not the time to let her vanity get in the way. She must stay calm and focused. The opportunity for a new life is close. If she can pull off the kidnapping and make it work to her advantage, she'll be free of Riccardo. She steels her heart against what she has to do.

Thirteen was her age when Riccardo picked her off the street. He prostituted her until she turned twenty. Then he told her she was too old to be of much value to him unless she was willing to become one of his minions. He said a pretty spy would be useful.

She witnessed what he did with people who were no longer of value to him, so she agreed to stay on. There was no family to miss her. No one waited for her. For twenty years, she lived a life of crime. Now she wants out. But how can she leave? Where can she go that he won't find her? Is she strong enough, angry enough, to escape? He considers her his property, so he would never let her go.

She has worked relentlessly to prove to him she was invaluable. He entrusted her with more important assignments. One of the biggest was to turn Marco into an informant. Word had drifted back to Riccardo that Marco had been bad-mouthing the Guardia in a local bar. He sent a message to Isabella, telling her to check it out. It had been a real coup for her to convince Marco to cross the line. She closes her eyes and recalls their first meeting.

She had chosen a navy dress that was conservative but sexy. A multicolored scarf emphasized the plunging neckline. The red stiletto heels turned every head when she walked into the bar. Men would do anything for a woman in spike heels—every little boy's fantasy.

It had been easy for Isabella to meet Marco—a few drinks, a little flirting, and he belonged to her. It wasn't an unpleasant assignment. Marco was handsome, fit and a clothing connoisseur. They had a lot in common, and spending time with him was a break from murder and mayhem.

They met several times. He'd been eager to buy her drinks and talk. His anger toward his boss spilled out. His vanity and ego were bruised when Commissario Faena didn't give him the promotion he thought he deserved.

Isabella was good at persuading people to cross the line, but Marco was a challenge. He was proud to be part of the Guardia, which meant his anger was situational and would dissipate. But she understood men and knew he wanted her.

She let him talk. She was quiet, thoughtful and comforting. Slowly, she invited him into her false world of wealth—the one Riccardo financed. Concerts, invitations to posh parties, and exclusive private clubs all designed to spin a web—to capture his soul. Marco liked the good life—the one he wasn't able to afford on the

Guardia's salary. With Isabella's attention and sympathy, he convinced himself he deserved better and that his boss was a jerk.

She remembered almost word for word the conversation that made him cross over. They were having dinner at *Ristorante Il Molo*, where they feasted on salmon tartare and lobster. She smiled at him over a glass of creamy Soave. She'd dressed in an off-the-shoulder black silk blouse and long black skirt. After a month of holding him off, she knew he was ready to do anything for her.

"Your talents are being wasted at the Guardia. Look at all the advantages I have. My boss is easygoing and quick to reward good work."

She let the thought of easy money sink in as she caressed his hand, running her fingers in and out of his. Beads of sweat lined his forehead.

"You wouldn't have to leave your job. In fact, it would be helpful if you stayed. Perhaps there's something small you can do for my boss —nothing illegal. Maybe your commissario is on the take. Who knows? Keep your eyes and ears open. You'll be surprised at what goes on. In the meantime, it would be fun for you and me to work on a couple of projects. What do you think?"

Marco loved the way her fingers caressed his. His ache for her was so strong he barely heard what she said. He managed to ask, "Who is your boss? What does he do? Is the work legitimate?"

"Of course, the work is legitimate. I can't divulge his name as he's a mover and shaker in the financial world. Everything he does has to be clean. Your nest egg will grow overnight without taxes to consider."

She waited. Lines creased his forehead.

"If the business is legitimate, why wouldn't I pay taxes?"

"So you are listening."

"What?"

She laughed.

"Oh, Marco. I wanted to see if you were really listening. You seem to be somewhere else."

He blushed. His sophisticated persona faded into vulnerability. She hated that, and even more, she hated that she had feelings for him. It would make it more difficult for her to extricate herself. Men fell in love with her all the time. Even the ones who paid her seemed to forget she was a prostitute. Now here was Marco with his bright, expectant eyes.

His grip on her fingers tightened.

"You know what I want. Give me that, and I'll gladly take care of a couple of small jobs. But remember, I owe allegiance to the Guardia. It's all I've ever wanted to do since I was a kid. As angry as I am, I'll get over it."

Isabella smiled—a slow, wide smile. The tip of her tongue touched the corner of her mouth.

"Pay the check, Marco."

That's how it began, but it didn't stop there. Being forced to sleep with so many men had filled her with hate for all of them. But Marco was different.

He bared his soul to her. He treated her as the princess she longed to be. He never questioned her absences. When she called, he came. He told her she was all he wanted. He was willing to do anything for her.

Little by little, she trusted him. Bits of her story of enslavement slipped out, although she didn't reveal she worked for the mafia. Instead, she told him she had escaped from her captors and found a decent job.

She snuggled in his arms as she told him she wanted to be her own boss, and she wanted to travel. But more than anything, she wanted to leave the country and begin a new life with him. They talked into the night about ways to make that happen. Marco fell into the trap.

"Can you get me more jobs?"

"I can, but you said you wouldn't accept any more jobs after the last one."

"Yeah, but that's because you asked me to do something illegal."

"But Marco, the file I asked you to copy on that man who interviewed with our company revealed he was a criminal. All you did was run a background check to confirm my boss's suspicions. It saved him from hiring a thief. Isn't that a good thing?"

He wanted to believe her, but what he did was wrong. He shrugged and poured more wine into their glasses.

"You said the jobs would be legitimate. I'm good with that, and the money can go toward our plan to leave. I'll do all the legal jobs you can find me."

And she had for a while.

Then Marco was given an undercover Guardia assignment as a manager at a posh resort. His role was to protect a woman who was arriving in Italy in a few weeks and staying at *Casoli di Casole*. Isabella informed Riccardo. It was just luck that the person Marco was hired to protect was someone Riccardo was looking for. He was pleased with the information and arranged for her to secure a position as Marco's assistant.

Marco was eager to tell her the woman was an important friend of the Guardia in Puglia. When Cat deposited her jewelry in the vault, Marco watched. He relayed to Isabella the necklace was a one-of-a-kind custom-designed piece with a large price tag.

Isabella remembered thinking this might be the break she'd been waiting for. She would steal the jewelry. Marco could help or not. She asked innocent questions about the woman. Where was she from? Why was she here? Who was her contact in the Guardia?

She mulled the information over before saying, "Marco, that piece of jewelry could be the beginning of our life together."

Marco's mouth dropped open, and his eyes darkened.

"You aren't serious, are you? That's stealing. That would be the wrong way to start our life together. What if we got caught?"

When he asked that question, Isabella smiled to herself. That was the opening she needed. She mentioned just in passing that she was a locksmith, and she had the technical skills to loop the camera feed.

He stared at her and shook his head.

"You've done this before, haven't you?"

Her voice was so low he had to lean in to hear her response.

"You know I had no choice. The only way out for me is death. I want to live. I want to start a new life with you. She has to have insurance. She won't lose anything."

Later, she told him she had contacts all over the world and could easily find a buyer. Little by little Marco had bought in. His job was to fine-tune the heist. It was supposed to happen in the early hours of the morning after the concert.

What Isabella hadn't counted on was jealousy. It reared its ugly head when the petit redhead arrived, and Marco seemed enthralled. When she questioned him, he told her it was necessary to get close to Cat. To her mind, intimate picnics and the special attention he lavished on the woman seemed more than necessary. From the time she was a child, she'd been trained to deceive. What if Marco was doing the same?

She was angry at her own insecurity. They both agreed there would be no strings, but that was at the beginning when she had no feelings for him. She laughed at herself, but the laughter faded. What if Marco was playing her for a fool?

Then the unthinkable happened. Their plans backfired when Riccardo intervened and stole the necklace at the concert.

Isabella glances again at the photo still clutched in her hands. She doesn't want to be this severe-looking woman. She looks into the mirror, pulls her bountiful hair into a knot, and tries on the glasses. She's sad, tired, and angry. She feels stupid to have let Marco into her life—maybe betrayal was the only game men knew.

She repacks the bag and adds her few belongings. The next phase was about to begin. She has to be very careful from now on. If Marco betrays her, she will kill him. Or, she may not have to. If Riccardo finds out they are together, he will eliminate both of them.

37

Conversations float endlessly around the bed. Although I've been awake for a while, my eyes stay closed. I drift in and out of consciousness. They talk about me as if I'm not in the room. Their arguments have me either shipped back to America or squirreled away in Castello del Mare while the Guardia searches for Riccardo.

Commissario Faena's attempts at whispering hover between high and low pitches.

"It isn't safe for her to stay here. Some of Riccardo's men may have infiltrated the staff. They're watching the place around the clock. She'll be safer if we send her back to America. Luigi can travel with her."

Hearing Luigi's name surprises me. Didn't Lorenzo send him? Gino's voice interrupts. It's low and gravelly.

"She has to stay in Italy. If we send her home, she'll be dead before she reaches the US. As remarkable as Luigi's skills are, he'll be outnumbered. Once Riccardo is apprehended, she'll have to testify unless you're planning on killing him. Even that means a deposition and lots of paperwork for her to complete. It makes no sense to send her home and call her back. It's best if we send her to Castello. Lorenzo will provide protection."

That statement almost makes my eyes fly open. I seriously doubt Lorenzo wants to protect me, much less see me. I let his face drift into my vision. If only it were possible for us to be together. My love for him has never wavered, from those early summer vacations to the present. Our desire is strong, but not strong enough to tamp down our ambitions. We are overachievers and are determined to be successful in our chosen careers. Neither of us is willing to move to another country and start over.

The commissario's voice breaks the silence.

"I hate that it's necessary to keep her on Italian soil. She's such a nuisance. If we didn't have to depose her, I'd put her on the next plane. Maybe I can convince the judge to let us video her deposition. Then we could send her packing."

The conversations continue as various people decide my fate without asking my opinion or permission. My eyes are heavy from the drone of their voices. I sink into that borderland between sleep and awake.

At some point, they must realize I need to rest. The shuffle of feet, the fading whispers, and the closing of a door tell me they've left the room. As soon as the door is shut, I open my eyes. I gingerly slide out from under the covers and hobble to the wardrobe for clean clothes. With great care, I step into the shower and let the hot water wash away my fears—well, at least some of them.

38

The morning mist hovers over the pool. Silvery wisps weave through the gauzy puffs of low-lying clouds. For twenty-four hours, I was scrutinized by Davide, Gino and Marco. This morning, the villa is quiet. I'm alone.

The scene outside the window is peaceful until it's interrupted by two armed guards patrolling the area. Their intrusion makes me sigh and turn away. While they're here for my protection, the sight of them reinforces I'm not safe anywhere until Riccardo is back behind bars or dead.

Yesterday, I was told to get ready to move. My fate has been decided. I'm being shipped to Castello until this mess is sorted. Arrangements have been made to fly me there. It's all very hush, hush. Sometime in the wee hours of tomorrow, I'll be spirited away. All I've been told is a car, a boat, and a plane. Lorenzo will be waiting.

Although he's angry with me, he's still in the business of protecting me. It's been almost a year since we've been together. My stomach clinches in anticipation. The passion that erupts when we see each other has had time to cool off. I often wonder if our desire is based on wanting what we really can't have. A future together isn't possible. The situation is manageable when we're apart but when we're in the same place—well, that's another story.

An ocean and our careers stand in the way. Plus, a glaring factor is he wants children. I'm close to deciding I don't want any. There's so much to sort through before I would consider bringing a child into a world as corrupt and angry as the present one. Maybe I'll just get a cat. Somehow, becoming a cat lady sounds like a more rational thing to do.

A pounding on the door startles me.

"Cat, it's Marco! Open the door!"

I turn too quickly, and the room spins. I grab the back of the kitchen chair and hold on until the room resumes its normal state. Instead of rushing to answer, I hold my head very still and take small steps.

When I open the door, Marco stumbles into the foyer. His face is a washed-out gray.

"The Hickmans are dead."

"What? I-I don't understand."

"Their bodies were found this morning."

"Oh no! Please, tell me it isn't true. Riccardo got what he wanted. I was hopeful he'd let them go. What happened?"

Marco leans against the door.

"Are you sure you want to hear? It's pretty gruesome."

My head nods, but my heart seems to have stopped. *Did I help get them killed?*

"Kids found them in some old ruins not far from the concert venue. Signora Hickman was stabbed straight through the heart with a musical note pinned to her chest. Oh shit! Forget I said that. According to forensics, she was killed a couple of hours before Mr. Hickman."

"Forensics? How would you know about that?"

His face flushes. The palms of his hands push back against the air.

"Let me finish."

I'm confused, but nod. The police wouldn't give a resort manager that kind of detail.

"Neil had a nasty knife wound in his side, but it was the stab to his heart that killed him. Poor bastard, he didn't die right away. It seems they wanted to torture him by letting him bleed out with Gladys lying dead in front of him. It must have been agonizing."

If not for the wall behind me, I would have collapsed. It was naive of me to believe the necklace would save them. And once Riccardo discovers it's fake, and that will be soon, none of us will be safe. The brutal murder of the Hickmans is a neon sign advertising my demise and possibly those close to me. *What have I done?*

"Marco, who are you?"

"What do you mean? I'm the manager of *Casoli di Casole*. Why are you asking? Are you not well?"

"Ha! For two years I've been on the solving side of a series of crimes. You're not just a manager of this resort. If you were, you wouldn't know about forensics, and you certainly wouldn't be privy to a clue like musical notes unless you're involved. So, who are you, and whose side are you on?"

Anger, fear and embarrassment cross his face.

"You're quite the little Sherlock Holmes, aren't you?"

"Not exactly, but I'm not stupid."

With arms crossed over his chest, he says, "Well, you'll find out eventually. No, I'm not the manager here. I work for the Guardia. Commissario Faena is my boss. He's going to be furious you found out."

"Don't worry. I won't say anything. That is if you tell me what's going on. Start with the musical note. Did Neil have one, too?"

"Cat, if Faena finds out, I'm going to lose my job."

"Marco, if you don't tell me, you'll lose your job. Why should he find out? Do you plan on telling him?"

He sighs and tells me about the crime scene. As he talks, I see the tiny musical note on each of the cards that were tucked in the roses. Disjointed thoughts cram into my head until he says something about someone else missing.

"Who's missing?"

"Isabella. She didn't come to work today. No one's seen her. She doesn't answer her phone, and she hasn't returned any of my calls."

"Is she sick? Or is she somehow involved? The way she questioned me about Neil made me suspicious. Is she part of the Guardia? Mafia?"

Marco's face goes from putty to alabaster. Beads of sweat pop out on his upper lip. He's too quick to defend her.

"No, no, I'm sure she isn't with either one. Like everyone that works here, she had to be vetted. Can you really see her in either role? I certainly can't."

"How would I know? She could be part of the plot, even if it's only to keep an eye on me. If she's working for the mafia, we haven't seen the last of her. Plus, we're lucky she didn't slit our throats."

Marco's mouth falls open. "You can't think Isabella is capable of murder. That's ridiculous."

I stare at him as his face goes from surprise to fear to anger.

"Is it? I'm already checking over my shoulder for Riccardo. Isabella has disappeared. I think that's a reason to be suspicious of her. Why are you coming to her defense? What aren't you telling me?"

He stops talking and walks away from me.

"Okay, so you're not ready to tell me about Isabella. What can you tell me?

"My job is to keep you safe. Nothing else. I'm not privy to the plan."

"But wasn't your job to keep the Hickmans safe, too? What's going on, Marco? Wait, don't tell me. I need coffee. This mess is too much to think about without something to drink, and it's too early for alcohol."

I storm down the hallway. Marco follows. He plants himself right next to the stove. I grind the espresso beans and fill the cylinder with water, tamp down the coffee in the basket, and set it over the flame. Once it's ready, we move to the terrace. I slump against the cushioned lounge. Marco remains standing.

"Okay, Marco, no more games. Tell me everything you know. My life is on the line. The only thing that will help me is knowledge."

He hesitates for a second. "I guess I owe you that much after everything you've been through. It was you who set the whole thing in motion when you called Maria and asked for Stella's dress. Maria and Gino knew you were going to attend the concert, and they told Lorenzo."

It would be easy to be angry with Gino and Maria, but I'm not surprised they would contact Lorenzo. They don't want the same thing to happen to me that happened to Stella.

Marco picks up his empty cup and puts it back down.

"Your name was placed on an alert list. Lorenzo was contacted as soon as it appeared on a flight manifest. He called Commissario Faena. They've worked together on several cases. Lorenzo asked Faena to protect you during your stay. Several weeks ago, they moved me and others in place to protect you without knowing exactly what might happen."

He fidgets with his espresso cup, swirling it in circles on the glass-top table until it creates an annoying screech.

"You weren't told because it was important for you to behave normally instead of suspiciously. I was warned that you tend to be in the wrong place at the wrong time with your nose in other people's business."

He laughs, but I don't.

"That would be Lorenzo who provided that bit of information?"

He nods. "He painted a vivid picture of what we were up against. And if you weren't enough, the Hickmans showed up. We weren't informed by the FBI who they were until after they landed in Rome. No one knew they were staying at the same resort as you. We had no clue if you knew each other or if there was something else going on,"

"Look, I don't know the Hickmans. I saw them for the first time at the Hilton Airport Hotel in Rome. Does anyone know why they were staying at this resort? Was it planned?"

"No one knew who they were or why they were here, but we considered them dangerous. We had to split the task force to keep both you and them under surveillance. We realized right away how incredibly naive they were. They were unaware that they were targets of the mafia. And they certainly didn't think the mafia here might be connected to the American mafia. By the time Neil caught on, it was too late."

I chime in, "So when Neil and Gladys acted all hostile toward each other, maybe that was to confuse all of us as well as the mafia?"

"Could be. Except everyone's plans were intertwined. Gladys' father wanted Neil eliminated. He underestimated the mafia. Money was their primary goal until Riccardo added the necklace. Then, you and the Hickmans showed up at the same resort on the same day. Everyone was confused."

If this were a made-for-TV movie, it would be unbelievable. I'd turn it off. No one seems to have a grasp of what's going on.

Marco stands and stretches. "I need to check in with Faena."

"Tell me about the wiretaps first."

"Oh shit. You figured that out, too?"

I raise an eyebrow. "It was obvious to me and perhaps illegal?"

"Not in Italy. Sure, the owners would have been upset, but they didn't need to know. We had to get intel on the Hickmans and learn why you were making plans with him. That's how we discovered Neil was supposed to steal the necklace."

The insanity of our conversation makes the serene backdrop of the resort seem ludicrous. A sort of hellish paradise with flames circling the perimeter.

"Once we listened to your conversation with Neil, we changed our plans to coordinate with yours. It was extraordinarily complex to pull together a plan without closing down the concert. We considered canceling, but the commissario didn't want 10,000 people angry at the Guardia."

"What if you had closed down the concert? Would that have saved the Hickmans?"

"No, maybe delayed the murders a bit, but they were on Riccardo's list. We think Riccardo was working with Signora Hickman's father. Maybe it was a private contact, and it was just happenstance that the Hickmans showed up at the same resort as you.

"That's bizarre. Why do you think that?"

"Riccardo rarely works with the Russian and Albanian mafia, but those were the thugs who worked Signor Hickman over. And they assisted Riccardo in stealing the necklace. The entire operation was confusing as no one was exactly sure who was doing what."

Marco shrugs and moves to the window.

"Bottom line is Riccardo wanted you at the concert so he could steal the necklace. Somehow, the Hickmans guaranteed you'd show up."

"So the Hickmans being at the same hotel and the same concert was just a coincidence?"

"As far as we know, Neil was supposed to be killed but not Gladys. We don't know what happened. Maybe she put up a fight."

I shudder. "What if it was our plan that got her killed? What if they got wind that the necklace was fake before the concert?"

"What? What are you saying? The necklace is fake? *Merde*, Cat, that changes everything."

Marco pulls out his cell phone and starts to punch.

"Don't do it, Marco. No one else knows. It complicates things a bit. Once Riccardo finds out, he'll speed up killing me. For now, I need you to promise not to tell anyone that the necklace is fake. Lorenzo needs to be the first to know. I'll tell him when I see him."

He pauses. "I have to tell Faena. Cat, the necklace is the reason we thought we had some time to get you out of here. A piece that significant has to be broken down and sold on the black market. That can take a while. By tomorrow, Riccardo will know it's fake. He'll blow this place apart."

He shakes his head and continues to hold his phone, poised to make the call to the commissario. "I can't believe you would wear a fake necklace and not tell us."

"How could I tell you? I didn't know you were part of the operation, and I only met Commissario Faena after the necklace was stolen. It was part of my plan all along before the Hickmans were involved. No one was to know."

"*Mio dio*, Cat, you should have at least told someone in the Guardia."

"Maybe, but I need more time. Telling may have gotten me shipped back to the States immediately. Don't you understand that Riccardo is a murderer? Everyone of you let him get away with only a slap on the wrist. It's not enough. I'm asking you to give me this one break and pretend you don't know the necklace is fake until after I tell Lorenzo."

"I can't do that, Cat. I'd be fired."

I hold my breath, trying to think of a way to stall him. One thing comes to mind when I remember the couple of times I saw Marco and Isabella with their heads together. And Marco jumped to her defense when I questioned who she was. I plunge ahead.

"Wouldn't you be fired if Commissario Faena found out about your fling with Isabella? Particularly since you don't really know who she is. You could be sleeping with one of Riccardo's spies."

He clenches his fist and raises his arm. I back away.

"I think you might want to keep your mouth shut."

39

There's nothing in the foyer that I can use to protect myself, but I refuse to take back what I said. I hit a nerve, so I press on.

"I'll keep my mouth shut if you do the same."

The grimace on his face says it all, but I keep going.

"It's my necklace, not yours. Why are you so upset that the necklace is fake? It means I still have the real one to bargain with."

"What do you mean—the real one?"

I shake my head and wish I hadn't let that slip. Although Marco says he's Guardia, I don't trust him.

"I misspoke."

Marco looks bewildered. "You're putting this entire operation in jeopardy. People could get hurt or killed. This is not a time to play games."

I shrug and continue with false bravado to lead him to another topic.

"I'm not the one playing games. I don't have anything to hide. Perhaps you don't know the back story of this operation. Riccardo killed my best friend. Then he came after me. I was kidnapped and tortured, And for what? A sentence of a couple of years. Now he's free, and the Hickmans are dead. And what about my friends in Castello? Who else is he going to kill? Maybe those of you in law enforcement need to feel guilty for allowing this to happen."

Marco's frown deepens. He struggles with what to say. "Okay, this conversation is over. I don't understand what you hope to accomplish, but I don't intend to be part of whatever your plan is. I won't tell anyone about the fake necklace. I'll take you as far as Castello, but that's all."

"That's all I'm asking. When I see Lorenzo, I'll tell him about the necklace and whatever else he needs to know. Neither he nor your boss will hear about you and Isabella from me unless what you're doing isn't in the best interest of the Guardia. You might want to tell your boss before someone else does."

While I don't need Marco as an enemy, I think his behavior with Isabella is unprofessional whether he's in the Guardia or the manager at this posh resort or something else entirely. All I know is my senses are yelling at me not to trust him.

Marco stands and stares off into the distance. When he turns and faces me, he nods in a noncommittal way and says, "Before we continue, I'll get us another espresso."

I start to protest, but he's already picked up my cup. I watch him move with purpose through the French doors. I walk to the edge of the pool and look toward the mountains.

Marco closes the door to the kitchen before clicking on Isabella's number. As soon as she answers, he says, "Listen to what I have to say. Then, hang up. We have to change our plans. The necklace Riccardo stole is fake. But I think the real one is still in the safe. I don't know where you are, but we have another chance. I'll call you later today or tonight with more information."

He hangs up and splashes coffee into the espresso cups. He stops just outside the door to the terrace and watches Cat gazing at the mountains. She looks innocent, but she's smart. It won't take much for her to become suspicious and start asking more questions. Those questions might start a chain reaction that will lead to him.

♩

Within an hour, Isabella's phone rings. Thinking it's Marco, she pulls off the highway. Instead, it's Riccardo. His anger rumbles through the phone as if somehow it's her fault the necklace is fake. He rages on and on.

When he calms down, he says, "They are moving tonight. We'll try to intercept them, but if we don't, your job is to kidnap Maria and Gino's grandson."

His laughter grates as he tells her that instead of keeping an eye on Cat's movements, she's to nab the kid. A teaching assistant's job is waiting for her in Castello. She's to use the resumé and clothes in the backpack. Someone else will be moved into place to shadow Cat.

Isabella's hand trembles as she writes down the information about the little boy and his family. He tells her the school board in Castello will be hiring several teacher's assistants. He says one of the jobs is hers. Since she already has a new identity, it will be an easy transition.

Once she has the kid, Cat will be contacted to bring the necklace in exchange for the child's release.

The call ends. Isabella closes her eyes and leans her head against the seat. Kidnapping? No. That's not possible. Of all the things she's done, children have never been involved.

She clicks on Marco's number. When he doesn't answer, she leaves a message. "Marco, my assignment has changed. Riccardo knows the necklace is fake. He says I'm no longer spying on Cat. Instead, I have to kidnap a child. He's the grandson of Cat's best friends in Castello. We need to rethink our plans. Call me tonight after I reach Castello. You can fill me in on what happened at the concert."

On the long drive to Castello, she revises what she needs to do several times. Maybe Marco can steal the necklace from the safe. When they looked at the video, they thought she did something, but they didn't know what it was. This means the real necklace could still be in the vault.

She turns on the blinker and eases off the gas. She needs coffee to continue. If the necklace isn't in the vault, or if Cat is moved before Marco can steal it and Riccardo doesn't intercept them, then kidnapping the child might work. The child's life for the necklace.

Yes, it just might work. She wouldn't harm the child. Instead of delivering him to Riccardo, she would keep him. Then, she would negotiate a deal directly with Cat. Maybe the kid was her ticket out of this hell hole. She'd need a place to hide out with him for a few days. Marco could help her with that. On her end, she would find a buyer, get new passports, and find passage out of the country.

The easiest route would be for Marco to steal the necklace. But if Cat left with it, they would still have several weeks to put the backup plan in place. While she doesn't like involving a child, Cat will easily give up the real necklace for the kid's life. Either way, she'd get what she wanted.

On her next birthday she will turn thirty. Long ago, she'd set up an offshore bank account, anticipating the day she'd find a way out. With the necklace, she'll have enough to disappear. She had hoped Marco would help her. But now, she's unsure about her feelings for him. Maybe he'll come with her or maybe not. If he doesn't, she'll have to kill him.

40

Casoli di Casole

Marco hands me the coffee. I set it on the table and wonder if he poisoned it. Maybe that's a little farfetched, but that raised fist tells me he doesn't have my best interest. His phone keeps vibrating, but he ignores it as I string out a series of questions.

"What about Riccardo? How long has he been out of prison? Who knew he was out?"

"He was released a few days ago. Higher-ups signed his extradition papers. Lorenzo had no choice but to sign, and Riccardo was delivered to the Albanian police. Lorenzo and Davide were both there. They saw him get on the boat and leave, but it was a setup. The boat had been hijacked by the Albanian mafia. They had the proper uniforms and the credentials. The prisoner was released to them."

"Didn't anyone at the Guardia think that might happen?"

"Why do you think we were at the resort? We were sure his henchmen would show up at the concert, but we had no way of knowing that Riccardo was on his way."

"Well, this is just a mess. Why didn't he kill me at the concert? It would have been easy to put a lethal dose in the syringe."

"As far as we know, stealing the necklace is just the beginning of his revenge for Carlo's death. He plans to make your life hell until he decides when and where to kill you. He will play games with you. His goal is for you to live in constant fear."

It seems to me that Marco is eager to stick the knife in my side and turn the blade. I walk to the edge of the pool and stand next to him.

"What else?"

"What else? Well, the death of the Hickmans was just another way for him to torture you—to make you feel guilty. And the fake necklace will increase his fury. In his mind, you're the only loose thread left. He intends to eliminate you as he chooses. Once you're dead, he'll disappear."

The way Marco speaks about torture implies he might be happy to see it applied to me.

"How was it possible for me to see Riccardo before the concert? He was at the hotel and the train station. Could he have been released earlier?"

"No, it's usual for mafia types to have a lookalike to stand in—maybe a brother or cousin. You never saw him up close, did you?"

"No, he was always a good distance away. But the man I saw at the concert was really Riccardo, right?"

"Yes. He was released a few days before the concert. He had to scramble to arrive in Lajatico in time. We're doing our best to capture him before he captures you."

"What happens now? I mean, what's being done to find him? Why wasn't he apprehended at the concert?"

"As I told you, Lorenzo dropped this bomb on us shortly before the concert. We barely had time to get people in place at the resort. The plans you made with Neil weren't on our radar until the last minute. I was the closest person on site, so I got the job of chauffeur. I never lost sight of you, but Riccardo's people were everywhere. Davide and his crew were late arriving. That's all I know."

He moves away from me as if I have a contagious disease.

"I'm not part of the inner circle. My next assignment is to keep you safe until I hand you off to Lorenzo. The commissario will stop by tonight and tell us what happens next and when."

It appears that's all the info I'm going to get from Marco. I switch topics.

"I know you don't want to talk about it, but I need to know about Isabella. You said she disappeared. What can you tell me about her?"

Marco's face flushes. He tugs at his collar. "Not much. She doesn't live on the premises, so the most I could do was bug the *l'ape* she used. The way she grilled you on the way back to your villa raised my suspicions. Plus, she neglected to mention to me that she had a conversation with you. Then she brought the so-called nurse into the house. Their little chat in the kitchen was enlightening."

"Was it necessary for you to become as close to her as you did?"

Marco turns away from me before answering. "Yeah, well, that was my mistake. It was stupid on my part. I thought I could find out more if we were friendly. But she isn't into sharing personal information."

"Hmmm, do you think she knows you are part of the Guardia?"

"No, I didn't share my personal life either. You suspected she was jealous, so that might be all it was."

"Is it a good or bad thing that she's disappeared? Do you think she's sick or she's somehow involved?"

"I really don't know."

I drum my fingers on the side table as the sun swings higher. The cicadas burst through the tranquility of our private thoughts with a cacophony of buzzing and clicking sounds. For a moment, it takes my mind off the crazy conversation we're having, but only for a moment.

"What else can you tell me?"

Marco's sophisticated charm has been replaced by tousled hair, a rumpled shirt and lines etched into his forehead. He looks across the undulating landscape to the mountain range before replying.

"What do you want to know? More about the Hickmans?"

"No, I believe I know just as much as you do or maybe more."

"Cat, you've got to stop this. You're sticking your nose into a dangerous area. It's not your business to do that. You did hear me when I said the Hickmans are dead, didn't you? You must realize what a nuisance you are. Davide wants you gone, and Lorenzo isn't excited about us shipping you to him."

Watching various expressions cross Marco's face, I decide to shut up. There's so much he's not telling me. I'm no closer to knowing what's going on.

"Yes, I'm sure they are furious with me. So what happens next?"

"Our job is to safeguard you and take Riccardo back into custody. Once that happens, you will be on a plane home."

"And exactly what do I do? Wait for Riccardo to kill me? Your protection didn't help the Hickmans. Why should I believe I'll be protected?"

Marco picks up his coffee cup in the palm of his hand. I pull out my phone as if I plan to make a call. My insides are churning. What if I've pushed him too far?

"It would be better if you stand down so we can do our jobs. We believe Riccardo will stop at nothing to kill you. It's our job, not yours, to see that you are safe."

I force myself to smile before saying, "Somehow, I'm not feeling very safe."

41

Castello del Mare

Analisa frowns as she scans the names on the list of potential candidates for the teacher's assistant position. Most of the names are familiar—from the village or the surrounding area. She taps the pencil on the table and chews on her thumbnail. There are ten candidates for three slots. In Analisa's opinion, only one stands out. She studies the name again, Lucrezia Cristina Barone from Milano. She smiles and hopes the candidate will relax.

"Your credentials are outstanding. Why are you applying for this position?"

Isabella's smile fades, and a flush travels to her cheeks. She looks Analisa in the eye and says, "The reason is complicated. My mother sent me here to look after her sister, who is ill. *Mia zia* lost her sight a few months ago. Then she fell and broke her leg."

She clears her throat and moves her hands to her lap before continuing.

"My mother and her sister are close, but age prevents my mother from traveling. She asked me to come and assess the situation. When I arrived, I realized my aunt needs full-time caregivers while her leg is healing and while I'm trying to find a more suitable place for her to live."

Analisa doodles on the sheet of paper in front of her. She wonders why the applicant didn't answer the question.

"What about your job at the Natural History Museum in Milan? Did you resign or take a leave?"

"Once I assessed the situation, I requested a year-long sabbatical from my job. It was approved. I will continue to write articles and conduct research while I oversee my aunt's care. I've already found two daytime caregivers for her. I'll only be needed at night. Since I'm staying for a year, it would be nice to fill my time with some worthy cause in the community, and as you said my credentials are outstanding."

Analisa nods and continues, "Wouldn't a part-time position take away from your research or the care your aunt needs?"

A moment of panic slides across Isabella's face.

"Oh, no. It would fit nicely into my schedule. I'd rather not be cooped up in the house all day. This position is perfect for me. In the evening, after my aunt is settled, I'll have plenty of time for research."

Something keeps niggling in the back of Analisa's mind, but she can't pull it out. She feels unqualified to be questioning this woman who has a slate of degrees and an impressive work history. Also, when they took a short break, the principal promoted this candidate.

"The work you currently do is not with children. In fact, it is quite an intellectual position. Perhaps you'd be bored working a few hours everyday with a group of unruly but enthusiastic kids."

The woman doesn't change her tone or smile.

"Becoming a teacher's assistant will help me become part of the community. If you check my resumé, it lists my volunteer work. Much of it involves children. The caretakers will work eight-hour shifts on a rotating basis. If I'm needed, I'll be close by. I really want to participate while I'm here. It's a lovely village, and I really enjoy being with children."

Analisa studies the face devoid of makeup—the long black hair pulled back in a low, severe bun and the oversized eye glasses. The attempt at homeliness doesn't hide a certain polish in the candidate. With a little makeup, and a flattering hairstyle and a stylish outfit, she'd be beautiful. She wonders why the woman has dressed down, particularly coming from Milano. Is it intentional?

Analisa had watched each of the applicants during the time they interacted with the children. That was the deciding factor for her.

Giorgino hung back. Most of the candidates didn't seek him out or even question his reluctance to be part of the group. He was small for his age and shy. The sickle cell disease isolated him during those early school years when he was home-schooled. He didn't have the same level of social skills as the other kids. Analisa's top priority during the interviews was to find someone who noticed the marginalized children.

There are several in Giorgino's class. Little Andrea whose parents were recently killed in a head-on collision, Matteo who was held back because he's dyslexic, and Laura with a droopy eye and a speech impediment. Only three of the applicants sought out these children. Giorgino, after a few minutes, had gravitated toward Signorina Barone.

Annalisa listens intently to the responses given by each of the candidates as they're interviewed. She meticulously studies all the resumés. Lucrezia's name is the only one that receives a star from her. Yet, she wonders why she feels so hesitant.

She peruses the list again and checks off two other names who recognized all the children and not just the healthy ones. Each of the three she favors has solid qualifications. She gives Lucrezia one extra point because of the principal's backing, but somehow it doesn't feel right.When she looks back up, Lucrezia is smiling. It's such a lovely smile, yet it doesn't quite reach her eyes.

Isabella holds her breath, knowing Analisa is scrutinizing her, but she's sure she sucked her in. After all, that's what she has been trained to do.

42

Casali di Casole

Commissario Davide Faena's face says it all, something along the lines of *I'm a nuisance, and he will be greatly relieved to get rid of me.*

Marco texted me earlier to let me know he and the commissario would be outside my door at 2 am. With that as a wake-up call, there was no point in going to bed. Instead, I packed a bag and dressed in head-to-toe black as I was instructed. I dozed on the sofa in the dark, too afraid to turn on any lights.

For the past ten minutes, the commissario has been lecturing me. I should be listening, but I've heard it all before from Lorenzo. Marco stands by the front door, phone in hand. It looks like he's texting someone. The commissario's voice is impatient and demanding. I tune back in.

"Where's your bag? Why aren't you ready? We're leaving in five minutes. Whatever you leave behind will be packed up and sent to you. Gino and Marco are going with you, as well as an armed guard. A boat will take you down the coast a short distance to a private airfield. From there, you'll fly to Castello."

"Why are we sneaking out in the middle of the night?"

He works at composing his face before he snarls.

"Because you've created big problems for us. This resort has too much wide open space, and my officers are already spread thin. I can't offer you enough protection. Marco tells me one of the employees disappeared. We're pretty sure the staff here is compromised, which means it's no longer safe. Be thankful Lorenzo offered protection for you in Castello. If he hadn't, I would have locked you up."

He barks more than laughs. I don't join in.

"Riccardo and his friends are infiltrating the area. If they arrive before I get you out of here, you'll be trapped, and so will we. The danger is both inside and outside these gates."

Great, now I have another lecture. Yes, I was wrong to come. This pilgrimage for Stella has turned from honoring her to endangering everyone who crosses my path. The commissario has a right to be angry.

"Sorry. Of course, you're right. I certainly don't want to put anyone's life in danger."

The commissario continues as if I hadn't spoken. "The most difficult phase of protecting you will be during this time on the run. They are watching the airport and train station and probably all the roads leading in and out of here. We expect to be followed but not for long."

Headlights flash through the windows. Faena looks at his watch.

"If the first part of our plan misfires, they still won't be prepared for us to take a boat. As far as we know, they don't have access to the private airfield we'll use. No one is supposed to know where that airfield is except the pilot of the boat and me. Once you reach Castello, you're under Lorenzo's care. He's secured your house, and he has the staff to protect you until we apprehend Riccardo."

He pauses long enough for me to ask, "What's being done to capture Riccardo?"

He ignores me and says, "We're wasting valuable time with your questions. You should have used this time to pack. We're leaving now."

I stand up, grabbing for the tote that I packed earlier. Marco reaches for it, but I shake my head. I can't take a chance of losing the necklace. Marco was furious when I insisted that Luigi accompany me to the vault. He babbled about Luigi's security clearance not being good enough since he was only a chauffeur.

To put my mind at ease, I scrounge around in my bag on the pretense of locating my prescription for Meclizine—a necessity for my vertigo when flying or on a boat—another result of being whacked on the head two years ago. I break off half a pill and swallow without water. Then I slip the velvet bag with the necklace inside my jacket just in case my backpack falls into the wrong hands.

"Commissario, I'm ready."

This time, I let Marco grab my bag and my arm. We run to the waiting car. Gino is inside. He nods as I slide in next to him. Before Marco closes the door, the car is moving. There's absolute quiet as the car accelerates in the direction of the coast. Luigi, the man Marco said didn't have the correct security clearance to go in the vault with me, is now driving us to the boat. I'm not sure either Gino or Marco realize he works for Lorenzo. Whether they do or don't, I feel safer with Luigi along on this great escape.

He drives without headlights at a speed that has all of us grabbing for the assist grips. Chatty banter isn't a good idea. After a few minutes of high-speed driving, he abruptly turns into a wooded area and cuts the engine.

We wait. Two cars whiz past at breakneck speed. When Luigi is satisfied there aren't any others, he starts the car. But instead of returning to the main road, he continues on a cow path for a few miles before he cuts through a pasture to a small paved road, where he resumes the same reckless speed.

I look across at Gino and Marco.

"Since everyone seems to have been aware that I was coming to the concert, I'm guessing the driver is part of this, too?"

Marco looks at Gino. Gino shrugs. "We don't know who he is. Maybe he works for Davide or Lorenzo. Once you asked Maria to send Stella's dress, we knew you'd show up at the concert. I know you're not happy with me for contacting Lorenzo, but we love you,

Caterina. Maria would never forgive me if you were killed too. Losing Stella was almost too much. She couldn't handle losing you."

While part of me wants to be furious, the other part understands. If they hadn't told Lorenzo I was attending the concert, I might be dead.

"Oh, Gino. I'm sorry. I believed Riccardo was in prison and that it would be safe for me to return. It wasn't my intention to worry you and Maria."

Gino continues, "We know that. You had no way of knowing Riccardo would be extradited or that the Hickmans would show up and create so much chaos. No one was sure who they were and what they were doing."

"Before all the chaos, what was supposed to happen?"

"Members of the Guardia were to be posted at the entrances and exits to the concert and also in the audience. Lorenzo planned to attend the concert with you. Things got out of hand when the Hickmans showed up, and you and Neil decided to rescue Gladys."

"Sorry about that."

"Faena told Lorenzo about what Marco overheard on the wiretap. Lorenzo was too irate to be objective so he handed everything over to Commissario Faena. That last-minute change created all sorts of delays. Well, you know the rest."

"So Lorenzo washed his hands of me, right?"

There was a long silence until Gino said, "*Vero*, he is very angry with you. He said his anger would only impede the operation."

The two men look at me expectantly. What could I possibly say other than I'd screwed up again, and Lorenzo was right?

Less than an hour later, we pull into the port of Livorno. Luigi grabs my bag and my arm, pulling me into a fast trot. Marco and Gino bring up the rear with guns drawn. Not exactly what I was expecting.

Pre-dawn blackness permeates the night. Cranes, trucks, containers, and tangles of heavy ropes become dangerous obstacles as we move further into the jumbled maze. Huge cargo and cruise ships throw imposing shadows across the docks. We turn sharply away from the main port. Luigi jerks my arm at each turn. We run toward a long stretch of warehouses, squeeze in between buildings, and wind our way through a labyrinth of equipment and more containers stacked so high I can't see the top—not that I have time to look up. We follow unknowingly like a small herd of sheep until we arrive at a rundown marina full of tattered sailboats and half-sunken yachts. I stop and dig in my heels.

The sudden change in pace surprises Luigi. He drops my backpack. Marco and Gino plow into us.

"Oh, no," I whisper, "What is this? Some kind of ship cemetery? You're not getting me on one of those. I don't want to drown."

Luigi puts his face up close to mine and says, "Be quiet. You don't have a choice. Now move."

With that reprimand, he picks up my bag and pulls me until my feet move forward. We stop at the water's edge. He pauses for a second, looks in all directions and then throws my bag into the arms of a man waiting on the boat. A narrow plank shimmies with the motion of the waves. There's no way I'm going to walk that plank.

Two seconds later, Luigi lifts me and places me on the narrow board. Before I land, he whispers in my ear, "Don't be frightened. You won't see me, but I'll be in Castello del Mare. Remember, don't trust anyone. Call me anytime you need me."

My legs turn to jello—both from his whispered message and my fear of gangplanks. The trembling starts in my legs and continues until I'm shaking from head to toe. I can't move either backward or forward. The urgent whispers to move fall on deaf ears. I am paralyzed on the plank.

A small yelp emits from my mouth when the board shifts. Another body joins me on the precarious plank. A hand is placed solidly on my back. It nudges me forward until the man standing on the boat leans forward, grabs me around the waist and swings me to safety. I crumble onto a pile of ropes.

Before I can recover, Gino and Marco join me. The roar of the engine propels us away from the dock. When I look back, Luigi has already disappeared. We are underway at full throttle.

The early morning breeze is cold. I shiver without a jacket. The mate who helped me aboard tells me there's room for one person in the wheelhouse with the captain. I knock on the glass and receive a curt nod to enter, nothing more.

There's a small spot where I wedge myself against a tiny table littered with an overflowing ashtray and an assortment of maritime maps. I hang onto the edge of the table as the boat bounces up and down. I pray the ride isn't too long.

Dawn breaks as we pull into Calafuria Nature Reserve, a place with numerous hidden coves. Treacherous rocks jut out of the water —clearly a dangerous place unless you know the area. The captain knows it well.

The mate jumps off the boat and ties off the line thrown to him by the captain. Gino maneuvers the plank in place. Marco is first off. Gino nods. I have no choice. I step gingerly onto the plank. Gino keeps a steady hand on my back until Marco, waiting on the other side, grabs me.

My *grazie mille* blows out to sea as I'm pushed toward a waiting panel truck. After a bumpy ride of only a few minutes, the doors open, and I tumble out to find myself facing a Piaggio P180 Avanti. I only know this because it's written on the nose of the plane. Again, my arm is grabbed, and I'm running toward the steps. Before my seatbelt is securely fastened, we're racing down the dirt airstrip and are airborne.

♩

Frank Woodlee steps out from behind the trees. He puts the binoculars back in the case and touches the number on his mobile.

"They just took off. The girl, Marco and Gino. Yes, I understand. You'll provide me with the number of guards at the villa along with the schedule for the change of guards. I'm on my way to join you in Castello."

The silken voice on the other end asks, "And Isabella?"

"I don't know. She slipped away during the night."

The silence was thunderous.

"If you want to keep working for me, that's the last time you'll say I don't know."

43

Castello del Mare

As we swoop into the sky, the wind batters the plane like a paddle ball. We head toward dark layers of clouds heavy with rain. Within minutes after takeoff, the plane abruptly banks to the east. An hour or so later, we descend to a muddy field. A thump and skid tell me we're back on earth. The plane taxies close to a tumbled-down shed. With my sleeve, I wipe the moisture from the window and peer out. The plane bumps and groans until the brakes grip and the wheels dig into the soil.

The night turns into a dreary gray morning. The engine idles. He turns and faces the plane. His hair is tousled by the wind and rain. His jaw is clenched as his eyes glance my way without seeing me.

Lorenzo. My heartbeat thunders.

The door opens. The stairs deploy. Marco glares at me and says, "This is where we part company. You're in Lorenzo's hands now."

Gino has my bag and is pushing me toward the door. I make a last effort to neutralize Marco.

"Marco, you think your anger is justified. That's okay. I made a promise not to betray you, and I won't. But if you hear from Isabella, please let me know."

He ignores the business card I place on the seat next to him. Gino propels me to the door. I step out into the wet morning and gaze to the bottom of the stairs where Lorenzo waits. He reaches out his hand and pulls me close. A sob originates from the deepest part of my soul. I settle against his chest. A moment of self-pity surfaces. He holds me for a few seconds longer than necessary and whispers, "Cat."

The passion between us spirals until he abruptly pulls away. He turns from me and reaches for Gino's hand. He salutes Marco and strides to the waiting van. The plane is airborne before we pull away from the airstrip.

♩

Sofia watches from the wood line until the plane lands and the door opens. She crouches low into the brush and brambles until the vehicle starts up. She makes her way back to the car that she parked on a ridge above the airfield. Once inside her vehicle, she calls Frank Woodlee to let him know the plane has landed and Marco stayed onboard.

She reminds him to be vigilant, but loses her temper when she discovers that he's let Isabella slip away. Worthless comes to mind as she considers what to do next. Woodlee is only one of a handful who were willing to side with her as she tries to take over the SCU. She'd have to keep him until she was fully ensconced as *la padrone*.

She waits until the van pulls onto the road before starting the engine and following. She hangs back until they're far enough away not to notice they're being followed. Of course, there's no hurry. She knows where they're going.

♩

Once Gino, Lorenzo and I are in the van, I tell Lorenzo the necklace Riccardo stole is fake. He grits his teeth and turns away from me. I keep on talking long after I should stop. There are times when my mouth operates without any input from my brain.

"I guess you know about the musical notes. It's so weird, don't you think? First, they show up on the notes attached to the roses, and now the same note shows up on both of the Hickmans."

"What musical notes? What roses?"

"Didn't Marco or Davide tell you about the musical notes? I think Riccardo is giving us a riddle to solve."

"Why the hell would he do that? His only plan is to kill you, and you're doing everything to make that easy for him."

His comment is enough to shut down my mouth. He doesn't speak again until we're almost to Villa Fiori, but my mind keeps right on working. *Does Davide know about the musical notes or only Marco?*

Lorenzo's deep voice interrupts my speculation.

"Cat, this is the last time the Guardia will protect you. You're not invincible. You're also not part of this investigation. You keep forgetting that it's not only your life you're jeopardizing."

What can I say? There's no further conversation until we pull up at my villa. Gino retrieves my bag and opens the door. I step out but turn back and look at the angry face of the man I once thought I'd spend the rest of my life with.

"*Spero che un giorno mi perdonerai*—I hope one day you will forgive me."

I slide across the seat. Before I reach the open door, he grabs my hand, and turns it over and brushes his lips across my palm.

♩

Maria stands in the doorway of my villa. She waves her arms and yells my name. Her smiling face waits at the top of the stairs, her arms open. She pulls Gino and me into her love and warmth, all the while clucking like a mother hen before she starts fussing.

"Caterina, you must promise never again to do something so foolish. You could have been killed."

Gino intervenes. "Hush, Maria. Caterina is exhausted. She hasn't had much sleep."

"I won't hush. She's probably starving. Food is what you need, *carissima*. Once I feed you, then you can rest."

In spite of my fatigue, I laugh. From our first meeting, Maria decided she would be in charge of my eating habits. She treats me as if I know nothing about food. It doesn't matter that I'm a caterer or that I worked at *Ristorante Il Cantico* for months when I was last in Castello. In some ways, she's right because I don't know all the old-style ways of an Italian mamma, and their cooking is always the best.

Maria releases me from her embrace.

"Gino is right. You look like hell. So first you sleep, then you eat."

As she guides me to the bedroom, she chatters about how the villa has been cleaned from top to bottom and tells me the pantry and fridge are stocked. She says something about dinner and Analisa stopping by, but I fall on the bed without getting out of my clothes. I'm asleep before she closes the door.

The musical rise and fall of Italian chatter wakes me. It sounds like a houseful of people, but it's probably only two. When Italians get together, the noise level sounds like it's far more people than it actually is. I listen to the beauty of the language and feel safe. The harmony lulls me back to sleep.

♩

When I next rouse from sleep heaven, it's to the scrumptious whiff of intense garlicky tomato sauce. The aroma permeates my sleepy mind. My stomach rumbles as I try to remember the last time I ate.

I stumble to the bathroom, throw cold water on my face, pick through my tangled red curls and tuck my wrinkled shirt into my jeans.

Approaching the kitchen, I see that Maria and Analisa are the only two people in the house besides me. Their chatter is so intense the windows are steaming up. Analisa grabs me in a sisterly hug and plants an air-kiss on both my cheeks.

"Ah, Caterina, Mamma tells me you are in trouble again."

I nod in agreement because clearly, I'm not only in trouble, I'm creating most of it.

"Where's little Gino?"

"Oh, Papa and Enrico are on the way to school. They'll be back with him in time for lunch. If it's okay, we'll eat here. We're so happy to have you back."

She lowers her voice as if to reveal some great secret and says, "This is very important. Our little Gino has declared that we must all call him Giorgino. He says he's a big boy, and little Gino is a baby name."

She laughs and hugs me again.

"Sit. You must still be tired after the long journey."

She pulls out a chair. I obediently flop down. She hands me a hunk of warm-from-the-oven bread, and pours a glass of intense red wine and shoves it in my hand.

"Eat the bread first and then drink. You'll feel stronger."

I bite into the yeasty slice of olive-infused bread. I chew slowly and carefully to avoid the olive pits. The salty, slightly spicy flavors fill my stomach. Then I tip back my head and take a big swallow of wine. The deep richness of ripened grapes, sunlight, and blackberries slides down my throat and settles on my bread-padded stomach. All the angst and exhaustion of the last few days melt away.

"Mmm," involuntarily slips from my lips along with little grunts of pleasure for these uncomplicated flavors and the way these two women nourish my body and my soul. In my fear, I stayed away too long. For the moment, and I know it will only be a moment, I luxuriate in the simplicity of this good life.

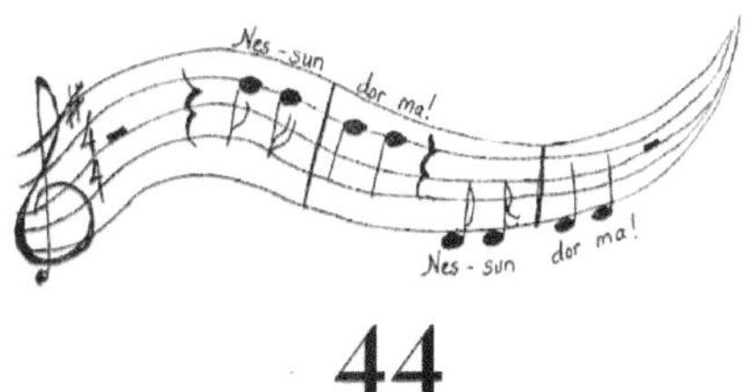

44

The villa explodes with energy when Gino, Enrico and Giorgino arrive.

"Zia Caterina," Giorgino yells as the door bangs open. He rushes me with his body and a multitude of words—school, the name of his new best friend, the plane his daddy helped him build.

"Come fly the plane with me," and he's out the door. Gino goes after him. Enrico stays on the threshold. Analisa grabs his hand and pulls him into the room.

"You haven't met my husband. The last time you were here wasn't a good time. Enrico, this is Caterina. You've heard us talk about her."

He smiles and shakes my hand. What little I know about him comes from Maria. He farms the land. He's quiet. He loves Analisa and Giorgino. He's a good provider.

The man standing before me is short and stocky. His hand, as he reaches for mine, is rough and shows signs of soil under his nails. The sun has creased his face. His handshake is firm.

"*Piacere*...Pleased to meet you."

"*Allo stesso modo*...the same."

He blushes and backs out the door. Analisa shrugs. The three of us continue to chatter as we set the table and prepare the food.

We feast on fresh pasta loaded with seafood—tiny shrimp, mussels, squid and chunks of fish. A salad of fresh greens, tomatoes, shredded carrots and paper-thin slices of onion are dressed with a drizzle of Enrico's golden olive oil.

The men hurry off—Giorgino back to school, Enrico back to the farm, and Gino to wherever Gino disappears on most days.

Maria, Analisa and I spend the next few hours reminiscing. We speak of Stella—sharing only our good memories. We forego all the painful ones. Analisa fills me in with all the news about Giorgino's health and how Dr. Tony returned from prison a better man. I notice the sly smile between the two women but decide I'll pump them for information later as there's a reason behind those smiles, and that reason involves Antonio.

Giorgino, who has been home-schooled for several years because sickle cell anemia sidelined him, has now joined his classmates—all because of Dr. Tony's wonderful care. Analisa claps her hands with delight. Her little boy is finally able to grow up in a normal environment.

That conversation leads Analisa to fill me in on her interviewing skills and every detail of the interviewing process for the new teacher assistant positions in Giorgino's class.

"I was astonished when I was selected to participate. I was the only parent, along with the principal and some board members. Since I don't have a stack of degrees and a long list of credentials, I was so nervous. While I think I selected the three best candidates, it was a nerve-racking experience. Have you interviewed people?"

It had been a while, but a big part of my job in management with the accounting firm had been interviewing. With the catering business, it's different because it's so small. I listen as Analisa chats about qualifications and expectations.

Maria interrupts us to refill our wine glasses and place a platter of cheese and salumi on the table. We laugh at her attempts to fatten us but quickly fall back into discussing the pros and cons of good interview techniques.

"Analisa, interviewing is like anything else we do. If we practice enough, we build up experience. We get better. It's important to weigh the resumé, references, the answers to the questions during the interview, but it's also important to allow your instincts to help with the final decision."

A frown crosses her face.

"What do you mean by instincts?"

"Instincts—your gut reaction. Of course, you consider the tangible assets of a person, but also the intangible ones. How the person behaves during the interview. Are they nervous? Uncomfortable? The tone of their voice. Body and facial movements. And your natural ability to analyze the level of comfort you are experiencing with the person. All these little things add up."

Analisa's face turns from attentive to concerned. A crease appears on her forehead. Her lips compress. Her hands, usually so animated, lie still.

"It takes practice, but once you become aware of these things, you step back and reflect. Instinct provides you with nuances that aren't on the resumé or in a person's responses."

I lean back in my chair, take a sip of wine and put one more thought on the table.

"The other thing I like to do is put the person in a team-building exercise. If that's not possible, ask questions about times they've worked as part of a team. It's one of the most important qualifications, in my opinion."

Analisa's face flushes before she asks, "Are you sure about that?"

"Why do you ask?"

"Well, if what you say is true. I may have made a mistake by selecting one of the people as my top choice."

"Tell me why you think that."

Analisa reaches for the wine bottle and pours a little into both glasses before continuing.

"One of the applicants ticked all the boxes. She's intelligent, her credentials are excellent, her answers to all the questions were well thought out, and the children loved her, particularly Giorgino."

She stops and fidgets with her napkin.

"My instinct told me her credentials are too good for a part-time job. On the surface, her reasons made sense, but there was a disconnect as if she was trying too hard to be the perfect candidate. I don't know exactly what made me uncomfortable, but something did. Do you think I should tell the principal about my concerns? I really don't have anything to back them up, and the principal indicated to all of us that she was the best candidate."

"Where's she from?

"She said Milano, but she had a southern accent. I barely detected it, but it was there. She appeared to have taken great pains to make herself plain and unattractive. With makeup and the right clothes and hairstyle, she would be beautiful. That was another red flag, as all the other candidates were quite fashionable."

I smile and reach for her hands. "Why don't you drop in from time to time to observe? It would be even better if you could do that without her knowing in advance."

"That's a great idea. I already checked on one thing. During the interview, she said she and her mamma often visited this aunt—the one she's taking care of. When I asked around town, no one remembered a child named Lucrezia and her mother visiting. Was that instinct?"

"Yes, it is."

The crease between her lines disappears with her smile, "I hope I didn't make a mistake choosing her."

I laugh and gather her hands in mine. "It was your first time. You were nervous, but you are asking yourself the right questions."

Analisa sips the last bit of wine in her glass.

"Giorgino is so smitten with her that I can't say anything negative about her around him."

She smiles and ducks her head, "But maybe I'm a little jealous, too. He can't stop telling me how wonderful she is."

We burst into laughter. Maria says we've gossiped too long. She tells me there's plenty of food, and she'll be back tomorrow to check on me. After many hugs and cheek kisses and promises to call if anything frightens me, they leave. I lock the door and breathe in the silence. In the pit of my stomach, the churning goes on.

45

The ear-splitting ring of my phone startles me out of a toss-and-tumble sleep. My hand gropes around on the night-stand until I clasp the monster and check to see what miserable person is calling me in the middle of the night. I click on the bedside lamp and look at the caller ID.

"Cassie, what's wrong? Are you okay? Sam? Diana? The business?"

"Oh, shucks, Cat. I forgot to look at the time. Sorry. No, everyone and everything is fine. I just finished up for the day and didn't think to check before I clicked on your name. I'll call back tomorrow."

"No, I'm awake. Catch me up."

"You sure? It's two your time. Really sorry."

I put the call on speaker and push my hair out of my eyes.

"It's okay. I miss you—all of you. Tell me what's going on."

"It's kind of embarrassing, but the main reason I called is to find out where you are. When you didn't answer my texts or calls, I contacted the resort. They said you left a couple of days ahead of your scheduled check-out time. What happened?"

What do I tell Cassie, my dearest friend? Rubbing the sleep out of my eyes, I consider how to respond.

"Oh, Cass, I'm not sure where to start. It's a long story. I'll give you the condensed version."

"Oh, no, you don't. I want every detail. Knowing you, it's going to be one of your over-the-top adventures."

"Cass, it would take me the rest of the night to fill you in. I don't have the energy, and you would be getting on the next plane to rescue me. Please believe me when I tell you I'm protected by security cameras, motion lights, and round-the-clock protection from the Guardia."

"Well, that's enough to make me want to hop on the next plane. What in the hell happened to dictate that kind of safety net?"

"Riccardo was extradited to Albania, but he escaped and paid me a visit at the concert. He stole the necklace."

"He what? Stole the necklace? Did he hurt you?"

"Not really, but he did scare the heck out of me. I'm not sleeping well as it was bone chilling to see his sneering face."

"Oh my god, you had to be frightened out of your mind. I can't imagine the horror of seeing that bastard again. Are you sure he didn't hurt you?"

"Other than a needle in my neck to sedate me I wasn't hurt. You can stop worrying, okay?"

"A needle in your neck? Cat, that's ghastly."

"I promise you I'm okay—well, at least physically. My mental status is a bit off course, but I've arranged for a Zoom with Dr. Ginny."

It's quiet on Cassie's end. I don't interrupt the silence as I know she's processing what to say next.

"I'm glad you made the appointment. Dr. Ginny wasn't happy when you didn't show up for your last session. So the necklace was stolen?"

"Maybe."

"What do you mean maybe?"

I hesitate. After Cassie's disastrous relationship with the sleazy senator, we agreed there would be no secrets from each other.

"Cass, if this information gets out, it could kill me. Promise me you won't tell anyone, even Chuck."

Cassie is silent for a few seconds before she says, "That's a tough one, but I know you wouldn't ask unless it was important."

"It's life or death important to me, Cass."

"If it's too risky, don't tell me. But I promise you I won't tell anyone—not even Chuck. If you think it's too dangerous to tell me, then tell Dr. Ginny. But you know I won't betray your trust. You're all alone there. You need someone you can talk to, and I'm listening,"

Taking a deep breath in, I exhale in one big gush.

"You're right. I'm overwhelmed, and I do trust you with my life. If you're ready, sit down. This is a long story."

46

Cassie and I have grown close over the past year—a year that was a total disaster for both of us. She fell in love with a corrupt senator, and I found myself pursuing a human trafficking ring with links to the same senator. From those devastating experiences, we learned to listen with compassion and understanding and to trust each other. As a result, a solid friendship was created in our personal lives, as well as a stronger partnership in our business lives.

We know each other well, so it's easy for me to imagine what chair she's sinking into—the navy blue one with wide white stripes by the large bay window overlooking the marshes. It's late summer and early evening in the South Carolina Lowcountry. She has a glass of Nages rosé in her hand. She'll switch to red when the weather cools.

Her feet are tucked up and curled under her. Her mop of black hair is twisted in some type of knot and secured with a clip. I can almost hear the sigh as she lets go of a busy day.

"Okay," she says, "I'm comfy. Let's hear your story."

While she's settling into her favorite spot, I open the shutters to the darkest night—that brief time before dawn when the world waits for the first light. A soft breeze from the sea stirs the air.

"Cassie, I've never shared much about Stella with you because it was an unusual relationship—imperfect and complicated. Most of the time, I can't explain it to myself. Maybe the best way to start is with our birth."

I pause long enough to wonder how to explain my off-and-on friendship with Stella. But there's no clear direction, so I plunge in.

"We were more siblings than friends and more twins than

siblings. We were born on the same day, in the same hospital, to mothers who were best friends. Stella was born a few minutes before me. I've never been sure why that was significant, yet it was. She used those few minutes to control me. The thing is, I let her."

My breathing is shallow as I pause and wonder if I can continue.

Cassie's sweet voice says, "I'm here."

"Stella was the only constant in my life. By the time I realized we weren't sisters or twins or related by blood, it didn't matter. The intensity of her love and hate for me was all I knew about friendship. One day she loved me, and the next day she hated me. It took years and a lot of therapy to recognize her controlling behavior. But even that couldn't break the bond."

I plump up my pillow and lean back against the headboard. Taking a sip of water, I close my eyes and continue.

"Once we went our separate ways, I found my footing. She didn't have as much control over me. In our late teens we drifted apart, but those early childhood bonds were too strong to be broken entirely. The last year before her death, we made inroads into restoring the friendship. When I received that last phone call from her, the one where she begged for help, I had to go."

Cassie's voice breaks into my thoughts, "I remember that day when you told me she'd disappeared. You were a wreck. On the drive to the airport, I tried to convince you to let me come with you. But you were hellbent on going alone—just like for this trip. Cat, please come home. These people aren't going to stop until you're dead."

"Cassie, if that would solve the problem, I'd be on the next plane. But it won't. Wherever I am, Riccardo will find me. His is a personal vendetta. He believes this is what Carlo wants him to do. It's almost like a suicide mission for him. I'll never be safe until he's stopped."

"But what if he can't be stopped?"

"He has to be. There's no alternative for me. It's one of those situations where it's either him or me."

"Oh, Cat, I'm sick with worry. I need to be with you. Since you introduced me to Chuck, I've become an expert in self-defense. And

Sheriff Blackwell has taught me how to shoot a bull's eye. I'd have your back every waking second until Riccardo is found."

"I know you would, Cassie. I love your fierce, protective nature, but I can't afford to lose you. Riccardo would take you out as soon as your plane landed. I'd never forgive myself if you were eliminated simply because we're friends. *Allora*, let me fill you in on the rest of the story before I run out of steam."

"Cat, if you change your mind, I'll be on the next plane."

I take another swig of water as I consider what words to use to continue the story of Stella and me. I don't check the time during our conversation, but first light hovers against the black horizon before I wind down.

"Stella was much smarter than people thought. She took every precaution with the necklace. Not only is the necklace priceless, but it was the gift Antonio gave her on their wedding day. It was the one thing she valued. I didn't know until after her murder and after the estate was settled that she had a duplicate necklace made of paste jewelry. When she was in the public eye, she always wore the fake necklace as her signature piece."

"And no one knew?"

"Well, her insurance company would have known, but no one else."

"Wow, that's remarkable. Don't you think that's what all the Hollywood celebs and royalty do?"

"Probably."

The sun creeps through the slats. It casts horizontal bars across the duvet. I stretch and shift my body into a more comfortable position and continue.

"Stella was notorious for disappearing for a day or few weeks. Those around her understood her need to be away from the limelight. For the first few days after her disappearance, no one thought it was unusual. But after she missed photo shoots and the filming of her next movie, the Guardia was alerted. Antonio made the assumption she was kidnapped for the necklace."

As the sun moves higher in the sky, I pull on a t-shirt and slip into a pair of jeans.

"But you were the one who found the necklace. Right?"

"Yes, it was just crazy luck that I discovered the location of Stella's last photo shoot. At some point, she must have tossed it into the brambles. Of course, no one, including me, knew it was a fake necklace and not the priceless masterpiece. A lot of people wanted that necklace."

I chuckle with the memory of Gino stealing the necklace to keep me safe—all the missteps we took.

"Shit, Cat, how can you laugh? I'm petrified for you."

"It's always in retrospect that I laugh at myself. I was thinking of Gino and his plan to protect me by stealing the necklace. Well, you know the rest of that disastrous story. Do you know that I've never worn the real necklace? As far as I know, Stella only wore it two times —her wedding and for the private gala at the Metropolitan Museum of Art."

Cassie blurts out, "Now that's just dumb—to own something so valuable that you can't wear it."

"True, but the necklace is only one reason she was killed. Carlo really didn't care about the necklace. He was all about revenge. Stella humiliated him when they were kids, and he never forgave her. The necklace was just part of the revenge package. What killed her was when she discovered his drug smuggling operation. When she attempted to take him down, she signed her death certificate."

"Oh, Cat. I'm so sorry."

"It's okay, Cass. Dr. Ginny and I have discussed all of this endless times."

"And she still thought it was okay for you to return?"

"She did. She said making this journey for Stella and myself was important. But neither of us had a clue that Riccardo would escape. It's no one's fault I'm here. The thing I fear the most is that Riccardo will come after my friends first before he comes for me. If he's like Carlo, he wants revenge."

A low groan comes from Cassie.

I slide my feet into flip-flops. The sound of rubber slapping the floor follows me to the kitchen. I set the kettle over the flame and find a cup, a jar of honey and a tea bag.

Pushing my hair out of my eyes, I whisper, "Cassie, I'm scared. Riccardo probably knows by now that the necklace he stole is fake. He'll be furious. He will come after me with a vengeance. The necklace and my death are the only two things that will satisfy him."

I don't mention the pleasure he will receive in torturing me before he kills me.

"Cat, get out of there! Come home. You'll be safer here. Sheriff Blackwell won't let anything happen to you. In fact, he's in awe of you and all you did to blow up that human trafficking ring last year."

The kettle wheezes as the steam builds up. I turn it off quickly before the piercing sound blows out my eardrums. When the boiling water hits the honey and teabag, the aroma fills the air with exotic spices.

"The problem is I wouldn't be safe at home. Riccardo has connections all over the world. He'll find me wherever I am. Cassie, I can't live in fear, and I can't bring this problem to the Lowcountry. I'm well-protected here, better than I would be at home. Lorenzo has the entire Guardia at his disposal."

"Lorenzo? How's that going?"

My laughter is hollow and as fake as the necklace that Riccardo stole. "Oh, Cass, every time I see him, I lose my sanity. As usual, we're at odds. I hate it that I can't let go of loving him."

"Cat, I'm booking the next flight."

"Cassie, you're not only my best friend, you're my partner. I need you to stay there and keep our business going until I return because I am coming home. I promise you."

"Okay, but let's figure out a signal, so I know you're safe. How 'bout you send me a thumbs-up emoji before you go to bed and again in the morning? If you do that, I swear I won't get on the next plane."

This time my laugh is genuine. "I think I can manage that. Plus,

I'll text you Lorenzo's number just in case, and you already have Maria's."

Cassie joins in the laughter and then falls silent before saying, "Oh crap, Cat, I forgot the real reason I called you. I wanted to give you a heads up about what's happening with our business, and then there's Al."

"What's going on with the business? And what does '—and then there's Al—' mean?"

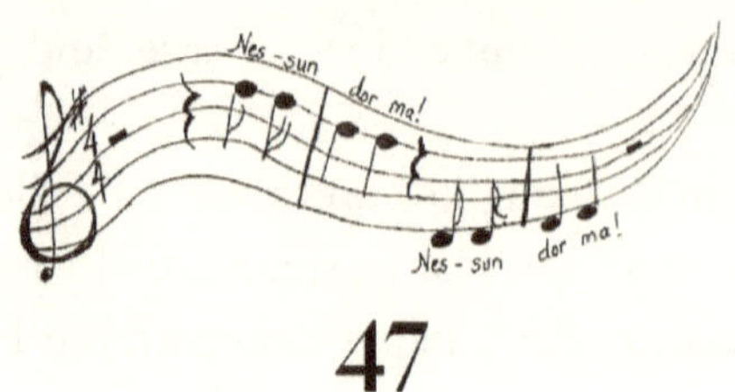

47

Cassie's pause spirals across the Atlantic and settles heavily in my ears.

"I'll start with Al. He's leaving."

"What do you mean he's leaving? Why? When?"

"His father is ill and not expected to live much longer."

"Oh, that's dreadful. I'm so, so sorry, but he's coming back, right?"

"That's the problem, Cat. He's undecided. He's the oldest son, and by all rights, he'll inherit the estate, including the title of duke. But his brother will contest the will, and it may take time to settle in court."

"That must be why he's been trying to reach me. I haven't answered his calls or texts. I'm not up to talking with him."

"Well, one of the reasons he was calling is to ask you to come home and take over his business. If you agree to this, he'll return. If you don't agree, I don't know. He's in love with you."

"Oh gosh, Cass. I'm fond of Al. I've even considered him as someone I could grow to love. He's a wonderful man. It's just that every time I see Lorenzo—well, you know how I feel about him. Al deserves better."

"So Lorenzo is still in the picture?"

I open the door to the terrace and breathe in the salty air. The sea is a brooding gray, and the morning sun has slipped behind dense clouds.

"He's the only person, Cass. I know it won't work, but my heart isn't willing to give up. But you need to tell me what Al means when he wants me to 'take over his business.' "

"It means he wants you to come back now so he can leave. He

says you understand his business more than most would because you helped him start it."

"Cass, I could be here for weeks or even longer. I can't leave until Riccardo is back behind bars or dead."

"I understand, but would you be interested in taking on his business and running ours too? Seems a bit much."

"I haven't thought about it. Maybe. Our business is doing well, and you're just as capable as I am to manage it. How are things? Our August schedule was pretty light unless you've picked up more events since I left."

"No, it's the same, although we've booked more events in September and October. November is always slow because we pace ourselves for the big hit in December."

"Cassie, you're as capable as I am to handle his business until I get back."

"Oh gosh, no. I'm not. I don't have the expertise. I can plan the events and assist with the food but that's it. The business end, the financials, and the menu planning is your forte. Plus, all those spa guests. You know I'd push back when they got all wonky about stupid stuff like the towel has a wrinkle in it."

Our laughter filters through the connection. For a few minutes, its warmth wraps around me.

"Hmm, what about if we hired a couple more people? I did that for those last two big events we catered. You and I discussed expanding before I left. Have you had time to think about that?"

"Yes, that's another reason I called, and I'll get to that. Right now, it's Al and his business that are our biggest concern."

"Oh? Why is that?"

"Al knows the odds of your returning immediately are slim, so he's been interviewing for a chef/manager position. He's counting on you to take over the management of his business when you return. If you do, you'll have to deal with the person he hires. He told me when he finds someone, he will offer them a bonus to take on the entire business until you get back. Don't you think that it would be awkward for that person? Wouldn't they feel like they were getting a demotion when you returned? Wouldn't that create all kinds of problems for you?"

I close the door to the terrace and return to the bedroom. The papier maché Madonna on top of the wardrobe appears to open her hands a little wider as if welcoming me into her arms. Her blue gown is gracefully draped over the pure white inner garment. Her face is a gift of serenity in this uncertain world.

"Hmmm, well, that could be a sore point. Since our work and Al's are so connected, I hope he'll choose carefully. At least, with this information, I won't be blindsided. I'll have time to clear my head and develop a list of questions before I call him. But I want to be sure that it's a business arrangement and not personal."

"Gracious, Cat. You know from his point of view it's personal."

"That concerns me. I'm fond of him. We have grown closer, but I haven't been fair with him. I didn't tell him before I left that I was returning to Italy. I'm sure he thinks I came back to see Lorenzo. And he'd be right."

"That's exactly what he thinks. Since you left, he's been wearing that hangdog look. From my perspective, his decision to leave immediately is based more on his broken heart than on seeing his father. They've never been close. The younger brother has always been the favorite son."

"Cassie, Al is a wonderful man. I wish I could fall in love with him. We have a lot in common, and he's been so kind to me—both as a friend and mentor. I've learned so much. Without him, getting our business back on track would have been far more difficult. But I can't create feelings for him that I don't have."

Before Cassie has a chance to say more, I change the subject.

"What about the hiring project? You were going to fill me in."

"Only if you're agreeable, I'd like to start the interviewing process. We have a bunch of candidates. One of the women you hired for the last two events before you left is really good. I encouraged her to apply. I also advertised on that industry website you recommended. "

"Go ahead and start interviewing. There's no clear-cut plan for me to return yet. With the busy season coming up fast, you're going to need the help."

"Okay. Now, the hard part is going to be my telling Al you don't have a scheduled return date. He'll be devastated."

I glance again at the Madonna's beatific smile. In the span of a few minutes, her outstretched arms no longer offer comfort. Her beauty fades. Her smile is stiff and fake, like the stolen necklace.

Our lives are made up of fakery. We are born into a mixed-up world. One full of hatred, injustice, favoritism, corruption, greed and power brokers. We add our own madness to the mix.

Thank goodness there are friends like Cassie and kind people like Al to keep me from becoming cynical and inclined to withdraw from the world.

Donna Keel Armer

In the early hours before dawn
the street cats sleep.
The breeze rests as I climb the curving sweep
of the hill to the cathedral—
ancient, regal, still pulsating with the spirits
of past generations who have moved in
and out of this piazza for thousands of years.
Their footsteps play a tune,
a sacred tune of beginnings and endings,
of stories told or not,
of songs written and sung,
of life and death
Told with connection and continuation.
Shadows flicker across the cobbled passageways,
my footsteps the only sound except for
the music that lives on in my heart.

~ Donna Keel Armer

48

nalisa waits while the school secretary finds Lucrezia. She could leave a message, but she wants to talk to this person who has won Giorgino's heart. Every day, he comes home from school with new-found energy and excitement as he spills out stories of what he's learned and how Signorina Barone let him lead the class on a recent field trip or how she singled him out to be in the school play.

"Sì, this is Lucrezia."

"Oh, hi, Signorina Barone. It's Giorgino's mamma, Analisa."

"Please, call me Lucrezia. If you're calling about his progress, don't worry. He is the best student. He's so loving and never causes any problems. Is something wrong?"

"No, no, no. He thinks you are *Donna Meravigliosa*—Wonder Woman. From the time I pick him up until he goes to bed, he talks about you. I'm calling to let you know that I have to work later than usual today, and my mother will pick him up."

"Oh, alright, but if you like, I could keep him here with me. Although the after-school program ends at seven, I could stay a little later if that would help. I have papers to grade, and the room has to be straightened. Giorgino could help me. He's so eager, and it's a pleasure having him around."

Analisa twirls a strand of hair around her index finger, not quite sure how to respond. It's a kind offer, but she feels uncomfortable. It's that intuition stuff she and Caterina discussed a few days ago.

Isabella senses her hesitation.

"Are you still there? It's really no trouble. You have to pass right by the school on your way home. I could help him complete his homework which would free up your weekend to do fun activities with him.”

It's so tempting, but it's Friday, and as usual he's spending the weekend with her parents. It doesn't make sense to leave him at school under those circumstances.

“Signorina Barone—Lucrezia, you are so kind to offer, but my mamma can't wait to pick him up. He's spending the weekend with my parents. But thank you so much.”

“Sure, anytime. If it happens again, it would be okay for Giorgino to stay with me. Most of the time I'm the one staying for the after-school program.”

Analisa mumbles another thank you and hangs up. Relief tingles up her spine. It's such a strange thing to feel this way when Giorgino is so taken with Signorina Barone. Maybe she really is a little jealous. She shakes her head and texts a message to her mamma that the school is expecting her to pick up Giorgino after his last class.

♩

Isabella takes a deep breath. This job is taking much longer than she anticipated. Her instructions were to develop the relationship with the child slowly so there are no glitches later on. Still, she's sick of being penned up with these snotty-nosed kids. Their screechy voices penetrate her skull even after she leaves for the day. One thing she's learned from the experience is she won't take on another assignment that includes children—they are such exhausting little monsters.

49

Isabella forces herself to walk back to the classroom and smile at the child waiting to hear the verdict.

"Giorgino, your Mamma is sending your Nonna for you. You didn't tell me that you were spending the weekend with her."

His smile, although sweet and mischievous, doesn't break through the ice that entraps her heart. If she's to kidnap this child, she can't get close to him. She cannot care about him.

"*Perché* Signorina Barone, I want to spend the weekend with you. Please call my mamma again. Explain that I want to stay with you."

Isabella squats in front of him. "I can't, Giorgio. Your Nonna will be here in a few minutes. You'll have a wonderful time with her."

Giorgino sticks his hands in his pockets. His bottom lip quivers, and one tear slowly trickles down his cheek. "But I can see Nonna anytime. You are more fun."

Isabella pastes a smile on her lips and says, "We'll plan another time. Okay? Now help me move these books into storage, please."

♩

Maria is punctual but is perplexed by Giorgino's behavior. His usually sunny disposition disappears behind a frown.

"Giorgino, what's wrong?"

"Nonna, I want to stay and help the teacher. If I leave, she's alone. She promised to read to me."

Isabella laughs and says to Maria, "He's such a help when he stays in the after-school program. He's one of the few children who enjoys keeping the classroom organized. He must be a big help around the house."

Maria smiles. "No, actually, he's very little help to his mother. He'd rather be outside playing."

Maria watches Giorgino as he stands between the two women and looks back and forth. She finds his adoration of the teacher uncomfortable.

"Okay, Giorgino, hand me your backpack and put on your jacket. I've made your favorite meal."

Giorgino drags his feet all the way to the door. He turns back and says, "You'll be here Monday, right?"

Isabella nods. As the door closes behind them, her phone rings, and Riccardo's number flashes on the screen.

"Why haven't you called me with a plan?"

Heat rises in Isabella's face. Sweat trickles between her shoulder blades.

"You said you weren't in a hurry. Has something changed?"

"I ask the questions, not you. Where's your plan? I want the boy delivered to me by the end of next week. If you can't do that, I'll get someone else."

The cruel, abrasive voice echoes in her head. She fully understands Riccardo would kill her as easily as he would squash a spider under his shoe.

"No, Riccardo. I can handle the situation."

"Good. There are only two reasons for me to talk to you again. One, to receive your plan and two, when the kid and you are on your way."

She composes her thoughts. She has to be tough if she and Giorgino are to get out of this alive. Her heart pounds. Her palms ooze sweat. She's sure he can read her mind. He's done it often enough in the past. If he knows she's hoping to sabotage his plans, he'll kill her. She has to get out of his clutches.

"I'll contact you Wednesday with a date."

50

This morning, Maria stops by with a jar of honey and freshly baked bread. While I'm making coffee, she chatters about what's happening in the village. I never tire of the local dialect she drops into the conversation. I'm in a half-dozed state when she mentions she's having a few people over for dinner on Friday, and I'm to come. Maria believes no one in their right mind wants to eat alone.

"Maria, you don't have to keep feeding me."

She pretends not to hear and goes right on talking about who's invited.

"Of course, you'll come. It's only a few people: Analisa, Enrico, and Giorgino because he's spending the weekend with us."

"Okay, since it's just family, I'll come."

There's a long pause before she continues.

"Well, mostly family. Dr. Tony is sort of family, and we love his new friend, Chiara."

She let that slip into the conversation, knowing I'd catch the last bit.

"His new friend? Chiara?"

After prodding, the story unfolds. A few months ago, a lovely woman arrived in town and opened a mosaic shop. Maria persuaded Antonio to go to the open house, and that's where he met the owner Chiara. She's from Milano and is an accomplished restorer of mosaics in the grand cathedrals of Europe. Although the lovely Chiara, who is now often seen in the presence of Dr. Tony, moved to Castello for a simpler lifestyle, she continues with her restoration work during the off-season.

According to Maria, Antonio was smitten by Chiara before he finished the first glass of Prosecco.

"Dr. Tony is hopelessly in love with her. I can see it."

Maria rambles on and on about Antonio's new friend while I check the pantry for lunch possibilities. Antonio and I have a long history of mutual disdain. Although he and Stella were ill-suited, I didn't agree with his public humiliation of her, his indifference to her disappearance, or his inability to hide his contempt for her.

He and Lorenzo both loved Stella. After Antonio married her, the two men put aside the past and fell right back into the childhood friendship all of us had shared. I haven't been able to forgive Antonio. Being in the same room with him and sharing a meal would be awkward. I'm still angry Stella is dead, and Antonio is making a new life for himself.

The pain is unhealthy, but it lingers. While Stella was difficult, the marriage breaking up was created by both of them. In my heart, I believe Stella would be alive if Antonio had found time for her in his life.

Of course, Maria insists that I come. So tonight I'm meeting Chiara, the new woman in Dr. Tony's life. As I pull the black sweater over my head, my anger mounts. If I didn't care about Maria and Gino, I'd pass on the dinner invitation.

♩

Maria and Gino's house oozes with love. Chiara is warm and friendly but not pushy. Warily, Antonio and I exchange greetings and move apart. Giorgino's enthusiasm for Signora Barone has us laughing. I stop when I see the lines around Analisa's mouth drawn tight.

The long trestle table is laden with enough food to feed twenty. As Maria calls us to the table, there's a knock. A familiar voice calls *permisso?* May I?

Maria leaps from her half-sitting pose and says, "*Certo, certo, si accomodi*—certainly, certainly, come in."

Recognizing the voice sends me into a tailspin. How could Maria ask Lorenzo to join us? Chiara is standing next to me. As I turn my back and start to move to the other side of the table, she reaches out her hand and touches my arm.

She pats me in a comforting motion and says, "I don't understand, but I can see you're upset. Please sit next to me. I've heard so much about you. I would like to get to know you."

I murmur *grazie* and turn toward the door as Lorenzo embraces Maria.

The night, at first, seems endless. I think of a million ways to excuse myself, yet I stay rooted to my chair. Lorenzo sits across from me. We avoid looking at each other. Chiara constantly pats my hand or arm and engages me in conversation. She shares her life's story and regales me with funny incidents involving some of the world-famous cathedrals and the deities that run them. She invites me to her shop and suggests we meet for coffee.

After a glass, well maybe two, of the intense 2021 Primitivo di Manduria with a three-glass designation from Gambero Rosso, the angst settles. I'm able to participate without directing my comments or looks at Lorenzo.

The conversation centers on Enrico and his olive grove. When Analisa insisted on marrying Enrico, Maria and Gino weren't happy. At the time, Analisa had been engaged to another young man, and both families approved. Once Analisa met Enrico, she fell hopelessly in love. She refused to change her mind. They said he was too old, too reserved, too involved with farming. She was too young. She would be bored.

Little by little, Enrico won them over through his many kindnesses to them and Analisa. He is a strong, silent, patient man. He loves the land, but he loves Analisa more.

It is a joy to watch the two of them together. Enrico approaches fifty. He's handsome in a rough-and-tumble kind of way. His face is lined from hours in the sun. His shoulders are broad and strong. When he moves, his muscles flex and bulge.

Analisa is barely thirty and looks younger. She's elegant with her shoulder-length dark curls. Her eyes are dark and fringed with thick lashes. When Antonio asks Enrico to tell me the story of saving the olive groves, she looks at her husband with adoration.

Of all the stories told tonight, Enrico's is the best.

"The government said we had no choice but to destroy all the infected trees when the culprit bacteria *Xylella* attacked the groves. But I wasn't satisfied that was the correct solution. After conducting some research, meeting with some prominent agricultural scientists, and inspecting all my trees closely, I discovered insects were carrying the bacteria."

Murmurs around the table support Enrico's story.

"Better scientific minds discovered the destruction of the olive tree started in the leaves and branches and not the roots, as the government told us. A group of us decided to take a different course of action. Instead of burning our trees, we pruned the infected areas."

Analisa's face brims with joy, and her eyes with tears.

"He saved our groves."

Enrico nods, "But still, the region has lost millions of trees. It will take many years to return to our status of highest producer of olive oil in all of Italy."

Everyone congratulates Enrico. Conversation and numerous toasts flow around the table. At some point, the evening ends. I'm full of happiness as I leave the warmth of friends. My guard nods and follows in step behind me as I walk home.

When footsteps move rapidly in our direction, the guard pushes me behind a stone wall and draws his gun.

"Sorry, Officer, I didn't mean to alarm you. You can return to the signora's house. I'll walk Signora Gabbiano home."

Before I can protest or pull away, he tucks my hand in his. I shiver. He wraps me in his jacket and gathers me under his arm. For a single moment, I lean into him. But it's no good. We're headed for trouble unless I stop it. As we reach the villa, I pull away. I fumble with the key. He takes it from me and turns it in the lock. The gate opens with a loud creak which reminds me to anoint it with WD-40.

"Buonanotte, Lorenzo. *Grazie* for walking me home."

"Cat, we have to talk. I'm madder than hell, and so are you. We need to put our anger aside and talk. It's critical for your safety that we're on speaking terms."

"Not tonight. I've had too much wine."

He stands with his hands in his pockets.

"Give me five minutes. The locks have to be checked, and I need to make sure the guards are in the correct positions. The best place to determine that is from your terrace. I won't leave until I see that everyone is in place."

We face each other. The twitching of Lorenzo's jaw reveals he's as unsure as I am. The cool air seems to have cleared my head, so maybe I can manage a quick conversation.

"Okay, but please, no more than five minutes. I'm exhausted."

I count the sixty-eight steps in silence as I remember the first time I climbed them. Back before I knew Stella had been murdered. Back when there was still hope.

Even sixty-eight steps don't last forever. We reach the terrace. I stand outside the door while he walks from side to side and front to back. He counts heads and seems satisfied.

"Okay, let me have the key. It's my job to ensure you are safely inside and your door is locked before I leave."

I place the key in his hand. He smells like sandalwood, citrus and the salty sea air. The key clicks in the lock. He pushes the door open and steps back to let me enter first. His hand is warm on my back.

He closes the door and grabs me by the shoulders, "Why? Why did you put yourself in harm's way again? What is wrong with you? Don't you know if anything happens to you, I'd never forgive myself?"

I put both hands on his chest and push back, but his grip is too tight to break.

"Cat, I let you down. My anger put you in grave danger. I came very close to not calling my colleague in the Tuscana di Guardia. Can you forgive me?"

I have no choice but to look at him. When I do, I'm lost. We are lost together.

He whispers in my hair as he lifts me in his arms and pushes the door to the bedroom open, "You are all I ever want."

51

Of course, there's only an empty space beside me in the morning. No sweet note or cornetti on a napkin-covered plate or the tantalizing smell of coffee brewing waits for me when I stumble into the kitchen.

He's gone. What little energy I have dribbles away. I'm left with my own fury for giving free rein to my passions. We are two magnets drawn to each other. We cannot be in each other's company. We've agreed that our relationship is hopeless. But the minute we lock eyes, the passion overcomes every rational thought. That's all it is—passion, and that isn't enough. We have to let each other go.

The tile floor is cool against my bare feet. I climb back into bed and pull the covers over my head. I bury my face in the pillow and weep.

Days go by without hearing from him. I adjust to the constant patrols that invade my space. On several occasions I catch a glimpse of someone who might be Luigi. The man shows up unexpectedly, but he's not part of the regular patrol group. He never looks in my direction or indicates in any way that we've met before. The guards know him, so I have to believe it's Luigi. I have to trust Lorenzo sent him to protect me.

Lorenzo's instructions to the guards restrict me from leaving the premises unless he approves my request. My sleuthing days are over, at least for a while. This morning, I sit in the shade on the terrace with a list of guests in one hand and a menu in the other. The event is a small dinner party for Chiara and Antonio—one that doesn't include Lorenzo's name on the guest list. The menu is easy except for the problem of what to do about Maria. She'll be hurt if she's not involved with the food preparation.

Maria's approach to cooking goes beyond the preparation of food. For her, food is life, love, compassion, family and friends, and all the goodness there is in the world. Feeding people is her sacred commitment. It's who she is and what she does. Knowing this makes it difficult for me to invite people to dinner without letting her help with the cooking and allowing her to feel like she planned the whole thing. Hmmm, an impossible feat.

A beep on the computer screen notifies me that Al is asking if I have time to Zoom. I sigh loudly and send a message back: *in 15 m.*

Al and I haven't spoken since I left the Lowcountry. He's called and texted, but I haven't responded. With everything on my plate, I'm not up to a conversation about business or our personal lives. But I've put him off long enough. To keep delaying isn't fair. His critically ill father is more important than my feelings, or lack thereof at this moment.

My track record with men makes me leery of forming relationships. Only recently, and with Dr. Ginny's help, have I been able to confront these issues and realize I'm in charge of my life. The decisions I make have to be in my best interest. She reinforces over and over that living my life according to everyone else's plan for me isn't healthy.

I sigh again—this one so deep I shudder. Al deserves an honest discussion about our relationship, but that has to be face-to-face. I'll do my best to keep today's Zoom all about business.

Thanks to Cassie, I'm at least informed. I've had time to think about his business proposal. If I help him, it has to be because it will be a good experience for both of us versus me agreeing to accommodate his needs.

Over the year or so since Al arrived in the Lowcountry and particularly because of all the trauma we suffered together during the human trafficking operation, we've grown close—he more than me. He's an incredibly kind and generous person. If I give him a chance, he will try to fulfill my every need and desire. That's not a partnership. That's not what I want.

When I question why I'm not jumping at this chance, I remind myself that it's too soon for any kind of commitment. The situation with Lorenzo is precarious. My feelings for him still run deep. Until I can let go of him, there's no room for another relationship. The best way for me to heal is to go it alone.

The Zoom starts. I accept and begin with our standing joke.

"Ciao, *You Can Call Me Al.*"

His chuckle takes away some of the pressure I'm feeling.

"You'll never let me forget that, will you?"

"Of course not. It's still one of my favorite stories about our meeting."

"Mine too."

The dreaded silence permeates my office. I hate silence unless I'm alone, so I do my usual rush to fill the empty spaces.

"Well, you look grand as always."

Al straightens his cuffs and pats his perfectly smooth hair,

"Thanks, Caterina. Seeing your beautiful face is particularly difficult. You left so suddenly. Why didn't you let me know?"

This time, I let the silence go on. Anything I say will be wrong.

He breaks it by saying, "I'm not going to pressure you, Cat. You know how I feel about you, but that's a topic we'll put on hold until we're in the same place at the same time. So, let's focus the conversation on what's happening with the business end of things. I'll start with why I really need your help."

"Okay."

Another dramatically long interlude before he stutters, "Would you be willing to take over my business? I have to return to Spain. I don't know how long I'll be there. I want someone I trust to be in charge. That person is you."

"Al, in case you haven't noticed, I'm in Italy."

"Cat, please don't joke. I've worked so hard to develop this business, not only the resort but the Moringa Tree Nursery. As you know, Josh Campbell has been managing that part of the business for six months. He's trustworthy and knows what he's doing, but..."

The smile fades from his face.

"But what?"

He pulls at the sleeves of his jacket before saying, "Josh is working on this. He says it's under control, but I think I need to tell you since I'm worried."

Oh lordy, these days, no matter the conversation, everyone seems to have a problem.

I take a sip of water and say, "Okay, what's going on?"

"Immigration paperwork stalled on some of our employees. There are rumors of immigrants being picked up by ICE and not seen again. Josh says it's a paperwork glitch, but others are saying it's more than that."

I fiddle with a loose paperclip on my desk as I try to retrieve anything from my brain about immigration. Al and I felt strongly about helping the immigrants who were the victims of the human trafficking ring we broke up last year. We found jobs for many of them in the spa, nursery, and as kitchen staff. We organized housing and resources to help them obtain citizenship. I thought everything was moving smoothly in that direction.

"Does Josh have everything he needs? Immigration attorneys? Sponsors? Resources?"

"Yes, he's working with the Citizenship Resource Center. I've given him absolute *carte blanche* to do what needs to be done. These are honest hard-working people who have experienced the worst kind of trauma. Having their requests for citizenship stalled is unexpected. The visa process to live in the United States was a quick and easy experience for me."

Al is white and rich so it would be an easy process for him. I'm silent for a while longer. I want to come up with words that don't belittle him. He's a natural leader. He gets down into the dirt as required, but his last remark tells me he's out of step with the current situation.

"Keep me informed. Tell Josh if he needs my help once I return to please reach out."

"I will, Cat and thanks. Let's move on to the part of the business that you'll be handling. You're the only person who understands the operation of the hotel, spa and restaurant. It's a huge enterprise. There's not enough time to find someone who knows the business as well as you do."

"Can you tell me what your plans are?"

"That's why I called. I wanted to talk with you before someone else calls you—like Cassie. Although I imagine she already has, hasn't she?"

I search for words somewhere between the truth and a slight alteration of the truth.

"She mentioned your father is ill, and you needed to return to Spain."

"Well, that part is correct. My father is ill. I've spoken with the doctors."

There's a long pause before he says, "This time, he's not going to recover. I've never been close to him, but I am the oldest son. While I'm in line to inherit the estate, the assets and the title, my brother has done his best to stop everything from passing to me."

"Have you spoken with your brother?"

"I tried on several occasions without success. I must arrive before my father dies. It's not about me inheriting as much as it's about getting the estate settled for the sake of my mother and sister. They deserve to stay in the family home. My brother will force them out."

"Sounds like you need to get there in a hurry."

"Yes, it would be easier if I had my father's support. While I'm sure he wouldn't want his wife and daughter to be destitute, he's been subjected to misinformation. If my brother gets his hands on the will or the property, he'll turn my family out and then proceed to mismanage the estate."

"Oh, Al, I'm sorry. Your family needs you now. When do you leave?"

"As soon as I can turn the business over to someone I trust."

"Well, that explains your sense of urgency. What exactly are you asking me to do?"

"I'm asking you to manage the hospitality end of my business. You can name your price."

How do I respond? He's desperate to leave, and I'm an ocean away.

"The problem is I'm in Italy. I would love to help you out, but it's not possible until I return. The circumstances are unresolved, so there isn't a return date."

"Cat, forgive me. I've been so caught up in my personal mess that I didn't ask you if you enjoyed the concert?"

My fingers latch onto a pen. I roll it back and forth on my desk until I realize the noise must be annoying. This is when I hate Zooms. I decide to tell the truth.

"The concert was magnificent except the man who killed Stella was released from prison. He showed up at the concert."

"*Dios mío*, Cat. What happened? Are you okay?"

A small sob-laugh escapes.

"Yes, I'm okay now. It was a bit harrowing. I'm back at my villa, and the Guardia is protecting me while they look for the guy. Until he's found, I have to stay here. It's not safe for me to travel."

There's another long silence while all the ways Al has helped me tumble through my mind. He's pretty much been my patron saint. He aligned himself with me against my nemesis, Mrs. Randolph Augustus Harrington. His aristocratic title and impeccable manners have opened numerous doors, and my business has flourished as a result. He's taken on Diana and Sam as if they were his own daughters. I want to help him.

"Al, is there any way you can find someone to temporarily manage your business until I return? I know that's not what you want, but I don't have anything better to offer."

"I'm working on a solution and might have something to run by you in a couple of days. Whatever I come up with needs to be manageable for both of us. I hope that's possible."

52

The evening of the dinner party, it rains. That doesn't dampen the spirits of my guests. They tackle the 68 steps and shake off the wetness before leaving their rain jackets and umbrellas on the hooks provided under the overhang on the terrace.

A bright blaze from the fireplace takes the chill out of the almost fall air. The room is washed with a soft glow. Chiara and Antonio are the first to arrive. Chiara has an armful of yellow and red flowers, which she thrusts into my arms. Antonio has a bottle of chilled Prosecco. They wait until I arrange the flowers in a vase, add them to the centerpiece, and put the sparkling wine in the fridge before grabbing me in a joint hug. Their happiness dumps equal doses of joy and sadness into my heart.

They are well suited. When their eyes seek out each other, everyone else disappears. At one time, Antonio worshipped Stella, but Stella loved Lorenzo. She never gave herself fully to Antonio, yet she had expected his adoration to continue regardless of her behavior. When it didn't, she blamed him.

Of course, he behaved badly. I mean, sleeping with his nurse is not a particularly intelligent activity. The one thing I hate the most is that Stella was in the process of redeeming herself when she was murdered. Few people, other than myself and Maria and Gino, knew that. Sadness cloaks me in its clutches until the sound of laughter pulls me back to the present.

A charcuterie board of olives, cheeses, nuts, spicy tapenade and focaccia has been discovered, and everyone has gathered. Antonio keeps everyone's glasses full. We toast each other and the goodness of our lives. Everyone is in a celebratory mood. Riccardo is forgotten.

The warm hum of conversation continues as I return to the kitchen with Maria hot on my heels. She's harassed me all week by popping in unexpectedly with questions about the menu, how she can improve it, and ways she can help. My way of dealing with her was to request she make dessert. That seemed to satisfy her. Now she's determined to do more.

"Caterina, let me help. You are making me unhappy. You cannot prepare food alone. It has to be done with those you love. If not, it won't taste good."

Mercy, I love this woman, but she's driving me crazy. It's like we're dueling cooks and scribes of perfection—that is, when it comes to the food we bring to the table. If I give her busy work, she'll do it, but she'll take it as an insult. I settle on asking her to finish the soup. It's complicated enough to satisfy her importance in the kitchen. Plus, she, along with her best friend Beatrice, created the recipe.

The first course is already in the oven—plump mussels stuffed with bread crumbs, parmesan cheese, parsley, Italian spices, and a dash of mussel juice, olive oil, salt and a squeeze of lemon. They require ten minutes in the oven and three minutes under the broiler. Cheesy focaccia accompanies the juicy mussels and the sound of laughter and compliments reach me in the kitchen until Maria shoos me out to join the others while she reheats the soup base.

My choice for the soup course is *vellutata di ceci e fave*. The first time I experienced this dish, because it was an experience, was at *La Pignata*. The creamy deliciousness of the dish implies it's full of rich cream, but it's the pureed beans and olive oil that create the creamy texture. The recipe Maria and Beatrice created has a soup base of beans slowly cooked with garlic, onion, carrots, celery, tomato sauce, rosemary and bay. The shrimp are sautéed with garlic, parsley, fresh chopped tomatoes, sun-dried tomatoes, olive oil and a secret ingredient. It is that one secret ingredient that makes the soup over-the-top wonderful.

Initially, when Maria discovered that Beatrice's daughter, Doriana had given the recipe to me, she was furious. It was, after all, only to be passed from mother to daughter. Only Analisa and Doriana were eligible to have a copy. I am so thankful that Doriana and Analisa argued long and hard to convince Maria and Beatrice that I was a sister to them. They finally relented.

I stand in the doorway and watch as Maria adds the secret ingredient. She smiles and says, "You are sworn to secrecy. You can never tell anyone."

I promise as we ladle the soup in warm bowls. I let Maria do the honors of topping it with the shrimp mixture and another drizzle of olive oil.

The 'oohs and ahhhs' hum around the table. I replenish the focaccia and refill glasses. Chiara insists I stop waiting on everyone and join them. As I settle in the chair next to her, she says, "You are a fabulous cook. Maybe you can give me lessons. The only thing I can do is make broken pieces of stones into something whole. I have no talent or patience for cooking, but I love the eating part. If Antonio and I decide to be together, what will I do? I think I must be the only Italian woman who can't cook."

We laugh. I suggest she ask Maria for cooking lessons.

"She's the best. She's taught me so much about fresh ingredients and the joy of cooking. She reminds me so much of my Nonna. Plus, I'll be leaving soon."

Chiara leans closer. "You'll come back when it is safe, sì? I don't understand much, only that your life is in danger. But with Lorenzo protecting you, I think it's okay. Tell me about Lorenzo. He's not here, yet you have very strong feelings for him."

I honestly don't know how to answer her question, so I say, "Can you take a break from your work this week? We could meet for lunch."

"Yes, I'd like that."

When I leave the table, Maria follows me back to the kitchen. The pasta water has been simmering, so it's only a matter of minutes before a platter piled high with spaghetti lightly sauced with fresh tomatoes, garlic, peperoncini and olive oil is passed around the table.

The real surprise for the evening is Enrico. I enlisted him to grill sea bass. Earlier, realizing rain was in the forecast, we'd moved the grill in the back under the eaves. A dozen, whole perfectly grilled fish are brought to the table along with platters of grilled tomatoes, zucchini, eggplant and thick slabs of sweet onions.

Of course, Maria is the star of the evening with her over-the-top array of desserts: a cherry crostata, a lemon olive oil cake, and the traditional cream-filled pasticciotti. After we can't eat another bit, she places bottles of Capo d'Amaro on the table. The night rings with laughter, and love floats around the table. I savor every moment as if it might be my last.

53

The final dish from last night's dinner party is washed and tucked away in the appropriate cabinet. I settle in front of the fire with my laptop to start work on a reading-in-English program Analisa wants me to put together for Giorgino's class.

As I open the computer, a Zoom invitation comes through from Al. He's responding much quicker than I anticipated. I open the invitation and enter the chat room.

Al pauses before looking at me. "Ciao, Caterina. Forgive me for not notifying you in advance, but after our last conversation, I wanted to act quickly."

"I understand. Did you find someone?"

"Yes, I did. He's waiting for me to invite him into the Zoom with us. Since you two will be working together, I want you to meet him before anyone else."

I push my hair out of my eyes and wonder if I have food on my shirt or in my teeth. I'm surprised and startled that Al found someone so quickly.

"Sure, it would be nice to meet him."

"It won't take very long. Do you have time?"

"Yes, I do."

"After you meet and assess him, he'll leave the Zoom. I'd like you to stay on so we can discuss how to make this work for all of us. Is that okay with you?"

"Of course it is."

Out of the corner of my eye, I watch as the screen opens to an unknown place and man. He's seated at a table in what appears to be a restaurant. He's fidgeting with a salt shaker. I give him a once-over and turn my attention to Al.

"Cat, I'd like you to meet JAB."

"Who?"

Al's chuckle is halfhearted, "Caterina Maria Lucia Gabbiano, let me introduce Jacob Augustin Benoit LeBlanc or JAB LeBlanc."

One of my many flaws is the ability of words to jump out of my mouth before I process them.

"JAB, what kind of name is that?"

The man opens his mouth. His drawl is so long that I fear I might grow old and die before he finishes a sentence.

"Hello, ma'am, JAB here." He lifts his hand in a slight wave. "I'm originally from New Orleans."

His *New or-lee-yuns* sounds like the Deep South rolled around a French accent, all spoken while eating a beignet. Laughter gurgles from the depths of my stomach. I try to hold back, but it spills out in wheezy snorts. I grab a tissue and pretend to sneeze and cough while wiping my tears.

He waits until my barely concealed hysterics are contained before he shrugs and says, "It's the kids who named me, ma'am. Y'all know how it is when y'all are growin' up in south Louisiana, huh?"

I look at Al and ask, "What did he say?"

They both laugh. Then this JAB person says in a clear voice free of dialect, "Once my classmates discovered my name spelled out JAB, there was no going back. It stuck and served me well as the middleweight champion in high school, college, and the military."

"Oh."

Al watches our short exchange. When we're both silent, he says, "Cat, JAB is going to run the restaurant. That's all he wants to do, but he says he'll manage the entire business until either you or I return."

"Well, JAB, I hope you don't find me rude, but what's your background?"

He waves his hands like he's conducting an orchestra and has come to the tricky part. I notice how blue his eyes are and how little lines crinkle around them when he smiles. He smiles a lot. His hair is tousled with streaks of blonde, red and brown from long days fishing in the sun off the bayou. JAB is written in the upper left-hand corner of what I now realize is a chef's jacket. It's unbuttoned at the neck, and the sleeves are rolled past his elbows. When he moves, a *fleur de lis* tattoo emerges on his left forearm.

"Went to the CIA, ma'am. You know, the one up there in New York. Ever heard of it?"

He's making fun of me, but I don't take the bait.

"Hadn't thought of being a cook until I went in the military. Somehow, they figured a boy from Louisiana should know something about beans and rice. I didn't, but I learned real quick. I liked it, so I decided after my four-year stint to give culinary school a try. Then I moseyed on back to New Orleans and did some cooking until the owner of Jubans hired me and transported me to Baton Rouge— working on my first Michelin until this here count decided he needed my services."

When he finally stops jabbering, I ask, "And if I take over the management of the business when I return, how will you feel about that?"

"Long as you stay out of my kitchen, I won't give a damn how you run the business. But I think that might be hard for you to do, seeing as how you're a chef yourself."

I splutter all over the place about how I understand boundaries, before I realize he's teasing me again. None of this bodes well for us having a healthy work relationship.

"Al, it could be weeks or even months before I return. Surely, JAB will want to continue as both the manager and the chef. I think it would be foolish for me to waltz in and presume to know more than he does about your business. My business is far smaller than yours, and I barely stay on top of it. Mr. LeBlanc seems to be quite capable, don't you think?"

"Now, hold on there, ladybug. Don't be giving me a job I didn't apply for and don't want. The kitchen is my home. That offer alone was enough to entice me to leave a place I dearly love. I wouldn't even consider the management part, except the count here offered me a bonus so big I didn't have the balls to turn it down. By the time you or the count return, the business will probably be bankrupt, but not the restaurant."

The nerve of this JAB person, calling me ladybug. The heat rises from my face like a red beet being pulled out of the ground. He doesn't seem to notice and keeps right on running his mouth.

"Both of you need to understand my only love and my only job is to create Michelin quality food for others to enjoy. Oh, and write an occasional cookbook, and perhaps, from time-to-time entertain a film crew. Al understands that. I hope you do too."

Interrupting him, I say, "Well, you certainly seem to know what you want, but what about our current staff? Are you willing to work with these people, or are you a one-man show?"

He laughs long and heartily. "I want people in the kitchen who feel the same way about food as I do. It sounds like the count already has them onboard. I'm willing to run the day-to-day operation for the count, but only until you get your butt back to the Lowcountry."

I'm struck dumb. Al's head is bobbing like one of those wacky bobblehead dolls. *How did this happen? How am I going to work with this rude man?*

Al must sense my tension because he jumps in, "Unless there's anything else you two need to discuss, I'll let JAB go. Cat, I need you to stay on a little longer to work through the details."

Before I can respond Mr. Jabby's mouth jumps in, "Now don't y'all forget about me, Cat. I'll want a Zoom with you every Monday. Don't want you saying I'm not keeping you in the loop. Plus, I have a lot of questions, and I bet you can answer them all. I'm counting on you to hurry back and take over the business end of this deal."

Lordy, he's cocky—so sure of himself. He's lucky I'm thousands of miles away; otherwise, I'd be considering what poison to put in his drink. The only way I can deal with him for now is to ignore him.

"Mr. LeBlanc, Mondays may not work for me as my time can't be scheduled at the moment."

Nothing I say diminishes his grin. He's so pleased with himself for some reason—a reason I hope never to discover. What is it about him that's so irritating, or maybe it's just me? In fact, I'm sure it's me. Neither of these men knows about the mess I'm in. There's no need for them to know. So I put a smile on my face.

"I'm sure we can find a time that's agreeable for both of us."

"Yes ma'am. You let me know when it's convenient for you. It's been a pleasure. Y'all have a good time in Italy."

He nods and turns his attention to Al.

"Al, I've already given my notice and will be packed up and out of here by the end of next week. Give me a call later as we still have a few logistics to work out."

His spot on the Zoom turns to black. Al and I are left on the screen. We stare at each other through the screen. Al breaks the silence with a laugh. I join in.

"Where in the world did you find this JAB person? No, that's the wrong question. What possessed you to hire him?"

"Believe it or not, I like him. He has a bit of an ego, and he's a bit showy."

"A bit? Don't you think it's more like over the top?"

"Now, Cat, I interviewed a lot of chefs. JAB is the only one that's going to make my restaurant a world-class place. That's what I want. The restaurant is good, but so far, we're only making ends meet. I want more than good. This man has those skills."

"Did you consider whether or not our personalities would mesh or clash?"

Al smooths back his perfectly groomed hair.

"Actually, I did. You'll like him."

"Hmmmm. I'll do my best. You must have a million things to do. Let's discuss how this is all going to work."

"Cat, the papers are drawn up with your responsibilities and your salary. I'll send them as soon as we hang up. I need you at the helm far more than I'm able to say."

"Okay, send them. Al, I do understand the pressure you're under with your family situation. I'm glad I can help. JAB and I will work it out."

Al's smile radiates through the screen. "As soon as you return the papers, I'll get my plane tickets. At least we'll be in the same time zone. It will be easier to stay in touch. I'll let you know when I arrive in Spain, and you let me know the minute you have a date for your return. Maybe we can meet up before you leave for home."

"Al, the reason I'm helping you is because you've been such a help to me this last year. My business wouldn't have fared so well without your going to bat for me. I really appreciate it. I'll do everything to ensure your business continues to prosper. But come back as soon as you can. Who knows—maybe we can arrange to fly home together?"

He bows his head in his courtly nod. When he looks back up, our eyes lock, and his feelings for me radiate through the screen. Although I don't feel the same, my heart moves closer to his. It would be a good life without conflict or pain.

I click on the leave meeting button, and the screen goes dark.

54

Enrico looks up when Analisa calls out that she's leaving to take Giorgino to school. He removes his wide-brimmed straw hat and waves both arms as the car passes him. He stands at the edge of the olive grove and stays there until the car disappears.

His smile always takes Analisa's breath away. Eleven years they've been together, and her heart still flutters. Most of her friends grumble about their husbands, and many of them work full-time because they have to or because they want to get away.

Enrico is a successful farmer. His olive groves survived the horrendous bacteria that hit so many other farms—all because he let go of the old ways and created a new path. There's no need for her to work, yet she struggles with wanting to.

She's a creative person and wishes to express herself in ways other than as a wife and mother. Although Enrico is an amazing provider and loves having her at home, he supports her decision to find gratifying work. She waited until Giorgino was at the age when he wasn't so dependent on her. And now, under Dr. Tony's care, he's healthy enough to attend school. This has allowed her to try a few part-time jobs without feeling guilty.

When a friend told her the high school library needed a part-time assistant, she applied and was hired for the position. She loves books and thinks it's a good match for her. The job allows her to drop Giorgino at the elementary school and drive another ten minutes to the high school.

This morning, Giorgino is unusually quiet in the back seat. She glances in the mirror. Her heart skips a beat. She's been so busy with her new job, along with interviewing for the teacher's assistant position, that it's been a day or two since she looked at him closely. Dark circles and puffy skin frame his eyes. The calendar says it's another week before they see Dr. Tony, but maybe she needs to push that up.

"How are you feeling today? Are you excited about staying in the after-school program with Signorina Barone?'

"Sì, Mamma."

"Bambino, listen. If you aren't feeling well, tell me. I can take you to Nonna's house, or I can stay home from work."

"No, Mamma. I'm okay."

Analisa pulls to the curb in front of the school and watches with a sinking heart as her little boy opens the door. He reaches for his backpack and gives her his usual crooked smile and a half wave.

"Don't forget I'll be back after lunch with Signore Gabbiano for the reading hour."

She watches until the door closes behind him, and an impatient parent honks at her to move on. Glancing at her watch, she gasps. If she doesn't hurry, she'll be late for her job. She steps on the gas and pulls out into the traffic.

♩

The bell chimes before I reach the bottom step. I've been waiting for Analisa. We are both excited about the new program called *Read in English,* which she's asked me to introduce into the lower grades at the elementary school.

The teachers are excited to have an American living in their town and asked Analisa if I'd be willing to help them. She wrote the proposal, and it was accepted.

When Analisa approached me, I couldn't stop laughing.

"Me teach English? You know I'm a chef and not a teacher or writer?"

She said, "Of course, I know that, but the teachers and students don't care about what you do. They're thrilled you are an American and you speak English. That's enough for them. Only a couple of teachers speak some English. They all want to learn. The best way to learn is to start with children's books in English."

"But what do they want from me?"

Analisa grins. "You know many people in America. Don't you have friends who are teachers or authors who write children's books? Couldn't they help us?"

Of course, how could I say no? I figured it would pass the time while I'm in exile. After numerous Zooms with teacher and author friends, I put together a program and met with Analisa and the teachers who could speak English. They specifically wanted an American experience with American books for themselves and the children.

The South Carolina Lowcountry nourishes the souls of writers. I'm often called on to cater book launches because I offer a steep discount to writers. It turned into a fun adventure to ask for input and assistance from authors who write children's books.

To kick off the program, I selected *The Sea Island's Secret* by Susan Diamond Riley for the eight to twelve year olds, and *Percy Goes Camping...Maybe* by Joy Corley for the four to seven year olds. The authors were excited and generously mailed me copies of their books to share with the students.

I sling the sack of books over my shoulders and open the gate. Analisa's sad face has me asking what's wrong.

"Giorgino isn't feeling well today. I should have kept him home."

I link my arms through hers. "Since his class is the first one I'm reading with, you'll get to see him. If he's still not feeling well, call Antonio. I'm sure he'll see you today."

She smiles and pulls me into a warm embrace, "Thank you, Caterina. That's so true. Now I feel better. *Andiamo.*"

We walk arm-in-arm to the school with two guards flanking us.

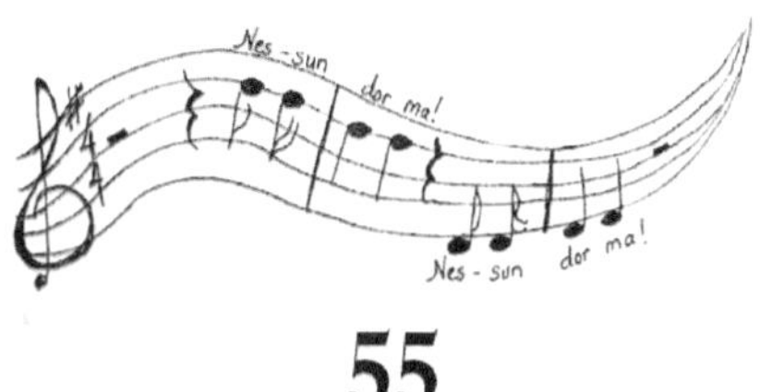

55

Analisa and I peek through the glass panel in the classroom door to make sure they're ready for us. The teacher stands at the front. Another woman leans against the cabinets in the back of the room. She must be the teacher's assistant. Her head is turned away from the door. Her choice of wardrobe colors blends in with the dull brown of the cabinets.

I nod, indicating the woman in the back, and whisper to Analisa, "Is that the new teacher's assistant, the one you interviewed?"

"Sì, I'm still not sure it was the right decision, but so far, she seems okay. Giorgino adores her. If he's well enough, he's staying with her today in the after-school program so I can finish up some cataloguing at the library."

The teacher sees us and waves us in. The woman in the back glances over. Her hand flies to her face. A startled expression behind the oversized glasses gives her that deer-in-the-headlights look. I wonder which of us elicited the fearful expression. She abruptly turns away. I crane my neck to get a better view as I have this weird sensation I've seen her before. Maybe she's just one of those people who looks familiar. Once I meet her and get a better look, I'll know.

The teacher reaches the door and invites us in. The kids crowd around me as I'm still a novelty in this part of the world. Giorgino proudly introduces me as his *amica Americana.* The kids jostle, giggle and pull on my bag for a look at the books. Analisa and I exchange looks over Giorgino's head. He's full of energy. Whatever was troubling him has disappeared. She smiles and nods.

As I move toward the front of the room, the door to the hallway opens and closes. I glance up and catch a glimpse of Signorina

Barone's back. Strangely, she's leaving just as we arrive. From the look on her face, perhaps she's ill. I hope not, as I'm interested in meeting her.

When I reach the front of the room, Analisa asks the teacher if Signorina Barone is returning and if we need to wait for her before starting.

We're told to go ahead with the lesson. Signorina Barone doesn't return.

♩

Isabella locks the door to the bathroom and leans against the wall. She sucks in some air as she attempts to slow down her jagged breathing. After throwing cold water on her face, she unlocks the doors, checks the hallway, and moves rapidly to the teacher's lounge.

She's furious. Riccardo assured her she wouldn't run into Cat. He said the Guardia had her grounded. She wonders if Cat recognized her. She stays in the teachers' lounge until she's sure Cat and Analisa have left. When she returns to the classroom, she apologizes profusely and explains to the teacher.

"I'm not sure what happened. I felt faint. No, no, I'm fine now. I saw the school nurse. It seems I forgot to eat breakfast this morning, and I skipped lunch. Momentarily, I felt lightheaded. There's no need to cancel the after-school program. So far only Giorgino has signed up, and he's an easy pupil."

The teacher smiles with relief as she has an appointment.

"Look, I can cancel if you aren't feeling well."

Isabella isn't concerned, as she knows the teacher is anxious to leave. Most of the teachers and assistants don't want to be stuck with the after-school program.

"No, no, I'm fine now. I ate and then rested. That's all I needed."

She pretends to grade paperwork until the teacher leaves. Her anger eases. Since Marco wasn't able to steal the necklace before Cat left the resort, she has to put the new plan in motion. Giorgino will be used as a bargaining tool for the necklace. Her thoughts are interrupted as Giorgino bounces into the classroom. His cheeks are flushed, his face dirty, and there's a rip in his jeans.

"Signorina, I'm here. What are we going to do today? I have my plane."

He reaches into his backpack and pulls out what looks like a miniature Piper Cub.

"Do you want to fly it with me?"

Isabella tries to hide the frustration spreading across her face. *How will I ever pull this off?*

"No, Giorgino, not now. I promised your mother we'd tackle your homework. If you get it all done, then we can fly your plane."

Giorgino groans and slumps at the table. Then he bounces right back up. "Let me help you. What do you need me to do? I help my mamma all the time. She says I'm a good helper."

"The best way to help me is to sit down and start your homework assignments. As you finish each one, let me know, and I'll check your work."

"But Signorina, I thought the after-school program would be fun. Can't we play some games, or maybe you could read to me? I loved the book about the dog. I want a dog just like Percy. Please? I can read it to you."

Lucrezia grits her teeth and puts on her fake smile. "Giorgino, if you finish all your homework before your mother comes for you, we'll read the book about the dog. *Va bene?* Until then, I don't want to hear another word."

Giorgino stares at her. He wonders what's happened. Maybe she's grumpy like Mamma is sometimes. He pulls out his homework and opens his notebook. He bends his head over his assignment, but his eyes follow her. She moves across the room with her phone to her ear. She looks angry.

56

Both my trip to Castello two years ago to find Stella and this visit have had Lorenzo locking me up inside the villa. During my first visit, when I was searching for Stella, there was no reason for me to explore the property because the villa was Stella's, not mine. Thanks to Stella's generosity, I own the villa.

Although it's been a bit difficult with officers everywhere, I've been exploring the property. Most of the time, they don't bother checking out the back of the house. With their first search, they discovered there was very little opportunity for anyone to enter or leave via the rocky terrain.

But I'm determined to find a way out. Two years ago, when I was kidnapped, I didn't have an escape plan in place. Now, I'm committed to finding a way out of this place if I need it. Each day, I spend a little time outside. Sometimes, I hang the laundry or exercise or garden. All normal activities so I don't arouse the guards' attention.

The back part of the yard extends only a few meters and then drops away into a rocky ravine. It would take a great effort for someone even in the best physical shape to scale the slippery stones. There are no footholds, or tree branches or even shrubs for support. When facing the front of the villa, the left side of the house is a sheer rock wall. With those thoughts in mind, I approach the right side of the property.

Buried beneath the thick foliage, I discover bits and pieces of an ancient wall. Every day, I trace the wall a little further. I would love to tear through layers of brambles, but I don't want to attract attention. The wall stops at a thick briar hedge that connects to the villa.

Every morning and every evening with the changing of the

guards, Lorenzo shows up. He gathers the men in front of the villa for debriefing. During those few minutes today, I pull back a portion of the hedge and discover a wrought iron gate.

I push, pull, and grunt with the effort, but it doesn't move. It's locked, and the lock is corroded. After arranging the brambles back in place, I spend the remainder of the afternoon looking for a key that might fit the rusty lock.

This evening when Lorenzo arrives, I scramble on all fours to the gate, oil the lock, and try a series of keys. None fit. I sit on my butt and slam my feet against the gate. It moves a fraction. On my knees, I lean into it with all my weight and push. It doesn't budge. The guards' voices drift into the backyard. I stop what I'm doing and scurry back to the house.

♩

Early the next morning, with the changing of the guards, I hack away at the vines until a space is created. I push with my whole body until the gate finally bends and opens wide enough for me to squeeze through.

A series of stone steps crumble into more thorny vines. It's an easy place to break my neck. With the right tools, I can clear it enough to determine how far it goes and if there's an opening at the end. Closing my eyes, I visualize my escape route.

Murmuring voices from Lorenzo's instructions creep through the vines as I test a few of the steps. By observing, I've learned that Lorenzo's visits last about ten minutes. Eight minutes have passed, so I scamper back up as quickly as the broken stones allow. I brush the leaves and debris out of my hair and off my clothes and race through the back door just in case he decides to check on me. Just in case he's changed his mind.

But the bell doesn't chime. I listen as the engine starts, and he drives away.

57

Lately, it seems as if I'm spending my life on Zoom. Today, it's Cassie and Diana. Ever since Diana came into my life with the human trafficking ring, I knew she'd be a star. She was willing to die to save her little sister. She came close. Her determination, persistence and keen understanding of life at such a young age have served her well.

To anyone who listens, she says Sheriff Blackwell and I saved her life. After it was all over, she didn't waste time feeling sorry for herself. Instead, she finished her senior year and entered culinary school and will graduate in the spring.

She has the drive, the intelligence, and that no-fear attitude that reminds me of my younger self. While Cassie's daughter Sam is content to stay in the background, Diana wants to be involved in every aspect of the business. Before I left, Cassie and I had a long talk about giving Diana more responsibility. Cassie had to be onboard, or it wouldn't work.

Cassie suggested that she and Diana conduct the interviews for the sous chef/front-of-the-house person. Today, they want my input on some of the candidates.

♩

Diana's mop of blonde hair appears first, then Cassie's dark head bobs in next to her—both waving and smiling. Diana is bouncing around at the table, which indicates she is excited about something. Cassie puts her hand on Diana's arm in an attempt to calm her down. But it's no use.

"Oh, Cat, you won't believe who called and wanted to hire you and only you to cater her next event."

She doesn't wait for me to guess before the words burst from her mouth.

"The one and only Mrs. Randolph Augustus Harrington. When I told her you weren't available, she dropped the phone. Then she sputtered and demanded to know why. She was on speaker, and Cassie was listening in. We almost couldn't contain ourselves. Cassie was shaking with laughter, and I about peed in my pants trying not to laugh."

The two of them are giggling and snorting as Diana continues, "Once I hung up, we danced around the kitchen like crazy people— laughing and whooping like we'd won the lottery. Oh my, it was a delicious moment to turn her down."

I join in the laughter. Once they settle down, Cass says, "I guess you're worried about our mental state, but it was intoxicating to tell her she was out of luck. Although we knew you'd love to hear that news, that's not the main reason for the Zoom."

She shuffles some papers on the desk and continues, "We've found some good candidates for the position, and we want your input before we make an offer. Diana is leaning toward one and I toward the other, so we need you to weigh in."

"Okay, thanks for sending me their resumes. Cassie, you go first and tell me why you think Lina Douglas is the better candidate."

"Well, her qualifications speak for themselves. I mean, she studied at the Culinary Arts Academy in Switzerland, and she's worked at some of the best restaurants in Europe."

"That's impressive, but we're small-time in comparison. Why would she want to work with us, and how did she get to South Carolina?"

"She told us she's been in the food business since she was eighteen and wants to make a change. She took some time off to visit some extended family in the Greenville area. She saw the ad in iHireChefs."

"Hmmm, doesn't that seem a little unusual?"

"Yeah, I thought so too, but she said the constant pressure in Switzerland to become the best chef was too much. She gave it considerable thought and decided she'd like to slow down and work in a friendlier and less competitive environment. Her father is an American diplomat, and her mother is Swiss. Lina has dual citizenship so that eliminates any problems on whether or not she can work in the US."

"What did the culinary school and her former employers say about her?"

"There was a problem at the school. Lina was accused of cheating and was kicked out. But she was reinstated with a full apology and was able to complete her education."

"Wow! That's a story. What did she say about it?"

"Not much. Just that another student had it in for her and set her up. She said she was able to prove to the faculty that it was the other student who did the cheating. She was uncomfortable talking about it. When I asked her why, she said that the other student committed suicide, and she felt she was to blame."

"What a nightmare experience. Did the school corroborate her story?"

"They said they weren't at liberty to discuss the situation because of privacy laws."

I glance through the resume again before asking, "What's your take on her mental state?"

"It happened ten to fifteen years ago. Based on our exchange during the interview, I didn't pick up on any residual effects."

"What did her previous employers have to say?"

"Well, I'm still working on that. In the current environment, employers don't want to talk for fear of lawsuits, so I'm not getting much information. I get comments like 'she was a hard worker', or 'she did her job', or 'she was passionate about her cooking.' All vague responses that really don't reveal anything. I have a couple more calls to make, but you know how difficult it is with the time difference. I'll reach out to all of them before the final decision, but I think she'd be an asset."

"What qualities did you pick up on that made you decide she was the right candidate?"

Cassie glances at her notes before responding.

"Her answers during the interview indicated a lot of motivation and creativity. She's eager to please. She's reserved, although that could be her style for the interview."

"What about being part of a team?"

"I'm going to leave that to you, Cat. You're the one who can see whether or not a person has that skill. On the surface, I'd say yes, but until we work with her, who knows."

"Diana, what did you think of Lina?"

Diana didn't hesitate and blurted out in her usual manner.

"Oh, I don't like her. I know that's not reasonable since I don't know her. It's more of an instinctive thing."

My ears perk up as that's one of my own criteria when interviewing. How does this person come across? Conniving, cunning, controlling, a straight shooter, or a team player? I listen more intently as Diana explains.

"She was pleasant, but her answers seemed rehearsed. When I asked her inane questions like what was her favorite course or favorite food, it seemed to throw her off her script. She tried too hard to provide answers she thought we wanted."

Cassie interrupted, "Oh, I disagree. I didn't pick up on that at all. She was sincere and intelligent. Her answers were well thought out. I would have prepared the same way. I guess you would have thought my answers were scripted, too."

Diana rushes to respond, "That's not true, Cassie. You don't come across as scripted and you don't strive for perfection, which I think she did. But, yes, she's knowledgeable about cooking and the hospitality industry. As I said, I didn't like her, but that doesn't mean we don't consider her."

Cassie and Diana avoid looking at each other. I'm dismayed they are on opposite sides, as we've always worked well as a team. Hiring more staff could possibly be more of a headache than it's worth.

"Okay, we don't have to settle this now. Diana, it's your turn to tell me about Destiny Clarice Booker. Why have you selected her?"

"First, she's a local from Saint Helena Island. She graduated from the Technical College of the Lowcountry's Culinary Institute of the South. She's been working at Magnolia's in Charleston. I love that place. The food is consistently good, and it's more along the lines of what we prepare. She was a straight-A student. The professors loved her and her work ethic, as does the management at Magnolia's. She has a great sense of humor, is down to earth, and everyone I talked to said she's a team player and not a prima donna."

"Cassie, your thoughts on Destiny?"

"Well, she's all those things that Diana said, but she lacks polish. I think she'll be fine in the kitchen, but I don't see her in the front of the house."

Diana frowns and opens her mouth to speak, but I decide to jump in as I see a stalemate looming.

"Okay, good job—both of you. Out of fifty candidates, you came up with two great choices. Are there any others?"

"Yes," they say in unison and laugh which eases the tension.

Diana nods at Cassie. "Go ahead."

"Actually, there is one more candidate we both think is the number one applicant."

I lean toward the screen. "Why didn't y'all talk about her first?"

They look at each other, and Cassie says, "Well, she's the woman you recently hired for a couple of events. We did the interview together."

"Okay, but tell me everything just like you did with the other two."

Cassie starts to protest but decides against it.

"Her name is Sarah Martin. Based on her resumé, she's probably in her late thirties. She owned a small, successful catering business in upstate until her husband became ill. When caretaking became her full-time role, she closed the business. Her husband died about a year ago."

My heart hurts at the thought of losing someone you love. The death of my parents and Stella still haunts me. Losing a loving spouse must seem like the end of the world.

"How did she get to the Lowcountry?"

"After her husband's death, a friend invited her for a visit, and she says she's going to stay. The thing is, she's not ready to work full-time. She wants to ease back into the job. Plus, she said she is still settling the estate and is out of town frequently. We thought maybe hire her for special events if you're agreeable. We're hoping to phase her in as a full-time employee. We both think she's excellent."

Sarah Martin had all but slipped from my mind with all the chaos in my life. I vaguely remember she didn't have the usual nerves that most new staff do. The one thing I do recall is she didn't mix with the other staff. Of course, that doesn't mean anything when a person is only working for a specific event.

"How about we utilize her skills to help me with Al's business? She could still help out with special events too. Let's give her a try. In the meantime, what do y'all think about offering jobs to both Lina and Destiny?"

Both heads nod their approval.

"Since our business has picked up, I think there's room for both of them—at least for a few months. Maybe a six-month trial period to determine if one fits better than the other. One of them might turn us down. Whether one accepts or both, keep a close watch. We're too small to hire someone who isn't a team player or doesn't pull their weight."

Diana responds immediately. "That sounds fair to me, Cat. What do you think, Cassie?"

I can tell Cassie doesn't quite agree to hiring both candidates.

"Cass? What's troubling you??

"Maybe I'm wrong, but hiring two people makes me think you've said yes to helping Al."

Cassie always sees through my smoke screen.

"You're right. Just as you told me, Al asked me to manage his business. With two more on staff, as well as Sarah, I might be able to swing it. Since she previously owned a catering business, she can help me with the overall management. Then I suggest we have Lina and Destiny spend time both in our business and in Al's. It would be a great experience for both of them. How does that sound?"

They nod their heads vigorously in agreement.

"If Lina isn't a team player, we'll soon find out. We can determine with some training if Destiny can manage the front of the house. If they both work out, we'll slot them in positions that let them shine with the understanding that they have to be backups in all aspects of the business. Agreed?"

Both heads nod.

"Diana, I can tell you're ready to get on to the next thing on your list. Thanks for all your hard work."

"Oh, Cat, I loved every minute. But I do have to run. Sam asked me to help her finish up the last of the hors d'oeuvres for tonight's event. Come home soon. We miss you."

She blows a kiss, waves, and is gone.

58

I wait until I hear the office door close before saying, "Are you and Diana going to be okay?"

"Sure, she's a great kid. In some ways, with her brutal abduction last year, she's wiser and older than I am. But in other ways, she's young and inexperienced. I'm not too concerned that she doesn't like Lina. She's young, and already on to the next thing. She'll forget about it right away."

"As long as you two are okay, then I'm okay. Are we ready to wrap up?"

Cassie fidgets.

"What?"

"Well, I asked Al to interview all three of the candidates. He was quite taken with Lina and Sarah. He thought Destiny had good skills, but he said Lina and Sarah were more polished and professional. He actually said he'd be happy working with either of them."

Cassie giggles, "He appeared to be dazzled by Lina. I don't blame him as she has those beautiful classic features—blonde, slim, clear complexion, perfect nose and ears."

Funny how a little bit of jealousy stirs in my blood. Al never mentioned interviewing the candidates. I plaster a smile on my face and focus on Cassie. During our Zoom, I've been watching her. It's hard not to focus on Diana's jubilant personality, but there's something going on with Cassie.

"What's up, Cass?"

Cassie glances up from the resumés with a silly grin on her face.

"Are you going to tell me why you're grinning from ear to ear?"

She blushes and whispers, "Oh, Cat, I've been waiting all this time to tell you."

She giggles like a teenager before saying, "Chuck asked me to marry him."

My mouth falls opens—not because I didn't expect it to happen, but because I'm not there to hug Cassie and do the stupid dance we always do when we're over-the-top excited.

"Yikes! That's wonderful. Why are you whispering?"

"Because no one at work knows. We don't want to announce it until you get back. But I've been dying to tell you. I need you here with me. The wedding will be small and intimate. There'll be an elegant brunch for the wedding party, but that evening we want a grand reception. I can't do that without you."

"Oh gracious, what fun we'll have planning everything together. You know we don't have to wait until I come home. We can get started now. Do you have a date?"

"We don't have a definite date because everything hinges on your return. Once we know, we'll pick a date far enough out so we don't feel rushed. Maybe a few months after you come home. Will that work for you?"

"Of course. Let's schedule our next Zoom so we can start planning. Will the wedding be at Al's place?"

"Yes, and as soon as we hang up, I'm going to see him. He's great at keeping secrets. But I can't have the wedding without both of you attending."

"Oh Cassie, with all the chaos in my life, this is the best news. Chuck's a wonderful man, and he adores you."

Cassie's smile is dazzling.

"Do you remember when I dragged you down to his studio for my Krav Maga lesson?"

"Do I ever. I was so furious with you for interfering in my life and my misery. If you hadn't kicked my butt, I'd still be moping around over that disgusting senator. You are the best friend."

As I get ready to hit the *leave* button, Cassie leans in close to the screen and has another fit of whispering.

"Cat?"

"Hmmm?"

"There's one more thing. Well, actually two. I asked Sheriff Blackwell to walk me down the aisle. And, I was wondering if you'd be my maid of honor?"

I shriek with joy.

"Oh, Cassie, you know I will. It was my lucky day when we collided in the grocery store. I can't believe it—you and Chuck—it's perfect."

Cassie beams. "Chuck wanted me to wait to tell you, but I said there was no way I was going to keep it from you. You're my best friend. Plus, I'm the one who will have a difficult time keeping my mouth shut."

At this moment, I want to be home. If I were, we'd be whirling around the kitchen doing our wild women dance.

"What about Sam? What does she say about your getting married again?"

"She's happy for us. She likes Chuck a lot. He's always there for her but not pushy. She's never had a father. The deadbeat left before she was born. She was inquisitive when she was a teenager, but several years ago, she told me I was enough mom and dad for her. Plus, having Sheriff Blackwell endorse Chuck doesn't hurt."

My face hurts from the constant smile that won't release my jaws.

"Oh, Cassie. I wish I were there or you were here. Zoom will never take the place of a bear hug and our happy dance."

Cassie throws back her head and laughs until she's gasping for air.

I join in the laughter.

"If you don't quiet down, everyone's going to know your secret."

We both snort, wipe our noses and eyes and put our business faces back on.

"Well, the timing is good to hire more staff. You and Chuck will need some time off. Where will you honeymoon?"

"I was wondering—will your villa be available?"

Laughing with delight, I say, "Of course, it's yours. My wedding gift to you. Now tell me how he proposed—I want all the details."

59

Matera

Isabella parks below the city walls. Working in the school system, even half days with those kids who never shut their mouths, has taken a toll on her disposition. The first week is behind her, and it was worse than any prison sentence she could imagine. During the three-hour drive to Matera, she hopes she regained some of her sanity.

The coins drop into the parking machine, and the ticket pops out. She places it inside the vehicle so it shows through the front windshield. This is not the time to get a parking ticket.

Wearily she takes in the steep incline as she leans against the stone wall. She hasn't slept lately. The climb doesn't look inviting. *How can people live in a place where their homes are carved out of the side of a stone mountain? How did it happen that people lived excruciating existences in caves?*

She couldn't imagine Marco growing up in a place like this. She thought Sicily was the end of the earth, but gracious, this place was the ass end. Of course, she wouldn't mention that to him.

Perhaps the trek is what she needs. She's angry and exercise might clear her mind before she knocks on his door. Until Cat came along, she thought she and Marco had an understanding. But he hasn't responded to her calls or texts since she left the resort. If he thinks she is some naive bimbo he can use and toss away, he is wrong. She can easily crush him.

She focuses on the rough stones beneath her feet. Some of the anger dissipates as she settles into a rhythmic stride. She knows

Marco has feelings for her. Like all men, he's frightened of commitment. Plus, he's dabbling with two devils—Riccardo and Commissario Faena. He's wondering about her, too, and he's as uneasy as she is. Before she came along and lured him to become an informant, he was a decent guy. She's sure the reason he hasn't called is because he's wondering how he got caught in the middle between doing the right thing or basically becoming a criminal.

And now this weekend she's going to hit him with her plan to sabotage Riccardo. She'd worked and reworked her scheme to steal the necklace before Riccardo could put his hands on it. Each time she streamlined it, she knew the odds for both of them to be murdered were high. For her, it was an easy choice, but not for Marco. Commissario Faena not promoting him didn't come close to the years of slavery and prostitution she had endured. Marco's ego was hurt—something he'd get over. When he did, he might regret everything and her most of all.

Isabella shifts her backpack from one shoulder to the other and stops to take in the view of the valley far below. It isn't beautiful or picturesque. Instead, it's harsh and dramatic. Marco had shared with her stories of his birth place and the toughness required to grow up in a city that at one time was Italy's shame.

The history of Matera is ancient, dark and dated back to 7500 B.C. Along with Petra and Jordan, Matera is the oldest continuously inhabited settlement in history. In the 1950s, the cave dwellers were moved en masse, and the city was cleaned up. Now it's called a hidden gem, and global travelers clamor to stay in the caves that once housed the poorest of the poor—a rags-to- riches story for a town built on depravity and poverty.

By the time Isabella reaches the main piazza, a fine sweat covers her face. She searches in her purse and pulls out a scrap of paper—a diagram of the streets leading off the piazza to Marco's place. He had given it to her before she left the resort.

She drove all this way to convince him to be part of her kidnapping scheme. Matera is the ideal place to hide a kid and hold up for a couple of days before moving on to the next safe house.

Marco's house is hidden in an obscure passageway. His timing to take vacation couldn't have been better. Since he hasn't returned her calls or texts, she decided to turn up this weekend without letting him know. He would either be happy or furious to see her. The thing is, she needs him. Kidnapping Giorgino requires two people to pull it off. Once she reveals her plan to him, she'll know whether or not to continue the relationship. If he won't cooperate, she'll eliminate him.

She drops the piece of paper back in her purse. It lands on the small snub-nosed revolver. As much as she cares for Marco, she won't allow him to stand in the way of her freedom from Riccardo.

60

Castello

This evening, when the guards change, the chime rings. I release the gate and wait, not breathing.

We haven't seen each other, spoken or texted since our night together—almost a week ago. I'm dreading this encounter, as I'm sure he is.

I walk onto the terrace as he clears the last step. We both pause. My heart hurts when I look at him as if it knows before I do that this is really about saying goodbye. He says my name with such tenderness. Unleashed tears gush.

He holds me, and his words, while muffled against my hair, are clear in their meaning.

"That was the last time, Cat. You know it. I know it. We have no future. Neither of us is willing to change our lives, our careers, or our countries."

Through my sobs, I ask, "So you really didn't mean it when you said maybe you'd consider a consultant's position with the FBI?"

He tenderly traces a tear.

"Cat, I love you. I can't change that, but it's time I settle down. My work is here. My life is here. I want a family. You're not willing to move, and you're ambivalent about creating a family."

I pull away, but he holds on.

"Listen to me. Unless you've reconsidered, you're not willing to upend your life and neither am I. You're building a business, and children aren't part of your dream right now. That might change, but you know as well as I do that we have to make decisions that are best for us as individuals. You've said that to me often enough, right?"

Nodding, I use my shirt sleeve to wipe the tears from my face.

"I want a woman in my life who wants children, who isn't interested in a career other than wife and mom—a woman I will never have to worry about what kind of trouble she will get into next. I won't have to hold my breath every time she walks out the door because I fear she won't return."

He pulls me back into his arms. I nod into his chest and mumble, "You already have someone in mind, don't you?"

"She will never take your place, Cat, but it's time. I'll stay through this operation. I'll do everything in my power to protect you. When it's all over, I'll personally put you on the plane home. That's all I can do."

Words I long to say remain buried. He's right. We have danced around our relationship long enough. My entire body aches. The words 'I'll stay' lodge in my throat and die there. The longing to change my entire life to be with him is strong. But if I do, over time, the relationship will erode. My life and my career are things I fought and suffered to obtain. Lorenzo and I are alike in that respect. We refuse to give up our dreams.

We cling to each other, and then we step apart. Tears gather in his eyes. He squeezes my hands and turns away. I stay rooted on the terrace until I hear the gate clang. It's over, and I was too stubborn to tell him I love him. No, I think, it was the right thing to do. If I'd said those words, we would have been right back at the beginning with no place to go. It's over. This time, there will be no resurrection.

61

Matera

The weekend, other than a quick bite to eat, is mostly spent in bed. Isabella doesn't mention the kidnapping to Marco until Sunday afternoon when she's packing. His eyes follow her as she moves back and forth across the room. After she zips up the tote, she sits on the bed and pats the space next to her.

"Marco, are you with me or not? It's not an easy thing I'm asking. You're concerned about throwing away your career with the Guardia. You must realize that whatever jobs you did for me, you were doing for the mafia—specifically for Riccardo, whose plan includes murdering Cat. At some point, that will all come out. Whatever expectations you had for a brilliant career will be over."

Misery crosses Marco's face. He thinks he loves Isabella, but *mio dio* she was a prostitute. *How had he fallen in love with a prostitute? And now she's planning to kidnap a kid. What sane person does this?*

"I need more time. That's why I came here. Why don't you kidnap Cat? I'd be okay with that. A little kid shouldn't be involved."

Isabella shakes her head.

"You know Cat is being watched around the clock. How do you suggest we kidnap her? Look, the kid won't be hurt. Cat loves him and his family. She'll meet me, give me the necklace, and the boy will be released unharmed. We'll be out of the country and start a new life."

Marco tugs at his shirt, pulls at his hair and frowns.

"It sounds good, but a million things could go wrong."

"They won't. Wednesday, I'll bring him here unless you've changed your mind. Are you telling me not to come?"

"No, maybe, I need more time. Can you give me until Tuesday evening? I can't afford to make the wrong decision."

Isabella pulls her hair into a knot and secures it with a barrette.

"Okay, but I'm counting on you, Marco. If you want us to escape together, then stock up on food a kid would eat and games. We'll stay here twenty-four hours and then move out to the next safe house. It's already stocked."

"Where's that?"

"You'll know when it's time to move. After we make the second move, and I'm sure we haven't been followed, I'll arrange to meet Cat and get the necklace. While I'm doing that, you'll move Giorgino to the last safe house."

Marco cuffs and uncuffs the sleeve of his shirt as Isabella lays out her plans.

"We'll have to keep the kid sedated until we're ready to board the boat. Just before we leave him, we'll give him a dose of sleeping powder and release the restraints. You'll text Commissario Faena and tell him you've seen the kid."

"Why would I text the commissario? Won't that make him suspicious?"

"Why would it? You simply say you saw a woman with a little boy that fits the description. You'll ask for backup and give him an address. We'll be long gone before they figure out what happened, and the kid will be reunited with his family."

Marco shrugs and nods okay. Isabella touches his face and runs her fingers over his lips.

"It will be worth it. You'll see."

62

Castello

Lorenzo picks up his mobile and scrolls through the contacts until he comes to the Guardia di Finanza in Tuscany.

"Davide, how are things in your area?"

"Ah, Lorenzo. I should be asking you the same question. Is the redhead Wonder Woman still causing you grief?"

"Well, at the moment she's staying put, but we're watching her 24/7. She really can't move without my knowing about it."

"Ha, I suspect she's planning a great escape. I don't trust her one bit. She's a hard one to keep track of. I don't envy you."

"Look, Davide, have you noticed any mafia activity? I mean more than usual?"

"No, in fact, it's been too quiet since Cat left us. What are you thinking? Is there something I need to be on the lookout for."

"I'm not sure. It's quiet here as well. No activity at all which is strange. One of the reasons I'm calling is I need to speak to Marco, but I wanted to clear it with you first. He probably spent more time with Cat than anyone else when she was at the resort. I've been meaning to follow up with him. The thing is, he doesn't answer the number I have for him. Why is that?"

Davide's hearty laugh echoes through the phone. "Always the investigator—don't worry—he's on vacation. When he was walking out the door, he told me he was leaving his work phone in the desk drawer."

Lorenzo leans back in his chair and takes a sip of coffee. "Why's that?"

"He said babysitting Cat had changed how he felt about the Guardia. He wanted time to think about his career without being interrupted."

"Was he serious or joking?"

"I'm not sure. He was up for promotion a few months back, and I chose another officer. He was angry. Maybe he'll ask for a transfer to your jurisdiction."

"Well, he seems like a good man. With your okay, I wouldn't mind taking him if he decides to transfer."

Davide fiddles with the paperclips on his desk.

"I don't know. One of the guys working with him at the resort seemed to think he was overly fond of Cat. And another thought he was hot for one of the employees. Neither had proof, and I don't listen to gossip. But when he came into my office and asked for time off, he sure had a hangdog look."

Lorenzo wonders if any of this is relevant to the case, but it's often the smallest piece of information that solves the puzzle.

"I hope during his time away, he realizes how fortunate he is to be working for you."

"I hope so, too, because he hinted at requesting a sabbatical or possibly resigning. I'm not sure what's going on, but I thought it best to give him some time off. Let him rethink things. He's a good officer, but managing a posh resort was a bit more than he bargained for."

"He has the look of a smooth operator. He was a much better choice than you would have been with your ugly face and 1980 outfits."

Davide laughs.

"Well, he might have fit the description of a resort manager, but throw Cat in that mix along with the very disgruntled Gladys Hickman, and it was a firestorm. No amount of training could have prepared him for those two. So I'm not too sure what direction he will choose."

"Let's hope we don't lose a good man. Is there any way I can reach him?"

"He said he was going home. Not sure where that is—somewhere in the south probably closer to you than me. I'll check his personnel file and text you the address."

"Sure, thanks. Oh, Davide, while you're looking at records, see if you have anything on a Sofia Vallario."

"Anything specific?"

"No," Lorenzo hesitates before deciding between fact and fiction. He chooses fiction. "Her name turned up in case. It's just a routine check. No hurry, and thanks."

"Sure, I'll be back in touch."

Lorenzo clicks off the call and wonders why he didn't tell Davide that Sofia is the woman he's seeing with thoughts of a long-term relationship. He could have looked up the information but felt it might be invasive. He didn't want Sofia to know he was checking on her. If later on she found out someone was researching her, the request would show another officer's name on the paperwork. He needs to spend more time with her. Learn more about her. She seems too good to be true, and that makes him suspicious.

63

La Cucina di Nonna Tina's is my go-to place for comfort food. Chiara texted earlier to say she'd be a few minutes late, but to go ahead and order her a glass of wine.

It's a short walk down the Lungomare. I pause often to soak in the sun and the beautiful Adriatic, which today is a brilliant turquoise with undertones of aquamarine. The guard hovers in the background. He's irritated with my slow stroll and having the job of babysitting me.

As I turn away from the splendid view, Francesco, the owner, sees me and waves me over. After cheek kisses, I slide into my usual corner booth. I order a bottle of Aka because Chiara mentioned it's her favorite. Plus, I'm hoping, much to my guard's chagrin, that we'll have time for a leisurely lunch. It's the first time Chiara and I've had a chance to meet alone.

My text pings again. *I'm on the way.*

And she is. She rushes through the crowds of tourists. Her hair, a mass of brown tangled curls, moves with the breeze. She wears loose-fitting clothes to accommodate long hours creating mosaics, giving classes, and interacting with the public. Marble dust is scattered across her cheeks, in her hair, and on her olive green blouse.

She arrives in a flurry and bends to embrace me. Her eyes are bright, her cheeks are flushed, and she's gasping for breath.

"I'm so sorry. People came to the shop just as I was closing. They said they knew exactly what they wanted and would only take a moment. Ahhhh, they lied."

She drops her purse and then herself into the seat across from me.

"Mamma mia! I believed them and let them in. After closer inspection, they decided the piece wasn't exactly right, and maybe they should look around a bit more. Sometimes, it is so difficult not to be rude. Of course, I cannot afford to ruin my reputation, so I smile and listen and make suggestions. And guess what? They leave without making a purchase."

During this exchange, Chiara's well-worn hands flutter in a language all their own. Suddenly, she looks at me and laughs, "But you see, I am here with you, so all is okay. *Come va?*"

And just like that, she leaves behind her frustration. Our conversation sprinkles the air with lightheartedness until after our order is taken.

"I'm sure you are curious about me. You wonder if a successful woman from Milano can be satisfied in a small town with a doctor who's been incarcerated. *Non è vero?* Isn't that true?"

There's no point in hedging, so I say, "Yes, that's true, but only partially. You were so kind to me the first time we met. I want to know who you are because I'm interested. I'm sure you're curious about me too and even more about Stella. *Non è vero?*"

She laughs with delight. "Yes, of course. I want to know about Stella. I've had Antonio's version and Maria's, but no one knew her better than you. You will show me the real Stella. You will tell me if I'm wasting my time competing with a ghost."

The waiter arrives with two steaming vessels of *Tajeddha*, the house specialty and my favorite. The crock is loaded with layers of thinly sliced onions, potatoes, mussels, rice, tomato sauce and topped with a mixture of bread crumbs, parmesan, chopped parsley, seasonings and drizzled with olive oil—it's baked to perfection and then broiled so the top is crusty and gooey.

The Aka rosato pairs perfectly. Our table by the sea allows us privacy. The waiter, following Francesco's instructions, doesn't seat anyone near us. Service in Italy is all about allowing people to enjoy their food and never feel rushed.

We dig into our *Tajeddha* while it's hot with only an occasional comment. Chunks of the olive-studded bread sop up every morsel. I pick up my wine glass, lean back against the cushioned bench, and sigh with contentment.

"Salute, Chiara."

She takes her last bite, wipes her mouth and raises her glass.

"Salute, Cat."

After sucking in a deep breath, I begin.

"We were so young. Both of us were in love with Lorenzo. He was a demigod to teenage girls—tall, bronze skin, muscular, a smile that made each person feel special. He chose Stella. It broke my heart for two reasons."

I stop. It feels too personal—I guess it still hurts. Chiara leans across the table and takes my hand.

"This is causing you pain. We must talk about something else. I do not wish to hurt you."

"No, it's really okay. I should be over it by now. I loved Lorenzo, too, but Stella was my best friend. I didn't fight for him. Then she dumped him for Antonio."

"Oh, no one told me Antonio was not her first choice. A love triangle, no?"

"Yes, and one that was never resolved. Stella chose money over love. She knew from birth that she was destined to be a star. She saw Antonio as a step to make that dream come true. His royal connection was too much to turn down. She scripted the entire romance and wedding only to discover when she woke up, she didn't love Antonio —never had."

Chiara sighs and takes a large gulp of wine.

"She broke him, didn't she?"

"In a way, she finished what his family had started. He was willing to do a lot for her, but he withheld a lot, too. His family interfered, and he let that happen. They considered themselves superior to Stella. They made her life miserable. He worked six days a week and would spend every Sunday with his family. Stella drifted away and turned inward. She turned to drugs to ease the pain of her tortured soul. For a long time, Antonio supplied her the drugs because he felt guilty for neglecting her. When he realized what he'd done, he cut her off. She turned to the mafia for her fix. You know the rest, I'm sure."

Chiara pushes her fork into the crock. She picks up and discards the remains of rice and potato.

"Yes. He told me he was indicted for the illegal distribution of drugs, but thanks to your testimony and Lorenzo's his sentence was reduced and his license was only suspended not revoked. Why did you do that for him?"

"For a lot of reasons. He accepted Giorgino as a patient when sickle cell disease was first diagnosed. Giorgino's grandparents and parents are as dear to me as they were to Stella. Antonio gave that family hope."

Chiara smiled and nodded so I continued.

"Stella was more than Antonio could handle. She was needy and required too much from him or anyone. When the dust settled, I realized this community needed a doctor. To let my personal feelings prevent him from practicing would be wrong. Besides, he's a good man who made bad decisions."

"How do you see Antonio now? Broken or healed?"

"On the road to recovery. He was broken, but from what I've seen, you've given him hope that love is possible. Do you love him?"

She smiles a slow smile, starting with a tilt at the corner of her mouth until it blooms in her eyes.

"Yes, but I'm not sure it's enough for both of us to love again. When your heart is bruised and broken, trust isn't easy to obtain. I lived with a man in Milano for years. I believed we had a happy, normal relationship, only to discover he was married and had a wife and children in Turin. So loving someone is tricky business."

"Hmmm, I understand. Every time I give it a try, I fail. Either I meet the right man, but the timing is wrong, or the timing is right, but it's the wrong man."

"And it's not right for you and Lorenzo?"

"No, and it won't be."

"I'm sorry. You clearly love each other."

"True, but we live in different worlds, and neither of us is willing to compromise."

64

At four o'clock, Isabella hears footsteps in the hallway. The principal peeps in and waves. Isabella smiles and waves back. She sighs with relief. The principal is always the last person to leave the building. Still, she waits another half hour to be sure no one sees them leave.

The visit with Marco lingers. She questions whether or not he'll come through for her. She understands that kidnapping a kid is repulsive to him. But he crossed the line when he took on the jobs she'd given him. The Guardia would discover his betrayal, and he'd serve time. And there's no place for him in the mafia. Riccardo would laugh in his face and shoot him in the back.

She checks Giorgino's homework and assigns him the task of picking up trash around the desks while she pretends to read through the next day's lesson plan. Her thoughts are interrupted when the last bell of the day rings. The room is too quiet. She looks up. Giorgino is slumped at a desk in the back of the room.

"Giorgino! What's wrong?"

He doesn't respond. She runs to him and touches his shoulder. He pushes her hand away. "I don't feel good. I want to go home."

She feels his brow. The heat against her hand isn't a good sign. Oh crap, just what she needs—a sick kid. She sits in the chair next to him.

"Giorgino, is it time for one of your medications?"

"No, I want to go home. Call my Mamma."

"Your mamma is working. Why don't we go for a gelato? That will make you feel better."

A soft wail comes from his core.

"I want my Mamma."

Maybe Marco was right, involving a kid isn't the best way to break free of Riccardo. Children are unpredictable, but it's the only chance she has to get out of the mess she's in. Riccardo will soon discard her. She has five days before she has to deliver Giorgino to Riccardo. She silently prays it's enough time for her to make this plan work. But with a sick kid, she's not sure what to do.

Every single step is timed. Five days is just enough time to take Giorgino to Marco, send the ransom note, meet Cat to retrieve the necklace, and leave the country. She can't delay her plans for a minute, even if the kid is sick. After all she's been through, her life is worth more than his. She has to manage this new glitch.

"Tell you what. Put your head back on the desk. I'll call your mamma. If she says it's okay, I'll drive you over to the high school. That will be quicker than waiting for her to pick you up. Let me get you a Coke, then I'll make the call."

The only sound is a sob.

Isabella rushes into the small storage area off the classroom. She composes a text to the teacher.

> Received emergency call. Mia zia fell.
> Transported to the hospital in Bari.
> Dropping Giorgino off at the high school to
> his mother. She's expecting him. Need a
> few days off. Contact you Monday with
> further details.

She puts the text in draft. She'll send it once they're on the road. Next, she drafts a text to Annalisa.

> Sorry to do this, but my aunt fell and was
> rushed to the hospital in Bari. I'm bringing
> Giorgino to you around six.

This text also goes to her draft file. Satisfied, she opens the fridge and removes and opens a can of Coke. She fishes around in her purse, pulls out a packet of white powder, and dumps it in a glass. She adds the soda and stirs until the powder dissolves. She wipes down the counter to make sure no traces of the powder are left behind. She surveys the room to ensure nothing is out of place.

She closes the door, walks to the desk, and places her hand on Giorgino's shoulder.

"Giorgino, I have a Coke for you. Take a sip. You'll feel better right away. When you finish, I'll drive you to the high school. Your mamma will be waiting for you. She'll take you home."

She waits until he swallows the last bit of the doctored beverage then returns to the storage room, washes and dries the glass and returns it to the back of the cabinet. Panic rises in her throat when she walks back in the classroom and Giorgino is slumped at his desk. She gently shakes him.

"Okay, let's go. I'm parked behind the stadium. Can you make it that far?"

She hopes the amount of sleeping powder isn't too much.

Giorgino struggles to pick up his backpack.

"Sì, Signorina. I can walk."

She lifts the backpack from his shoulder and slings it over her own before opening the classroom door. She checks in all directions. When she's sure no one is in sight, she takes his hand and guides him to a side door.

His small hand trembles in hers. He stumbles but stays upright. When they reach the car, she props him against the door. Once she unlocks the car, she throws his backpack in the passenger seat before opening the back door. She steers him onto the seat and gives a little shove. He collapses. She grabs a pillow from the floor and shoves it under his head and covers him with a blanket.

After sliding into the driver's seat, she pulls out her phone and clicks on a number.

"Okay, I have him. If all goes well, I'll be in Matera in a few hours. It could be later as I'm taking the back roads. But there's a problem. He has a fever."

The silence is broken on Marco's end.

"How sick is he? What do you plan to do?"

"I thought maybe you'd have a suggestion. I don't know what to do with a sick child."

"Maybe you can find a pharmacy and get something to reduce the fever. Be careful. If Riccardo's on to you, he'll have a tail on you. Be vigilant. If you see anyone following, don't come here."

"Where would I go?"

"Don't you have another safe house?"

"Yes, but the drive is further."

"Isabella, if you're followed, don't bring him here. Do you understand?"

Isabella ends the call. A lot of help he is, she thinks as she starts the engine and pulls onto the road.

Instead of heading to Lecce, which would be the shorter route, she turns toward Nardó and the back roads to Taranto. Her plans include using the back roads all the way to Matera. She maintains the speed limit until she turns off the main highway.

She drives until she finds a clump of trees. The car bumps off the road. She opens the door and walks back to the road to make sure the car can't be seen. She checks on Giorgino. He's still out, but his pulse is steady, and his head isn't as hot.

She waits fifteen minutes to make sure no one is following her, and then she sends the two drafted texts. It's only five, so she'll be further away before Analisa becomes concerned. Next, she hunts through Giorgino's backpack. She feels stupid when her fingers close around a prescription bottle. Of course, he'd have his medications with him. She reads the directions before jostling him awake long enough to swallow a pill.

His cell phone is in a side pocket. She pulls it out and sees Analisa sent him a text. She says she'll be waiting for him at the front door at six. Isabella thinks a minute and decides she needs more time. She texts:

> Nonna & Nonno picked me up from school I can spend the night okay

65

My nightmare fades into reality when pounding on the door and yelling pull me out of the crazy, circular dreams that drain me of sleep most nights. Either I'm under siege by some unknown enemy, or the guards recognized the person who's going to kill me and let them through the gate. I glance at the clock. It's just after midnight.

In seconds I throw on jeans and a shirt and race to the door. Maria, Gino, Analisa and Enrico are gathered in a knot behind Lorenzo, who is intent on beating my door down.

"What? What's happened?"

Maria and Analisa are clutching each other and sobbing.

The whole group files into the house. One look at Lorenzo and alarm bells and whistles bombard my ears.

"Lorenzo, why are you here?"

"Giorgino is missing. Has he contacted you?"

"No, but let me look at my phone. Maybe I missed a message."

Analisa lets loose with a wail full of grief and angst. Tears flow as she cries out, "He's our baby! He's sick!"

"Lorenzo? What happened?"

Lorenzo's phone buzzes. He steps away from the group. Everyone starts to talk at the same time.

"He stayed after school."

"Signorina Lucrezia was supposed to drop him off at the high school."

"She texted."

"He texted."

"Stop!" I shout over the disjointed explanations.

My eyes rush over the group until they land on Gino. He appears reasonably calm.

"Gino, tell me what happened. Everyone else sit down."

Gino clears his throat and begins, "Giorgino stayed in the after-school program with the new assistant teacher, Signorina Lucrezia Barone. She texted Analisa with a message saying she had a family emergency and needed to drop Giorgino off at the high school earlier than anticipated. But she never dropped him off."

Analisa's wail interrupts. "He's just a little boy. He's sick. Where could he be?"

Maria grabs her in a strong embrace. "Hush! We'll find him."

Gino continues, "Later, Giorgino texted Analisa and said he was spending the night with us. That's not unusual, so she wasn't alarmed. Around eight, after Analisa returned home, she called Maria and asked if Giorgino was feeling okay. That's when we discovered he was missing."

The room is deadly silent until Lorenzo returns and takes over. I look in his direction and ask, "What's been done so far to find him?"

Creases I've never seen before gather around Lorenzo's eyes and his mouth. It hits me hard that my pilgrimage to celebrate Stella's life is probably at the bottom of Giorgino's disappearance. I pray I'm wrong.

Lorenzo begins a litany of facts.

"We searched the school. No one saw them leave. The principal was the last one to see them, around four. She said they were both in the classroom, and everything seemed to be okay."

"Do you think something happened to both of them or did Giorgino leave the classroom and wander off without her knowledge? Maybe she's looking for him? What about her car?"

"That's the funny thing. She didn't register one for a parking pass, so there's no information—no license number, nothing. I've sent out an alert and requested information from Milano on Lucrezia Cristina Barone to see if she's registered anywhere."

Analisa quits sobbing long enough to say, "She's dropped him off at the high school before, but I never noticed the car—only that it was dark—either navy or black. I knew something was wrong with her, and I still recommended her. This is all my fault."

Enrico pulls Analisa into his arms.

"Hush, we have to stay calm and think about the possibilities. Who is this woman? Why would she take him? Where would she take him? Lorenzo, what do we do now?"

All eyes turn to Lorenzo. He exudes calmness, but the muscles in his jaw twitch. He probably doesn't wish to discuss his plans in front of all of us.

He quietly says, "Analisa, can you write down a timeline for all the texts and then add the last time each of you saw Giorgino? We need to know what he wore to school today and what's in his backpack unless that was left behind. Does he have his medication, and does he know when to take it? Cat, we need coffee. I'll help you."

Once in the kitchen, I ask, "How many hours has it been?"

"The closest we can tell is between six to eight hours. We contacted the teacher. She said she left the classroom right after Giorgino arrived, which was around three. And the principal saw both of them in the classroom around four."

"Were there any signs of a struggle?"

"No, but Lucrezia is the only one who had an opportunity to take him. I'm not sure why—maybe she wants a child and stupidly thought this would be a good way to get one. If he had just wandered off, she'd let someone know."

"Lorenzo, I think I recognized the woman, but I can't recall who she is or where I've seen her. I only had a quick glimpse of the side of her face, but there was something familiar about her. The strange thing is she left the classroom and didn't return the entire time I was there reading to the children."

He thinks about what I've said and adds, "Analisa said something similar. She told me she interviewed the woman, gave her high marks, and recommended the school hire her, although she had misgivings.

She said she couldn't identify anything in particular, but she felt uneasy about the woman."

I nod in agreement. "Yes, she told me that also. It looks like she may have been right. Okay, what can I do to help?"

"Nothing is what you can do, and you already know why."

I ignore him and continue, "So you think Riccardo is behind this, right? I do, too. I'm guessing this happened because of me. So I have to help. If you won't let me, then I'll find another way."

"Cat, stop! You already know Riccardo plans to kill you. This is a trap. I won't let you walk into it."

"You're right. Riccardo knows I won't tolerate him hurting any of you, but particularly Giorgino. It's his way of manipulating me. Doing nothing won't work. Giorgino is the bait. I'm the target. I'll be hearing from him or one of his people soon, don't you think?"

He shakes his head and doesn't answer right away. He looks for espresso cups and fidgets in the utensil drawer until he finds little spoons and a bowl of sugar.

"You are probably right. He'll want to exchange Giorgino for the real necklace and you. I need to get back to the office, so we can put together a plan where neither of you will be hurt."

"Lorenzo, the game is over. I'm tired of the cat and mouse. He wants me, so that's what you'll give him."

"He'll kill you."

"I know, but I've had a good life. Yes, I'd prefer for it to be much longer, but Giorgino's is just beginning. He's already suffered too much for someone so young. For the first time, he's able to have an almost normal life. We can't let that be taken away from him."

"Cat, everyone's life has value—even yours although there are times when your absence would make my life easier."

I look up and see that he's smiling, but I turn away.

"Riccardo will figure out a way to get a message directly to me. We have to let that happen."

"Okay, but the minute you get his message, you're to let me know.

I'll send you a supply of burner phones with my number coded in. You need to stay in constant contact."

He places his hand on my arm. I push it away.

"No, Lorenzo, I'm not going to stay in contact with you. This is my fault. If I hadn't been so determined to honor Stella's life, none of this would have happened. If anything goes wrong, Riccardo might kill Giorgino."

"But giving him your necklace and yourself doesn't guarantee Giorgino's safety."

Tears threaten to consume me. I refuse to give in to them. My only focus is Giorgino.

"If I do what Riccardo says without interference from you, I believe he'll hand over the child. But he won't do it until he has both me and the necklace. Although Riccardo is despicable, his word is his sacred honor. I'll insist he guarantees Giorgino's safe return. He won't harm him if we give him what he wants."

66

Matera

"I'm going back to Castello."

"Isabella, *Sei pazzo?* Are you crazy? If you show your face, you'll be captured or killed. Is that your goal? Or is this part of your plan I don't know about?"

Isabella glances over at Giorgino. His small body is slumped under a blanket. He's lying on a cot in the far corner of the room, still in a drug-induced sleep.

On the drive over when Giorgino finally woke up, he was so confused and groggy that he didn't question where he was or what they were doing. She assured him she was dropping him off at the high school, and his mamma was waiting for him. She'd given him his meds, doctored his Coke with more sleeping powder and arrived in Matera without having to stop at a pharmacy. She was relieved. If she had stopped at a pharmacy, she could be traced. There was no sign that anyone was following her.

"While they know I kidnapped Giorgino, they won't expect me to return. They'll figure out I work for the mafia. They'll wait for Riccardo to send Cat a ransom note. I've already devised a way to deliver a message to Cat without anyone suspecting it's from me and not Riccardo."

"What will you do with Giorgino? You can't leave him with me? That wasn't part of the plan. You'll get us killed. If Riccardo is even a little bit suspicious of you, he's been tailing you."

Marco paces the room, scowling at Isabella.

"He probably knows you're in Matera. If you go back to Castello, you have to take the boy with you. Then what will you do? Tie him up? Leave him in your car? Stash him in a room? Riccardo will find you."

"Don't panic, Marco. There's enough time to pull it off before Riccardo becomes suspicious. I have five days to deliver Giorgino to him. He's in no hurry to kill Cat. His only interest now is to make Cat suffer. He wants to break her before he kills her. He'll dangle Giorgino's life in front of her. What better way to torture her than to kidnap a little boy she loves?"

Marco stares at her and shakes his head.

"I want to help you Isabella, but pretty soon both Riccardo and the Guardia will come after me. Either way, I'll end up dead by Riccardo's hands or imprisoned by the Guardia."

"Marco, there's a way out for both of us, but you have to help me. We'll disappear before either the mafia or the Guardia catch on to what we're doing."

Marco's face is an open book of disbelief.

"If I go back to Castello, I can arrange a meeting with Cat by tomorrow night. Cat will deliver the necklace. We'll deliver the kid. No one will be hurt, and we'll be on our way to another country. I already have a buyer for the necklace in Morocco. No questions asked."

Marco pushes back from the table and opens the door to the tiny balcony overlooking the strange and enchanted city.

"If we do this, there's no turning back. I'll never be able to come home."

"Home? This shit hole of a city where you grew up with nothing?"

She picks up her bag and slings it over her shoulder.

"Think about it, but don't take too long. I'm going to get us something to eat. Make up your mind by the time I return."

♩

Maria and I are side by side in the kitchen. Tension is thick. We don't speak. Every once in a while, Maria sighs. I start another pot of coffee.

Lorenzo returned to the station a few hours ago. Everyone stayed here for the remainder of the night. There was no sleeping. We mostly stared into the fireplace or listened with broken hearts as Analisa and Maria sobbed.

Enrico has murder in his eyes. My fear is if something doesn't break soon, Enrico will take matters into his own hands. He moves back and forth between Analisa and the terrace. He's been busy making calls. At first light he'll be searching.

Lorenzo has made it clear. I'm not to involve myself in any way. What he doesn't understand is that, just like Enrico, I don't have a choice.

♩

Over a giant pizza, Isabella works on Marco. Without his help, her plan won't succeed.

"First, I'll contact Cat. Believe me, she will cooperate. She isn't about to be responsible for this child's death. These people are her family. She'll hand over the necklace. No one will be hurt."

Isabella is surprised when Marco finally speaks.

"Why?"

"Why what?"

"Why did you choose me?"

"*Allora*, Marco. I didn't choose you. Riccardo did. I was just the messenger."

Isabella opens the backpack and pulls out a bunch of papers.

"Look, Riccardo worked for a year from prison on his plan. The meeting in the bar was arranged. You put a target on your back when you showed up at the bar as a disgruntled employee. You're part of his plan, just as I am."

Marco's face goes on alert. He squints, shakes his head in disbelief and asks, "How was I part of the plan?"

"Riccardo needed both of us at the resort to keep tabs on Cat. More than that he needed you to pass on the Guardia's activities. Are you saying you didn't understand that?"

Marco turns to the balcony once more. He steps out and opens his eyes to the place he's always called home. Never once had he ever thought of leaving Italy or betraying the Guardia. Isabella's voice turns the ancient, peaceful view into a nest of vipers.

"Are you listening? We only have a few days. I'm asking you to do this with me. We'll split the proceeds from the necklace. What do you want me to say? That I love you? Okay, I love you. I hope you'll stay with me, but once we reach a safe country, you're free to move on."

He turns back to Isabella and takes in her beauty. He knows she's been through far more than he has. She's offering him a chance to get out and start a new life.

"What about new passports and paperwork?"

She smiled that beguiling smile that had trapped him the first time he'd met her in that bar. He'd been dumb enough to think she was coming on to him. Instead, she had been assigned to turn him.

"Here's your new passport. Here's your plane ticket to Laos. There's also money along with the name of the boat and the time and where we'll meet. In Laos, we can live without fear of extradition or fear that Riccardo will find us. He wants to get out of the business. Killing Cat is his last act. What will make him angry is not obtaining the necklace. He might even consider coming after us, but I don't think he'll find us."

"You don't think he'll find us? You can't be that naive."

"Maybe, but I know him well enough to think he won't bother. It's our only chance to start over. We can live comfortably off the proceeds for a long time. We're a good team, and there will be plenty of freelance work for us."

"Isabella, I took two weeks off after I delivered Cat to Lorenzo, so no one is suspicious of me or what I'm doing. I wanted the time to decide what to do—confess to Davide or join ranks with Riccardo. When you left so suddenly, I decided it was over."

"Ah, you didn't trust me."

"Why would I? You'd tricked me once. Why wouldn't you trick me again? What prevents you from leaving me with the kid, while you take off with the necklace? If the Guardia catches me, I'll serve time. If that happens, Riccardo would find a way to kill me in prison. If I'm caught by Riccardo, which is more likely, I'll be dead before I can beg for mercy. And the kid? What would happen to him?"

Isabella laughs. It was low—more of a smirk than a laugh. "Riccardo has you exactly where he wants you. Don't you understand? Your fear of him has you stalled. I won't let him continue to ruin my life. Don't let him ruin yours."

He walks back to the balcony and looks down at the brightly lit piazza. He loves Matera. It was his birthplace. Although he'd left many years ago, it was the only place that he called home. He'd grown up in poverty and hung out in the caves with the unsavory characters. As soon as he was old enough to hold a gun without dropping it, he began his life of petty crime.

It was either a saint or satan who'd found him and offered him a better life. The armed robbery had gone wrong. The shopkeeper had his own gun pointed at Marco's head. The defining moment was when the guy handed him the gun and said, "You can continue down this path of self-destruction, or you can come work for me."

The sirens were close. He knew if he killed the shopkeeper, he would be taking a step over the line. If he let the shopkeeper turn him in, he'd be in the slammer for years. The shopkeeper was giving him a third choice. One he'd never considered before—a different life. He took that choice, but it turned out to be a mixed blessing.

Because he was a juvenile, his records were sealed and eventually expunged. With the shopkeeper's support, he'd done well in school and then enrolled at the police academy. When the time came, he chose the Guardia di Finanza. His benefactor had died believing he'd done a good deed and turned a wayward child into an upstanding citizen.

But here he was, right back where he'd started. He'd accepted the jobs Isabella had given him so he could supplement his lousy income. Once that happened, he began to live a parallel life between the Guardia and the underground. Now, he was in Riccardo's clutches.

Her offer was tempting, but deep down, he knew and she knew that Riccardo would find them. It might take a year or two, but in the end they'd be dead.

He turned back to face her.

"What if we kill Riccardo first?"

67

Now is one of those times when I question my intelligence and my sanity. The note in my hands is creased from numerous readings. Uncontrolled shivers torment me. Each time I read the words, I shrink back as if a venomous snake is ready to strike.

What can I possibly do? Call Lorenzo? Ask him to come back? Call Gino? No, he would involve Enrico.

If I were reasonably sane, I would turn the note over to the Guardia, but Giorgino's life is in the balance. Lorenzo made it clear he isn't providing anything for me other than protection. I'm sure he's angry that protecting me takes valuable resources away from finding Giorgino.

If Lorenzo read this note, he'd tie me down. If that happens, Giorgino's life will be over. Contacting Gino won't work either, as he's out of his mind with worry. He'd insist on going with me to save Giorgino. I have to go alone.

My mind replays over and over what we all could have done to prevent Giorgino's kidnapping. Analisa's intuition was correct, as was mine when I thought the woman in the classroom looked familiar. But neither of us pursued what we considered minor concerns.

While we all knew Riccardo would stop at nothing to get to me, not one of us considered he'd be so evil as to kidnap a child. The only choice left for me is to follow through. No one else can do this but me. I have only a few hours to prepare.

The note was left on the terrace sometime during the night. I woke at one point but only heard the hoot of an owl and a low buzz, maybe a small plane. There were no other sounds. The only people who have keys are Lorenzo, Gino and Maria. The note did not come from any of them. Does that mean one of the guards works for Riccardo?

The note flutters in the evening breeze.

MEET ME MIDNIGHT FRIDAY
CHAPEL OF THE SKULLS
BRING THE NECKLACE IF YOU WANT GIORGINO ALIVE

There is no choice. I have to go. I cannot risk the life of an innocent child.

♩

For the next few hours, I work on putting together a plan so I can leave the villa without anyone knowing. The sun hides under encroaching clouds as I practice descending the crumbling stone staircase. I slip a couple of times and hold my breath for fear the guards might hear me. The sea birds continue to circle, and no one appears. My shins have knots and bruises, but I reach the bottom without killing myself or causing too much pain.

Days ago, I discovered a small tunnel after the last step. While I count and organize utensils, I've never thought of myself as particularly claustrophobic. But the thought of forcing my body into that tiny space is a nightmare I don't want to live. Except I have to.

With a mask and headlight, I start my exploration. With every move, dirt dislodges and blinds me. Creepy things slither next to me. Waves of nausea and fear race through my body. Reaching the end is my only thought.

Focus on the light, I mumble over and over. Move, move, move. The tunnel finally comes to an end, with a tangle of shrubbery covering the exit. What little I can see looks like the parking lot of L'Aragonese.

I shimmy in reverse, praying I won't get stuck. As I move backwards through the tunnel, the thought comes to me that I'll be using this escape not to find freedom but to meet my death.

♩

Today, a mask, a headlight, and hedge cutters are arranged on the table—my tools for tonight. Nothing can prevent me from the rendezvous at the Chapel of Skulls. I make an espresso and wait.

Before Giorgino was kidnapped, Maria and Analisa stopped by or called everyday. Now I hear nothing from Analisa and very little from Maria. I'm the reason Giorgino was kidnapped. I understand their anger.

The entire village, with Enrico and Gino just steps behind the Guardia, is searching for Giorgino. Lorenzo alerted all law enforcement agencies, and an amber alert has been posted. Officers from other regions have joined the search on their days off.

I stare at the note again. Something niggles in my mind. It seems far too benign—not at all Riccardo's style. The language is more matter-of-fact without malice. Riccardo's style is to make his prey suffer—drag the agony out. He'd send me pieces of Giorgino's clothing or his backpack, or in the worst case, he'd send an ear or a finger. He would be brutal. This note is clear about what I'm to do and when. The threat level is low.

If Riccardo is behind the kidnapping, then perhaps the woman at the school is working for him. Maybe she sent the note at his direction. I place myself in the woman's shoes and follow her from the classroom to a car placed out of sight. *Where would I go with a small child?*

Since the kidnapper wants the necklace, Giorgino was probably taken to a safe house somewhere close by. *But what if the woman is working alone? What if Riccardo isn't aware of her actions?* I focus on the woman's face—the hair, the eyes, the clothes. Recognition is close, but it slips away until a lightbulb goes off.

I place a call to Analisa, but it goes to voice mail. She's probably with her mother so I call Maria. My heart breaks with her hesitation to take my call and the abrupt voice saying *Pronto!*

"Maria, I know this is my fault. I'm so sorry. But I want to help. Can you ask Analisa a question for me?"

No one seems to be at the other end.

"Sì, what do you need?"

I fight back the tears.

"Please ask Analisa if the resumés of the candidates had photos attached."

When Maria repeats the question, I hear Analisa shout, "Yes! I'll go to the school now."

Before I change my mind, I shout, "I'll meet you there."

The guard yells as I pass him at full speed. I'm at the door to the school before he catches up. I don't wait but push through the door and race down the hall to the principal's office. Relief clutches my heart, but it's short-lived. Analisa is already there and has learned that Lorenzo thought of this possibility before we did. The good news is the school's secretary is a friend of Analisa's and shares what she knows.

When she pulled the file on Lucrezia Cristina Barone for Lorenzo, the resumé and photo were missing. The concerned secretary, mindful of Analisa's agony, tells us she remembers the name of the Signorina's employee and provided Lorenzo with the information. When he stepped outside her office to make the call, she couldn't help but overhear the conversation. I want to roll my eyes but catch myself in time.

Our hearts sink when she says, "Lucrezia's boss confirmed she's a real person, and that she's also on sabbatical from the Natural History Museum in Milan."

With a shy smile the secretary says, "But listen! This is the best part. Lucrezia's boss said she's conducting research in Africa. He sent a photo of the real Lucrezia. It wasn't a good match for the woman the school had hired. Isn't that great news?"

Analisa is pale. Silent tears trickle down her cheeks as she walks away. I thank the secretary and hurry to catch up. Our steps are hollow against the pavers as we approach the car lot. The guard trails behind as I'm sure he's on his cell, providing Lorenzo with a blow-by-blow description of my escape.

"This is my fault, Analisa. If I hadn't returned, Giorgino would not have been kidnapped. Saying I'm sorry isn't enough, but it's all I can do—along with my promise that I will do everything to bring him home safely."

Analisa leans against her car. She turns her face away from me and sobs. I stand very still. It would be foolish of me to try to comfort her.

When she starts speaking, she doesn't look at me.

"Maybe one day I can forgive you, but right now, I can't. I know it wasn't intentional on your part. I know it was Signorina Barone who kidnapped him. I must also accept part of the blame. But still, what you say is true. If you hadn't returned, this would not have happened. I can't think past that."

She walks to the other side of her car and drives away without looking back. I can only hope that Giorgino is found alive and healthy. If so, maybe time will heal this open wound between us. If something happens to him, there will be no room in their lives for me. I push the negative thoughts away and focus on what to do next, which is nothing since the guard has me by the arm and is pulling me down the street.

♩

It doesn't take long for Analisa to let Enrico and Gino know that Lucrezia is probably the person who kidnapped Giorgino. They storm the Guardia. Lorenzo calls me to join them. He explains that he doesn't have the time or the inclination to keep us informed. Analisa weeps. Enrico scowls. Gino is furious. Maria gives him a piece of her mind. I'm quiet as I look at the photo of the real Lucrezia against the frumpy, contrived look of the woman in the classroom.

A weird question comes to mind, so I ask, "Have you contacted the people at the resort where I stayed?"

Lorenzo looks puzzled.

"No, why should I?'

"I don't have a reason. It's just that maybe someone there would recognize her. Perhaps Marco or one of the drivers?"

"Look, I know you want to help. The best way to do that is stay out of my way. The Guardia is working the case, not you. Please, stop interfering."

Part Three

Vincerò

I Will Win

Visibly shaken, Turandot asks the final question:

The ice that gives you fire, what can it be?"

Calàf tarries, then triumphantly cries

TURANDOT!

~ Turandot, Act III

68

Dressed in black with my red curls tucked under a stocking cap, I slip through the gate in the back garden and teeter on the top step before crouching down. I have thirty minutes before the midnight hour. I concentrate on not sneezing, coughing or falling down the steps.

I stumble and stones scatter. They tumble like giant boulders. The sound reverberates like thunder to my ears, but no one on patrol pauses. At the bottom, I pull back the tangle of brush from the tunnel's entrance and wait. The officer patrolling the area is so quiet I don't hear him until he stops right next to the vines I'm plastered against. I close my eyes and don't breathe. He must not be breathing either. There's only a whisper of movement when he leaves the area. I wait five minutes before I open my eyes and start the treacherous descent into the tunnel.

My fear is far greater at night. Only the thought of Giorgino keeps me moving forward. When my head butts against thick vines, I pull the clippers from my jacket pocket. There's little room to do much but hack, heave, and hope.

When the opening is large enough, I squeeze through. After standing, I breathe in the cool air until my heart settles. I brush dirt and leaves off my body. Then I reach back and pull the vines over the hole.

The night air is soft and wet. The sea crashes against the rocks just a few steps away. I check for movement. Seeing none, I trot to the end of the parking lot and climb the stairs. My face and body flatten against the still warm-from-the-sun stones on the wall. I stay smashed against the wall until the patrol passes by. Once out of sight, I rush toward my destiny.

When I reach the cathedral, I climb the side stairs and push against the door. The latch clicks open to the above-ground crypt. Musty odors assail my nostrils. I sneeze. The sound rattles around the hallowed space—loud enough to wake the dead. I step into the small chapel. A dim glow radiates from a few battery-operated candles near the altar. When I release the door, it thuds behind me.

The ancient walls whisper stories I don't want to hear. With Giorgino's face firmly planted in my mind, I force one foot and then the other to move across the marble floor. To reach the Chapel of the Skulls, I have to cross the entire length of the crypt, ascend the stairs and walk down the right aisle of the cathedral. Either I forge ahead, or I turn back.

To quell my sense of doom, I sort through all I know about this place. The crypt dates back to the 11th century. There are 48 cross vaults supported by 42 monolithic columns—some are raw marble, some polished marble. The columns are not original to the cathedral but were recovered from ancient buildings in this region. They date from Antiquity to the early Romanesque period. Some are carved with Christian symbols, some with acanthus or palm leaves, and still others feature animals or monsters.

The most interesting tidbit for me was learning that these columns were not chosen at random. They were selected because of the diversity of the foreign pilgrims traveling through the area. Whether the pilgrim was from the Corinthian, Ionic Asiatic, Egyptian, Islamic, Lebanese, Byzantine or Persian capitals, each would have recognized the style of the column representing their country. It's a clever and astounding display of kindness and diversity, as is the mosaic floor full of religious and pagan symbols.

But the history of this place isn't enough to keep me calm. The craziness of what I'm doing goes around in a never-ending circle. Nothing makes sense. It can't be Riccardo who wrote the note. *What would he gain by stopping the cat-and-mouse game he's playing with me?* The way the note was written, the timing, the meeting place all say it's someone else. But it's someone on the inside. Someone who knows what Riccardo and possibly the Guardia are doing.

I tiptoe past the statue of Mary. Her penetrating eyes reinforce my recklessness in coming to this place. But it's her face that startles me. For a brief second, the face of Giorgino's teaching assistant, Lucrezia, and the face of the Madonna merge. I close my eyes and try to decipher the meaning.

My eyes flutter open as the face of Lucrezia reshapes into Isabella. The pieces fall into place. She's been here all along. At the resort, she eavesdropped on all of my conversations. She knew about the fake necklace. She knows I still have the real one. *But why? Is she a greedy free-lancer? Is she connected to Riccardo? Does Marco know? Lorenzo?*

If it's Isabella who wrote the note, she's placed both of us in a precarious position. Maybe she's the messenger, and her only job is to get the necklace for Riccardo. Which means she won't have Giorgino. The pieces of the puzzle fall to the floor. They scatter like falling leaves. There are no answers. My only choice is to keep moving.

Focusing on something other than my fear has brought me to the stairs leading to the main cathedral. My foot touches the bottom stair, and I begin—one step at a time. At the top, I stop and listen. A faint rustling movement freezes me in place. The cathedral stretches in all directions. The Tree of Life mosaic floor spreads from the narthex to the silver-encased altar. One minute the air is static; the next, it's filled with air currents and whispers. For the first time, I wonder if more than one person is waiting for me.

Every possible bleak thought congregates in my mind as I stand locked in inertia. The bell tower tolls the midnight hour. The low resonance of the bass bong propels me toward the Chapel of the Skulls.

The red glow from the candleholders reflects against the glass cases containing the skulls. The hollowed eye sockets are black pits of despair. The bone fragments shimmer white. The light from the beheading stone is warm and gentle. It belies the brutal truth of its role in the systematic beheading of 800 men and boys.

As I cross the threshold, Isabella rises from behind the altar.

"Put the necklace on the altar," she demands.

"Where is Giorgino?"

"Give me the necklace, and I'll tell you."

Relief at seeing only Isabella tricks me into thinking I'm safe. My sassy mouth opens.

"Isabella, there's no way in hell I'm giving you the necklace without you giving me Giorgino. Do you realize the mess you're in? Are you doing this with Riccardo's blessing? No, I don't think so. I'd say you're motivated by greed."

She moves from behind the altar. In the dimly lit area, the light from the candles plays off the knife clenched in her hand.

"Don't be stupid, Cat. You don't know my history. If you did, you'd know I have nothing to lose. If you don't give me the necklace, I'll kill you and Giorgino. He's nothing but a pest. But it's a fair trade —him for the necklace. Put it on the altar, and I'll let you live. And I'll release the kid."

"Isabella, Giorgino is the only important part of this exchange. I'll gladly give you the necklace. But unless you can magically produce him from behind the altar or he's waiting outside, I won't give you anything. Once I have him with me, the necklace is yours. Until he is safe, there's no deal."

The smirk on her face turns her beauty into ugliness as she advances toward me, the knife lifted in a stabbing position. I back away.

"You have all the answers, don't you, Cat? You think you're smart. You even thought Marco was under your spell. But he isn't. You're stupid and indifferent, and I'm always a step ahead of you. If you keep it up, Giorgino will be killed, and others as well. Give me the necklace and Giorgino will be sleeping in his bed tonight."

While she's talking, I continue to back away. I've forgotten there's a step up into the chapel. My foot drops off into empty space. My arms flail as my feet slide out from under me. Isabella reacts as if I'm trying to escape. She lunges. The knife whizzes past my heart and slides across my arm. It takes seconds for the searing pain to motivate me to run. I heave myself up and rush toward the exit, but it's too late. Her grip is powerful as she grabs me around the neck. The knife digs into my throat. Blood drips onto the mosaic floor.

Her lips press against my ear. "You stupid woman. You don't understand. By trying to trick me, you aren't going to get out of this alive. Where is the necklace?"

Everything Chuck taught me about Krav Maga kicks in. I arch my back, move my right leg forward and swing it with enough force to catch her leg. With every muscle in my body, I pull.

We tumble onto the floor. The knife flies through the air and lands a few feet away. She scrambles for it. I grab her foot. She falls. Her head smashes against the base of a fat cherub. The crack is loud. Then, nothing but the sound of my breathing. A puddle of blood forms around her head. I kneel next to her and search for a pulse—it's there, but barely. *What have I done?*

With the hand that still works, I dial 112. I sob out that a woman fell in the cathedral and needs an ambulance. Then I run.

The horror of what I've done latches onto my brain. I am as evil as the others. I am part of the darkness that invades the human soul. I am one of the slayers who systematically behead one person after another. I have committed this act of violence against another person. If she doesn't survive, I am a murderer.

69

Darkness wraps me in black velvet. The circular nightmares come true. I race through the narrow passageways. Tears blind me. My heart pounds erratically. Blackness engulfs the piazza and all passages leading away.

Fear pumps through my veins. *Do I keep straight? Do I turn? If I turn, which way?* A sob rises in my chest. I push it back. Keep moving roars in my ears. The emergency call I made minutes ago will alert everyone that I'm on the run, a moving target for Riccardo and his minions.

The horror of what I've done latches onto my brain. I am responsible for all this madness. The soul of inhumanity rumbles through the narrow streets. Giorgino's small face invades my darkest thoughts. I have failed him.

Lorenzo warned me not to slip away from the guards he had posted. He was right again, but I could not allow an innocent child to die in my place. If Riccardo sent Isabella, I have signed Giorgino's death sentence. I push forward into another dark passageway. The night and panic thicken around me.

The metallic odor of blood fills the air as I run. Blood saturates my clothes. My hands are covered in stickiness. It drips down my useless arm. With my right hand, I touch the tender spot on my throat and then the knot rising from the cut on my forehead.

If Isabella dies, I am a murderer—the slayer of another human. I am not so different from the Ottomans who decapitated 800—one or eight hundred. It is still murder.

As I reach the piazza, the wind shifts. The clouds move away from the moon and reveal dark figures moving in my direction. Panic ratchets up my throat as the shadowy arms reach for me—sucking me into their evil vortex. There is no escape. I am powerless to stop those who will kill me.

I turn back toward the darkness and spot a small opening. As I slip through the narrow passage, a large hand covers my mouth, an arm encircles my waist and pulls me inside an arched doorway. No amount of Krav Maga antics on my part allows me to get close enough to the body holding me to render it off balance. A mouth is planted against my ear.

"Don't struggle. It's Luigi. We have seconds before we're overtaken. Run toward the light at the end of this passageway. You'll see the castle. Reinforcement is on the way. When I let you go, run. Your life depends on it."

70

Outside of Castello

Giorgino wakes to the sound of Marco's pacing. He opens one eye and then the other but doesn't say anything. He doesn't know this man. He doesn't see Signorina Lucrezia. His mind feels heavy. He wants something to drink, but he's too frightened to ask. He closes his eyes.

Marco moves back and forth over the rough flooring in the old hunting lodge. Before she left, Isabella handed him a map with directions. She said if she wasn't back by dawn, he was to pack up and move the boy. She assured him the place was completely off the grid. When Isabella didn't return and didn't call, he followed her instructions. He hoped no one saw him carry the kid to the car. He drove them to the lodge near Casamassella, a small town only a few kilometers from Castello.

Just as she said, there were backpacks with enough supplies to get them out of the country. If she didn't show up in 48 hours, he would take the boy to the next location. Then, he'd board the boat to travel across the Strait of Otranto. She told him there would be several burner phones in the backpacks. He was to use one of them to call the Guardia when the boat left the marina.

His message would be short, only to say he spotted the boy being taken into a house and to give them an address. Once he crossed into Albania, he was to keep moving. She gave him a contact in Morocco who would arrange for him to fly to Bangkok, and then on to Laos.

Before she left, she embraced him. He thought she whispered I love you, but he couldn't be sure. She left unspoken that if she didn't return, she would be dead or captured—either way, it meant Riccardo found her. He would be next.

He's not sure what to do. It doesn't seem right to leave the boy alone. Would anyone find him? Maybe he should drop him off somewhere closer to a town? He doesn't want to leave until he knows for certain that Isabella is dead or alive. He realizes he doesn't want to leave without her.

He clicks on his cell and calls one of his off-the-grid contacts. He hopes one of them will know what happened to Isabella.

$$\d$$

A man, hopefully a doctor, is stitching up my nasty knife wound. People hover in the background. Their faces distort and blur. I feel nothing, but I hear a slight buzz—an annoying last-fly-of-the-summer sound. From nowhere, tears flow. My nose grows big, and even in this out-of-body state, I can imagine the red splotches popping up on my face.

"What did you do to her? Why is she crying?"

The man with the big needle keeps on pulling the thread. "Keep calm, Lorenzo. The wound isn't major. First, she's in shock. Second, I gave her enough painkillers to put an elephant under, but she's fighting against them. Third, she's been stabbed. Is that enough, or do you want me to go on?"

Lorenzo squats until his face is level with mine. He takes my hand, turns it over, uncurls my fingers and kisses my palm. I cry harder and louder. Snot is dripping from my nose and lands on our clasped hands. That seems like a deal breaker to me, or at least enough to make him leave. He does, but he returns with a paper towel, wipes my hand and my nose, and pats away my tears that keep right on gushing.

"Ok, Doc. What's the deal?"

"She's lucky. The knife just grazed her enough to split her arm open but not enough to slice the muscles. She'll experience a fair amount of pain for a couple of weeks. I'll send a physical therapist over tomorrow."

"What else?"

"She'll regain about 90% use in a short time. The other 10% will come more slowly, but it'll happen. From these few minutes with her, I'd say she's going to try harder than most. That could do more damage than good. I recommend a watchdog for her."

Lorenzo shakes his head from side to side. "Yeah, that I already know. Anything else?"

"Well, in my professional opinion, she might need a therapist. She keeps repeating that she's a murderer. Do you know what she's talking about? Is that why the Guardia is here?"

I wonder who they're talking about. Their voices ebb and flow. The man with the needle has a flat voice; Lorenzo's voice is deep, heavy with sadness. Voices in the background jumble up with sounds of weeping and other shrill, sharp tones with edges of panic. I quit fighting the drugs and give in to the delicious warmth and safety of sleep.

♩

Lorenzo is in my face again. He hands me a cup of tea. His face is dark and frowny, and he wears a black, dejected look that I've seen before. Well, okay, he has reason. After all, I was able to sneak past the guards—all except Luigi. He's the only one I didn't fool—thankfully.

The other bit of good news besides not being murdered is to discover that I am not a murderer. Isabella didn't die. I didn't kill her. The ambulance arrived in time. She was air-lifted to Bari and is now under guard at the hospital. She has a bad concussion, but she'll survive.

Riccardo, it seems, didn't trust her and was tracking her movements. When he discovered she'd stolen one of his drones, he sent a group of his lieutenants to keep a watch on her. Those were the shadows that I thought were coming after me. They were actually after Isabella. Luigi, who I now realize tracks my every move, showed up with reinforcements from the Guardia and captured some of them.

But Giorgino is still missing. There are no clues as to where he is or who has him. *We know it's probable that Isabella kidnapped him. But who has him now? Riccardo? Who would she trust?* Marco's name comes to mind.

For now Isabella is in an induced coma so we wait. Time is running out.

71

When his mobile rings, Lorenzo reaches over to silence it. He wants to finish the pile of paperwork on his desk and get to the hospital. The swelling and bleeding in Isabella's brain has subsided. The doctors are gradually bringing her out of the induced coma. The hospital is adamant that he not stop by until tomorrow, but he isn't going to wait. Giorgino's life is at stake.

When Commissario Davide Faena's name shows up on the screen, he hits the speaker button.

Pronto.

"Buongiorno, Lorenzo, how are you? What's the status of your cat lady?"

"Ha, you think it's funny that I'm stuck with her. As of this moment, I can report she's behaving. The incident with Isabella subdued her. She thought she'd killed her. What's up? Anything special going down?"

"Can you meet me outside? I'm in the area for a conference. We're on break, so I only have a few minutes. I have the file you requested."

"Thanks, but why don't you come up?"

"Don't have time."

Lorenzo senses an underlying meaning. "Okay, on my way." He shoves the phone in his pocket and takes the back steps two at a time. Davide wouldn't be outside waiting for him if it weren't important.

When he reaches the car, the passenger door is already open. Davide nods and drives out of the parking lot.

"Good grief, Davide. Is all this secrecy necessary?"

Davide glances over at Lorenzo and nods.

"It seems we both have our hands full of women who misbehave."

"What do you mean?"

"Two things. First, we've lost contact with Marco. He's supposed to be vacationing, or as he liked to say, 'recovering' in Matera for a couple of weeks. After a week, he put in a request for more time off which I refused. I told him to report back in after the approved vacation. The two weeks were up on Thursday. He hasn't returned."

"I'm guessing his behavior is unusual?"

"Yes, very unusual. I sent a couple of officers over to check on him, and he wasn't at home. He's disappeared. The neighbors were questioned, but only one whose dog needed to go out late at night said she noticed anything. She said she saw a dark-haired woman and a young boy arrive at Marco's place a couple of nights ago. The description matches Isabella and Giorgino."

"Hmm, if the neighbor did see Isabella and the boy, it sounds like we have a big problem. Somehow, Marco is involved and the intel says Isabella moves in the same circles as Riccardo. Could the neighbor be mistaken?"

Davide pulls into a parking lot behind the Conad Mercato and turns off the engine.

"While I know it's something neither of us wants to do, we need to ask Cat if she noticed anything going on between Isabella and Marco when they were at the resort."

Davide's fingers tap out a drum roll on the steering wheel as he gazes out the window and waits for Lorenzo to respond.

"*Va bene*, I'll check in with her right away."

"Good. Let me know what she says."

While this is an urgent matter, Lorenzo doesn't understand why they couldn't have discussed it over the phone. There has to be more.

"You said you have a file for me?"

"Sorry, Lorenzo, you're not going to like what's in the file. Your friend Sofia leads an interesting life. It took a lot of digging, but her history, while not exactly illegal, is pretty close to the edge."

"How's that?"

"One of her specialties is surveillance. Your office is probably wired. I suggest you have your debugging crew do a thorough check of your office, your home, your phone and your car. The problem is whatever is found can't be traced back to her. She's good at her job."

Heat creeps around Lorenzo's collar and rises up his neck. His first reaction is to spew out every obscenity he can think of but that won't solve the problem.

Davide reaches into the back and hands Lorenzo a file.

"At one time she and Carlo Rossi were involved. There's a strong possibility she's the daughter of the infamous Don Luciano. Seems she and Riccardo both have designs on becoming *il prossimo padrone* so they are enemies. I imagine she didn't tell you about her father."

Lorenzo looks out the window. How could he have been so stupid. He turns back to Davide and says, "No, I interviewed her briefly about a case. I don't recall anything on record about her parents."

"Although you were young, you might remember her father. He was *padrone* about twenty years back—un *figlio di puttana brutale*—a brutal son of a bitch. Based on informants, it appears she has Cat and Riccardo on her hit list—and possibly you as well.

Lorenzo stops perusing the file.

"I'm not following you."

"Which part? That you're on her list, too?"

Lorenzo closes the file and hands it back.

"Yes, why would I be on her list?"

Davide throws the file in the back seat.

"Don't know. Maybe it has something to do with the case you were working on. If you turned your back or left the room, she's the type that would plant a bug. Are you still investigating that case or her?"

"No, but I'll make sure the office is swept. I'll also post a photo of her in case she shows up on our radar."

Davide pats Lorenzo on the shoulder and starts the car.

"Glad you didn't get close to her. It would be easy to do. She's a looker and experienced. I imagine she could charm milk out of a snake."

Lorenzo grunts and turns away from Davide. He hopes he was able to pull off his nonchalant look of not knowing who the woman is and not caring too much. He's seething and needs to get out of the car before he explodes.

72

Every day is full of fear—waiting for Giorgino's body to be found, waiting for Isabella to regain consciousness, waiting for my own death.

My physical therapy sessions are painful. My arm has a mind of its own. The therapist ignores my protests. He pushes, pulls and twists. Maybe it's a trial run on the torture I'll experience at the hands of Riccardo.

With the clock ticking, I want to use my time wisely to map out a plan, starting with how Riccardo will contact me—because he will. I also need to figure out how Isabella got the note to the terrace without being seen. *Or was she seen by someone who allowed it to happen?*

Although the note is evidence, I still haven't given it to Lorenzo. When Isabella goes to trial, it will disclose her malicious intent to harm a child. Yet I hesitate. I've held on to the note too long. When he finds out, it's going to alienate him further. Since I'm not sure I'll be alive much longer, it's crucial that I do the right thing.

I find a notepad and write a short message providing Lorenzo with the details. I attach my note to Isabella's. Both go into an envelope. I seal it, and address it to him.

The biggest part of the puzzle is how Isabella got the note on the terrace. Could she have found the tunnel opening? I don't think so, as Luigi would have seen her like he saw me.

My mind goes around in circles with more questions. *Who is Luigi? Am I the only one who knows him? Has he been questioned? Does he really work for Lorenzo?* Even in my dazed state, I gave him credit for rescuing me, which means Lorenzo has to know him. Yet it's strange that he's never said a word to me.

One Note Murders

When my heart accelerates, and the needle on my level of sanity is bucking into the red zone, I back off my deadly thoughts. Although it's early in the day, and I'm still on pain meds, I pour a healthy splash of red wine and move to the terrace.

The lone tree still stands, waiting for me to recognize the need for deep meditation. Stella found solace here as I did during that frightful time I was searching for her.

Like a one-armed bandit, I place my wine on the table and push one of the chairs closer to the railing. Another one-armed trip to the storage cabinet to pull out the cushion and drag it to the chair is necessary. It's a funny thing, although not haha funny, that I've been remiss in acknowledging the difficulty people with physical challenges deal with every single day of their lives.

How small my life has been. If I'm allowed to live, that will change. Having my life so close to being over is opening me up, particularly my heart. Each heartbreak I've suffered closed the door until even a crack of light and happiness were too painful to let in. Yet we all deserve a stab at goodness. Life is difficult, too difficult to walk alone.

Maybe it's the tree. I gaze at its gnarled branches hung with the last bit of summer greenery. Trees communicate with each other and with humans. They listen and protect. Stella knew to listen. The last time I was here, I heard the message, too.

My mind floods with memories of Al and I standing side by side in the field of Moringa trees. We held our breaths. We listened. The young saplings whispered as they stretched their leafy branches to the sun. That was the first time he'd reached for my hand, and I didn't pull away. A moment that now seems so far away.

The cushiony lounge chair is warm against my body. My eyes and ears tune into the tree. The erratic beating of my heart slows to a normal rhythm. Closing my eyes, I listen deeply. At first, there are normal sounds: the bird tweets, the hum of bees, the occasional car, and a passing conversation.

Then I hear another sound—one that isn't a normal occurrence.

It's the same sound I heard when the doctor was stitching up my arm - that pesky last-fly-of-the-summer sound or maybe it's more like a giant swarm of bees. Without moving, I open one eye and then the other. My head is already tilted back against the cushion. As my eyes adjust to the sun and afternoon shadows, a speck appears on the horizon.

At first, I think it's one of those floater thingies that my eye doctor told me about at the same time she said I needed readers. I blink several times, but the speck grows bigger and the buzzing a little louder.

What the? It's closer now, close enough to solve the mystery. Isabella delivered her message by drone. But that means someone—at least one of these officers had to see it or hear it like I'm seeing it and hearing it now. But maybe it's a drone from the Guardia. That would explain why none of my protectors would take any interest in it or report it.

If Riccardo and also Isabella know the Guardia uses drones for surveillance, then they both would know exactly when to slip a drone into the mix without raising suspicion. Isabella must have been part of Riccardo's original plot to kidnap Giorgino. She would have been privy to his plans. So, it means she also decided to break with him and the mafia. *What if she wants the necklace for herself?*

Clarity arrives. This is how Riccardo's message will come to me. In gratitude, I nod at the tree. I close my eyes, and a sense of *all will be well* surrounds me. A sense that arrives too soon and doesn't hang around.

73

Lorenzo calls and wants to meet for coffee. The Blu Bar is just down the street. The officer is waiting for me at the gate. The constant protection brigade that trails behind me is reminiscent of Marie Antoinette being led to the guillotine.

Lorenzo pastes a halfhearted smile on his face. Pasticciotti is piled high in a basket. As I pull out the chair across from Lorenzo, Giovanni arrives with our cappuccini.

I wait until he leaves before asking, "An hour of freedom? What's the occasion?"

"Cat, I know it's a royal pain to be a prisoner in your own villa. I'm sorry, but until we find Riccardo, I don't have a choice. I thought you could use a break. How's your arm?"

I automatically look at the bandage still swaddling from shoulder to elbow.

"It's better. The stitches came out yesterday. There was a little bleeding, which is why it's covered, but the movement is good. But I'm pretty sure that's not why I'm here. What do you want?"

He looks sheepish before saying, "I need some information."

"Hmm, I see. There are strings attached to my few minutes of freedom, and here I thought it was because of my good behavior."

He laughs. "I'm glad you still have a sense of humor."

"Not really. But I do appreciate being out of the slammer for any opportunity, even to have coffee with you."

I can tell that hurts, but I don't have any magical words to make our time together comfortable.

"Okay, what information do I have to relinquish for this jailbreak?"

His eyes soften, but I'm not having any part of it.

"Let's get it over so I can go back to my cell. What is it you want from me?"

He fiddles with the cream-filled pasticciotto instead of looking at me.

"Tell me everything you heard or observed between Marco and Isabella."

"Well, that's a surprise. But then maybe it isn't. What happened?"

"We think Isabella kidnapped Giorgino and took him to Marco's house in Matera. We have a witness who saw a woman and a little boy show up late at night the same day that Giorgino disappeared."

I take a sip of my coffee and a bite of the sweet, creamy pastry and watch the shop cat across the way stretch in the sun. Lorenzo's voice calls me back.

"Does that seem possible to you?"

"It does. I walked up on them several times. They were close and their body language was intimate."

Anger flashes in his eyes.

"This is all speculative, but we think she wanted the necklace for herself so she could sell it and disappear. While the scheme to kidnap Giorgino was supposed to be Riccardo's way of torturing you, we think she circumvented him. We also think she left Giorgino with someone, and the only candidate we have is Marco."

"While that's a harsh speculation, it's probably the correct one."

We both pick at the pasticciotto.

"Last night I visited her, but she was too groggy to question. I'll try again this afternoon. The thing is, when you tackled her at the cathedral, her plans would have failed unless she had a partner."

"You think that's Marco?"

"Yes, I do, and so does his boss."

There's no point in asking how in the hell Marco got himself involved so I often conjecture.

"But by now, Riccardo knows what she did and possibly where she is. Right?"

"Yes, we're sure he does. I don't have a lot of men to watch her, but there are two on her room and two at the entrance to the hospital. Plus, the security people at the hospital are on alert."

Scenes of walking up on Marco and Isabella surface. When I confronted Marco with their intimacy, I was just guessing. This kidnapping seems to substantiate their relationship. There's no reason to keep their little secret now.

"Initially, I had no proof except for my interpretation of their behavior. Several times, I walked in on them with their heads together. They jumped apart, which gave me the impression they were more than coworkers."

"What else?"

"When I let it slip that the necklace Riccardo stole was fake, Marco's reaction didn't make sense. He was more than surprised. He was angry as if somehow I'd done something wrong. I took a chance that somehow he and Isabella were involved. I pretended I was privy to the affair they were having. I told him I'd report him if he told you or Commissario Faena the necklace was fake."

Lorenzo scrutinizes my face.

"Well, you continually surprise me. How did Marco respond?"

"For a moment, I thought he might hurt me, but he backed off. That's when I realized they were involved. I don't know. Maybe he's a decent guy who's been led astray. Although if he's involved in the kidnapping, he's crossed the line."

Lorenzo sips his espresso and nods.

"All of this means Marco has Giorgino. But where? Any ideas?"

"No. I didn't overhear any of their plans. I was suspicious because neither of them fit the posh resort profile. The only other thing I can add is I felt in danger after I told him I knew about their liaison. For just a moment, it appeared he was ready to murder me or at least hurt me."

His hand reaches across the table for mine but drops back down before it arrives.

"You have that effect on people, Cat. Did you notice anything else? Any small detail that might give us a clue?"

"No, I can't think of any. So much of my time at the resort is a blur. I'm surprised I was astute enough to recognize something was off about their behavior. But from the first day, I was on alert."

"Really? Why?"

"Luigi. You don't send a big, burly guy with bulging muscles and a gun in his waist to pick up a resort guest. Or, in my opinion, you don't."

He nods and says, "Most guests wouldn't notice. You always seem to be looking for people or things to be other than who they're supposed to be. You'd make a good spy."

"Lorenzo, I just want to go home. Catering is my line of work, not espionage."

I take another bite of the half-finished pasticciotto. It's crispy on the outer edges. My teeth sink into the thick, buttery pastry cream. For a moment, I pretend we're still lovers out for our morning coffee. The sun flickers across the corner of our table. Shop owners with brooms briskly sweep thresholds and place colorful displays of products outside their doors.

"There are a few little details, although I don't think they'll help. But since you asked about noticing small clues, here are a few. Isabella was very possessive of Marco during our first meeting, which indicated to me she'd never worked at a posh resort like Casoli. She seemed to think I was a threat—again, strange behavior toward a guest who had just arrived."

For a few seconds I close my eyes. The sun warms my face, and the taste of pastry lingers on my tongue.

"Initially, I thought it was an innocent fling between an employee and management and figured they were headed for trouble if their employer found out. But when Isabella made it clear she could barely tolerate me, it only increased my observation of her behavior."

Giovanni pokes his head out of the door.

Avete bisogno di qualcosa? Do you want anything else?

We shake our heads in unison.

No, grazie.

Lorenzo leans toward me.

"What did you observe?"

"You understand it is only my observation, right?"

He nods.

"When Marco asked me to babysit Mr. Hickman, I became suspicious as that's not something you'd ask a guest to do. I decided he was either at the resort because you hired him to protect me, or he worked for Riccardo and was setting a trap for me."

I pause before saying, "But it was what Isabella said when she didn't know I was eavesdropping on her and the nurse that was the trigger. She asked the nurse to interrogate Mr. Hickman. That put me on high alert."

Lorenzo fiddles with the pastry on his plate.

"It turns out you were right on both counts. Isabella works for Riccardo. Luigi works for me, and Marco is an officer in the Guardia. He works for Commissario Davide Faena. I guess I should say he used to work for Davide. Now he's on the arrest-on-sight list along with Isabella."

I shake my head at the complicated aspects of this debacle.

"When did you learn about Isabella?"

"Only recently. It took a while because her fake paperwork was almost flawless. When we realized she was on Riccardo's payroll, it was too late to change our plans without revealing the Guardia had infiltrated the resort. What we didn't know is that Isabella was the reason behind Marco's sudden interest in the project."

"What do you mean?"

"Well according to Davide, he'd recently passed over Marco for a promotion. He said Marco slacked off after that happened and had made a point of arriving late and leaving early. Then suddenly, he asked to be assigned to the resort as part of your protection force. He fit the description perfectly—elegant dresser, good looks, lots of charm."

My stomach curdles. I drop the pastry back on the plate.

"Any other observations?"

"Oh, yes, when I was in Mr. Hickman's villa, I detected surveillance cameras. That's when my discomfort level changed to high alert. Also, both Isabella and Marco grilled me after I'd been with Mr. Hickman. Again, neither of them had enough savvy to realize that intense questioning of a guest at a posh resort isn't normal behavior."

Lorenzo's head shakes back and forth and sighs.

"Looks like we need to do more specialized training, although throwing people in positions that put them out of their element is a job hazard in our business."

"That's why I'm a caterer and not a spy. You'd have to be a little off-kilter to be someone different every time you receive a new assignment. The saddest part of this whole thing is at some point, Isabella convinced Marco to switch allegiance."

"Yes, as of yesterday, he's an enemy of Italy."

74

My villa used to be like the crossroads of a busy intersection. Maria would appear everyday with food. The door to my refrigerator would groan in protest every time I approached it. Often, Analisa or Gino would come with her. Giorgino would run in and out, and neighbors would drop by with more food. In the past, there was always an abundance of food in the house—not anymore.

The house is silent except for my feet pacing back and forth. Maria occasionally sends food through one of the guards. She never delivers it herself. They have reason to be angry with me, but I miss them.

Tonight I've invited Chiara and Antonio for dinner. They have continued to be visible in my life, and I am grateful. I halfheartedly make ravioli stuffed with mushrooms and ricotta. I toss together a panzanella salad and marinate a piece of branzino that I'll bake in parchment with potatoes, peppers, olives and capers and slices of lemon.

I slip on a pair of black jeans and a red sleeveless blouse and tie my unruly mass of hair with a black ribbon. As I'm setting the table, I hear the gate open.

Chiara calls up the steps. *Sono io, Chiara.*

Greeting her at the top of the steps, I ask, "Where's Antonio?"

"He's coming later," she answers and sniffles at the same time.

"What?"

"I was interrogated this morning."

"Don't you mean questioned?"

"No, yesterday Antonio was interrogated. He came away feeling responsible for Giorgino's disappearance. As if he could have prevented it—that's just foolishness. And today, they did the same to me. I felt like I was the kidnapper."

I pull Chiara into the living room and close the front door.

"I don't understand. I haven't been questioned yet. In fact, everyone seems to be tiptoeing around me as if what I have to say doesn't matter."

"That's really strange. You know more than all of us put together. You know all the players—or at least most of them. What's Lorenzo up to?"

"I have no idea, except he thinks I have a loose screw."

Puzzlement crosses Chiara's face. "*Una vote allentata?A* loose screw? What is this?"

"*Sono Pazzo*! I'm crazy! Which is possible with all the whacks my head has taken. Maybe I'm lucky that my arm was slashed instead of taking another hit to my head."

Chiara laughs until tears drip down her cheeks. "*Allora, capisco—Hai una rotella fuori posto*! I understand. You have a loose screw."

She carefully wraps her arms around me, avoiding my injured arm.

"Oh, Cat. We're all a mess. You most of all. Here I am whining about being treated unfairly by the Guardia, and you've just been through hell and back. Is the therapy okay?"

"*Braccio o testa?* Arm or head?"

Chiara's laughter flies through the apartment. My sadness disappears. We both collapse on the sofa. She sputters, "I need a glass of wine. Please!"

Her laughter follows me to the kitchen. I smile in spite of all the tension that's knotted across my shoulders and in my neck. I raise my voice so Chiara can hear me, "I asked Lorenzo to stop by for a few minutes to give us an update on Isabella. He was supposed to visit her today. Instead, he's sending Luigi, so I asked him to eat with us. Is that okay?"

Chiara joins me in the kitchen. She pops a chunk of caciocavallo in her mouth and reaches into the cabinet for wine glasses. For someone who doesn't cook, she's comfortable in the kitchen. All the ingredients for a charcuterie board are on the counter. Together, we assemble cheeses, nuts, olives, taralli, prosciutto and salami.

"*Si, certo!* We want to know as much as possible so we can be helpful."

Antonio arrives after seeing his last patient. He grumbles about his interrogation by the Guardia. Chiara tells him to hush, as there are more important topics than the inconvenience they suffered at the hands of the Guardia.

The bell to the gate chimes. I hit the release button, and in a few seconds Luigi's large frame appears in the doorway.

It's difficult not to stare at Luigi. He is a surprise. He looks nothing like the person I remember, although I can't say I remember too much about his looks. Tonight, his form-fitting jeans, a navy turtleneck and an aviator jacket made me blink twice before I blush and look away. He takes off his jacket and hands it to me. His muscles flex and ripple and take me back to the first time I saw him at the Florence train station. I was right when I thought he was more than a chauffeur. When I glance up, he's staring at me like he knows what I'm thinking.

Although I'm still not clear about his role, I do know Lorenzo trusts him above all his other officers. By saving my butt after my altercation with Isabella, he's proven to me that he's trustworthy. But then, I never really saw him that night. He'd grabbed me from behind, and once he released me, I'd taken off like he told me to.

He catches me watching him and smiles in such an intimate way that my knees quiver. *What's going on?* His smile says he knows something that no one else knows. *But what?* The only thing I can think of is the drone. He saw it. He must realize that I saw it too. Crap is all I have time to think before Chiara calls from the kitchen.

The meal is a mixture of joy and sadness. We keep the conversation light over wine and the apperitivo. The mushroom ravioli is a success, as is the baked fish. The only thing I didn't prepare was dessert. Maria sent a tiramisu over this morning. I serve it with tiny cups of espresso and fortifying glasses of Amaro or Limoncello.

The table is cleared of everything except the bottles of Amaro and Limoncello.

Chiara speaks first. "Today, I was interrogated by the Guardia."

She turns her angry eyes on Luigi. He holds up his hands and says, "I'm not part of the Guardia. It's why Lorenzo asked me to join all of you tonight. Lorenzo and I have a friendship that goes back many years. We only call on each other in times of severe need. I'm a free-lance contractor. When dealing with the mafia, it's best to have someone on your team who can re-interpret the law."

All eyes remain on Luigi. Finally, Antonio breaks the silence.

"Is there a chance Giorgino will be found in time?'

"There's always a chance. There's always hope until there isn't. My only goal is to find him and return him in good health to all of you."

Our heads nod in agreement.

Chiara continues, "Okay, then my anger isn't directed toward you. But the Guardia totally invaded my privacy. They searched through every bit of information they could find on me, including my dentist, and what work I'd had done on my teeth, to when I started my menstrual cycle. They dug up every past relationship, every bit of information on my family, as well as my personal history. Then they questioned me as if I were a criminal."

Antonio puts his arm around her, but she pushes him away. "I'm sorry, Antonio, but this won't go away with a hug. It has to stop before they pull in everyone in the village and interrogate them. Why is all this time being wasted?"

Luigi clears his throat. "It's a nasty business, Chiara, but it seems people other than Riccardo are involved. It's a precautionary procedure, but anyone who knows the family is questioned. I'm sorry if you were questioned in a manner that offended you."

Chiara eases against the back of her chair. This time, she allows Antonio to put his arm around her. He leans in close and whispers something indecipherable into her mass of beautiful spiraling curls.

Although I think I know the answer, I ask the question. "Can you tell us who else is involved besides Riccardo? Or do you want me to guess?"

He arches an eyebrow at me and retorts, "I'm not planning on telling you or letting you guess. That would only hamper the investigation."

His response is off-putting, but it doesn't deter me from continuing to pester him.

"Well, what can you tell us? Is Isabella still in a coma? Was she working for Riccardo or herself when she arranged the meeting at the cathedral and demanded the necklace?"

"What do you think?"

"I think she wanted the necklace for herself. The problem is she has an accomplice. Someone had to stay with Giorgino. That's the person we need to find. That's the person who has Giorgino."

I know better than to bring up Marco's name, but I give Luigi a knowing look.

"Hmmm," is all he says.

Antonio jumps into the conversation. "Well, if Isabella is no longer in a coma, has she been questioned yet?"

Luigi turns his intense stare on Antonio.

"I didn't say she wasn't in a coma. You are jumping to whatever conclusions you find suitable."

Antonio isn't used to being rebuffed. He clenches and unclenches his hands.

"In case you are uninformed, I'm a doctor. Any idiot would know from the hit to her head that she'd be in a coma, whether natural or induced."

I jump in before tempers flare.

"Antonio's only concern is Giorgino. That's what we're all concerned about. The more we know, the more we can help."

Luigi nods and pours another Amaro into his glass.

"The thing is, Cat, we really don't want or need any assistance from civilians. Without being rude, I need all of you to understand that."

The congenial atmosphere around the table disappears.

"Okay, Luigi, what do you expect us to do? We have no answers, and Giorgino is out there somewhere. He's frightened. He will soon run out of his medications. What do you suggest?"

My pause hangs heavy in the air. When Luigi doesn't respond, I say, "Okay, don't answer. If you do, you'll say exactly what Lorenzo says: *Stay out of our way. Let us do our job.* Am I right?"

75

Marco watches the hours tick by. When Isabella doesn't return, he fears the worst. Something has to be done with the kid, but he knows from experience an amber alert has been issued. The chances of being seen with a child in his car increase. He has to come up with another plan.

It upsets him that he has to tie the kid up every time he leaves the lodge, but he can't trust him not to bolt. Food and water are running low, and he needs more of the sleeping powder. He worries about overdosing the kid, so he has reduced the amount from what Isabella was giving him.

Because he started his life on the streets, Marco knows his way around. He toggles the dark web for information and reads the story about a woman attacked by an unknown assailant in the cathedral in Castello. Next, he calls a contact to check hospitals in the area.

The information he receives is sketchy, but it's enough to learn that a woman with a severe concussion was admitted, and the Guardia has been seen coming and going to one particular room. The description and details are vague, but they give Marco enough hope to think Isabella might be alive.

The most important piece of information he receives is that the woman in the bed is recovering. The description of the woman is enough for him to believe it's Isabella and not Cat. The bad news is there are two armed guards outside her door and one at the entrance to the hospital. What surprises him most is there's no mention of another woman, which means either Cat survived or she's dead. His contact, who works inside the hospital, agrees to slip a message to the woman.

Tonight, after they eat, he gives the boy an extra dose of the sleeping powder. He doesn't want to tie him up in case he doesn't return. At midnight, he leaves for the hospital.

A door at the back staff entrance is propped open for him. He slips inside the dark hallway. Once inside, he listens for movement. A dim glow lights the way to the staff room. In the early morning hours before shift change, it's empty. A doctor's white coat, stethoscope, badge and chart are on the table, as he requested. The coat fits well enough. He pins on the badge, drapes the stethoscope around his neck, and picks up the chart.

Footsteps in the corridor send him running to a small toilet room. He locks the door and waits. The handle rattles, and a voice says, "How long are you going to be?"

"Too long for you to wait."

After a string of curses, the footsteps move away. After a few minutes, Marco unlocks the door and surveys the hallway. All is quiet. He follows the arrows painted on the floor to the elevators but walks past to the exit sign at the end of the hall. He keeps his head down and walks rapidly. Once the door closes behind him, he climbs the stairs to the sixth floor and looks out the small window into the corridor. The lights are dim, but there are several people at the nurses' desk. Two have their backs to him, but one appears to be looking directly at the door. He moves against the wall and waits.

After the group disperses, he pushes through the door. Room 610 is at the end of the corridor. Only one officer stands outside the door. Marco gives him a cursory nod and puts his hand on the door handle.

"Hey, wait a minute. You're not the usual doctor. What's your name?"

Marco turns slowly enough to catch the name at the top of the list.

"Oh sorry, maybe the head nurse forgot to tell you. I'm filling in for Dottore Santi.

The emergency room needed him. I'm Dottore Zappulla."

The guard shakes his head.

"I have orders not to let anyone into this room unless their name is on this list."

"Yes, of course, but I've been assigned to see the patient. You don't want something to happen to her, do you? Her situation is critical. Why don't you come in the room with me while I check her vitals?"

"Nah, go ahead. I need a short break if you're going to be in there for a few minutes. I'm overdue for a stretch, and my partner has wandered off. I need coffee and something to eat to get through these long, boring nights."

"Take your time. I'll stay until one of you returns."

"Hey, thanks. Most of the doctors don't even speak to us."

He tips his hat and shuffles to the elevators. Marco waits inside the door until the officer steps on the elevator.

The curtain is drawn around the bed. Marco pulls it aside, expecting Isabella to be dressed and ready to go. His contact assured him she knew he was coming tonight. The sheet and a blanket are pulled up around her neck. He's irritated that she's asleep. He worries it's too soon to move her. But he knows if he doesn't get her out tonight, they are doomed. The wheelchair he asked for is in the corner, and the drip has been disconnected.

He approaches the bed and whispers, "Isabella, get up. We only have a few minutes before the guard returns. We have to get out of here now."

There's no movement. He approaches the bed cautiously, not wanting to startle her. He places his hand on her arm. Still nothing. He peels back the covers. A knife protrudes from her ribs. Blood saturates her hospital gown and the bed linens. It covers most of the paper attached to the knife—one musical note stares back at him.

76

Twilight crawls along the horizon on a cloudy day when earth, sea and sky blend into a thick gray soup. The low hum of a drone reaches my ears before I see it descend through the mass of clouds. It hovers over the terrace for only seconds, deposits a small package on the table, and disappears into the fog rolling in from the sea.

There's no point in retrieving the package until I'm sure the Guardia has no interest in the drone. If they're suspicious about its appearance, they'll be on the terrace in a few minutes. After fifteen anxious minutes of waiting, I crack the door open. Recently, in a local you-can-find-anything store with my escort leaning against the counter with half-closed eyes, I discovered a dusty can of WD-40. I slipped it into my purse and vowed I'd return and pay the shopkeeper when this was over.

Every door and window in the villa received a squirt of the WD-40. There's no chance any of the officers will hear the doors open or close or see me slip in and out unless they're on the surrounding rooftops. Several times, I've spotted a couple of sharpshooters on nearby roofs, but this evening's gloomy weather indicates it's not a good day for rooftop surveillance.

Creeping to the table, I grab the package and slink back inside. It's small and very light. There are many possibilities as to what might be inside, but none of them are good. I peel the brown paper away and open the box.

The child's finger nestles against the white satin lining. Tears gush. I reach for my phone and pull up Lorenzo's number. I stop. I need to think this through. Maybe I'll call Luigi. Before he left last night, he reminded me to call him if I needed anything.

Between big gulping breaths, sobs, and wails, I try to think what is best for Giorgino. Riccardo probably has eyes on me at all times. If Lorenzo shows up at my gate, he'll know I contacted him. I can't put Giorgino in any more danger than he already is.

After blowing my nose and wiping my eyes, I force myself to study the box, and the human finger inside. I focus on being objective.

A piece of paper is tucked in the side. Knowing enough not to touch the evidence, I find tweezers and pick at the paper until I grasp it. Using tweezers and a fork, I unfold the note.

EVERY DAY ANOTHER PIECE OF HIS BODY WILL BE SENT TO YOU

There are instructions as to what I must do each day for the next three days. At the bottom is the date and time I'm to meet Riccardo, but not the location. He adds that Maria is next on his list. Then Gino. After that, he'll eliminate every single person I love if I don't comply.

The instructions tell me I won't receive directions until I'm in my car and on the way. He's smart enough to know Lorenzo has a tracker on my car, so I'm guessing another vehicle will be waiting for me somewhere.

Again, I consider who to contact. If Lorenzo sees the note, he will hogtie me and set up an ambush, except he won't have a location. The good news is I don't think Riccardo knows about Luigi. He's the kind of guy who would stay in the background until I need him.

The more I think about this package, the more I believe Marco has Giorgino. This makes Riccardo's note all the more confusing. Except there is the possibility that Riccardo has found Marco and Giorgino or perhaps he hasn't found them.

My thoughts are a senseless jumble. I read the note again. All I know is if Riccardo has Giorgino, he might kill him if I don't follow his instructions. Still, I wonder if this is some kind of ruse.

Although my stomach is heaving, I study the finger carefully. It doesn't appear as if it was just cut off. What if this isn't Giorgino's finger? What if Riccardo doesn't have Giorgino and is in a panic and has changed course?

If he has, his only goal would be the necklace and me. He could care less about a little boy. He knows that without the boy he has no leverage with me so he's added others to the list. I can't take the chance that he doesn't have Giorgino or that he won't kidnap Maria or anyone else I care about.

I brush away my tears. In control and calm has to be my credo. I have to think like a vindictive murderer. Every possibility has to be considered. I need to study Riccardo's instructions over and over and think of ways to rescue Giorgino and get out alive.

But first, I have to find Giorgino. If I can do that, perhaps I can stop this madness. Since we all believe Isabella is behind the kidnapping and Marco is part of the scheme, then Giorgino has to be with him.

Where would Isabella hide until she felt safe to leave the country, and how would she leave the country? Airports and train stations are on alert. But boats moving in and out of the coastal areas are more difficult to monitor. That's where Marco will be, somewhere close to the water. But Puglia has a vast coastline. If only Marco would reach out to me or one of his friends in the Guardia. Although my anger is huge for what he's done, I don't believe he's a bad guy. I don't think he'll hurt Giorgino. I hope I'm right.

Puzzling through all the possibilities, I decide the odds of Riccardo having Giorgino are small, and the note is a bluff. It's a huge risk, but I'm going with my gut. If I'm wrong and Riccardo has him, I can only hope he won't kill a child.

During Riccardo's trial, the story of Carlo rescuing him from the sea came out. It gave me insight into his fierce feelings of loyalty to Carlo and why he had blindly followed him. He believed he owed

Carlo his life and his total allegiance. As evil as Riccardo is, he still remembers what it was like to be saved when he was a little boy about the same age as Giorgino. But he'll have no qualms about killing Maria or Gino.

My thoughts are a confusion of relief and fear. Riccardo wants me. Everyone else is collateral damage. I have the necklace, so I'm going to show up. But since I'd like to live a bit longer, I'm going to plot my next moves carefully.

77

Luigi texts me and says he's on the way over. I text back that I'm busy writing my memoir and don't wish to be disturbed. He doesn't appreciate my humor and says he's already at the gate. He's not one for small talk. As soon as he reaches the top step, he says, "What's in the package?"

What a snoop.

"What package?"

"Don't play games, Cat. You know I have eyes on you 24/7. I waited for you to call me as soon as the drone left. Why didn't you?"

Ever since I opened the package, I've been practicing what I'd say to Luigi. Now he's here, and I'm stumbling all over the place.

"Giorgino's life is the only thing that matters to me. If Lorenzo finds out, he'll make sure I'm under lock and key. Then he'll set up an ambush. If he does that, Giorgino will be killed."

"That doesn't answer the question of why you didn't call me?"

"I was thinking about it, but what stopped me is I knew you'd want to come with me. Riccardo will have a small army waiting. He's outsmarted all of us at every turn. The note inside the package provides no information about the location. If you follow me, he'll know. My only goal is to make sure Giorgino comes out of this alive. So, I don't want to include you or anyone."

"I agree."

Oh shit, I hate it when people agree with me. It usually means they see through my act of bravado. They'll put some kind of spin on what I've said and confuse me. These are usually people with bizarre minds like Riccardo and now Luigi.

"Just what are you agreeing with?"

"Your goal is to keep Giorgino alive. It's the only goal. Tell me how I can help you make that happen."

Now what? He's outsmarting me. I'm not sure how, but he is. The only thing I can do is question his motivation.

"Why are you doing this? Is Lorenzo behind it?"

"Lorenzo hired me to protect you."

My sputtering interrupts. "I, I don't need more protection. You can leave now."

He waits until I regain my composure.

"Cat, let's work together. You didn't let me finish. Right from the beginning, I realized you needed a partner—someone to have your back. You don't need me watching over you. You're an intelligent woman. You run a business. You know martial arts and how to protect yourself most of the time. Okay?"

I nod but don't add anything.

"The difference is I've had more experience with lawless criminals than you have. They don't have diverse portfolios. Crime is their job. It's not yours. But ferreting out criminals is mine. Is it possible for us to work together to rescue Giorgino?"

There it is—the outsmarting. There's nothing in Luigi's approach I can challenge. He's a savvy hunter of criminals and has probably had to placate a few wanna-be solvers of mysteries like me. But he's right. Crime isn't my job. Rescuing people is.

"Exactly what are you suggesting we do together that will increase our chances of extracting Giorgino alive?"

"The first hurdle is trusting each other implicitly. If our partnership is to work, we can't withhold information. Without that agreement, one or both of us, as well as Giorgino, will be killed. I'm willing to trust you. Are you willing to trust me?"

My phone chimes. The number doesn't have a name attached, so I ignore the call.

"Do you need to take the call?"

"No, it's just a robo-caller."

Luigi continues, "If we trust each other, the odds of us rescuing

Giorgino are greater. Can you do that? Are you willing to share what you know?"

Doubt floods me as I really don't want to trust anyone.

"Trust is hard for me. It goes hand-in-hand with betrayal."

He nods and offers another perspective. "Often trust is based on friendship or love developed over time. Betrayal gets into the mix when things go awry. I'm not asking for that kind of trust. We don't have a relationship of any kind other than me being hired to protect you and you being suspicious of me from the first time you met me."

"You knew?"

"Well, I wasn't a very convincing chauffeur, was I?"

He's working me. The guy is good at his job.

"It was clear that you hadn't received any training in how to transport a guest to a posh resort. Even putting your clumsiness aside, having a firearm in your waist band was a dead giveaway."

"Ah, next time I'm offered that job, I'll confer with you for the appropriate chauffeur training."

We laugh, which eases the tension. My phone pings a text. I glance down and read the text:

It's Marco call me

"Sorry, my business partner needs me to call right away. There's some sort of problem."

"Sure, do you need privacy? I'll step outside."

With my fake smile in place, I say. "I need some fresh air. You stay. It'll only take a minute or two. Cassie tends to overreact."

Instead of the terrace, I walk through the dining room, the kitchen and out the back door. I want as much space as possible between myself and Luigi. At the moment, the trust thing is an issue for me.

"Marco, do you have Giorgino?"

"Cat, stop. There's not much time, so let me talk."

"I have to know if you still have him. Is he okay? Please."

"I have him. He's fine. They killed Isabella."

"What? When? Wasn't she under guard at the hospital? I thought she survived."

"Riccardo and his gang did it. I managed to get a message to her. She knew I was coming to get her out of the hospital and take her into hiding. When I arrived, she'd been knifed and pinned with the same damn musical note as the Hickmans."

His voice cracks, but any empathy I might have had for him left when he involved himself with Giorgino's kidnapping. Anger wells up, but I can't afford to upset him.

"Marco, the only thing I want from you is Giorgino. What do you want from me?"

"I want the necklace. Call it an exchange for Giorgino. You cannot involve anyone else. Do you understand?"

78

The next few minutes are life and death for Giorgino. I have to convince Marco to release him to me. Giving him the necklace isn't a problem.

"Marco, Riccardo contacted me. He sent a package with a child's finger in it."

"*Merde*, the guy's a psycho. Giorgino is fine. He has all his fingers."

I want to weep joyful tears, instead I say, "Does he have enough meds?"

"He's good for another week. He'll be fine if we make the exchange."

"Why are you doing this? I don't understand."

"Look, Cat, there's not a lot of time for storytelling. I met Isabella shortly after I had a showdown with Davide. I was angry. She was beautiful and convincing. The few jobs she asked me to do were just shy of breaking the law. I chose not to ask about her connections. I realized too late that she was part of the mafia."

"But why? I thought you were loyal to the Guardia and justice."

"I am or was, but I let my anger get in the way. When I tried to break it off with Isabella, she said I couldn't."

"Why didn't you go to Commissario Faena? You may have been reprimanded and put on desk duty, but *mio dio*, Marco!

"It's too late. I signed my own death warrant when Isabella recruited me. When Riccardo assigned Isabella the task of kidnapping Giorgino, she saw it as an opportunity to break free of him. She wanted me to be part of her scheme."

"And you agreed with her—to kidnap an innocent child?"

"Isabella was an innocent child when Riccardo plucked her off the street. She was thirteen. He turned her into a prostitute. After he used her up, he recruited her for other aspects of his business. I know you don't like her, but perhaps if you understand her background, you'd be more forgiving. I'm not excusing her, but she saw a way out and took it. Now she's dead."

"Sorry, Marco, there's no forgiveness for people that kidnap children. Not to mention that she tried to kill me."

"I didn't know. I'm sorry. I can't excuse that, but she was desperate to get away from Riccardo."

"And you plan to pick up where she left off?

"Guess so. The plan might have worked if she'd just asked you up front for the necklace. But she couldn't see her way to do that. I can. I won't harm the boy. But it's a fair exchange, don't you agree?"

"There's nothing fair about kidnapping a child. But what do you expect me to do? I'm locked up in the house. Both Riccardo and the Guardia watch my every move. The one night I slipped out to meet Isabella, Riccardo's minions almost got me. Are you going to send a big drone to pick me up?"

At least my last remark elicits a sort of laugh.

Luigi maneuvers his way to the back of the house. From the kitchen door, he catches glimpses of Cat as she paces back and forth. Her reaction to the text was big. She lied to him about who it was. When she looked at the phone, all the blood drained from her face. Their only hope to rescue Giorgino is for her to tell him the truth. If she does, the trust part will be sealed. If she doesn't, he's not sure how to proceed. He walks back to the living area and waits.

"Marco, Luigi is here. He thinks this call is from my business partner. If I stay on the phone much longer, he'll get suspicious. When do we make the exchange?"

"You can't tell him. Promise me."

"But what if he can help?"

"I don't trust him not to tell Lorenzo. If he does, a manhunt will start. I'll have to flee and take the boy with me."

"Please don't do that. You know Riccardo is looking for you too."

"No, I'm good. For the moment, Riccardo isn't suspicious of me. The first thing I did after leaving the hospital was contact him. I told him Isabella dumped the kid on me and left. I said I didn't know where she was, and she wasn't answering my calls. I asked him what I was supposed to do with the kid. He said my job was to bring the boy to him."

"You called him? Marco, that's the dumbest thing you could do. He's looking for you now."

"And if you keep stalling, he'll find me. Do I get the necklace or not?"

"Of course, you get the necklace. Giorgino's life is worth more than a few jewels. When are you supposed to deliver him to Riccardo?"

"The good news is he asked me to wait a couple of days. He said he'd let me know when and where to deliver the boy. My guess is he needs time to set up the location where he'll meet you. He thinks you'll show up with the necklace, and you'll expect him to hand over Giorgino. Keeping Giorgino is part of his plan to torture you."

"Okay, tell me what to do, and I'll do it."

"We've talked too long. I have to move to another spot. I'll call you back in a few hours. That should give you time to figure out a way to sneak out without alerting anyone. But I'm guessing you already have an escape plan. Whatever you do, don't involve anyone else."

"Marco, please take good care of Giorgino."

My words fall into space as he's already gone.

79

Luigi looks up when I enter the room. "Did you get everything resolved with your partner?"

"No, I didn't. Look, the only way I'm willing to trust you is if you promise that you will not tell another soul about the information we share. Can you do that?"

"Yes!"

"Even Lorenzo?"

"Yes!"

"And you are willing to tell me everything you know."

"Yes."

"Then why didn't you tell me Isabella is dead?"

He rises halfway out of his chair and then sinks back down. "I didn't know."

"You mean Lorenzo didn't tell you?"

"That's exactly what I mean."

"If I call Lorenzo now and ream him out for not telling me and ask him if he told you, what will he say?"

"If he's honest, and I believe he is, he'll say he didn't tell me or anyone because he hasn't been informed yet. Please call him if that's what it takes to trust me."

"That was Marco on the phone. He has Giorgino, but he assured me he's okay."

"He's proposing something, right?"

"Yes. He wants my necklace in exchange for Giorgino. He wants to leave the country. It's what he and Isabella planned to do. According to Marco, Isabella was brutalized for years by Riccardo."

Weariness engulfs me as I turn away, wondering if this nightmare will ever end.

"When Riccardo asked her to kidnap Giorgino, she saw it as her opportunity to get away from him. She enlisted Marco to help her. He stayed with Giorgino when she met me at the cathedral. If you hadn't found me, I'd be dead like Isabella."

He frowns, stands, and stretches. "It's time for a glass of wine, don't you think?"

"Sure, I could use a wine break. I'm a bit tense."

"How did Marco know Isabella was dead?"

"He snuck into the hospital last night with the intention of bringing her out. Instead, he found her with a bloody knife in her ribs and a musical note attached to her body."

"Holy Shit! That's definitely the work of Riccardo and his crew. It's the same signature as the Hickmans. Has anyone analyzed the musical note?"

"You're asking me? Did you forget I'm not part of the Guardia?"

Luigi's eyes crinkle and a smile replaces the scowl.

"No, I was just testing you."

"Well, I think it's from an opera. It's significant to Riccardo in some way. Can you find out if the notes for each murder are the same or different?"

"Sure, I'll check with forensics."

Once in the kitchen, I peruse the wine rack and ask, "Red okay?"

"It's my preference."

I blush and ignore the innuendo. Without thinking, I try to open the bottle of Negroamaro. As the pain ricochets up my arm, I drop the wine opener and let out a yelp.

Luigi pulls out a chair at the kitchen table and commands, "Sit. Don't move. I guess you've heard it before, but your head is certainly hard."

"Yeah, it's not the first time. Why don't we see if there's something to eat? Maybe some cheese, olives and prosciutto. And grab that loaf of bread right behind you."

He pokes around in the fridge and comes out with his arms full. He arranges everything on a tray and then cuts big slabs of yeasty bread. He lays the wine glasses on the tray and hands me the bottle.

As we walk back to the living room, I say, "About the musical note."

"What about it?"

"If I could see it, I might have an idea. Do you think you could send me photos? It might be a clue, or maybe it's just Riccardo's way of thumbing his nose at us—first with the roses, then at the concert and now in the hospital. He could simply be letting us know that he will win."

"What note? What roses?"

"It's another story if you have time."

"I sure do. First, let me send a text asking for photos of the musical notes."

We sit in silence while he chews on bread and sends the text. After a big swallow of wine, he says, "Okay, what has Marco proposed?"

80

When the knock on the door comes, Lorenzo isn't sure he's ready. He takes a deep breath and lets it out slowly before saying, *Si accomodi.*

The door opens, and Sofia, all smiles, enters. She's stunning in a sea green dress that fits every curve and moves with the air as she saunters toward his desk.

He watches. Her smile fills the room. He doesn't ask her to sit, although she does.

"Well, this is unexpected. I thought maybe you'd forgotten me. Is this an invitation to lunch? If it is, I can stay over."

She says all this with a pretty pout. He wonders how pretty she'd feel if he jerked her across the desk and throttled her. Of course, he's the one who needs the throttling. How could he be so stupid, so willing to be deceived?

"I have something for you."

"Oh," she exclaims, placing her perfectly manicured fingers against her cheeks. "How exciting. I can't imagine what it is."

"I believe you can. It belongs to you."

He reaches across the desk and hands her the small piece of surveillance equipment.

"Did you really think you could pull that on me? Did you?"

She has the decency to blush before she says, "Really, Lorenzo, what is it? Why do you think it belongs to me? Is this a joke? Am I supposed to laugh at some clever meaning that I don't understand?"

"A joke? Well, perhaps it is—on me. Did you really think you could waltz into my life, invade my office, and expect me not to do a thorough background search on you?"

She stands up abruptly, "Are you crazy? You really think I would do something so stupid? Do I look like a spy?"

"I have nothing on you, but this piece of surveillance equipment. You're clever enough not to leave fingerprints, and a slick mafia lawyer would have you released before I could get you to the jailhouse."

Her composure slips a little. She sputters, "You can't possibly suspect me of doing this. Someone is setting me up. Why is it so easy to believe I'm the culprit? Maybe that pretty redhead? I heard she has your heart. Maybe she put it there to check up on you?"

He shakes his head and wonders how he considers himself an investigator when he can't control his personal life.

"It was my colossal mistake to let you get close to me. I'm letting you walk out of here. But you're on my radar and the radar of the entire Guardia. You have twenty-four hours to pack and leave my jurisdiction. If you come back, I won't be so easy on you. Is that understood?"

A scowl replaces her normal radiant smile. "You're making a huge mistake. Too bad, isn't it? While our children would have been beautiful, I wouldn't want to take the chance they'd be stupid like you."

"Get out!"

Once the door closes, she smiles. While she's a little miffed he found the bug, it was inevitable. Now, she's ready to roll out the second part of her plan. Leaving the area is exactly what she has in mind. Her father will be avenged, but she's in no hurry. It's the only thing she and Riccardo have in common. The bonus for her will be to eliminate Riccardo, Lorenzo and his sweet little girlfriend.

♩

The bottle of wine stands empty. Only a scattering of crumbs remain on the tray. Luigi and I have gone over and over the plan and the possibilities—both likely and unlikely. The only goal is protecting and rescuing Giorgino. The odds are reasonable for doing that, and they're fairly reasonable for us to come out of the exchange alive. While we both feel confident Marco only wants the necklace, Luigi is determined I can't meet him alone.

Before we review the plan one more time, I ask Luigi, "How do you and Lorenzo know each other?"

He's quiet. I wait.

"Many years ago, in another lifetime, we were in the military—both stationed in Afghanistan. Italy offered 5,000 men to the cause. We were in the 13th Command and Tactical Supports Unit out of Bari. That's all you need to know other than Lorenzo saved my life."

The silence is poignant. Imagining the two young men in their twenties in a hostile and life-threatening situation is easy. I don't need to know anything else. The bond between men who've served together is the most powerful bond of brotherhood.

Luigi sighs, taps my hand and says, "Okay, when Marco calls, he'll give you the time and place to make the exchange. In the meantime, I'll call Gino and tell him to be on standby. I'll also arrange a safe house for the family."

I stretch and push back from the table.

"Luigi, this is such a fragile plan. It will fall apart if we don't get to Giorgino before Riccardo finds them."

"Yeah, I understand."

He pushes back from the table and picks up the tray.

I blurt out, "What about provisions at the safe house?"

"What?"

"If Riccardo doesn't kill me, Maria will. You can't take her to a place that doesn't have enough supplies to feed an army. Don't neglect that part, or she'll figure out a way to get past the guards to go grocery shopping."

Luigi looks at me in bewilderment. "It's amazing how you manage to keep a sense of humor when your life is on the line."

"What else can I do? I'm sure weeping and wailing won't get me very far with you."

He deposits the tray in the kitchen and puts on his jacket.

"I'm glad you're a strong woman. See you soon," he says as he squeezes my hand.

The door closes softly. I stand at the window and watch him slip into the night.

81

Sofia pulls off the highway into the parking lot of an Autogrill. She knows Lorenzo put a tracking device on her car. When he unexpectedly called her to stop by his office, she figured he was on to her. It didn't matter. Her plans were already in place.

She leaves the car and walks slowly into the Autogrill. She sashays among the aisles packed with tourists and locals. She attracts as much attention as possible with her brilliant smile for everyone. In a few minutes, she spots one of the escorts Lorenzo sent to watch her. She dawdles for a while before entering the women's restroom. She walks with style and grace—a beautiful blonde in a sea-green dress with stiletto heels. Every male head in the place turns to admire her.

Inside the stall, she pulls a collapsible bag from her large purse. From it, she pulls out a dark pixie wig. She pins up her hair and tops it with the wig. Next, the dress and the heels come off. She slides into a pair of faded jeans, a black t-shirt and a roughed-up pair of sneakers. She adds a pair of glasses, a rumpled cardigan and a cap with the logo of Milan's soccer team. Before leaving the restroom, she washes the makeup from her face and fluffs up the mousy brown wig.

She stops at the food counter and purchases a sandwich. She spots a different escort standing in the aisle looking at candy choices while keeping his eye on the women's rest room. She casually walks out the exit and heads to the opposite side of the parking lot where a black Nissan SUV waits. She lingers for a few minutes to see if any of her escorts or any other suspicious characters appear. No one notices when she pulls away and takes the highway to Brindisi. When she's sure she isn't being followed, she doubles back to Castello and drives to the highest point. She parks outside the penthouse—the one her Papa left her—the one Carlo stole when he killed him.

♩

Luigi and I understand the risk we are taking. If Giorgino is harmed in any way, it will be because of us. Even Gino, who has supported every crazy scheme I've come up with, is not onboard.

As far as Marco is concerned, I'm coming alone. He's desperate enough to trust me, but only so far. We're sure there will be changes in the instructions along the way. Luigi refuses to tell me how he will track me without being seen. His assurances that he will be there are all I have plus the tracker he says is on my watch.

♩

The text comes at three in the morning. I have a few minutes to text Luigi that the instructions include leaving my phone behind. Luigi is camped somewhere close by, so he can see the signal we've rigged, indicating I'm leaving the premises. It's some kind of trip-wire circuit strung across the last step at the bottom of the crumbling stairs. Once I'm out, the instructions say to pick up a dark green car in the parking lot of Ristorante L'Aragosta.

The face mask and headlamp are in place before I leave the house. I maneuver the stairs without breaking my neck and wiggle my way through the tunnel. I push the pile of debris aside and slide through the opening. I trot off at the fastest pace I can muster in a crouching position. There's only one car in the lot. The key is in the planter, just as Marco said along with a burner phone.

Five kilometers down the road, the phone vibrates with a text.

Take road to Palmariggi

The GPS indicates ten kilometers.

As I reach the outskirts, the phone chimes again.

> Continue to Bagnolo di Salento

Another twenty minutes pass before the welcome sign appears and the phone pings.

> vegetable stand on right as you leave town.
> leave key in ignition and phone in car.
> pickup blue Mazda. key on wheel driver's
> side. burner phone in car

As I switch cars, I pray Luigi is close by.

The next message takes me to *Cursi* and the following one to *Melpignano.*

Exhaustion and fear settle between my shoulders. At every small town, I slow down and search the landscape. It doesn't make sense that Marco has created this runaround. Of course, he's frightened, but this is excessive. A scary thought enters my mind. *What if he and Riccardo are working together?*

I constantly check my mirrors for a glimpse of Luigi. It would be helpful to have a tiny bit of reassurance that he's near. There are no vehicles on the road but mine.

The next town is *Castrignano di Greci.* As the small sign welcomes me to the town with a population of 4,107, the next text appears.

> Cross over railroad tracks drive behind
> building and park

I do as instructed. A black car with the motor running is parked behind the building. A masked man stands next to it. His hand holds a gun leveled at me. I park, cut off the engine, and open the door.

"Lay the keys on the hood along with the necklace and back off."

"Who are you? Where's Marco and Giorgino?"

"Don't worry about Marco or the kid."

The voice sounds vaguely familiar. I attempt to keep him talking.

"Marco agreed to meet me. Where is he?"

"Like you agreed to come alone?"

"Do you see anyone with me?"

"I don't have to see anyone to know someone is watching us."

While he's talking, I try to envision the person behind the mask. Tall, muscular, good haircut and clean hands—not a typical thug. The Italian spoken is Tuscan with an American accent.

"No more talking. Do as I say."

I place the key and the velvet bag on the hood of the car. He pockets the key and opens the bag. The necklace spills out, and for a moment Stella's face full of regret flashes before me. She cherished the necklace more than anything.

My legs are trembling, and my hands are shaky but I don't waiver.

"Are you satisfied? Now, where is Giorgino?"

He moves closer. As he scopes up the necklace, I notice a *stiddari* tattooed between his thumb and index finger. The faint odor of cigar smoke drifts my way. He notices me staring and steps back. He places another key on the hood of the car.

"The key is for an old hunting lodge just outside of *Cannole*."

"Where's that?"

"Go back the way you came. When you get to *Bagnolo di Salento*, take a left. Go about four kilometers. Drive through the town. After about two kilometers, take the dirt road off to the right. Keep going until you reach the lodge. It's maybe another five kilometers from the road. It's buried pretty deep in the woods."

During those few minutes of conversation, I focus on the speech pattern. Nothing occurs to me until that nauseating faint hint of cigar smoke wafts into my space. The face of Frank Woodlee pops up. Wanting to prolong the conversation to be sure, I say, "Those directions are a bit complicated. Can you draw me a map?"

He laughs, and I have no doubt it's the despicable man who sat next to me at dinner at the resort and later tried to hit on me.

"How will I get to the lodge without a car?"

He strokes the necklace and tucks it in his pocket.

"Since you didn't come alone, I'm sure you'll find a way. Even if your friend lost your trail for a while, he'll pick it up."

"Why isn't Marco here? What have you done with him?"

He laughs sardonically. "Don't worry, Marco's waiting for you at the lodge."

He shakes his head, mumbles some obscenity and drives off. I watch the taillights disappear. Night sounds surround me. I pick up the key that may or may not be to some unknown lodge. If the tracker on my watch works, Luigi will find me.

The road is unwelcoming. It stretches ahead with thick woods on both sides. My choice is to stand still and wait or start walking. I walk.

A hum gathers from a long way off. In a matter of seconds, the volume picks up. I step off the road and hide in the tree line. A super-charged motorcycle whizzes past, does a 180° and skids to a stop at the exact spot I'm hiding. The helmet comes off. Luigi appears.

"What in the crap is that? How in the hell are we going to rescue Giorgino without a car?"

He laughs and says, "Here's your helmet. Hop on. Bet you've never been on a MV Augusta F4 RR super bike before?"

"Can't say I have. It looks pretty wild."

"This babe can hit 198 mph and goes from 0 to 60 in 2.9 seconds."

"I'd rather walk."

"Ha, I thought you were Wonder Woman. You've now shown me two weak points: gangplanks and motorcycles."

"Let's just say that most of the time I make informed choices, and they don't include warped boards over water or souped-up vehicles."

He laughs again and makes sure I'm secure before saying, "I'll take it easy. There's a car waiting for us in *Bagnolo di Salento*."

82

I wrap my one good arm around Luigi, lean in and hold on tight. All of a sudden, the night seems friendlier, the breeze softer against my face, and the road less bumpy. I'm thankful not to be alone. I lean into his back and force tears not to fall.

In a matter of minutes, we retrace our steps, are in the car and on our way to Cannole. Finally, Luigi speaks.

"So you gave Marco the necklace?"

"No, I didn't."

"What?"

"Marco didn't show up. I gave the necklace to a man I didn't recognize at first."

"What do you mean 'at first'?"

"Well, it wasn't so much what he said, but it was his smell."

"Wait a minute. Don't tell me you're part bloodhound, too?"

In all this shit, I am grateful that I'm in it with Luigi. His warped sense of humor matches mine.

"Yes, smell. I met this guy at the resort—a nasty piece of work. He tried to get too close to me. He not only repelled me with his conversational skills, but it was the vile smell of cigars that was a major turnoff. He said his name was Frank Woodlee. Does that mean anything to you?"

Luigi frowns and shakes his head.

"No, but I'll alert Lorenzo and ask for a background check. American?"

"Yes. Maybe he works for Marco."

"Could be. We'll find out soon enough."

"What if he works for Riccardo? The more I try to make sense of this, the more confused I become. This isn't going to end well."

"Can you explain?'

"Well, like you said, Marco was supposed to meet me. Maybe Riccardo found out and intervened?"

Luigi doesn't answer. He turns off the main road onto a dirt path. He spots the lodge before I do. After parking the car in a wooded area, we wait like sitting ducks. Luigi indicates I'm to stay in the car while he walks the perimeter. After making a complete circle, he nods. I bolt out of the car, race to the door, and insert the key. Luigi pushes me aside. With his gun drawn, he crashes through the door.

The odor assaults my nose and latches onto my throat. I recognize the metallic smell of fresh blood. I gag but stay close to Luigi. The room is dark and full of shadows. Luigi already has a small pinpoint light moving slowly around the floor and bouncing off the walls.

A lump lies in a corner on a dirty mattress covered in blankets. I'm across the room in two seconds and pull back the cover. I stifle a cry as Marco's sightless eyes stare at the ceiling. A knife protrudes from his chest. Pinned to the knife is a bloody piece of paper with one musical note, turning red with Marco's blood.

I drop the blanket and back away. A wail starts in the pit of my stomach, but Luigi is right beside me.

"Come away. Whoever did this is close by. We need to do a quick search and get out of here."

"Where, where is Giorgino? Who has him? What are we going to do?" spills out in one breath.

"Take a deep breath. Let's take a minute to think. Is there anyone else who wanted the boy besides Riccardo?"

"Of course not—well, I guess not. I mean, who? Why?"

"Something doesn't seem right. Marco said he and Riccardo were okay, and the delivery of the boy had been arranged, right?"

Throbbing wraps around my head. I press my knuckles against my temples as I try to make sense of the jumble of information.

"Yes, but Riccardo is smart. What if he didn't trust Marco? He didn't trust Isabella. So maybe he knew about their plans and about the safe houses. He could have been watching them the entire time. Do you think the person I gave the necklace to works for Riccardo?"

"Could be, but he'd have to scramble to organize all of this in such a short time."

Luigi didn't want to push the possibility that another person might be involved. Lorenzo told him only a little about the woman who bugged his office. She had not only been the daughter of one of the most brutal mafia bosses in history, but she'd also been Carlo's lover until Cat arrived on the scene. Lorenzo seemed to think that she might have some vendetta against Cat. This woman, Sofia, was supposed to have left Puglia, but Lorenzo said they lost her.

"Luigi? What are you thinking?"

"Nothing. I'm sure you're right. Riccardo is probably behind this. Let's head back to the villa and map out what we need to do next. Okay?"

"I'm not leaving until I find Giorgino." I respond angrily.

83

The black car pulls off the road and parks next to the driver's side of a navy Alfa Romero. Windows are rolled down. The velvet bag exchanges hands.

"Where's the boy?"

"He wasn't there."

"What do you mean he wasn't there? He was there with Marco. I had the place staked out. I saw him, you stupid idiot. Get out of the car."

He takes his time. He hates working for a woman, but she is in control now. Her father had been a fine man. Frank had been the go-between for the Italian and American dons. When the *padrone* selected Carlo to take his place, he had sighed with relief and forgot about the girl—the daughter. Forgot she was handling all the finances and would eventually take her place as *la padrone*, as her father intended.

He partially opens the door and slides out of the seat. He stands but stays behind the door. His eyes glance down at the gun sticking out of the side pocket. He leans forward until his fingers touch the barrel.

"Did you interrogate Marco?"

"Of course, I did. He said the kid ran off. I searched the lodge. No kid, nothing that belonged to the kid. So I'm guessing he escaped. Not that it matters. You have the necklace."

"You stupid fool."

He didn't see the swift movement or the gun, but he felt the searing pain as he crumbled beside the car.

Sofia didn't bother checking whether he was dead or alive. He didn't matter. She had more work to do before she could call herself *la padrone.*

84

Pulling the blanket back for another look makes me sick, but it was necessary. A few days ago, Luigi sent me photos of the musical notes pinned to Gladys, Neil, and Isabella. They are all the same as this one attached to Marco—the closing note of the opera Nessun Dorma. This must be Riccardo's feeble attempt to assert himself as *il padrone,* or maybe it's a sick joke. The closing victorious lines of the opera are **I WILL WIN! I WILL WIN!**

There's some underlying madness in the message, but what is it?

Luigi touches my shoulder.

"We need to get out of here."

"We can't leave Marco, and I won't go without finding evidence that Giorgino was here."

"Don't worry. I texted Lorenzo. A team is on the way. We need to clear out before they arrive. We have time for one quick look."

Luigi takes one side of the lodge and I the other. We search every corner. A kitchen chair leans against the wall. I walk past ready to say I've finished and there's nothing when I notice a large scrape across the floor.

Squatting for a closer look, I see a ridge outlined in the floor. I push the chair. It topples and crashes. Luigi races into the room.

"What? Did you find something?"

I point to the uneven groove in the floor. "Might not be anything, but let's take a look. Do you have something to pry it open—a screwdriver, knife, anything sharp?"

Luigi pulls out one of those complicated pocket gizmos and squats beside me. As he pushes what looks like a mini crowbar into the crevice, we hear the sound—a tiny mewing. We look at each other.

"Well, even a litter of kittens deserves rescuing, right?"

His raised eyebrow gives him a we-don't-have-time-for-this-nonsense look, but the tilt at the corner of his mouth tells me otherwise. He lifts the panel. At first there's nothing to see. My eyes take a moment to adjust to the black hole. An outline of a backpack inches further back into the hole. Luigi reaches in and grabs the bag.

A sound, at first almost a growl, turns into a howl that nearly shatters my eardrums. As Luigi pulls on the front side of the bag, two small hands cling to the backside. I throw myself into the hole and land on top of the bag and the small body underneath.

"Giorgino, Giorgino, it's Zia Caterina."

He howls even louder as he flings his body into my arms.

I kneel in the black hole and sob with him until Luigi pulls us both out. I clutch Giorgino as tightly as I can as his wails vibrate off the walls of the lodge. We rock back and forth, our sobs joining forces.

Luigi whispers in my ear, "We've got to get him out of here. I need you to focus. Calm him down as quickly as you can. I'll call Gino and have him move everyone to the safe house."

He disappears out the door.

"*Stai zitto, bambino*—hush baby. *Va bene, sei al sicuro*—It's okay, you are safe."

The wails subside into sobs, and then he says, "*a casa, zia Caterina. Mamma e Papà.*"

"Sì, bambino. We are taking you to your mom and dad. We must be very quiet now, and you must do whatever Luigi and I say. Okay?"

He nods, and together, with his body still attached to mine as tight as a tick, we rise from the floor and join Luigi outside.

85

ist rolls in off the sea and through the open doors as I slip into my jeans and tie my shoes. I pull a bulky gray sweater, the same color as the fog, over my head.

If only time would stop or even better if it would reverse—reverse to that moment so long ago when Stella stood in this same spot. If she had canceled the photo shoot, I wouldn't be here now. I wouldn't be headed to certain death. The only difference is I know I'm headed to my death. Stella did not.

There's no choice for me, although others would disagree. But it's me Riccardo wants, no one else. There will be no early stakeouts or sharpshooters to come to my rescue simply because no one but Luigi knows about my plan. He's the only one who knows Riccardo contacted me. It's me he wants. I agreed—my life for Giorgino's. And although I know Giorgino is safe, it's only a matter of time before he's kidnapped again or Maria or someone else. This insane game would go on indefinitely. My friends cannot live in fear. It has to stop. I'm the only one who can stop it.

Dread fills every molecule in my body. My neck and shoulders pull taunt, and pain radiates in my left arm with the slightest movement. My stomach clenches and unclenches as bile rises in my throat. A fit of coughing has me running to the bathroom. Dry heaves echo throughout the stillness of the house.

Washing my face in cold water doesn't help. If the man who took the necklace from me is Frank Woodlee, then Riccardo has the starfish necklace by now. The only thing left for him to do is kill me.

Il vento rattles the window. It whirls around the villa built on strong, enduring rock. The thought gives me strength. Moving both my body and my thoughts out of the paralyzed stage I've been in, I close my eyes and imagine I will survive.

The small revolver tucked in the waist of my jeans is a steadying factor, even if it won't do much damage unless Riccardo gets close enough. But the gun will be long gone before I see him. In the worse possible scenario, he'll take me to some isolated place where he'll take great pleasure in letting his men rape me before he begins to cut off pieces of my body while I'm still alive.

From an old back injury, I keep a supply of pain pills. They're in my pocket. I hope I get a chance to take them all at once.

Luigi tried to dissuade me. He believes the Guardia will find Riccardo. Maybe. *But what do all of us do in the meantime? Live in fear?* I tried that route. I can't continue. After Luigi failed to talk me out of my madness, he devised some ridiculous plan that he refused to share with me. He promised to be somewhere close by. He swore he would protect me.

Yet even if Luigi finds the location, he has little chance of getting through.

We both think Riccardo will lead me to the same place where he killed Stella. Maniacal personalities have a tendency to do that. Although I think it's a stupid move on his part to return to the scene, he must feel safe knowing a small army of his men will provide protection.

My phone vibrates.

> Drive to the old lighthouse no phone or weapons

I text Luigi.

It begins.

The thirty-five-minute drive to the grotto seems to take seconds. I park and watch as one car with dark windows pulls directly in front of mine and another behind me. A door in the front one opens. As I leave my car, I'm joined by a big brute who pats me down. My gun and watch are removed along with the pills. I'm handed a burner phone. A blindfold is pulled taunt. The feeling of helplessness produces a sob in my throat. I force it back. As long as they don't find the tracer in my shoe, there's still hope.

After what seems like hours, the car stops. A door opens. I'm pushed out. It speeds away. The burner vibrates. Ripping the blindfold from my eyes, I read the text.

> I'm waiting

The road is easy to recognize. It leads to the cliffs above the caves.The red flowers still bloom along the top of the ridge. Memories of the day I climbed the cliff to pick the flowers and instead found Stella's starfish necklace come flooding back. Another memory takes its place—Lorenzo rescuing me when I almost slid off the cliff. The memory of him holding me in his arms and later picking the red flowers for me.

My eyes cloud with tears. I won't see him again. If I had one more chance, I'd tell him I love him.

As I climb the sandy path to the top, I spot the strategically placed men. I wish there were some way to let Luigi know there aren't as many as we thought—maybe ten or twelve. Still, one man against this many is useless.

I crest the hill. Riccardo waits. He smiles like a friend welcoming me into his home.

My feet refuse to go further. I yell across the space. "You have the necklace. Have you released Giorgino?"

"Ah, you're never one for small talk, are you?"

We're standing about fifteen feet apart. Riccardo doesn't answer my question, so I try again. I want him to admit he doesn't have Giorgino. But he's smart. He holds up his phone. Somehow, he's managed to get a photo of Giorgino and Analisa in an embrace with a time and date stamp. While it's been doctored, it's still frightening to know that either Riccardo or one of his henchmen could get that close. For now, Giorgino is safe. He will remain safe if I'm out of the way.

After the three of us left the hunting lodge, I dropped Luigi and Giorgino off. I didn't have to worry about Giorgino going with Luigi because as soon as he laid eyes on the MV Augusta F4 RR super bike, he forgot he'd been kidnapped. He was out of the car and rushing around the powerful bike as he squealed with delight.

Although I didn't actually see Luigi take Giorgino to the safe house, I know he's there with his parents and grandparents. I talked to all of them last night. They assured me they were all safe. It will take time to determine if the impact of the traumatic kidnapping will have long-range implications for Giorgino. Dr. Tony checked out his physical wellbeing and a Guardia therapist is onsite with the boy.

My thoughts are interrupted when Riccardo's voice floats across the space between us.

"I don't have a beef with the boy, so I let him go. So, where is the necklace?"

With my shoulders thrown back in defiance, I say, "I gave the necklace to the man you sent. If your own man didn't give it to you, then I suggest you find him. You know the necklace is bad luck. It killed Stella. It killed Isabella and Marco. It's going to kill me. Then it will kill you."

"Ha, as beautiful as it is, I have no intention of keeping it. It's part of my retirement plan. You're my last hit. Although I'd love to put a bullet in Lorenzo, it's time I move on. The only thing I want is the necklace."

I feel like I'm shouting across a huge abyss. I hear traffic on the road below which is seldom traveled. I focus on Riccardo and say, "I can't give you something I don't have. I followed all of your instructions. The man was waiting for me. He took the necklace. If you don't have it, who does?"

"Good question. If you're not lying, describe the man you gave it to."

My mind is paralyzed with fear as it dawns on me that Riccardo doesn't have the necklace.

"He was big and burly with a tiny blue star tattooed between his thumb and index fingers. He smelled nasty, like stale cigar smoke."

A fleeting look of surprise crosses Riccardo's face.

"Well, well, it appears that the new *padrone* has taken over before I leave."

"New *padrone*? There's a new *padrone*? Who is it?"

"Ha! I suppose you'd like that bit of information to give to Lorenzo. It doesn't matter if you know, as you won't live to see Lorenzo. He's in for a shock when he discovers the woman he's been seen with around town is the new *la padrone*."

The noise below the cliffs increases. For a moment, we're both distracted until I blurt out.

"Woman? *La padrone*? What are you talking about?"

He checks his phone and shakes his head. The gun moves steadily in my direction.

"Looks like we might have company. You know how stupid it was for you to bring reinforcements. Your friend Luigi will go down with you."

My heart thumps in my ears. No, not Luigi. I cannot think that he will also die because of me, so I change tactics.

"Why did you kill Stella?"

"You're wasting my time, Cat, and the answer won't save you. But it doesn't cost me to tell you. Carlo hated Stella for a lot of reasons: she was intelligent, she saw through him, and she dumped him after a quick fling. When she discovered his drug smuggling ring—the one he was conducting under the noses of the Guardia—he had to stop her. He had hated her most of his life, because she'd laughed in his face when he was a poor boy. He never forgot that slight. It festered and grew larger over the years as he watched her become more successful."

"So why didn't Carlo kill her? Why you?"

"You know the answer. Carlo never got his hands dirty. Carlo promised if I carried out his request to kill Stella, I'd be next in line as *il padrone* whenever he stepped down."

"But you knew Stella. How could you kill her?"

"It wasn't easy. She tried to talk me out of it. When I told her I didn't have a choice, she fought back. The gun went off. I'll never know which of us pulled the trigger."

All this killing—for what? My time is running out. I try one last way to reach him.

"It's a strange phenomenon, Riccardo, but you and I are alike in some ways. I loved Stella, and I was loyal to her just as you loved and were loyal to Carlo. We're both standing here out of that misplaced love and loyalty. Why don't we stop it?"

As I'm talking, that irritating last-fly-of-summer sound floods the sky. The drone must be large, but unless it's armed and on my side, it's not beneficial to this tense situation. Maybe it's a voyager wanting to be a sensation on social media.

Riccardo hears it, too. He glances up. I shift toward the rocks— my mind creating an escape route out. A larger boulder is within reach.

"Don't move," he yells and fires a shot close to my feet. I freeze.

The thump, thump noise grows louder until it far exceeds a magnitude a drone could make. It's the sound of a million birds beating their wings. A cloud of sandy soil swirls as the thumping, pulsating sound of the rotary blades of a helicopter draws near. The downward force of air lifts debris off the ground and hurls it in all directions.

Riccardo is momentarily blinded. He brushes dirt from his eyes and aims. My eyes automatically close. Then I force them open. I want to see with my last breath. The world is still beautiful; the sun still shines, the sky is still blue—streaked with a white dusting of clouds, and the red flowers still bob in the breeze. Rescue is so close.

Riccardo aims and pulls the trigger as a body hurls from behind the rocks. The blast jolts through both our bodies. The full force of the impact knocks us to the ground. Hands cradle my head as we hit the rocks. The world explodes. Blasts continue as helicopters, sirens, and a military presence invade the cliff.

The earth shakes and pounds against me until I stop breathing, and the world goes dark. My breath returns as the heavy body on top of me is pulled away. My only thought is to thank the person who saved my life. Hands press against my body. A voice says, "No broken bones, but we need an ambulance.

I'm eased into a sitting position. A cool cloth swipes across my face. I push the hand aside to see my rescuer. His dark blue eyes, fringed by black velvety lashes look back into mine.

"Lorenzo," I scream as I fling myself at him. His smile is weak and fading. Blood puddles around his head. Hands grab my arms, and the cry for a medic rings out. I jerk away from the hands holding me and touch his face.

"Lorenzo! Don't leave me."

His eyes open.

"Lorenzo, *ti amo sempre.*"

Sì bellissima, ti amo anch'io.

Hands reach for me. Strong arms lift me. My face is pressed against another face that is wet with tears.

"Hush, Cat. You're safe."

"No, no, no!" I shout as I struggle against Luigi's strong arms. "Let me go with him."

"You cannot. Nor can I. It's not time for us. He loved you, Cat. Let him go. He died the way he wanted—rescuing you. He once told me that it didn't matter how many times you got into trouble; he would always be there. He said that if the day came that he was no longer able to be there for you, I must promise to take his place. We loved him. He loved us. You and I are forever joined through his love."

One Note Murders

Castello del Mare stands on a hill overlooking the Adriatic Sea.
It isn't Rome, Tuscany, the Amalfi Coast or Venice.
It's a place all its own
A place off the beaten track—
A place in my heart—both real and imagined.
There's a hint of poverty interlaced in the karstic rock,
the rugged coastline, and the people who understand
the music of love and loss.
A place I carry in my heart with me wherever I go.
I pack the memory of it carefully,
wrapped in tissue paper
the colors of the sea
Acqua, emerald, slate
On rain-filled days when my heart is heavy,
I remember the intense Salento Sun,
The strands of Moorish music drifting
Through narrow passageways,
The sounds of laughter—
The love of one man
All fill my heart
with
Sadness
And
Joy.

Part Four
The Circle of Life

Your task is not to seek for love, but merely to seek and find all the barriers within yourself that you have built against it.
~ Rumi

86

Cassie and I fall into each other's arms. We don't bother with hello. My sobs are too loud for further conversation. We cling to each other. She moves her hands in soft circular motions on my back. We pull apart to search for tissues, then hug again. We gather her luggage, and, in silence, leave the airport.

Luigi stands next to the car. He reaches for Cassie's luggage, and, with a grin, asks me if he's doing the chauffeur thing right. Every day, he tries to find ways to make me smile—sometimes it works, but most often it doesn't.

During the hour-long drive, Cassie and I keep our hands tightly entwined. She asks me to talk about what happened. Luigi's eyes catch mine. He nods. The healing begins. Cassie never lets me down.

After sobbing through what happened, I share the happy ending of Giorgino being reunited with his parents and grandparents. He's in good hands with Dr. Tony and a therapist. Both are available anytime he's frightened. The good news is he actually didn't see anything that was too disturbing. His questions have been about Signorina Lucrezia and why she took him away and what happened to her and who was the nice man who kept him when she wasn't there but made him go into the dark hole and he didn't like it.

As I share my story with Cassie, she says, "Oh Cat, as soon as I heard what happened, I booked the next flight. I hope you aren't angry with me. I promise you Diana and Sam can handle it. Al, Chuck and Sheriff Blackwell are looking out for them."

She squeezes my hand and says, "If you're upset that I left the business, too bad. You're my best friend. You're more important to me than the business will ever be. You stood by me last year even when I pushed you away. We're together, and somehow, we'll get through this too."

We pull up in front of the villa—finally free from patrolling guards. For the first time, Cassie sees my second home—a place I love as well as the Lowcountry.

Maria is waiting for us. She pinches Cassie's cheeks, bestowing many kisses on her, and triumphantly says it's her job to put meat on Cassie's body. She says we're too skinny to be chefs. She hugs me and whispers once more she's sorry she deserted me. We've had time for long discussions—the whole family—to ask for and to receive forgiveness.

Joy comes to me in small moments when I show Cassie around town and introduce her to my friends. Maria insists that Cassie learn to make several different types of pasta along with sauces and, of course, pasticciotto. I show her the cathedral, the lighthouses, and the end of the world in Santa Maria di Leuca. We stay up all night talking. She sits beside my bed and holds my hand when nightmares rob me of sleep.

This morning we move to the terrace with our cappuccino. I share with her the story of the Lone Tree—both mine and Stella's.

"Cassie?"

"Hmmm?"

"Is this the right place for your honeymoon?"

"Oh, Cat, it's gorgeous, and the view is spectacular. Looking out across the Adriatic makes me want to move the wedding date up. I don't want to leave. No wonder you love this place."

"It's your place too. Anytime you need to get away with or without Chuck. Same for the girls. Maybe one time, just you and me."

Cassie squeals so loud I put my hands over my ears. Then we fall into each other's arms laughing and crying as the bittersweetness of life overwhelms us. Our journeys, like all journeys, are a combination of tears and laughter, pain and joy.

Later, I stand on the terrace alone. Cassie is Zooming with Diana and Sam. She shooed me away, telling me she and the girls would handle the business for now. Since Riccardo is dead, I'm free to leave after my deposition is taken. It won't be long as everyone wants to close the case.

My solitude is broken when my name is called. Luigi stands below. After releasing the gate, I wait at the top of the steps. He's become my shadow. I've tried to convince him to move on. But here he is with a smile that always lifts my spirit. He hugs me in a brotherly way and pats my shoulder before saying, "Checking to see how you are."

His face has a few new squiggly lines, and there are a few more threads of gray in his hair. "In a week or two, I'll be going home."

He shrugs, but his smile disappears.

"Let me know the date. I'm coming with you."

"Luigi, you can't come with me. This is your home. Your work is here or all over the globe not in some small coastal town in the States. I'm safe. Riccardo is dead. No one else is after me either here or back home. I heard Commissario Faena asked you to work with him. You'd be crazy not to accept his offer. Lorenzo would want that for you."

He moves away from me and looks out to sea.

"The necklace disappearing bothers me. Someone has it, but who?"

What do I say? I haven't told anyone that I think the new head of the mafia has it. Luigi will learn soon enough on his own.

"I don't know. Does it really matter?"

"It worries me that the necklace has vanished. What if that Frank Woodlee person kept it? There's still danger. I need to stay with you."

I move closer and place my hand on his arm.

"Just like you, I'm curious about what happened to the necklace. I gave the sketch artist the description of the man. He must have worked for Riccardo, or maybe he's a rogue agent like Isabella? Someone with a personal vendetta? Maybe he decided to keep the necklace."

"I guess, but it's been long enough for the gemstones to show up on the black market, and they haven't."

I shake my head.

"I think the person who took it is smart enough to wait a good while before they try to sell it. Plus, don't you think they've left the country by now? We'll never see it again. I'm okay with that."

Luigi shakes his head.

"What you say might be true, but I can't help speculating that Riccardo had a rival. He told you Carlo was ready to name his successor. If it wasn't Riccardo, then who's in line for *il padrone*? There's a link we don't know about."

"Luigi, I have to believe it's the end of this story—that all the players are dead. I can't get on with my life if there's someone else who wants me dead."

"You're right. I guess there's nothing to be done until the necklace or gemstones turn up."

He turns and faces me.

"But just in case, I'm going with you. Lorenzo would want me to see you safely home."

Placing my arms around him, I pull him into an embrace.

"One day it will be okay for both of us. Cassie's leaving in a couple of days. We'll have plenty of time to talk again before I leave. If it makes you feel better, a friend is meeting me in Rome. We'll fly home together. Luigi, I'll be back, and we'll stay in touch."

I lean into him for a last warm hug. Luigi holds onto me for a moment, then pulls away. He nods and walks down the steps. Once outside the gate, he turns and gives me a salute. He disappears as if he were never here.

I wonder why I didn't tell him the friend I'm meeting is Al or that I'm meeting him in Madrid and not Rome. The strange thing is Cassie told me that Al was still in the Lowcountry when she left. That makes the text I received from him weird. He said he was in Madrid, and wanted to go over our contract and answer my questions. I dismiss my thoughts as irrational.

I turn toward the lone tree and let the tears come as I free Lorenzo into the universe. He will always be the person I love with my whole being. Now he is with Stella. Two brilliant stars at long last together. It was meant to be and should have been from the beginning. Except as humans, we force our lives into directions they don't wish to go—like square pegs in round holes—listening to others instead of the truth of our own hearts.

We hang onto friendships that we feel obligated to continue, even when they are toxic. We hang onto old, critical images of ourselves put there by others. We hold back from embracing life for fear of being hurt. If we are fortunate, we arrive at a time and a place when these brutally painful lessons wake us up to our own truths.

While it is a lifelong journey, I am finally on a healthy path. I plan on staying. Will I ever love again? Maybe. But these bitter lessons have taught me that while lovers come and go, true friendships endure even the roughest tempest. Luigi will always be one of those friends.

> *Step out of the circle of time*
> *And into the circle of love.*
> ~ Rumi

87

lone to face a world that isn't always kind, I stand on the cliffs above the Zinzulusa Caves. Those I love best are lost to me—Mom, Dad, Stella, and now Lorenzo.

Yet today, for this moment, I am surrounded by true friends—the ones who were willing to forgive me as well as ask for forgiveness—a huge step for all of us. Many of us are raised in a faith that demands forgiveness. Yet, it is impractical to imagine forgiveness if Giorgino had been murdered. In that instance, even if these dear people could forgive, they would never forget. *How could they?*

His family has every right to be hurt and angered by the circumstances. Although Giorgino wasn't harmed, my redemption came about only because Luigi and I rescued him. That spoke volumes to his family. The fear that separated us is gone. Forgiveness was sought and found on all sides. Still it's a miracle that we're here together as I was the instrument of their horror. Although Riccardo set the kidnapping in motion, I was the reason.

Together, we took the time to glue the broken pieces back into a stronger mosaic of friendship. There are no expectations that I am anything other than myself—a self that is sometimes riddled with insecurities, that often flounders, and isn't always lovable. Yet I'm loved and cared for, and I have found a home on two continents.

As I stand on the hillside within this circle of friends, I glance at Cassie. She leaves tomorrow and will take part of my heart with her. Soon, I'll join her and be welcomed back into my circle of Lowcountry friends.

I'm ready to go home. During long hours of introspection, I've decided to walk alone for now. A time for healing and restoration waits for me.

A magnificent *Circle of Life* mandala rests in my hands. The sun strikes the gold and black interwoven mosaic pattern. I clasp it in a tight grip. It's a gift from Chiara. She placed it in my hands, closed my fingers around the circle and said, "The broken pieces once put together create a pattern of wholeness. The circle of the mandala symbolizes the universe in its ideal form. It offers healing and transformation from suffering to joy. Your broken pieces will become whole again. Do not despair. You will move back into the circle of joy."

We have gathered in this place that claimed the life of Stella and Lorenzo. We have no ashes to scatter for either. Stella is lost to a watery grave. Lorenzo's family took his body back to Rome. Two red roses are tossed into the sea by each of us.

And so it is. The pain of losing Stella has lessened—it's a physical thing like being hunched over for hours, and suddenly, you sit up straight, throw your shoulders back, and breathe deeply and fully. Tension eases away. Life once again moves, flows, and circles throughout every part of your body.

The pain of losing Lorenzo is raw—a gaping wound without the promise of healing anytime soon, if ever. Yet, life is circular. The pain will ebb and flow. Over time, joy will embrace me again. But most importantly, these people—these friends of my heart will love me through the black days of my anguish.

Io sono sopravvissuta—I am a survivor.

Understanding and believing in my own strength has changed me. As I gaze around the rugged cliffs, I see life—the red flowers nod in the breeze, tiny wildflowers cluster in the rocky terrain, and song birds soar.

The sea is quiet today. The sun sprinkles diamonds on its deep blue surface. I breathe in and out—deeply, fully, rhythmically, sucking in life and letting go of death, at least for this moment.

Just as the sirens of the sea called to the sailors, the Lowcountry is calling my name.

♩

Turandot addresses the emperor and the people:
"I have discovered the stranger's name—
it is Love!"

Epilogue

From the penthouse, Sofia moves the binoculars across the group on the cliff. She smirks as the roses drift on the wind currents before plunging into the sea.

Carlo is dead. Lorenzo is dead. Riccardo, the wanna-be *padrone* that Carlo abandoned, is dead. At last, she is *la padrone*. The first female.

Her father, the supreme *il padrone*, groomed her from the day she was born. He told her to keep her own counsel, to tread lightly, to know everything about everyone, and to take no prisoners. He predicted that one day she would be *la padrone*. She believed him and continued to believe him even after Carlo had her father killed and schemed his way into the top position. He didn't know she knew. She bided her time.

She smiles as she remembers the bug she planted in Lorenzo's office. That had given her Isabella and Marco's names. The rest had been easy. Riccardo's plans to return to Albania had been discovered by a traitor within his trusted men. These same small, fickle-minded men now clambered for her attention.

Almost all the stumbling blocks are gone. Only one is left. The others failed to kill Cat. She would not. Just as she did not fail to steal the necklace—the one Carlo and then Riccardo pursued for years. Too bad they would never know she was the winner.

She glances in the mirror. Her fingers trace the red starfish and the clusters of diamonds. She smiles widely. Tonight, she will slip away without leaving a trace. She's ready to move on for her next kill.

She observes the people standing on the cliff. Not one of them is aware of her existence. She will keep it that way. She has one task left before she can assume her role as *la padrone*. She will kill Cat. Her father's voice told her not to leave anyone standing. Where others failed, she would succeed. Her bag is packed. Her next stop is the Lowcountry. She will arrive before Cat. Her plan is already in place.

The End ~ La Fine

Author's Reflections

There are moments in my lifetime that stand out. Some are small moments like the sweet sound of a child's laughter as they splash in the ocean for the first time or the trill of a robin in spring. Some are magnificent, like the Andrea Bocelli concert I attended on his family farm in Tuscany, which became the backdrop for *One Note Murders*—the third book in the Cat Gabbiano Mystery Series.

In *One Note Murders*, I share my love of opera through Cat and *Turandot*, a powerful opera written by Giacomo Puccini (22 December 1858 – 29 November 1924). Puccini's most renowned works are *La Bohème* (1896), *Tosca* (1900), and *Madama Butterfly* (1904). *Turandot* (1920-1924) was posthumously completed by Franco Alfano. It was Puccini's last opera.

Over the years, I've had the privilege of seeing many of Puccini's operas on stage, but I had only viewed *Turandot* on PBS. It never dawned on me that *Turandot* and Bocelli would come together on the gentle slopes of Tuscany.

I couldn't have predicted that my dream to see *Turandot* would become a reality or that it would take eighteen years to come true. I also couldn't have predicted the joys and sorrows of living. As my life's journey continued, the dream to see *Turandot* never wavered. Those rich musical notes of Nessun Dorma lived on in my heart.

After settling into our new Lowcountry life, my seventieth loomed large. My bucket list had dwindled to one item, seeing *Turandot* performed by Andrea Bocelli in concert on his family farm in Tuscany.

It's time, I said to Ray. He nodded in agreement. On a summer evening in 2015, we sit in orchestra seats on Bocelli's farm in

Lajatico, Italy. Our hands were clasped, and our hearts beat in unison. A limousine had transported us to the executive cocktail party before the concert. We had the best seats—center stage, row ten. We were living our dream.

There have been a few of these divine magical moments in my life when the world stood still, and the door to my heart opened wide. This was such a moment. The harvest moon rose, and the orchestra swelled. Maestro Bocelli and the music of the night took center stage.

<table>
<tr><td>Dilegua, o notte!</td><td>Vanish, oh night!</td></tr>
<tr><td>Tramontate, stelle! Tramontate, stelle!</td><td>Set, stars! Set, stars!</td></tr>
<tr><td>All'alba vincerò!</td><td>At dawn, I will win!</td></tr>
<tr><td>Vincerò! Vincerò!</td><td>I will win! I will win!</td></tr>
</table>

Donna Keel Armer ~ 2025

Acknowledgments

Stephanie Larkin and Red Penguin Books have made my publishing experience exciting and joyful. A special thanks to both **Stephanie** and **Denise Roman-Reichert.** They are always available to answer my questions, no matter how insane they are.

Tracey Tannenbaum—my extraordinary editor. A chance meeting in Beaufort, and I have both a friend and a professional editor who speaks her mind when I go off track—which I'm prone to do.

Line Editors: Susan Dickey and Carter Hoyt—your abilities to search out and attack grammatical errors and misspellings are amazing.

Jonathan Haupt and the Pat Conroy Literary Center — Jonathan, you are always there. I am grateful to call you friend and thankful for our conversations and your unending support, not just for me but for all our local authors, the DAYLO kids, Families Against Book Bans, Authors against Book Bans, and so many more literary endeavors that teach the goodness of words and the diversity of our global world.

Spirit Writers: Katherine Tandy Brown, Ellen Kelly, Virginia Hall-Apicella, Susan Madison, June Labyzon, Virginia Vogler Brown, Michelle Jerome, and Beth MacDonald—you have the arduous task of listening to the raw material that includes information dumps, characters gone astray, illegal grammatical terms, and whatever else I concoct. This is the ninth year I've been in your midst. I love every one of you.

A special thanks to Virginia (Cookie) Vogler Brown for permission to use her poem *Dark Lady*.

June Tante von Neumann —thank you for your assistance

with the musical notes. Your sketch is on the front cover and at the start of each chapter thanks to my creative publisher.

Donna Johnstone Bearden and her book *Mandala Messages: On the Way to Becoming.*

Local Authors—Beaufort, South Carolina is a community of writers. Wonderful writers who are supportive and who show up for book launches and presentations and provide support and encouragement. I applaud all of you. A special nod to **Joy Corley** and her debut children's book *Percy Goes Camping...Maybe* and to **Susan Diamond Riley** for her pre-teen mystery series featuring Delta and Alex. They graciously permitted me to use their book titles in *One Note Murders.*

Friends and Readers—both old and new—who buy my books, read them, write reviews and ask me to write another. Thank you!

Ray, my partner of forty-two years. We are growing older together like the rarest wine. I love you more with each passing day.

Coming in 2026...the Cat Gabbiano Mystery Series Continues

Book #4 ~ The Voyage Never Ends

Author Notes

After the agonizing debut of my first book *Solo in Salento: A Memoir* during the Covid pandemic, I turned to writing fiction. A wonderful author and Professor of Literature, Janette Turner Hospital, once said during her *Caught in the Creative Act* class at the University of South Carolina, "Oh please, do write fiction. It's so much more fun, and you won't get sued."

So fiction it is.

The Cat Gabbiano series goes back and forth to whimsical places in Italy and the Lowcountry of South Carolina. While locals in each place probably recognize the town(s), they'll also recognize what's real and what is imagined.

Castello del Mare is actually a combination of two towns in Puglia—Otranto and Castro Marina with most of the locations in Otranto, although *Villa Fiori* (not real name) and *Ristorante L'aragosta* are in Castro Marina. The Zinzulusa Caves are further down the coast and are very real and very scary. Ask any member of the Dazzling Dozen who ventured to explore them with me in October 2024. The names of most bars, restaurants and attractions are real, and I often use the names of real people.

Casali di Casole is a very posh resort that I've never been to and won't because the price tag is outside the depth of my purse. But if Stella were real, it would be exactly the kind of place she'd stay.

https://www.casalidicasole.com/?utm_source=Google& utm_medium=Yext

I spend copious hours researching things like paste jewelry, the Guardia, mosaics, crypts, cathedrals, and sickle cell disease. All my books have small underlying themes like the ecology of the ocean, recycling, mental issues, human trafficking, and diseases.

We live in a time when the medical community has transformed sickle cell disease. Although it is still a severe life-threatening disease of childhood that transforms into a chronic, lifelong condition, there is a better understanding of treating not just the health of the patient but also the physical, psychosocial, and emotional challenges it brings. Over twenty million people worldwide have the disease.

https://ijponline.biomedcentral.com/articles/10.1186/s13052-021-01109-1

In the uncertainty of our future and the future of our children, books still give us hope for a better world. Books are gifts that never stop replenishing our spirits—all books.

Just in case you think you finally read a book by me that doesn't mention Pat Conroy, you'd be wrong. Here's what he had to say about banning books in a letter to the editor of the Charleston, West Virginia Gazette:

You've now entered the ranks of censors, book-banners, and teacher-haters, and the word will spread. Good teachers will avoid you as though you had cholera. But here is my favorite thing: Because you banned my books, every kid in that county will read them, every single one of them. Because book banners are invariably idiots, they don't know how the world works— but writers and English teachers do.

Please read Pat's letter in its entirety at

https://patconroy.com/a-letter-to-the-editor-of-the-charleston-gazette/

This is a work of fiction. Any errors in this book are mine and mine alone. Mistakes are easy to make but painfully hard to catch.

About the Author

Donna Keel Armer resides in the beautiful Lowcountry of Beaufort, South Carolina with her husband of forty-two years. Ray sees to it that she is fed and clothed, as she sometimes forgets the necessities when she's writing. She graduated with honors from Mississippi University for Women with a double major in psychology and social sciences and graduate studies in theology. Her first job during high school was a gofer for a furniture company and her last position was president of the hospitality business owned by Donna and Ray. While she volunteers at numerous organizations, she is most often found at The Pat Conroy Literary Center where she will welcome you to Beaufort and give you the grand tour.

Her writing inspiration comes from her world travels, her personal experiences in Italy and from living in the Lowcountry. She has written numerous magazine articles on travel and food and is the author of *Solo in Salento: A Memoir* and the Italian translation *Un'Americana in Salento*. She celebrated her Italian book launch in Otranto, Italy in 2022. In October 2023 her first novel in the Cat Gabbiano Mastery Series, *The Red Starfish*, debuted. In 2024, Book #2 *Moringa~Tree of Life* was released. Book #3 *One Note Murders* followed and Book #4 *The Voyage Never Ends* is in the works.

Her essays have appeared in the following anthologies: *London - Smokes, Blokes and Jokes of FoggyTown*; *Paris - Love, Loss and Longing in the City of Lights*; and *Rome - Centuries of Stories of the Eternal City*. Donna and Ray split their time between the South Carolina Lowcountry and Italy.

What Readers
Are Saying

One Note Murders, Donna Keel Armer's latest in the highly addictive Cat Gabbiano series, delivers a sumptuous blend of mystery, music, and memory. Armer spins a story that moves with operatic grace—from the sun-drenched hills of Tuscany to the dark chambers of the human heart—familiar territory Armer readers will recognize and relish. Her heroine, Cat Gabbiano, brave, flawed, and unforgettable, moves through a landscape as stunning as it is perilous, where loyalty and fear share the same breath. The twists are breathtaking, the writing luminous, and the final note—like Bocelli's own—lingers in the imagination of the reader long after the curtain falls.

—Karen Warner Schueler, Author, *The Sudden Caregiver: A Roadmap to Resilient Caregiving.*

In the third installment of Donna Keel Armer's *Cat Gabbiano Mystery Series*, Cat returns to Italy, hoping for a chance to honor her murdered best friend—but trouble finds her first. Familiar faces resurface, new ones emerge with hidden motives, and Cat is pulled deeper into a mystery where every clue plays a part in a deadly symphony. Suspenseful and evocative, *One Note Murders* is Armer's most gripping adventure yet.

—*Dana Ridenour, author of the award-winning Lexie Montgomery FBI Undercover Series.*